全国翻译专业资格（水平）考试辅导丛书

英语笔译综合能力（3级）

（修订版）

总主编　黄源深
主　编　顾大僖
编　者　顾大僖　金　辉
　　　　周　曦　武　成
　　　　周孟华

外文出版社
FOREIGN LANGUAGES PRESS

图书在版编目（CIP）数据

英语笔译综合能力．三级／顾大僖主编．—北京：外文出版社，2009
全国翻译专业资格（水平）考试辅导丛书
ISBN 978-7-119-03754-7

1.英…　 II.顾…　 III.英语—翻译—资格考核—自学参考资料　 IV.H315.9

中国版本图书馆CIP数据核字（2006）第145586号

全国翻译专业资格(水平)考试辅导丛书

英语笔译综合能力（三级）（修订版）

主　　编　顾大僖

责任编辑　王　蕊
封面设计　吴　涛
印刷监制　张国祥

ⓒ2009外文出版社
出版发行　外文出版社
地　　址　北京市西城区百万庄大街24号　　　　邮政编码　100037
网　　址　http://www.flp.com.cn
电　　话　(010)68320579/68996067（总编室）　　68995875/68996075（编辑部）
　　　　　(010)68995844/68995852（发行部）　　68995852/68996188（邮购部）
印　　刷　北京外文印刷厂
经　　销　新华书店／外文书店
开　　本　16开
印　　张　16.25
印　　数　28001—38000
字　　数　260千
装　　别　平
版　　次　2009年第1版第6次印刷
书　　号　ISBN 978-7-119-03754-7
定　　价　42.00元

前　言

　　本书是依照全国翻译专业资格（水平）考试英语笔译3级考试大纲（试行）的要求，配合《英语笔译综合能力》（3级）指定教材而编写的专项练习。本书编写的宗旨是通过更多的练习，帮助读者巩固词汇和语法知识，提高阅读能力和词义辨析能力。全书共有16个单元，每个单元包括语法、阅读、完形填空三部分。鉴于本书用于准备英语笔译综合能力（3级）的考试，为了便于读者掌握有关应试内容和提高应试能力，练习的类型基本和考试类型相同。此外，本书还为读者准备了两套模拟试卷，以供练习使用。

　　本书的材料主要有三个来源：

一、网站

www. 4freeessays. com；

www. abcgalle. com；www. absolutearts. com；www. americanpolitics. com；

www. anyon. com；www. artdaily. com；www. beliefnet. com；www. biz. yahoo. com；

www. caller. com；www. cdc. gov；www. chinaview. cn；www. cnn. com；

www. CNSNews. com；www. customwire. ap. org；www. drkoop. com；www. enc. org；

www. fishing-hunting. com；www. healthcentral. com；

www. hosted. ap. org/dynamic/stories；www. mirror. co. uk；www. msn. com；

www. nytimes. com；www. okhere. net；www. politics. guardian. co. uk；

www. sciencedaily. com；www. sciencenews. org；www. science-of-speed. com；

www. story. news. yahoo. com；www. syllabus. com；www. time. com；

www. tourism. gov. my；www. washingtontimes. com；www. woe. edu. pl；

www. world-tourism. org；www. yahoo. com；www. zone10. com；

二、报纸、期刊

Banking Strategies（July/August 2003 & November/December 2003）；*Los Angeles Times*（Jan. 21，2004）；*Saturday Business*（February 24，2004 & April 24，2004）；*The Sunday Times* magazine（January 25，2004）；*The Times*（Jan. 24，2004）；*The Washington Post*（Jan. 30，2004）；*USA Today*（Feb. 20，2004）

三、书籍

Genuine Articles（《精选 I 阅读》英文版，Peking University Press，Cambridge University Press）；*Selected Articles from American & British Newspapers & Periodicals*（《美英报刊文章选读》，《2007年考研英语新教程》，《博士研究生入学考试英语模拟考场》，《考研英语新大纲高级教程》）等。在此对这些网站、报纸期刊和出版社及作者表示深深的谢意。

　　本书由顾大僖、金辉、武成、周曦、周孟华等人编写，由顾大僖审校统稿。

目 录

第三单元　副词

第四单元　冠词

第五单元　语态

第六单元　语气

第七单元　介词

第八单元　关系从句

第九单元　过去及现在分词

第十单元　状语从句

第十一单元　情态动词

第十二单元　固定搭配

第十三单元　时态

第十四单元　代词及其他

第十五单元　各种语法点

第十六单元　各种语法点

第一单元 名 词

I. Grammar: Nouns

A Multiple Choices

1. The committee _____ unable to agree on a policy, and so _____ decided to meet again next month.

   A. were... they   B. was... it   C. have been... it   D. has been... they

2. That not-well-planned proposal leaves _____ room for discussion.

   A. much   B. a big   C. a bigger   D. a much bigger

3. There are over seventy _____ in our hospital.

   A. woman doctors   B. woman doctor

   C. women doctors   D. women doctor

4. I had my hair cut at the _____ around the corner.

   A. barber   B. barbers   C. barber's   D. barbers'

5. The policemen hurried to the spot of traffic accident where there was a large crowd of _____.

   A. looker-on   B. lookers-ons   C. looker-ons   D. lookers-on

6. This tank is big enough for ten gallons. It is a _____.

   A. ten-gallon-tank   B. ten-gallons tank

   C. ten-gallon tank   D. ten-gallons-tank

7. That magnificent _____ temple was constructed by a famous architect.

   A. eight-centuries-old   B. old-eight-centuries

   C. eight-century's-old   D. eight-century-old

8. He was frightened by _____ lightning.

   A. bolt of   B. a piece of   C. a flash of   D. a

9. Everything, including the clothes in the closets, _____ stolen from the apartment.

   A. were   B. have been   C. was   D. are

10. The data _____ arrived just on time.

    A. has   B. have   C. have been   D. has been

11. Mathematics as well as physics always _____ me a lot of trouble.

    A. has been caused   B. are causing   C. cause   D. causes

12. "Do you want the pants?" "My pants _____ laid in bed. "

    A. is   B. was   C. are   D. being

13. There was _____ of complete silence.

    A. an instant   B. hours   C. three minutes   D. seconds

14. Doctor Adams explained that not all bacteria _____ harmful.

    A. were   B. are   C. was   D. is

15. I don't want to borrow Kent's big bicycle because I am too small to ride _____.

    A. that bicycle of him   B. that bicycle of his

    C. that his bicycle   D. his that bicycle

16. There _____ the last piece of cake and the last spoonful of ice cream.

    A. we go   B. goes   C. go   D. are losing

17. _____ sent from Florida for all the children in Cabin Six.

    A. A crate of orange were   B. A crate of oranges were

    C. A crate of orange was   D. A crate of oranges was

18. There _____ in that part of the country.

    A. are not much industry   B. is not many industry

    C. are not many industry   D. is not much industry

19. After four years in America, he got _____.

    A. a degree of doctor   B. a doctor's degree

    C. the degree of a doctor   D. a doctor degree

20. "Why is the university doing so much building?" "The number of students _____ that there aren't enough classrooms. "

    A. have increased so rapidly   B. has increased so rapid

    C. have increased so rapid   D. has increased so rapidly

21. The storm has caused _____ to this region.

    A. many damages   B. much damages

    C. much damage   D. few damages

22. Her house is within _____ from the police station.

    A. a stone's throw   B. a throw of a stone

    C. stone's throw   D. the stone's throw

23. _____ is really a burden to a small boy.

    A. Ten pounds' weight   B. Ten pounds weight

    C. Ten pound weights   D. Ten pound weight

24. "Have you ever gone water-skiing before?" "Oh, yes _____. "

    A. a dozen of time   B. dozens of times

    C. dozens of time   D. dozen of time

25. "What did you see?" "We saw _____ police there. "

    A. many   B. much   C. little   D. the

26. I was surprised to see _____ at the concert.

    A. those number of people   B. that amount of people

        C. that number of people   D. those amount of people

27. "Do you want to wait?" "Three weeks _____ too long for me to wait."

    A. is   B. are   C. were   D. was

28. Fifteen years have passed since we graduated from the middle school. I have found she has _____.

    A. some white hair   B. much white hair

    C. a few white hairs   D. a little white hair

29. If these shoes are too big for you, buy a smaller _____.

    A. set   B. cone   C. copy   D. pair

30. When you are at your _____ end, you should not lose your head.

    A. wit's   B. wit   C. wits'   D. wits's

B Error Correction

1. Newspapers are one of the most important sources of news, and its versatility and availability make it the most popular mass media at all levels of a community.

2. The students are told to take great pain to obtain good marks in their examinations.

3. Providing relief after the disaster necessitated the mobilization of vast amounts of food, medical supply and people.

4. We might say that the earliest tools were a means of extending the human being own bodily powers.

5. Amniocentesis can reveal whether a fetus is suffering from any of a variety of chromosomal defect.

6. The large bird house together with the numerous bird feeders under the eaves attract a considerable number of different species in the summer.

7. Considering their vast numbers in the seventeenth century, not much sheep are raised in Spain today.

8. The hundred thousand dollars were found, because the thief dropped the money while escaping.

9. The integration of independent states could best be brought about by first creating a central organization with authorities over technical economic tasks.

10. The number of days of vacation provided to university employees remain constant from year to year.

11. The news on the local radio station, as well as newspaper accounts, confirm that the prison riot was serious.

12. Digitalis is a drug which is prepared from the seeds and leafs of a plant with the same name and is used as a cardiac stimulant.

13. The most famous alumnus of the college were invited to participate in the graduation ceremony

and related activities scheduled for late May.

14. A diamond or ruby is a jewelry that is often used to decorate valuable ornaments or other special objects such as rings or necklaces.

15. Encyclopedias can be used to acquire knowledge in any field, to obtain informations on a particular subject, or to deal with other academic questions.

II. Cloze Test

A Sports 体育运动

Many animals engage in play, but homo sapiens is the only animal _____ (1) have invented sports. Since sports are an invention, a part of culture _____ (2) than an aspect of nature, all definitions of sports are somewhat arbitrary. _____ (3) sports are a human universal found in every known culture or a _____ (4) unique to modern society depends upon one's definition of sports. Men and _____ (5) have always run, jumped, climbed, lifted, thrown, and wrestled, but they have _____ (6) always performed these physical activities competitively. Although all literate societies seem to _____ (7) contests of one sort or another in which men, and sometimes women, _____ (8) in displays and tests of physical skill and prowess, sports may be _____ (9) defined as physical contests performed for their own sake and not for _____ (10) ulterior end. According to this strict definition, neither Neolithic hunters nor contestants _____ (11) religious ceremonies such as the ancient Olympic Games were engaged in sports.

_____ (12) on the stipulation that sports must be performed for their own sake _____ (13) the paradoxical elimination of many activities which are usually thought of as _____ (14), such as exercises done for the sake of cardiovascular fitness, races run _____ (15) satisfy a physical education requirement, ball games played to earn a paycheck. _____ (16) definition also means abandonment of the traditional usage in which "sport," derived _____ (17) Middle English disporter, refers to any light hearted recreational activity. In the _____ (18) of some 18th-century aristocrats, a game of backgammon and the seduction of _____ (19) milkmaid were both considered good sport, but this usage of the term _____ (20) become archaic.

B The Ancient Olympic Games 古代奥林匹克运动会

According to historical records, the first _____ (1) Olympic Games can be traced back to 776 BC. They _____ (2) dedicated to the Olympian gods and were staged on the _____ (3) plains of Olympia. They continued for nearly 12 centuries, _____ (4) Emperor Theodosius decreed in 393 A. D. that all such "pagan cults" _____ (5) banned.

The oldest myth which concerns the beginning of the _____ (6) Games is that of Idaios Daktylos Herakles. According to other _____ (7), Zeus, the father of humanity, fought and defeated Cronus in a _____ (8) for the throne of the gods. Finally, the well-known _____ (9) Herakles is mentioned who staged games in Olympia in honour _____ (10) Zeus, because the latter had helped him conquer Elis when _____ (11) went to war against Augeas.

Through the 12 centuries of _____ (12) Olympic Games, many wonderful athletes competed in the stadium and _____ (13) hippodrome of ancient Olympia's sacred area, moving the crowds with _____ (14) great achievements. Although mortal, their Olympic victories immortalised them. Of _____ (15) best athletes who left their mark on the sacred valley _____ (16) Olympia, some surpassed all limits and became legends by winning _____ (17) successive Olympic Games and remaining at the forefront of their _____ (18) for more than a decade.

The ancient Olympic Games were _____ (19) a one-day event until 684 BC, when they were extended _____ (20) three days. In the 5th century B. C. , the Games were extended again to cover five days.

III. Reading Comprehension

Passage One

My First Experience with AIDS Patients
我初次接触艾滋病人
by Marc Kielburger

I was ushered to the AIDS ward of a hospice in the slum. I would later learn that the ward did not exist, at least not officially. Not a single person in Thailand had AIDS, according to the Thai government at the time. People got "sick," of course, sometimes "very sick," but no one had AIDS. The hospice was home to an ever-growing number of "very sick" people.

I entered the ward and was greeted by two Thai nurses.

"Thank goodness you are here, Marc," said the first.

"You're a doctor, right?"

I shook my head.

"So you are a medical student then!"

I shook my head again.

"But you know medicine, right?"

"Kinda," I offered. "I watch *E. R.*, every Thursday"

After a rapid exchange in Thai, the first one said, "No problem. Get ready for your four-hour medical school training!"

"But in my country medical school takes years!" I protested.

"We don't have that long," she replied. "So we better get started."

During the next few hours, I learned to clean wounds, administer IVs, treat bedsores, and dispense medicine. The work was punishing, made worse by stifling heat, frequent blackouts, and an incredible stench in the air. I tried desperately to hide my weak nerves and queasy stomach, but more than once dashed for the bathroom to throw up.

Just when it seemed my training was coming to an end, the nurse took me aside. "There are only two more things you need to know," she said. "On the left-hand side of the ward, you will find what we call the Exit Area." As it turned out, she meant "exit" in the largest sense of the word. Terminally ill patients were hidden behind a curtain and then exited out of the ward after death. "The second thing you need to know," she continued, "is that we haven't had a day off in three weeks. You'll be looking after the ward by yourself for the next shift."

My jaw dropped.

"Don't worry, Marc," said the other nurse, patting me on the shoulder before turning to leave. "Think of this as the beginning of your residency!" And with that, they walked out. Alone and petrified, I tried unsuccessfully to keep calm.

I counted to twenty-four. That's how many AIDS patients were in my charge. What am I going to do? I thought. What *can* I do? I fell back on my training with the Canadian government and put my talents to work. I served patients water-some with ice, some without. Next, I tried to cheer up everyone, myself included, giving enthusiastic high-fives to patient after patient. Soon enough, everyone was laughing. Some were laughing with me, others most definitely at me, but I didn't care. As long as I could keep people smiling, I was sure it would all be fine. And it was. Until a short while later, when a patient in the Exit Area began to choke. He had fluid in his lungs and could not breathe. As I crossed the floor, I could hear the man gasping for air. Fumbling and scared, I pulled back the curtain and administered the medicine the nurses had recommended. The man didn't respond. With nothing left to offer, I sat down and held his hand, looking into his eyes as he breathed heavily for a while and then stopped. Watching him slip away, I was hit by a feeling of anguish such as I'd never felt, either before or since. It haunts me to this day.

1. Judging from the passage, what is the writer most likely to be?

    A. A doctor   B. A medical student   C. A volunteer   D. A government official

2. Why were the two Thai nurses happy to see Marc?

    A. Because Marc was an experienced doctor for AIDS.

    B. Because Marc could amuse the patients.

    C. Because Marc would offer them further medical training.

    D. Because Marc would work in the ward so that they could enjoy a day off.

3. What is the actual meaning of the phrase "Exit Area" by the nurse?

    A. A place where to wait for transferring to a good hospital.

    B. A place where to wait for bidding a final good bye to the world.

C. A place where to be treated by experienced doctors.

D. A place where to wait for checking out and going home.

4. What was the AIDS patients' response toward Marc's efforts to cheer them up?

A. They all appreciated his efforts.

B. They were all grateful for his efforts.

C. They all enjoyed his efforts.

D. Some of them thought his efforts were ridiculous.

5. Which of the following did Marc NOT do to the patients?

A. Giving them operations.   B. Amusing them.

C. Administering medicine to them.   D. Sitting by their deathbeds.

Passage Two

Timberwolves are Marching to a New Tune
森林狼按新的节拍在前进

For the past seven years, Kevin McHale has struggled to put the right combination around his superstar, Kevin Garnett. McHale brought in dozens of players to complement his main man, but in the end the Timberwolves always looked like the '70s band Wings — one star (Paul McCartney) and a bunch of people nobody noticed.

With apologies to all of you who still are jamming to "Silly Love Songs," Wings never could live up to the Beatles. They didn't have the star power.

Well, McHale finally has found his own personal John Lennon and Ringo Starr, and their names are Sam Cassell and Latrell Sprewell. The two veteran guards have given the Wolves an edge they've never had before, and suddenly Garnett doesn't have to do it all by himself.

Wednesday in San Antonio, Garnett struggled at the start, found himself in foul trouble and never really got into the flow of the game. As all superstars do, he still managed to put up good numbers (22 points and 10 rebounds). But Garnett never found his groove, and he certainly didn't control the game.

Fortunately for Kevin Garnett, he didn't have to. Cassell, who has hit more big shots than anyone this side of Reggie Miller, came through with a huge game. Displaying his uncanny knack for creating his own midrange shots, Cassell riddled the Spurs' defense for 33 points including several clutch buckets in the fourth quarter.

Some guys like to take big shots. Cassell *needs* them. When the game gets tight and his team needs a basket, Sam's eyes light up and he enters another world. He lusts for moments like those.

Sprewell also had a major impact in Wednesday's victory, scoring 24 points and sealing the win with a steal and a highlight-reel slam. He is playing with amazing energy and zeal, and a touch of attitude that we haven't seen from Wolves players in the past. Together, the "Big Three" have become a major force that has to rank with any combination in the league.

Wednesday's victory in San Antonio epitomized the type of team that Minnesota has been all season. The Wolves defended well, scored 100 points against the league's best defense, got major contributions from their bench and huge shots from their stars, and showed a resilience and confidence usually reserved for championship teams.

After several first-round flameouts, is this the year the Wolves finally make it over the hump in the playoffs? It's only January, so we probably shouldn't get ahead of ourselves. But the team I saw Wednesday night showed all the signs of being a major player in the NBA playoffs this spring.

If things fall just right for McHale, maybe he can finally stop fiddling with his roster and simply "Let It Be."

1. What kind of game of the following is talked about in this passage?

   A. volleyball game   B. football game   C. basketball game   D. badminton game

2. What is Kevin McHale most probably?

   A. a counselor   B. an officer   C. a player   D. a coach

3. The "Big Three" have become a major force that has to rank with any combination in the league. Whom does the "Big Three" refer to?

   A. Kevin Mehale, Kevin Garnett and Paul McCartney

   B. Kevin Garnett, Latrell Sprewell and Ringo Starr

   C. Kevin Garnett, Sam Cassell and Latrell Sprewell

   D. Kevin Garnett, John Lennon and Ringo Starr

4. "Fiddling with his roster" in the last sentence of the passage means _____.

   A. thinking of cheating in matches with false actions

   B. playing with the name list of the team in order to form a better combination

   C. preparing a cock to treat his players for Wednesday's victory

   D. contemplating about the timetable of competitions

5. The title of the passage "Timberwolves are marching to a new tune" means that _____.

   A. the team has changed from having to arrange a good combination of players around its only superstar into a new state in which more players are performing wonderfully

   B. the team has changed from having to arrange a good combination of players around Kevin Garnett into a new combination of players around the new stars Lennon and Starr

   C. the team has improved so much that it has entered a new stage

   D. the team has organized demonstration with some musical instruments playing beautiful tunes

Passage Three

Her Dual Citizenship Brings Prejudice
她的双重国籍导致了偏见

She is Vietnam's top-ranked female tennis player. Still, Noel Huynh Mai Huynh is criticized by the state-run press and jeered by Vietnamese crowds who do not accept her as one of their own.

"I play tennis for my family," Huynh said before the Southeast Asian Games, a regional competition that runs through Saturday. "There's a lot of pressure because I know a lot of people, they don't like me very much."

Huynh, 18, was born in the US territory of Guam. She is the first "Viet kieu," or overseas Vietnamese, to receive dual citizenship from the Vietnam government to compete for Vietnam.

Huynh was four years old when her family moved back to Ho Chi Minh City (formerly Saigon) in 1989. She did not speak Vietnamese then but has since mastered the language and now considers herself more Vietnamese than American.

Still, many are wary. She is thought of as spoiled because of her American passport. It doesn't seem to matter that she's never been on the US mainland.

She and her four siblings — all accomplished tennis players — have been passed over for less talented Vietnamese players.

"We practice in Vietnam, we grew up in Vietnam… and they cannot beat us so they try to keep us out of competitions so we don't beat them," said brother, Jean-Pierre Qui Phu Huynh Jr.

The 65-year-old family patriarch, also named Jean-Pierre, is their inspiration. In perfect English, he recounts the path that led him from Vietnam in 1975 and back 14 years later.

He fought for the US-backed South Vietnamese army and was the tennis coach for former President Nguyen Van Thieu. He put his wife and children on one of the last helicopters leaving the US Embassy before Saigon fell April 30, 1975. He spent the next six months searching for his family, finding them in California.

They moved to Guam, where French-educated Jean-Pierre became a top tennis player with a big house and booming business building tennis courts. Still, something was missing. So he decided to go home in 1987.

The family, all US citizens, returned to Vietnam two years later. Most refugees were too scared to think of visiting them.

The elder Huynh coached his children up to eight hours a day, six days a week, and tried to make sure they got to play.

He became friends with former Prime Minister Vo Van Kiet, a tennis fan, and built the country's largest tennis complex in Ho Chi Minh City. He brought in international tennis competitions and urged Vietnam to strengthen its national team. Still, the discrimination persisted.

"I don't care about anybody who cheers for the other player," his daughter said. "It's OK for me, but sometimes I'm kind of sad about that because I'm on the national team but they always want the other players to beat me."

With Vietnam hosting the Southeast Asian Games for the first time and encouraging about 2.5 million Viet kieu to return, she was given a chance at this event.

"With the participation of Huynh Mai Huynh, the Vietnamese tennis team will be stronger," said Nguyen Hong Minh, head of the Vietnamese SEA Games sports delegation. "This is in our policy to expand international relations as well as win the support of the overseas Vietnamese community."

She was eliminated from doubles and mixed doubles. Her strength is singles, but she said her coaches didn't select her for that event.

Huynh says all she wants is to represent the country she considers home.

"I'll stay here," she said, "and I'll play for Vietnam forever."

～～～～～～～～～～～～～～～～～～～～～

1. Why is Neol Huynh Mai Huynh not favored by Vietnamese crowds?

A. Because she was born somewhere other than in Vietnam and therefore she is not a pure Vietnamese.

B. Because she doesn't have a high opinion of the Vietnamese government.

C. Because she was born in a US territory and is both citizen of Vietnam and a citizen of America.

D. Because she often plays and defeats other Vietnamese tennis players.

2. Which of the following statements is true?

A. Huynh went to America when she was a child and later returned to Vietnam with her family

B. Huynh considered herself more Vietnamese than American. However, a lot of people have doubt about it.

C. Huynh cannot speak Vietnamese, and this is one of the reasons why she is not accepted by Vietnamese people.

D. A lot of people in Vietnam consider Huynh more American than Vietnamese.

3. The word "inspiration" in the sentence "The 65-year-old family patriarch, also named Jean-Pierre, is their inspiration" probably means _____.

A. encouragement　　B. ingenuity　　　C. support　　　　D. comfort

4. The reason for Jean-Pierre, the family patriarch, to decide to go home with family is mostly likely that _____.

A. the family was hard up in a foreign country

B. he couldn't find what he liked in Guam

C. his children wanted him to take them home

D. he is emotionally attached to his own country

5. The fact that Huynh is prejudiced can be seen from all of the following except _____.

A. Vietnamese crowds do not accept her as one of them

B. Other tennis players want to beat her

C. Not many people like to greet her

D. Huynh's coaches don't select her for single events she is strong in

Passage Four

Roger Federer Lights up the Arabian Night
罗杰·费德勒点亮阿拉伯之夜

Plenty of people will be glad Tim Henman was not here to trouble Roger Federer once more last night, as the seedings said he should have been. Popular with the expatriates though he may be, and capable of upsetting Federer though he undoubtedly is, there is nothing quite so stirring as seeing one of the most gifted world No 1s of all in full cry.

Instead of struggling with his jinx player, Federer imposed a spell of his own. He beat Andrei Pavel, whom Henman beat in the Paris Masters final, by 6 – 3, 6 – 3, and strode the court like a ruler who knows his aura is expanding.

It carried the Swiss imperiously into a semi-finals of the Dubai Championships, where he will face Jarkko Nieminen. The Finn earned his place by defeating the Dutch No 8 seed Sjeng Schalken 6 – 3, 6 – 3.

Federer insisted he was not at his best — "I haven't wanted to chase the lines as much as I should," he said.

Pavel was driven to distraction as it was. He had already lifted himself near the level he showed when he was in the top 20. But just when he looked as if he might prolong the second set, Federer struck.

He retrieved one ball from deep, outside the tramlines on the forehand side, turned and reached the next ball from short and outside the tramlines on the backhand side, and still somehow hit a controlled winner. It completed the decisive break of serve.

Pavel responded by launching a spare ball towards the sky and it landed on the whiskey tables in the Irish village below. The umpire uttered a code violation warning in little more than a whisper. It was as though he felt sympathy for the Romanian.

If Federer reaches tomorrow's final he will play Spain's Feliciano Lopez, whose Davis Cup debut came in the singles in the 2003 final in Melbourne, or Mikhail Youzhny, whose first Davis Cup experience was as a ball boy in the 1995 final in Moscow.

That spurred Youzhny to make a top-level breakthrough seven yearslater, and to develop perseverance which has been revealed this week in a 6 – 3, 1 – 6, 6 – 1 quarter-final win over Rafael Nadal yesterday in heat which would have made a camel protest, and in a recovery from two days' vomiting after eating Japanese seafood. "My cap felt as if it weighed five kilos," he said.

1. From the opening paragraph, it can be inferred that _____.
   A. Tim Henman and Roger Federer were not in good terms
   B. Roger Federer was hardly any match to Tim Henman
   C. Tim Henman avoided meeting Roger Federer in the match
   D. gifted world No 1s are usually reduced to a state of tears when having lost a game
2. Which of the following is NOT true according to the passage?
   A. Roger Federer is Swiss.
   B. Roger Federer beat Andrei Pavel by 6 – 3, 6 – 3.
   C. Jarkko Nieminen will be Federer's next opponent.
   D. Henman once beat Federer by 6 – 3, 6 – 3.

3. It seemed that Andrei Pavel _____.

    A. played nearly at his highest level during the match

    B. nearly beat Federer in the second set

    C. had a break of serve by Federer

    D. was completely controlled by Federer

4. It can be inferred from the passage that _____.

    A. Pavel lost the game because his last ball flew towards the sky

    B. Pavel was not happy with the umpire

    C. Pavel lost his temper when defeated

    D. the umpire felt sympathetic for Pavel for he was a Romanian

5. The author made a special mention of Mikhail Youzhny's win at the quarter final because

    _____.

    A. he was greatly impressed by Youzhny's experience as a ball boy

    B. he admired Youzhny's perseverance during the match

    C. Youzhny was as persevering as a camel

    D. Youzhny took to Japanese seafood which made him very weak

第二单元 形容词

.... **I. Grammar: Adjectives** ....

A) Multiple Choices

1. The town has a _____ bridge.
   A. nice old grey stone
   B. old stone grey nice
   C. grey nice old stone
   D. old nice grey stone
2. It is a good time to catch up on _____ readings and other assignments.
   A. a former   B. previous   C. back   D. before
3. Once you have developed a good study habit, try to keep it _____.
   A. living   B. alive   C. live   D lively
4. A good plan must be a little _____ so that special projects which are not included in the plan can be done well.
   A. flexible   B. loose   C. relaxed   D. smooth
5. The more civilized man has become, _____ he is limited by the disadvantage of his environment.
   A. and the more   B. the less   C. the lest   D. and the less
6. One of the differences between the Pacific Ocean and the Indian Ocean is that the former has _____ waves.
   A. largest   B. large   C. larger   D. the largest
7. The people in Taiwan consume _____ milk per person today as they did twenty years ago.
   A. more than twice as many   B. twice more than as much
   C. so much more than twice   D. more than twice as much
8. Since arriving in New York, Thomas has had over 15 job interviews. And this is _____ opportunity to be lost.
   A. too good   B. too a good   C. too good an   D. a too good
9. The man was left _____ in the empty land, but he was not lost.
   A. lonesome   B. alone   C. lone   D. lonely
10. What some TV serials present to the audience is simply a _____ picture of the reality.
    A. fault   B. false   C. fake   D. flake

11. He was so disappointed that he angrily chose _____ music he could find in the hope that it might at least seem funny.

    A. worse   B. the worse   C. worst   D. the worst

12. — I want to see Mr. Smith. We have an appointment.

    — I'm sorry, but he is not _____ at the moment, for the meeting hasn't ended.

    A. available   B. accessible

    C. approachable   D. advisable

13. The reason why so many people sit before the television tonight is that there will be a _____ game of World Cup.

    A. living   B. live   C. lively   D. lived

14. The Yangtze River is not _____ than the Yellow River.

    A. very longer   B. more longer   C. longest   D. less longer

15. Although she didn't have to worry about money, she chose the _____ expensive among those fashionable coats.

    A. less   B. one most   C. more   D. least

16. It's _____ much more than I paid for it.

    A. worth   B. worth of   C. worthing   D. worthy

17. This is _____ for me to do.

    A. far too difficult a job   B. too far difficult a job

    C. far too a difficult job   D. too far a difficult job

18. The seven dwarfs in "Snow White" are _____ seventy centimeters tall.

    A. almost more than   B. hardly more than

    C. nearly more than   D. as much as

19. I caught the last bus from town, but Tom came home _____ than I.

    A. more late   B. more later   C. even later   D. the later

20. Dubai is the capital of the United Arab Emirates, one of the world's leading _____ oil producers.

    A. raw   B. crude   C. rough   D. primitive

21. The twins are so _____ that I cannot tell them apart.

    A. alike   B. likely   C. like   D. liking

22. The road accident left at least 10 people _____.

    A. died   B. dead   C. death   D. deadly

23. After the seed is planted, new, taller shoots appear until the bamboo reaches _____ height.

    A. complete   B. total   C. full   D. whole

24. This is the _____ bacon of the first class.

    A. choose   B. choosy   C. choice   D. choosing

25. — Do you think that the labor bill will be passed?

    — Oh, yes. It's _____ that it will.

A.　almost surely　　　　　　　　B.　very likely

C.　near positive　　　　　　　　D.　quite certainly

26. The boys were _____ with excitement when they heard the news.

A.　insane　　　　B.　mad　　　　C.　insensible　　　D wild

27. The mouth is _____ intelligent than the ears, for they are both controlled by the brain.

A.　not so　　　　B.　not much　　　　C.　much more　　　D.　no more

28. I can't find you _____. You have no choice.

A.　a coat enough large　　　　　　B.　an enough large coat

C.　a large coat enough　　　　　　D.　a large enough coat

29. He knows little of mathematics, and _____ of chemistry.

A.　even more　　　B.　still less　　　C.　no less　　　D.　still more

30. "Do you regret paying five hundred dollars for the painting?"

"No, I would gladly have paid _____ for it."

A.　twice so much　　　　　　　　B.　twice as much

C.　as much twice　　　　　　　　D.　so much twice

ℬ Error Correction

1. The sooner you start, the quicklier you will finish.

2. It was considerable of the committee to cancel the speech by Robert because he was suffering from one of the worst colds he had ever had.

3. Strawberries can, of course, be frozen but they taste best when bought and eaten fresher.

4. Every country has its own historic background.

5. The stream ran coldly over their feet.

6. In fact, money alone is almost invaluable.

7. Her house with a good view of Mt. Rocky was located at the most east end of the village.

8. She stayed at home for a week to look after her ill child.

9. Of the two reports, the first was by far the best, partly because the person who delivered it had such a dynamic style.

10. As a developing country, China is making a continual development.

11. The invention of the computer has increased the speed of word processing, thus making possibly the rapid growth of the publish business.

12. Jack's voice sounds strangely today.

13. Film directors can take far great liberties in dealing with concepts of time and space than stage directors can.

14. Initially acting as a sports announcer in the 1930's, Ronald Reagan entered national politics when he campaigned on TV for Barry Goldwater in 1964 president race.

15. International situations will become less tenser when nations have reached some degree of peaceful settlement.

II. Cloze Test

Ⓐ **How to Use a Painting Knife** 使用画刀的方法

Painting with a knife is a bit like putting butter on bread and produces quite a _____ (1) result to a brush. Painting knives are excellent for producing textured, impasto work and _____ (2) areas of flat colour.

· What's the difference between a palette knife and a painting knife?

A palette knife is a long, straight spatula that is used _____ (3) mixing paints and scraping a palette clean. They're made from metal, plastic, or wood and _____ (4) either be completely straight or have a slightly bent handle. A painting knife has _____ (5) large crank in the handle, which takes your hand away from the painting surface. They _____ (6) in numerous shapes (for example pear-, diamond-, or trowel-shaped) and are used for painting _____ (7) of a brush. The edge of the knife is blunt, so that it doesn't cut the _____ (8).

· What shape of painting knife should I use?

Different shaped painting knives produce different effects. For example, a short blade produces angular strokes _____ (9) a long blade makes it easy to put down sweeps of colour.

· Why can't I use a palette knife to paint with?

You can. Painting _____ (10) just have the advantage of coming in more angular shapes and with sharper points. And _____ (11) larger crank in the handle means there's less chance of rubbing your knuckles into wet _____ (12). If you're unsure whether you're going to enjoy painting with a knife, first buy a _____ (13), plastic palette knife and experiment a bit with this before upgrading to a wood-and-metal knife.

· How do I use painting knife?

_____ (14) the handle firmly so you're got good control. Pick up some paint off your palette _____ (15) the tip, as you'd pick up some butter with a knife. Use the side of the _____ (16) to spread paint across your canvas, or press it onto the canvas, as you _____ (17) spread butter across a slice of bread. It'll seem strange at first as it's quite _____ (18) to using a brush. Using just the tip of the blade will produce small dots. _____ (19) the edge of the knife down will produce fine lines. Pressing the blade flat down _____ (20) the paint will produce ridges. Scrape back into the paint to reveal underlying layers (called sgraffito).

Ⓑ **The Beatles** 甲壳虫乐队

The English rock music group The Beatles gave the 1960s its characteristic musical flavor and _____ (1) a profound influence on the course of popular music, equaled by _____ (2) performers. The guitarists John Winston Lennon, James Paul McCartney, and George Harrison; and the drummer Ringo Starr, were all born and _____ (3) in Liverpool. Lennon and McCartney had played together in a group called The Quarrymen. With Harrison, _____ (4) formed their own group, The Silver Beatles, in 1959, and Starr joined them in 1962. As _____ (5) Beatles, they developed a local following in Liverpool clubs, and their first recordings, "Love Me Do" (1962) and "Please Please Me" (1963), quickly made them Britain's top rock group. Their early music was _____ (6) by the American rock singers Chuck Berry and Elvis Presley, but they infused a hackneyed musical _____ (7) with freshness, vitality, and wit.

The release of "I Want to Hold Your Hand" in 1964 _____ (8) the beginning of the phenomenon known as "Beatlemania" in the United States. The Beatle's first US _____ (9) aroused a universal mob adulation. Their concerts were scenes of mass worship, and their records sold _____ (10) the millions. Their first film, the innovative A Hard Day's Night (1964), was received enthusiastically _____ (11) a wide audience that included many who had never before listened to rock music.

Composing their own _____ (12), The Beatles established the precedent for other rock groups to play their own music. Experimenting with _____ (13) musical forms, they produced an extraordinary _____ (14) of songs: the childishly simple "Yellow Submarine"; the bitter social commentary of "Eleanor Rigby"; parodies of earlier pop styles; new electronic sounds; and compositions that were scored for cellos, violins, trumpets, and sitars, as well as for conventional guitars and drums. The _____ (15) disbanded in 1970, after the release of their final album, Let It Be, and during the 1970s _____ (16) individual careers, On Dec. 8, 1980, John Lennon _____ (17) fatally shot outside his Manhattan apartment by Mark Chapman, a 25-year-old former mental _____ (18) who, earlier that same day, had asked Lennon for his _____ (19). Lennon's murder was universally _____ (20) with an intensity of feeling usually inspired only by political and spiritual leaders.

III. Reading Comprehension

Passage One

Go Ahead — Cook with It
别怕——就用它来烹饪

It's grapefruit season. From now through March, the golden orbs are ripe for the picking. And they're not just for breakfast any more.

Hanging around on trees all about California: grapefruit — heavy with juice, tartly sweet, beguilingly perfumed. Round and yellow as happy faces or suns, they seem to ripe just as the general populace sinks into its annual round of post-holiday dietary self-chastisement.

Coincidence? Perhaps. But we say run with it.

Look beyond the obvious salvo of half a grapefruit for breakfast attacked with a jagged spoon and you'll find a marvelous fruit for peeling and eating out of hand. There's nothing like it for inducing simultaneous feelings of gastronomic piety and delight at recapturing a long-lost pleasure. It's sensual: the aroma of essential oils as they spurt daintily from the pores of the thick skin, the ripping sound of the tenacious segments being pulled apart, the juice dripping down. And it's delicious.

But don't stop there. Cook with grapefruit. Use its juice to flavor sauces. Section and scatter it. Bake with it. Candy its peel. Grapefruit is milder and sweeter than lemon, but it can be used in many of the same ways — squeezed on grilled fish, made into a brightly flavored curd. And if you're looking for gorgeous color, red grapefruit offers extra plate appeal.

The notion that red grapefruit is sweeter than white or yellow grapefruit is, however, a myth, according to citrus specialists. (The story grew out of a marketing campaign by Texas growers.) Red grapefruits get their color from lycopene, which has health benefits (its an antioxidant) but does not affect flavor.

Sweetness is determined, rather, by the length of time the fruit has been hanging on a tree. A grapefruit picked in December isn't as sweet as one picked in February, so if you have a tree, just pick fruit as needed.

If not, ask at your farmers market about the different varieties available, all of which have their fans. California reds include the medium-pink Rio Reds from the Caochella Valley and the Star Ruby from Central Valley (and Texas). Yellow Marsh is a familiar yellow variety and the Duncan, while not usually labeled as such in supermarkets, is a reliable white.

For those who don't like the tartness of a true grapefruit, Oro Blanco — the half-grapefruit, half-acidless pummelo — is sweeter and can be used in salads.

Our salad of jicama strips, thinly sliced snow peas, fresh pea sprouts (available in Asian markets) and red grapefruit sections has an appealing crunch. Its delicately harmonious flavors are pulled together with a faintly sweet dressing of grapefruit juice, tarragon and mint.

The strikingly pink sauce of our baked halibut dish contrasts with the white flesh of the fish for an artful plate — and it's easy to make. Before baking, marinate the halibut in grapefruit juice with garlic and thyme. Sauce it with a reduction of grapefruit juice combined with blood orange juice, which deepens the color and softens the flavor. Then whisk in bits of cold butter for silkiness.

A rich crust is a perfect foil for the tangy grapefruit curd filling in our pretty tartlets. Both grapefruit juice and lemon juice are used in the curd to focus the flavor; grapefruits zest enlivens the crust. Garnish them with whipped cream and candied grapefruit peel.

For cooking, select heavy fruit, which indicates juiciness. (If you're making a batch of candied peel, however, lighter fruit will indicate more peel.) Before juicing, roll a grapefruit under your hand on the countertop to help extract the most juice. Avoid lumpy fruit, which may be over-ripe.

And finally, for those whose resolute January superegos care about such things, here's a reassuring thought: Grapefruit is low in calories (40 to 60 each), high in vitamins C and A, and an excellent source of fiber. It contains no fat, sodium or cholesterol.

So peel away.

〰〰〰〰〰〰〰〰〰〰〰〰〰〰〰〰〰〰〰〰〰〰

1. The writer thinks that the grapefruit seems to ripe just at the right time. Why?
   A. The grapefruit becomes ripe just after a holiday in a year so that people can consume more food.
   B. The grapefruit matures in autumn to provide people with a kind of rich food.
   C. The grapefruit can provide people with a kind of favorite fruit when they have been on diet for a few days after the Christmas holiday during which they ate too many rich foods.
   D. The grapefruit matures as self-chastisement for people.
2. Which of the following is NOT the way to cook with the fruit?
   A. Fry it with meat.   B. Section and scatter it.
   C. Bake with it.   D. Candy its peel.
3. The sweetness of the grapefruit is determined by _____ .
   A. lycopene
   B. the length of time the fruit is exposed to the sun
   C. the length of time the fruit is hanging on a tree
   D. the specific nutrient the fruit takes from the soil
4. What is the meaning of "superegos" in the last but two paragraph?
   A. absolute selfishness of one's character   B. personal likings
   C. personal attentions   D. personal regrets
5. The reasons the grapefruit is good to health include that _____ .
   A. it is an excellent appetizer   B. it is sweet and juicy
   C. it contains no fat, sodium and cholesterol D. it contains no calories and fat

Passage Two

Whales
鲸

Whales are aquatic mammals belonging to order Cetacea. A few species live in fresh water, but most species live in the sea. They have a streamlined shape and a powerful tail to drive them forward. With its two large horizontal fins or flukes, the tail produces the driving force by beating strongly up and down. Flippers at the front are used for steering and balance. The hind limbs of whales have completely disappeared, apart from a few small bones inside the body. Body hair has also disappeared, giving whales a smoother outline and less resistance to water. Instead of hair, whales are insulated by a thick layer of fat, or blubber, under the skin. The blubber may be as much as 61 cm thick on some parts of the body. Besides protecting the animal against the cold, the blubber is an important food reserve.

Most of the best-known whales large creatures. For example, the blue whale reaches a length of more than 30 m. However, many whales, such as dolphins and porpoises, are small. Some are only 1. 5 to 1. 8 m long.

Whales live entirely in water. Sometimes, whales are stranded on the shore. Although they are air-breathing animals, they soon die because their great weight keeps them from expanding (opening out) the chest cavity. They can breathe easily when afloat, because the water supports most of their weight.

The bottle-nosed whale has been known to stay under water for about two hours. The sperm whale can dive down to depths of 500 fathoms. Such long and deep dives are unusual. Most dives last between 10 and 30 minutes. Whales have special mechanisms that help them to stay under water. When they breathe, they renew about nine-tenths of the air in their lungs. When human beings breathe in, only about one-fourth of the air is renewed. Whales therefore have a fairly large supply of fresh air to start with. They also have an additional oxygen supply in the muscles, where air is loosely held in combination with a pigment called myohaemoglobin. Another thing that helps whales hold their breath for long periods of time is their low sensitivity to carbon dioxide in the blood. (It is the carbon dioxide building up in human blood that affects the brain and makes the human being take another breath.)

When a whale surfaces to renew its air supply, it needs only to push the top of its snout out of the water. This is because the nostril or blowhole is at the top of the head. The expelled air is forced out strongly to form the spout or blow.

Living whales are divided into two groups — tooth whales and whalebone whales. Tooth whales, which include most species, generally have many conical teeth and eat mainly squids and fishes. The killer whale feeds on seals. One African river dolphin feeds mostly on plants. Other tooth whales include the narwhal and the sperm whale.

Whalebone whales have no teeth. Their mouths contain huge comblike fringes of baleen or whalebone. This horny substance is usually black. All whalebone whales feed by straining small animals from the water. The mouth is filled with water and the water is then forced out through the fringes by the tongue. The animals caught in the baleen are swept into the stomach by the tongue. All whalebone whales are large animals, which are usually found in cold seas. They include the blue whales, the right whales, and the rorquals.

The future of many of the larger kinds of whales is uncertain. Whalers have killed so many blue, bowhead, humpback, and right whales that those species are threatened with extinction. Overhunting has also greatly reduced the number of fin and sei whales. Also, if the human population does not stop increasing, people may have to compete with whales for food in the sea. Some nations have begun fishing for krill. Krill is the chief food of whales in Antarctic waters.

1. It is apparent from the first paragraph that whales can swim easily in the sea partly because they have _____.
    A. good bodily resistance to water
    B. only a few small bones inside the body
    C. neither hind limbs nor body hair
    D. a thick layer of fat under the skin

2. If they run onto the shore and are unable to get away from it whales will soon die because _____.
    A. they can't find anything to eat on the shore
    B. their great weight prevents them from breathing in
    C. they are left exposed to a lot of poisonous air
    D. their sensitivity to carbon dioxide in the blood increases to a fatal point

3. One of the reasons why whales can make long and deep dives is that _____.
    A. they are able to renew their air supply under water
    B. they don't need any extra oxygen supply in the muscles
    C. they renew only about one-fourth of the air in their lungs at a time
    D. they are little affected by carbon dioxide in the blood

4. Which of the following is true of whalebone whales according to the passage?
    A. They live mainly on plants.
    B. They are more dangerous than tooth whales.
    C. They get small water animals as their food.
    D. They are frequently found in warm seas.

5. We can learn from the passage all of the following about whales except that _____.
    A. their blubber performs two important functions
    B. they vary greatly in size
    C. overhunting places some of their species in danger of extinction
    D. they struggle hard to compete with humans for food in the sea

Passage Three

Junk Hunting
淘旧货

Anyone who thinks exploration always involves long journeys should have his head examined. Or, better, he should put on his oldest clothes and go off in search of a junk shop. There are three kinds — one full of discarded books, one full of discarded Government equipment, and one full of discarded anything. A junk shop may have four walls and a roof, or it may be no more than a trestle-table in an open air market; but there is one infallible test: no genuine junk shopkeeper will ever pester you to make up your mind and buy something. And you are no true junk shopper if you march purposefully round the shop as if you knew exactly what you wanted. You must browse, gently chewing the cud of your idle thoughts, and nibbling here and there as a sight or a touch of the goods that lie about you. Yet you must also possess a penetrating glance, darting your eyes about you to spot the treasures that may lurk beneath the rubbish. This is what makes junk shopping such a satisfying voyage of exploration. You never know what interesting and unexpected thing you may discover next. For in a true junk shop, not even the proprietor is always quite sure what his dusty stock conceals. There is always the chance that you may pick up a first edition, a pair of exotic ear-rings, a piece of early Wedgwood china, or a cine camera — and possess it for the price of fifty cigarettes.

But this kind of treasure hunt is only a sideline to the true junk shopper. The real attraction lies in finding something that catches your own especial fancy, though everybody else may pass it by. An ancient tarnished clock, whose brass beneath your hands will shine anew; empty boxes that you can see transformed into the framework of a bookcase; an old bound volume of magazines of three-quarters of a century ago, which will shed strange sidelights on the ways our great-grandparents behaved and looked at life.

When you begin junk shopping, half the attraction is that you go with absolutely no intention of buying anything. You spend your first couple of Saturday afternoons ambling around among dusty shelves, savouring a page or a chapter as you please, or fingering the piles of oddments that litter counters or tables. At first, be warned, don't try to buy. You may, indeed you should, ask the price of this and that; but just to give you an idea of what the junk shopkeeper thinks you might be willing to pay him.

Later, you will find yourself returning a second and third time to something that has caught your fancy. And when you can hold back no longer, bargaining begins in earnest. This is the other great attraction of the true junk shop. Not only may it hold every conceivable product from every imaginable country; it also transports you to the mediaeval market place or the oriental bazaar, where no price is fixed until buyer and seller have waged a friendly war together, and proved each other's mettle. And this is where your old clothes become important: let no one take you for a rich connoisseur, or you will find yourself paying a rich man's prices. And avoid at all costs the suspicion of an American accent, or in spite of the good nature of all good junk shopkeepers, you will be for it.

1. The author equates junk shopping with exploration because both involve _____.
   A. traveling long distances   B. careful preparation
   C. a spirit of adventure   D. discovering unheard of places
2. The part "gently chewing the cud of your idle thoughts" implies that the junk hunter is _____.
   A. eating sweets or gum as he wanders around
   B. not thinking of anything
   C. ruminating on this and that
   D. thinking of many things at the same time

3. According to the passage a true junk hunter hopes to _____.

    A. find something invaluable   B. discover something new

    C. discover something exotic   D. find a bargain

4. The author suggests that the junk buyer's main reason for bargaining is _____.

    A. to fix a price   B. that he hasn't enough money

    C. that it's expected   D. to ask a price

5. From the passage we understand that speaking with an American accent _____.

    A. arouses suspicion in the junk shopkeeper

    B. increases the price of the goods

    C. engenders friendliness in the shopkeeper

    D. increases the chance of bargaining

Passage Four

The Disaster of Terrorism
恐怖主义的灾难

by Craig Kielburger

New York has an energy of its own, and that late summer evening, I truly understood why. All around me the city was alive with activity as everyone headed in different directions. The Big Apple's fabled ambition, wealth, and power were on full display, in the sleek cars stopped by the curb, the bright windows of the bustling restaurants, and the studied nonchalance of stylish young people out on the town. As I cut through the financial district, I passed the Twin Towers, shimmering in the streetlights.

Then came the next morning. Even before I heard what was happening, it was clear that something was terribly wrong: there was an unfamiliar edge of desperation to the city's usual hectic pace. At a friend's house, uneasy but unsure why, I turned on the TV news. Within seconds, I saw one, then another, plane crash into the World Trade Center. Time stopped. I was hit by the sickening realization that what I was seeing was real. I found it difficult to breathe as I stared blankly at the television scene. The horror hit me in waves, each more intense than the last.

A short distance away, people were injured, trapped, and dying. America was under attack. Again and again, the brutal images flashed by. The city was in a state of emergency. People were being told to stay inside and off the phones. Airports were closed, bridges clogged.

That evening there was a knock on the door. On the doorstep stood a ragged man looking frightened and shaken, covered with a thick layer of dust. His eyes were wide and strangely glazed, and his body seemed to tremble. He turned out to be one of the few to have made it out of the World Trade Center alive. As my host and I later learned, this man had spent the day wandering the city in shock, trying to get through to his wife on his cell phone. When he finally reached her, tearful and happy beyond belief, she had reminded him that an acquaintance, my host, lived in the area. And so he stood there confused and full of apologies, unsure of what to say or do. Of course, he was immediately invited in. No sooner did he step across the threshold than he collapsed into a nearby chair. He would later say it was a miracle he was still alive.

The events that day rocked me to the core. Grieving for those affected, I realized that had things been different, I might have been at the World Trade Center myself. In the midst of my sadness and fear, I felt profoundly grateful to be alive. Twenty-four hours earlier, caught up in meeting after meeting, my biggest problem had seemed to be adding a few more hours onto the day. Now that world seemed so far away. Reeling from the tragedy, I realized that each and every hour I had was a blessing that not everyone would enjoy. I vowed never again to think of time as a problem-but only as a privilege.

1. The ambition, wealth, and power of New York City were fully demonstrated in _____.
   A. the dazzling cars, the brilliant shop windows, and the nonchalant stylish youth
   B. the dazzling cars, the brilliant shop windows, and the shimmering Twin Towers
   C. the Big Apple, the brilliant shop windows, and the nonchalant stylish youth
   D. the people in the streets, the brilliant shop windows, and the nonchalant stylish youth
2. What happened on the second day of Craig's stay in New York City?
   A. an earthquake
   B. a foreign invasion
   C. two airplanes crashing into the Twin Towers
   D. the collapse of many skyscrapers
3. The word *hectic* in the sentence "there was an unfamiliar edge of desperation to the city's usual hectic pace" is most probably in the meaning of _____.
   A. in good order   B. full of excitement or hurried activity
   C. in a terrible way   D. in rapidity
4. The man who showed up in the doorway was _____.
   A. a friend of Craig's   B. a friend of his host's
   C. a next-door neighbor   D. a fireman
5. In the last paragraph, Craig expressed the idea that time is _____.
   A. burden   B. sadness   C. fear   D. treasure

第三单元　副　词

······················· **I. Grammar: Adverbs** ·······················

A Multiple Choices

1. My dress doesn't fit me around the neck _____ right.
   A. quite　　　　　B. barely　　　　　C. nearly　　　　　D. rather

2. Which of the following sentences is correct?
   A. The family sent faithfully flowers all weeks to the cemetery.
   B. The family sent to the cemetery each week flowers faithfully.
   C. The family sent flowers faithfully to the cemetery each week.
   D. The family sent each week faithfully to the cemetery flowers.

3. The harder you work, the _____ likely you are to qualify as a doctor by the time you graduate.
   A. much　　　　　B. more　　　　　C. fewer　　　　　D. less

4. Tommy got 100 plus in his history examination because his paper was _____.
   A. extremely done well　　　　B. well done extremely
   C. done well extremely　　　　D. extremely well done

5. This pair of shoes isn't good, but that pair is _____ better.
   A. rather　　　　　B. over　　　　　C. hardly　　　　　D. less

6. My husband is leaving for America _____.
   A. soon　　　　　B. lately　　　　　C. late　　　　　D. sooner

7. I hope Margaret will _____ to go to the concert with us.
   A. enough early arrive　　　　B. early enough arrive
   C. arrive enough early　　　　D. arrive early enough

8. I didn't go to the football match because the ticket was _____ expensive for me.
   A. very much　　　B. so much　　　C. for too　　　D. a lot of

9. I go to the horse races often, but I only bet _____.
   A. scarcely　　　　B. frequently　　　　C. rarely　　　　D. occasionally

10. _____ superstitious beliesfs about the mandrake plant. .
    A. People have had long　　　　B. Have people long had
    C. People have long had　　　　D. Long have had people

11. Clever and intelligent as he is, he can never solve the problem _____ .

    A. alone   B. lonely   C. lone   D. alonely

12. He had _____ returned to his office when he was told to see his boss again.

    A. nearly   B. hardly   C. mostly   D. almost

13. My parents, _____ touring in Britain, are looking forward to a traditional English afternoon tea in a beautiful setting.

    A. nowadays   B. instantly   C. presently   D. intently

14. Little _____ that he would fulfil his task so rapidly.

    A. did we expected   B. did we expect

    C. we expected   D. we expect

15. He is always working _____ he can.

    A. as hardly as   B. as hard as   C. so hardly as   D. so hard as

16. When did you _____ see John?

    A. last   B. lastly   C. late   D. lately

17. _____ does she do anything important without asking her parents' advice first.

    A. Usually   B. Seldom   C. Sometimes   D. Often

18. Her second husband was _____ as rich as her first.

    A. quite   B. very   C. much   D. too

19. The students are _____ young people between ages of 16 and 20.

    A. mostly   B. almost   C. most   D. at most

20. Nuclear science should be developed to benefit the people _____ harm them.

    A. more than   B. rather than   C. other than   D. better than

21. English schoolboys often show the sense of sportsmanship to a _____ high degree in their relations with each other.

    A. precisely   B. surprisingly   C. clearly   D. essentially

22. A reserved person is one who _____ speaks a little and _____ gets excited.

    A. always... sometimes   B. often... never

    C. never... sometimes   D. always... seldom

23. _____ , I'm not going to tell him _____ .

    A. Speaking frankly... direct   B. Frankly speaking... directly

    C. Speaking frankly... directly   D. Frankly speaking... direct

24. Make sure the door is _____ shut before you leave.

    A. fastly   B. soundly   C. fast   D. sound

25. He went _____ to study _____ after he graduated from the university.

    A. abroad... further   B. abroadly... furtherly

    C. abroad... furtherly   D. abroadly... further

26. Most psychologists deeply believe that it is just _____ difficult to change a person's way of thinking as it does to rectify his deep-rooted habits.

    A. as   B. than   C. so   D. more

27. There are now _____ methods for studying color vision in infants than there once were.

    A. more sophisticated than   B. much more sophisticated

    C. much sophisticated   D. sophisticated

28. _____ does an individual find himself sought by both parties as their presidential candidate, as did General Eisenhower.

    A. Not only   B. Sometimes   C. Rarely   D. If

29. A survey has shown that Americans believe Kansas is _____ visited by foreign tourists than other states.

    A. rarely   B. never   C. fewer   D. less

30. I was _____ busy looking for the recruitement ads to pay attention to the other news in the newspaper.

    A. very   B. too   C. much   D. so

β Error Correction

1. Since it was so difficult for American Indians to negotiate a peace treaty or declare war in their native language, they used a universal understood form of sign language.

2. She turned up at the party last night, pretty dressed.

3. Alan, returning home very lately from his club, found an angry wife waiting for him.

4. First-aid experts stress that knowing what to do in an emergency can often save a life, specially in accident cases.

5. He got up, walked across the room, and with a sharp quick movement flung the door widely open.

6. The invitation to the conference indicated that everyone should be dressed formerly.

7. Influenza travels exactly as fastly as man.

8. To people from the northern parts of the country, tropical butterflies may seem incredible big.

9. We need an unusual gifted man to solve this sensitive problem.

10. The crucial time is drawing neraly.

11. He was dismissed by his boss not because he was inexperienced but because he was not enough careful.

12. The woman in the yard gathered her housecoat tightly about her and moved quickly indoor.

13. Buying the textbooks for his courses, paying his tuition, and renting a locker took most all the money he had saved from his summer job. He got only little money in his pocket now.

14. This is too far difficult a job for one fresh from college.

15. To become complete mature, a child has to pass through several different stages in development at different times and at different rates of speed.

II. Cloze Test

A Accommodation 住宿

One is never at a loss for a place to _____ (1) in Malaysia. The country's cities and major towns have a _____ (2) range of accommodation to suit all tastes and budgets. Most international-_____ (3) hotels cater to total living requirements and as such, one _____ (4) easily find restaurants, entertainment outlets and fitness centres within the _____ (5) complex.

Several resort hotels even have adjoining golf courses and _____ (6) parks with special privileges accorded to hotel guests. Family outings _____ (7) these hotels can be a practical yet fun-filled activity. Guests _____ (8) on longer stays may appreciate the serviced apartments situated within _____ (9) major cities.

Malaysia is also an excellent destination for romantic getaways, _____ (10) for honeymooners seeking an idyllic tropical retreat with _____ (11) amenities. The country's award-winning island resorts are paradises waiting to be _____ (12).

For budget-conscious tourists, there is an array of accommodations located _____ (13) to amenities and tourist attractions. Budget accommodations in Malaysia are _____ (14) according to the Orchid Classification Scheme and include hostels, bed _____ (15) breakfast establishments, inns, boarding houses, rest houses and lodging houses. _____ (16) Orchid rating is awarded to tourist accommodations offering basic facilities _____ (17) well as safe and clean premises.

Adventurous souls can try _____ (18) the innumerable value-for-money kampung-style chalets located along popular beaches. Nature _____ (19) seeking communion with nature in Malaysia's world-famous nature parks such _____ (20) Taman Negara will be amazed by the easy availability of chalets with modern facilities in these areas.

B Egyptian Villages 埃及村落

Most of the inhabitants live in mud-brick homes, their _____ (1) walls insulating against the afternoon heat. Flat roofs, exposed _____ (2) the northern evening breezes, serve as cool sleeping _____ (3) as well as storage areas. Villagers plaster the outer walls _____ (4) often trim them in blue, a color they believe _____ (5) off the evil eye. As a man becomes richer, _____ (6) can add a second story to his house perhaps _____ (7) his married son. Those villagers who have made the _____ (8) to Mecca paint the legend of their trip on _____ (9) outer walls of their homes. Such hajj houses, along _____ (10) the mosques, are the most distinguished buildings in a _____ (11).

Some villagers build ornate pigeon coops close to their _____ (12), using the birds as food and their droppings to _____ (13) crops. Many houses still have dirt floors and lack _____

（14）or running water; women with jars balanced on their ＿＿＿（15）make the trek to the community well, and children donkeys haul the ＿＿＿（16）liquid in jerry cans.

All ＿＿＿（17）said, government sponsored building programs have also brought newer ＿＿＿（18）residences and utilities to some villages, particularly those outside ＿＿＿（19）Nile Valley in the Oases and the Red Sea ＿＿＿（20）areas.

III. Reading Comprehension

Passage One

Vacationing in Mexico
在墨西哥度假

Each year more travelers are finding their way to the sun coasts of Mexico; where ancient civilizations once honored the sun, modern sun worshippers are discovering superb vacation destinations. Airlines now schedule weekly flights from major national and international points to a variety of sun coast resort areas.

The peninsula of Baja California provides one of the most splendid vacation sites in the Western Hemisphere. The peninsula is divided into two states: Baja California Norte and Baja California Sur, which are now connected by the Benito Ju rez Trans-peninsular Highway, so that the entire peninsula can be easily reached by car, as well as by sea and air. A chain of new hotels offer deluxe accommodations, but there are also numerous camping grounds, trailer parks and wayside inns for those who prefer casual-living vacations. At the southern end of the peninsula, La Pazi San Jos del Cabo and Cabo San Lucas offer rapidly expanding deluxe facilities to accommodate the growing influx of visitors. All have good accommodations, restaurants, sports facilities and meeting rooms. In addition, La Paz, with its duty-free zone, is a shopper's paradise.

Kino Bay, a coastal resort on the mainland near Hermosillo, is expanding and will soon offer new luxurious tourist accommodations.

South along the coast are Topolobampo and Los Mochis, the former a ferry terminus serving La Paz on the peninsula, and boasting the largest natural bay in the world; and the latter a starting point for the Chihuahua-Pacific Railway trip which goes through the breath-taking Copper Canyon to the city of Chihuahua.

Mazatlán, the sailfish capital of the world, has developed a large new resort complex to accommodate its many visitors. Famous for its jumbo shrimp and other delicious seafood, Mazatlán also offers seasonal bullfights, lively evening entertainment and big-game fishing. An international fishing tournament is held there each fall. Modern convention and sports facilities are available. Mazatlán is easily reached from other major cities by good high-ways and an international aiport.

Puerto Vallarta, once a sleepy fishing village, is now one of Mexico's fastest growing resorts. The red-tiled roofs and cobblestoned streets contrast with the luxurious new hotels. The annual temperature averages around 80°F. , offering a perfect climate for parasailing, skin diving, surfing and other aquatic sports. Evening entertainment includes seafood dinners, floor shows and disco dancing that lasts until daybreak. Big-game hunting and fishing are also popular within this region of coastal Mexico.

1. The Sun coasts of Mexico are excellent vacation destinations where in ancient times people _____ .

   A. worshipped the sun   B. built a pyramid to worship gods

   C. built roads leading to other places   D. went fishing in waters along the coasts

2. La Paz is an ideal place for shopping, because there _____ .

   A. people can buy whatever they want to

   B. people don't have to fulfill their duties

   C. people don't have to pay tax for their shopping

   D. people can buy things at reduced price

3. The world's largest natural bay is located in _____ .

   A. Topolobampo and Los Mochis   B. Los Mochis

   C. Mazatlán   D. Topolobampo

4. In Mazatlán, tourists can enjoy all the following except _____ .

   A. delicious seafood   B. watching seasonal bullfights

   C. visiting a famous aquarium   D. evening entertainment

5. This passage is most likely _____ .

   A. an advertisement   B. part of a tourist brochure

   C. the introduction to a book of travel   D. part of an essay

Passage Two

The Lagoon Show
礁湖秀

The most romantic time to arrive in Venice is at dusk on a winter's day. Your water-taxi ride across the lagoon from the airport will catch the last velvety-grey streaks of daylight. You'll arrive on the Grand Canal just as the upper windows of its palaces start to bloom with rose-coloured lamps or sparkle with chandeliers. In no other city does evening begin with such promise.

Strange, then, that Venice should be so emphatically not a night-time place. However mobbed it may have been in daylight, darkness falls with the abruptness of a hauled-down shutter. The crowds of Asian tourists and schoolkits milling around seem to vaporize. In a hundred closed cafes, the espresso machines give an expiring hiss, as if at last slipping off their shoes and wiggling their toes.

That is what makes Venice by night so magical, when the loudest sounds are those of footsteps and lapping water, and the modern world recedes so that in any Square or over any bridge, you wouldn't be surprised to meet a hurrying figure in a cloak and buckled shoes; Casanova on his way to some assignation, perhaps.

St. Mark's becomes an enchanted place, with pools of the day's flood still underfoot and mist wreathing the cathedral. But "nightlife" seems nonexistent outside the weeks of carnival each February. In a city so stuffed with historical treasures, the lack of a living, modern culture is achingly apparent, especially after dark.

Venice's only theatre of note, the Fenice, has only just reopened after almost a decade, following a fire. Clubs, discos, even cinemas are almost as hard to find as car parks. Nor is there the eating-out culture that governs the rest of Italy.

Venice is not usually regarded as a gourmet paradise. Even J G Links, author of the definitive, eccentric guidebook Venice for Pleasure, suggests it has few restaurants worth visiting outside the Cipriani hotel. As a rule, it's best to avoid canalside establishments with their *menus turisticos*; look for places down alleys. Remember, this is rice, not pasta country, offering some of the best risotto you're ever likely to eat.

When I first came here, aged 15, on a school trip, we were quartered in a girl's convent school. Ever since, I've stayed at the Gritti Palace, on the Grand Canal, overlooking the Salute. Apart from its mixture of elegance and old-fashioned comfort, I have two reasons for loving this hotel. Alighting at its private landing stage completes the thrill of arriving in Venice by night. And it was here, 13 years ago, that Sue and I decided to get married and have our daughter.

Gondolas operate until well after dark. It can be doubly romantic, with the Grand Canal in pitch-darkness and silent but for the churn of water buses and scraps of operatic arias that some gondoliers still perform.

Latterly, Venice has been making more efforts to get a nightlife. There is a disco named Casanova near the railway station and a music bar, Piccolo Mondo, near the Accademia bridge. The city's student population has created funkier areas around Campo Santa Margarita and in Cannaregio, the immigrant quarter to the north.

There is also street music after all the smart shops have closed and the only merchandise on offer is fake designer handbags, set out on the trestles used as walkways at times of flood. Around one corner, you may come upon a countertenor in an anourak, singing Handel; around another, two men will be playing selections from Andrew Lloyd Webber on a vibraphone of water-filled glasses. You think that sounds totally naff? I can tell you it sounded totally wonderful. Such is the alchemy of Venice by night.

1. The first and the second paragraphs are meant to tell the reader that on a winter's day _____.

   A. Venice is very beautiful in the evening

   B. Venice is beautiful at dusk, and so is it at night

   C. Venice is beautiful at dusk, however, it doesn't seem an ideal place for nightlife

   D. there are not many people out in the street in Venice

2. There is a sentence in the second paragraph: "In a hundred closed cafes the espresso machines give an expiring hiss, as if at last slipping off their shoes and wiggling their toes." How do you understand this sentence?

   A. It means that the coffee machines have been used for too much and cannot be used any longer.

   B. It implies that the owners of these cafes are so tired that they just want to have a good rest.

   C. It suggests that the owners of these cafes have lost their shoes and their toes feel painful with cold.

   D. The coffee machines are going to stop working; it is just like what a person does before he goes to bed after a day's hard work.

3. The author mentions a cathedral in the passage. What is the name of this cathedral?

   A. St. Mark.   B. St. Mark's

   C. The Fenice.   D. The name is not given in the passage.

4. It is implied in the passage that car parks _____.

   A. are difficult to find in the whole Italy   B. are easy to find in the whole Italy

   C. are difficult to find in Venice   D. are easy to find in Venice

5. Which of the following can best summarize the passage?

   A. Venice provides visitors with delicious food of Italian style.

   B. Songs and music are special features of Venice by night.

   C. If you want to enjoy nightlife, Venice is a wonderful place.

   D. Venice is not a good place for nightlife at present, yet the evening of Venice has its own glamour.

Passage Three

An Underwater Hotel
水下旅馆

In a bay near Almeria in Southern Spain will be built the world's first underwater residence for tourists. The hotel will be 40 feet down in the Mediterranean. As all the world opened to tour operators, there was still a frontier behind which lay three quarters of the globe's surface, the sea; in whose cool depths light fades; no winds blow; there are no stars. There even the most bored travelers could recapture their sense of romance, terror or beauty. For a submerged hotel is such a beautiful idea.

The hotel will cost? 170,000 and will be able to accommodate up to ten people a night. Up until now only scientists and professional divers have lived under the sea, but soon, for the first time, the public will be able to go down into the darkness. They will have to swim down in diving suits, but at 40 feet there would be no problem about decompression.

Design of the hotel was crucial. Most of the underwater structures used before had been in the shape of a diving bell or submarine. Professional divers could cope with such things but ordinary people would run the risk of violent claustrophobia. Then an Austrian architect had the idea of making three interconnecting circular structures, 18 feet in diameter, and looking much like flying saucers. They would be cast in concrete and launched from the shore. Towed into position they would then be sunk. A foundation of cast concrete would already be in place on the sea bed. Pylons would attach the structures to this. Once in position the structures would be pumped dry. The pylons, made to withstand an uplift pressure of 350 tons, would then take the strain.

Cables linking the underwater structures to the hotel on shore would connect it with electricity, fresh water, television, and an air pump, and also dispose of sewage. Entry would be from underneath, up a ladder; because of the pressure inside there would be no need of airlocks or doors.

The first structure would include a changing room and a shower area, where the divers would get out of their gear. There would also be a kitchen and a lavatory. The second structure would contain a dining room/lecture theater, and sleeping accommodation for eight people. The third structure would contain two suites. A steward would come down with the ten customers, to cook and look after them. Television monitors would relay all that went on to the shore so that discussions on the sea bed could be transmitted to all the world.

Around the hotel there are plans to build a strange secret garden, over 100 yards square, of plastic shapes, curves, circles, hollows. This would have a dual function. First, to attract fish who would see it as a shelter and hiding place; secondly, to allow guests looking out of the reinforced windows to see a teeming underwater life.

So far at the site a diving tower 33 feet deep has been installed for diving instruction. An aquarium has been built, and zoologists from Vienna University are in regular attendance to supervise its stocking. There are storage cupboards full of the plastic shapes for the underwater garden and there is a model of the hotel. All that is needed now is permission from the Spanish Government to start building.

1. From the passage we understand that tour operators were particularly interested in the siting of the hotel as _____.
   A. it was still undiscovered B. it was still unexplored
   C. it would offer new possibilities D. it would have unchanging weather
2. What design was finally considered most suitable for the new hotel?
   A. three separate circles B. three linked discs
   C. three connected globes D. three interlocked cylinders

3. The hotel would be able to float under water because it would be _____.

    A. made of light material   B. 350 tons in weight

    C. filled with air   D. attached to pylons

4. The purpose of television monitors under the sea would be to relay _____.

    A. instructions from the sea bed to the shore

    B. news from the shore to the sea bed

    C. information from the world to the sea bed

    D. information to the world from the sea bed

5. In the passage we are told that zoologists came from Vienna University to _____.

    A. study the fish in the aquarium

    B. decide which fish to put in the aquarium

    C. supervise the building of the aquarium

    D. help build the aquarium

Passage Four

My First Visit to Paris
我初次造访巴黎

My first visit to Paris began in the company of some earnest students. My friend and I, therefore being full of independence and the love of adventure, decided to go off on our own and explore Northern France as hitch-hikers.

We managed all right down the main road from Paris to Rouen, because there were lots of vegetable trucks with sympathetic drivers. After that we still made headway along secondary roads to F camp, because we fell in with two family men who had left their wives behind and were off on a spree on their won. In F camp, having decided that it was pointless to reserve money for emergencies such as railway fares, we spent our francs in great contentment, carefully arranging that we should have just enough left for supper and an overnight stay at the Youth Hostel in Dieppe, before catching the early morning boat.

Dieppe was only fifty miles away, so we thought it would be a shame to leave F camp until late in the afternoon.

There is a hill outside F camp, a steep one. We walked up it quite briskly, saying to each other as the lorries climbed past us, that, after all, we couldn't expect a French truck driver to stop on a hill for us. It would be fine going from the top.

It probably would have been fine going at the top, if we had got there before the last of the evening truck convoy had passed on its way westwards along the coast. We failed to realize that at first, and sat in dignified patience on the crest of the hill. We were sitting there two and a half hours later — still dignified, but less patient. Then we went about two hundred yards further down to a little bistro, to have some coffee and ask advice from the proprietor. He told us that there would be no more trucks and explained that our gentlemanly signaling stood out the slightest chance of stopping a private motorist.

"This is the way one does it!" he exclaimed, jumping into the centre of the road and completely barring the progress of a vast, gleaming car which contained a rather supercilious Belgian family, who obviously thought nothing to all of the two bedraggled English students. However, having had to stop, they let us into the back seat, after carefully removing all objects of value, including their daughter.

Conversation was not easy, but we were more than content to stay quiet — until the car halted suddenly in an out-of-the-way village far from the main road, and we learned to our surprise that the Belgians went no farther. They left us standing disconsolate on a deserted country road, looking sorrowfully after them as their rear lamp disappeared into the darkness.

We walked in what we believed to be the general direction of Dieppe for a long time. At about 11 p. m., we heard, far in the distance, a low-pitched staccato rumbling. We ran to a rise in the road and from there we saw, as if it were some mirage, a vast French truck approaching us. It was no time for half measures. My friend sat down by the roadside and hugged his leg, and looked as much like a road accident as nature and the circumstances permitted. I stood in the middle of the road and held my arms out. As soon as the lorry stopped as rushed to either side and gabbled out a plea in poor if voluble French for a lift to Dieppe.

There were two aboard, the driver and his relief, and at first they thought we were a hold-up. When we got over that, they let us in, and resumed the journey.

We reached the Youth Hostel at Dieppe at about 1:30 a. m., or as my friend pointed out, precisely 3 hours after all doors had been locked. This, in fact, was not true, because after we climbed over a high wall and tiptoed across the forecourt, we discovered that the door to the washroom was not properly secured, and we were able to make our stealthy way to the men's dormitory where we slept soundly until roused at 9:30 the following morning.

〜〜〜〜〜〜〜〜〜〜〜〜〜〜〜〜〜〜〜〜〜〜〜〜〜〜〜〜

1. The author and his friend decided to hitch-hike together in Northern France as _____.
   A. the other students didn't want to go with them
   B. it was difficult to find public transport
   C. they didn't want to stay with the other students
   D. it had never been explored

2. The travelers were able to reach F camp by getting a lift from _____.
   A. two men who had left their wives   B. two different lorry drivers
   C. two men driving different cars   D. two men without their wives

3. The bistro proprietor thought that cars wouldn't stop for the two students because _____.
   A. only gentlemen could understand their signals
   B. they only signaled to gentlemen
   C. they were too polite to signal
   D. their signals were too polite

4. The Belgian family made their daughter sit in the front of the car because they thought _____ _____.

    A. the students were too dirty to sit near

    B. the students wouldn't value her enough

    C. the students couldn't be trusted near her

    D. the students were too rude to speak to

5. The author's friend sat down at the side of the road because _____.

    A. he was too tired to walk any further

    B. he had had an accident and hurt his leg

    C. he thought the lorry driver would see him clearly there

    D. he wanted to give the lorry driver a reason to stop

第四单元 冠 词

········· **I. Grammar: Articles** ·········

A **Multiple Choices**

1. Although afflicted by _____ serious eyesight problems, Alicia Alonso was one of _____ principal stars of _____ American Ballet Theater.
   A. the... /... /   B. /... the... the   C. the... a... /   D. /... a... the

2. If laid out in _____ straight line, _____ human digestive tract would measure approximately thirty-foot long.
   A. a... the   B. /... the   C. the... /   D. the... a

3. Families like _____ Rockefellers have become _____ synonym for _____ wealth.
   A. /... the... a   B. the... a... /   C. the... /... a   D. /... a... the

4. _____ umbrellas are commonly used to protect _____ people from _____ rain.
   A. /... the... the   B. The... the... /   C. /... /... /   D. The... /... the

5. Western art of _____ 19th century shows _____ influence of _____ Far East.
   A. the... an... /   B. /... the... the   C. the... the... the   D. /... an... /

6. According to cognitive theories of emotion, _____ anger occurs when _____ individuals believe that they have been harmed and that _____ harm was both avoidable and undeserved.
   A. a... /... the   B. an... /... a   C. /... /... the   D. /... /... a

7. _____ religion used to have _____ strong hold on people.
   A. The... a   B. A... the   C. An... the   D. /... a

8. Jackie McLean's recordings have shown that he is one of _____ few jazz musicians whose style of playing has kept _____ pace with _____ evolution of modern jazz.
   A. /... /... the   B. the... a... /   C. /... a... an   D. the... /... the

9. _____ elasmosaur, _____ giant prehistoric sea reptile with fierce-looking jaws and flippers, had _____ muscular neck that accounted for more than half its length.
   A. The... /... a   B. The... a... a   C. A... /... a   D. The... a... /

10. Every one of us has _____ machine. _____ machine is _____ brain.
    A. a... A... the   B. a... The... the   C. the... A... a   D. a... A... a

11. Throughout the whole of _____ conversation, he never once looked me in _____ face.

    A. a... the   B. /... the   C. the... the   D. the... /

12. The old man is in _____ habit of going for _____ walk along _____ river every morning except that it rains.

    A. a... a... the   B. the... the... a   C. /... a... the   D. the... a... the

13. _____ Mr. White called you in _____ afternoon.

    A. A... the   B. /... /   C. The... the   D. The... /

14. _____ most common kind of fuel used by _____ peasants in our district is _____ wood.

    A. /... the... the   B. /... the... /

    C. The... /... the   D. The... the... /

15. I don't want to be _____ one to break _____ news to him.

    A. the... a   B. the... the   C. a... the   D. a... /

16. I have got _____ better understanding of _____ Einstein's special theory of relativity after attending a series of lectures on that topic.

    A. a... /   B. /... the   C. a... the   D. /... /

17. They bought _____ nice house in 1996. Years later, they bought _____ second house.

    A. the... /   B. a... the   C. a... a   D. /... the

18. _____ length, _____ breadth and _____ height of _____ cube are equal.

    A. The... the... the... a   B. /... /... /... a

    C. A... a... a... the   D. The... /... /... /

19. _____ good teacher should not do all _____ talking in _____ class.

    A. The... the... a   B. A... the... /   C. /... /... the   D. A... /... a

20. Professor Lee has _____ large collection of books, many of which are written in _____ foreign languages.

    A. /... /   B. the... the   C. a... /   D. the... /

21. It has been estimated that only 21 percent of _____ world's land surface can be cultivated and that only 7. 6 percent is actually under _____ cultivation.

    A. /... /   B. the... the   C. /... the   D. the... /

22. He is very famous. He is _____ poet and _____ novelist.

    A. a... a   B. the... the   C. a... /   D. the... /

23. Since _____ beginning of photography, _____ inventors have tried to make _____ photographs that duplicate _____ natural colors.

    A. the... /... /... /   B. the... the... /... the

    C. /... /... /... /   D. /... the... the... /

24. That is _____ very question he asked _____ last week.

    A. the... /   B. a... /   C. /... the   D. a... the

25. He was put in _____ charge of _____ reeducation of laid-off workers.

    A. /... /   B. the... /   C. /... the   D. the... the

26. Microwave cooking can be described as _____ first absolutely new method of preparing _____ food since _____ discovery of fire.

    A. a... the... the   B. the... /... the
    C. a... /... /   D. the... the... the

27. Without _____ use of money, trade will depend on _____ barter, _____ direct exchange of one commodity for another.

    A. /... the... the   B. the... /... the   C. /... a... the   D. a... /... a

28. _____ old man had _____ bad fall. Will somebody send to _____ doctor?

    A. An... /... a   B. /... a... /   C. The... /... the   D. The... a... a

29. If they have to share _____ apartment with _____ stranger, they may travel many miles without starting _____ conversation.

    A. a... the... the   B. an... a... a   C. an... a... the   D. a... a... the

30. Seeing _____ pictures, she couldn't help thinking of _____ happy days in _____ Vienna.

    A. /... the... /   B. /... /... the   C. the... the... /   D. the... /... the

β Error Correction

1. I started a rigorous program of running and dieting very next day.

2. If they will not accept a check, we shall have to pay in the cash, though it would be much trouble for both sides.

3. What a fine weather we are having!

4. Objects which fall freely in a vacuum have same rate of speed regardless of differences in size and weight.

5. Eleanor Roosevelt played leading part in women's organizations, and she was active in encouraging youth movement, and in promoting consumer welfare.

6. The earliest process for mining gold is panning, which involves using a circular dish with a small pocket at a bottom.

7. There were already four people sitting in the car, but we tried to make a room for her.

8. Several newspapers are on trail of some corrupt politicians.

9. All twelve of Henry's friends were shaking with the laughter.

10. He spoke at a length about the reforms in his college.

11. Sam, an university student, invented a new medical instrument.

12. The moon is a very silent world, for sound waves can only travel through the air.

13. The expansion of adult training program has resulted partially from the feminist movement, which encourages the women to improve their skills for the job market.

14. Long Island, an island that forms the southeastern part of New York, has greater population than before.

15. I held the opinion that a honest man is sure to receive high respect from others.

II. Cloze Test

A **Coast Along in Unspoilt Turkey（I）畅游在原始的土耳其（I）**

Turkey's Bodrum peninsula is different. The tourist boom in this part of the world _____ (1) turned some small villages into resorts yet left neighbouring beaches undisturbed, making it quite _____ (2) southern France or the Spanish Coasts where few stretches of coastline are undeveloped.

The _____ (3) for this happy set of circumstances is simple. For thousands of years, travel here _____ (4) easier by boat than by land. So when mass tourism arrived in the _____ (5) 1980s, there was no coast road for ribbon development to follow. So the peninsula, just _____ (6) hour from Bodrum airport, has not become one long littoral of resort.

The building _____ (7) new hotels has mainly been confined to places easily reached by then relatively _____ (8) roads. Such ease of access has made Gumbet, near Bodrum, a busy resort, while the little fishing village of Gumusluk, 12 miles further west and only recently reachable by _____ (9), remains tranquil and undisturbed.

It's worth thinking carefully about location when planning a family _____ (10) on the peninsula. Choose a place that is centrally located, preferably out of earshot _____ (11) Bodrum town's "lively" — which means nosy — nightlife, and you can then use _____ (12) area's comfortably small scale to your advantage. Today's new roads mean most places can _____ (13) reached in under an hour by taxi or the ubiquitous *dolmus*-minibus.

The _____ (14) of facilities at the Tamarisk Beach Hotel near the small village of Ortakent makes _____ (15) a good base. The family-run hotel — rooms and suites are in two-storey buildings _____ (16) by palm trees and flowers in terracotta pots — sits above its own sandy _____ (17) beach, shaded by tamarisk trees and sheltered by nearby islands.

The hotel is _____ (18) child-friendly, too. Children, from infants up to young teenagers, can take part in a _____ (19) of games and activities that include tuition in windsurfing, dinghy _____ (20) catamaran sailing.

B **Coast Along in Unspoilt Turkey（II）畅游在原始的土耳其（II）**

Pack such activities into a morning before it gets too hot, then take excursions in the late afternoon _____ (1) the heat starts to abate. This is the best time of day to catch the hotel courtesy bus _____ (2) nearby Bodrum, the Halicarnassus of classical history. It was the birthplace of the historian Herodotus and the _____ (3) of the Mausoleum, one of seven wonders of the ancient world.

The Mausoleum survived for 19 centuries _____ (4), in 1522, the Crusaders used its stones to build the castle of St Peter, _____ (5) still stands at the entrance to the harbour. It now housed a museum of underwater archaeology displaying items recovered from the seabed off the _____ (6), which is scattered with shipwrecks that date back to the Bronze Age.

Trips to most points on the peninsula _____ (7) through the high heartland, with splendid views, to the north and south coast. The interior is a timeless _____ (8) of windmills and citrus orchards, deserted villages and ancient monasteries. Donkeys, still the main beast of _____ (9), amble along the roads.

There are some busy resorts on the southwestern coast, including Karaincir, a broad sandy beach _____ (10) by hotels and restaurants, and Akyarlar. The Greek island of Kos is five miles away.

There's no real _____ (11) to hire a car in this part of Turkey. Minibuses are cheap and many hotels organize trips _____ (12) the peninsula as well as longer excursions to the great classical sties of Ephesus and Aphrodisias. If you want _____ (13) freedom, hire a car for a few days from Bodrum, where prices are competitive although it is worth _____ (14) that the quote you receive includes insurance.

The roads may have improved but the most evocative way to _____ (15) the area is till by boat. Bus boats and day trips operate from Bodrum and most other harbours _____ (16) beaches around the peninsula. From the port of Torba, for example, there are daily boat trips to Didyma _____ (17) view the Temple of Apollo. You can also negotiate your own boat hire if you have specific _____ (18) in mind.

Summer waters are usually placid, and the winds are light. Boats often _____ (19) anchor as they dawdle around the coast to allow passengers to swim. And as you look towards shore you see a landscape _____ (20) has changed little since antiquity.

III. Reading Comprehension

Passage One

The City of Winchester
温切斯特市

Many visitors to Great Britain who make a point of visting the famous cultural shrines of Stratford, Oxford, Cambridge and Canterbury are less aware of the equally rewarding historical interest and the friendly individuality of the ancient capital, the city of Winchester.

This Hampshire centre of around 30,000 inhabitants has welcomed (and, on various occasions, repulsed) a succession of visitors for nearly three thousand years. Early tribes occupied it from time to time, and much later the Roman colonisers established a commercial centre with solidly-constructed straight roads radiating from it. It was Alfred the Great who, in the ninth century, made the small town the national centre of learning, though his statue dominating the main street recalls the warrior with raised cross-like sword. Norman succeeded Sxon and soon the cathedral, one of the loveliest and richest in architectural interest in England, was being erected. A college was founded in the fourteenth century and even though a decline in the wood trade led to a period of economic stagnation, the college maintained the town's tradition of learning and is one of the most famous public schools of today.

Present-day traffic has destroyed much of the peace of the city centre. Private cars and buses which surge through the narrow streets at weekends may be supplemented on weekdays by lorries roaring on their way to Southampton. And yet away from the busier roads, the prevailing atmosphere remains one of calm meditation and contentment. From the smooth sun-flecked lawns of the Close, patterned with leaf-shadows from gently stirring foliage, rises the cathedral, its comfortable, square, late-Norman tower, its Norman transepts and severe Gothic nave suggesting that the beauty created by man, though not imperishable, may survive wars and revolutions, and represent the endurance of traditional values even in an age of undignified scurrying change. Certain houses round the Close may have provided homes for the loyal subjects of the first Queen Elizabeth when Shakespeare was learning to write. The youth Hostel, a mill standing on the city's river, is more than two hundred years old. In well-mannered unobtrusiveness, the old buildings of the main street blend with the new, and a walk through the town centre is one of enjoyable discoveries.

The rounded hills of Southern England, among which the city is built, shelter a country-side of farms and picturesque villages, where, despite motor transport and television, many of the old rural traditions and mental attitudes are preserved.

Winchester belongs to its surroundings: it is the appropriate centre of a region of prosperous, quiet, richly-green countryside. Lively, up-to-date and friendly, it maintains very many English traditions of fine domestic and ecclesiastical architecture, of graciousness and imperturbability, of richly inventive variety and peaceful dignity which are among the highest achievements of all those English planners and designers who created the heritage we now enjoy.

1. It appears that many visitors to Great Britain _____.
   A. find the city of Winchester very attractive
   B. think Winchester comparable to other places of interest
   C. are aware of the historical importance of Winchester
   D. know less about Winchester than about other famous cultural shrines
2. Who was responsible for the building of the famous cathedral in the city?
   A. The Roman colonisers.   B. The Saxons.
   C. The Normans.   D. Alfred the Great.
3. The word "severe" in "severe Gothic nave" (in Paragraph 3) is closest in meaning to _____.
   A. serious   B. simple   C. fierce   D. violent

4. It can be seen from the passage that the author _____.

    A. cherishes old traditions   B. opposes any social change

    C. works for a tourist agency   D. lives in the city of Winchester

5. Which of the following words can best describe the city's surroundings?

    A. Up-to-date.   B. Ecclesiastical.   C. Peaceful.   D. Lively.

Passage Two

Samuel Johnson
塞缪尔·约翰逊

    Visitors to St. Paul's Cathedral are sometimes astonished as they walk round the space under the dome to come upon a statue which would appear to be that of a retired gladiator meditating upon a wasted life. They are still more astonished when they see under it an inscription indicating that it represents the English writer, Samuel Johnson. The statue by Bacon, but it is not one of his best works. The figure ism as often in eighteenth-century sculpture, clothed only in a loose robe which leaves arms, legs and one shoulder bare. But the strangeness for us is not one of costume only. If we know anything of Johnson, we know that he was constantly ill all through his life; and whether we know anything of him or not we are apt to think of a literary man as a delicate, weakly, nervous sort of person. Nothing can be further from that than the muscular statue. And in this matter the statue is perfectly right. And the fact which is reports is far from being unimportant. The body and the mind are inextricably interwoven in all of us, and certainly in Johnson's case the influence of the body was obvious and conspicuous. His melancholy, his constantly repeated conviction of the general unhappiness of human life, was certainly the result of his constitutional infirmities. On the other hand, his courage, and his entire indifference to pain, were partly due to his great bodily strength. Perhaps the vein of rudeness, almost of fierceness, which sometimes showed itself in his conversation, was the natural temper of an invalid and suffering giant. That at any rate is what he was. He was the victim from childhood of a disease which resembled St. Vitus's Dance. He never knew the natural joy of a free and vigorous use of his limbs; when he walked it was like the struggling walk of one in irons. All accounts agree that his strange gesticulations and contortions were painful for his friends to witness and attracted crowds of starers in the streets. But Reynolds says that he could sit still for his portrait to be taken, and that when his mind was engaged by a conversation the convulsions ceased. In any case, it is certain that neither this perpetual misery, not his constant fear of losing his reason, nor his many grave attacks of illness, ever induced him to surrender the privileges that belonged to his physical strength. He justly thought no character so disagreeable as that of a chronic invalid, and was determined not to be one himself. He had known what it was to live on fourpence a day and scorned the life of sofa cushions and tea into which well-attended old gentlemen so easily slip.

1. We understand from the passage that most eighteenth-century sculpture was _____.
   A. done by a man called Bacon
   B. not very well made
   C. loosely draped
   D. left bare

2. "The body and the mind are inextricably interwoven" means _____.
   A. they interact with each other
   B. they are confused by all of us
   C. they have little effect on each other
   D. they are mixed up in all of us

3. Samuel Johnson's unhappiness was caused by _____.
   A. his melancholy nature
   B. his physical disabilities
   C. his strength of character
   D. his ill-temper

4. The author says Johnson found it difficult to walk because _____.
   A. he couldn't control his legs
   B. he generally wore irons round his legs
   C. people always stared at him
   D. it hurt his friends to watch him

5. According to the passage, Johnson had _____.
   A. never had enough money to live on
   B. managed to live on tea only
   C. lived frugally in the past
   D. always lived in easy circumstances

Passage Three

The Grand Canyon
大峡谷

The Grand Canyon, exceptionally deep, steep-walled canyon in northwestern Arizona, is excavated by the Colorado River. The Grand Canyon is 446 km long, up to 29 km wide, and more than 1,500 m deep. The entire canyon is extremely beautiful, containing towering buttes, mesas, and valleys within its main gorge. A spectacular section of the canyon, together with plateau areas on either side of it, are preserved as the Grand Canyon National Park, which receives about four million visitors a year.

The Grand Canyon cuts steeply through and arid plateau region that lies between about 1,500 and 2,700 m above sea level. This region, although lacking year-round streams in recent years, is sharply eroded, showing such characteristic forms as buttes; it is interspersed with old lava flows, hills composed of volcanic debris, and intrusions of igneous rock. The plateau area has a general downward slope to the southwest and in its upper reaches is sparsely covered with such evergreens as juniper and pion. Parts of the northern rim of the canyon are forested. Vegetation in the depths of the valley consists principally of such desert plants as agave and Spanish bayonet. In general the entire canyon area has little soil. The climate of the plateau region above the canyon is severe, with extremes of both heat and cold. The canyon floor also becomes extremely hot in summer, but seldom experiences frost in the wintertime.

The Grand Canyon has been sculpted in general by the downward cutting of the Colorado River, which flows through the canyon's lowest portions. Other factors have also played a part. The Kaibab Plateau, which forms the northern rim of the canyon, is about 365 m higher than the Coconino Plateau, which forms the southern rim. Water from the northern side has flowed into the canyon, forming tributary valleys, while the streams of the southern plateau flow away in a southerly direction without carving valleys in the canyon walls. The underlying rock beds also have a southwestern slant, with the result that groundwater from the north finds its way into the canyon, but water from the south does not. In the entire canyon region, the rocks have been broken by jointing and faulting, and fractures in the rocks resulting from these processes have contributed to the rapid erosion of the gorge.

The Grand Canyon is of relatively recent origin; apparently the river began its work of erosion about six million years ago. Coupled with the downward cutting of the river has been a general rising or upwarping of the Colorado Plateau, which has added its effect to the action of the river.

Although the canyon itself is of comparatively recent origin, the rocks exposed in its walls are not. Most of the strata were originally deposited as marine sediment, indicating that for long periods of time the canyon area was the floor of a shallow sea.

In a typical section of the canyon, toward its eastern end, nine separate rock layers can be seen, piled vertically like a stack of pancakes. Beneath these layers, at the bottom of the canyon, are the most ancient rocks of all, Precambrian schists and gneisses, from half a billion to a billion years old.

1. Which of the following is true of the first paragraph?
   A. The Grand Canyon National Park consists of the whole canyon.
   B. The Grand Canyon National Park covers a part of the canyon and plateau areas on both sides of it.
   C. The most impressive part of the canyon is just beside the Grand Canyon National Park.
   D. The Grand Canyon National Park contains towering buttes, mesas and the whole valleys.
2. Where does the desert plant agave grow in the Grand Canyon?
   A. It grows on the towering buttes.　　　B. It grows on the mesas.
   C. It grows on the plateau.　　　D. It grows in the depths of the valley.
3. Why does the groundwater from the north finds its way into the canyon, but the water from the south doesn't?
   A. Because there are fractures in the rocks in the south.
   B. Because the southwest part of the underlying rock beds are a bit lower than those in the opposite direction.
   C. Because the pressure of the upper streams forces the water to flow in from the north and

flow away from the south.

    D. The reason is not mentioned in the passage.

4. What does the author mean by saying that the Grand Canyon is of relatively recent origin?

    A. The river almost completed its work of erosion only about six million years ago.

    B. The Colorado Plateau only rose a comparatively short time from now.

    C. Volcanic debris and intrusions of igneous rock are of recent origin.

    D. The form of the canyon is the result of the recent work done by the natural force.

5. According to the passage, where can the oldest rocks be found?

    A. Near Precambrian schists.

    B. Below Precambrian schists.

    C. At the bottom of the canyon.

    D. In the strata deposited as marine sediment.

Passage Four

Tourism Enriched Campaign
旅游致富运动

    "Tourism enriches individuals, families, communities and all the world." This is a central, simple but straight-forward message of the new awareness campaign with which the World Tourism Organization (WTO) wants to raise awareness of the positive impacts tourism can have on life, culture and economy, in shourt on society at all levels.

    The "Tourism Enriches" campaign was launched at the First World Conference on Tourism Communications (TOURCOM) end of January in Madrid. "This is the first time WTO has aimed a campaign at the general public," said WTO Secretary-General Mr. Francesco Frangialli. "It is a simple, upbeat idea and a simple beginning, but ultimately the campaign is intended to be developed and used by the tourism industry, especially ministries in our member countries, as they see fit."

    The initiative came from the WTO Members last year and was discussed at the 15th Session of the General Assembly in Beijing, China, last October.

    "Governments have been putting a higher priority on tourism in the time of recent crises," stressed Mr. Frangialli, explaining that this resulted in recognition of tourism as the most prospective activity, important for environmental, cultural and social awareness, pursuit of peace and international cooperation recognition and in particular of its ability to alleviate poverty through the creation of small and medium sized tourism businesses and the creation of new jobs. "That same recognition has taken place at the highest level in the General Assembly of the United Nations, which unanimously agreed on December 23rd to make the WTO its newest specialized agency."

    "We are calling upon governments to implement this importance of tourism in practice and invest more funds in tourism development and communications," said the Secretary-General. "The success of Tourism Enriches' also depends in part on its diffusion in the media, so we are inviting them to become the third member in the already established public-private partnership in international tourism."

The aims of "Tourism Enriches" campaign are to promote tourism as a basic human right and way of life, to stimulate communication about the benefits of tourism as the most prospective economic activity for the local communities and countries, to enhance cooperation between destinations and the tourism industry with the local, regional and international media and to link individual tourism entities to the larger community of international tourism.

Cooperating in the campaign is offered to all destinations, tourist companies and the media, unconditionally with the membership status in the WTO. "While we believe that the principles of this campaign are acceptable for all, we in particular invite the developing world to adopt them and link them to the United Nations Millennium Development Goals," added Mr. Frangialli.

The campaign features five basic components that can be adapted and expanded for use by Member States, Affiliate Members of the WTO and the rest of the tourism industry in their own tourism promotion and awareness building activities: the slogan "Tourism Enriches", the graphic image or logo of the campaign, a six-page A4 size flyer outlining positive impacts of tourism, such as economic benefits, increased international understanding, rural jobs, environmental protection, etc., an attractive poster using the same artwork and a thirty second video public service announcement for free use on national television channels, airlines, and satellite TV (in progress).

The TOURCOM Network of Communications Experts, a new consultative body to the WTO Press and Communications Section, will be responsible for implementing the campaign within the scope of their own activities around the world.

Interested parties will be invited to use elements of the campaign at the local, regional and national level on destination brochures and advertising in the print media, on press familiarization trips, to publish the campaign materials in local languages, add the campaign to tourism websites, and to develop their own tools and practices, which will be shared through WTO with other tourism stakeholders.

Please note: Artwork, logo and flyers and other elements will be shortly featured on the WTO website under Newsroom.

1. Where and when was the Tourism Enriches campaign launched?
   A. It was launched in Madrid in January.
   B. It was launched in New York last October.
   C. It was launched in Beijing last October.
   D. It was launched in WTO end of January.

2. According to Mr. Frangialli, governments of countries have recognized tourism as the most prospective activity for the following reasons EXCEPT that _____.

    A. tourism can increase environmental, cultural and social awareness

    B. tourism is helpful to industry

    C. tourism can help to bring about world peace

    D. tourism can create new jobs

3. When mentioning media, the Secretary-General meant that media play the role of _____.

    A. investing funds in tourism development

    B. making advertisements for tourism industry

    C. spreading the message of Tourism Enriches campaign

    D. stimulating economic activities

4. What are the five basic components that the Tourism Enriches campaign features?

    A. the slogan of the campaign; the graphic image; six pages of paper; advertisements; a thirty minute video program

    B. its slogan; the graphic image or logo; a published book outlining positive impacts of tourism; national television channels; satellite TV

    C. its slogan; the graphic image or logo of the campaign; a six-page flyer; a poster; a video announcement

    D. the slogan of the campaign; the graphic image or logo; an A4 size advertisement; video announcement; airlines

5. According to the passage, the positive impact of tourism is that it can enrich _____.

    A. communities   B. families   C. individuals   D. all of the above

第五单元 语 态

I. Grammar: Voice

A Multiple Choices

1. A new big oilfield is reported _____ in the west of the country.
   A. to have been found
   B. to be found
   C. found
   D. having been found

2. When I returned home from a long journey, I found my house _____.
   A. had been broken in
   B. was broken into
   C. had broken in
   D. had broken into

3. The patient strongly objected to _____ like this.
   A. be treated   B. treating   C. being treated   D. treat

4. He had no idea how much a room in this hotel _____.
   A. was charged   B. charged   C. was charged for   D. charged for

5. He _____ in the emergency room when I arrived at the hospital.
   A. has been treating   B. has treated   C. had treated   D. was being treated

6. The decoration of the hall's _____ but it's not yet _____ with lamps.
   A. furnished, finished
   B. been finished, been furnished
   C. being finished, being furnished
   D. furnish, finish

7. She never expected _____ the chairwoman of the committee.
   A. to elect   B. to be electing   C. to be elected   D. be elected

8. Since the introduction of the new technique, the production cost _____ greatly.
   A. reduces
   B. has been reduced
   C. is reducing
   D. is reduced

9. The food shows no sign of _____.
   A. touched
   B. being touched
   C. having been touched
   D. having touched

10. No one can avoid _____ by advertisements.
    A. being influenced
    B. influencing
    C. having influenced
    D. to be influenced

11. The doctor said that the patient had _____ at once.
    A. to operate　　　B. to be operated　　C. to operate on　　D. to be operated on

12. The fifth generation computers, with artificial intelligence, _____ and perfected now.
    A. developed
    C. are being developed
    B. have developed
    D. will have been developed

13. Eighty-two people were reported _____ in the plane crash.
    A. to have injured
    C. injured
    B. to have been injured
    D. injuring

14. Greater efforts to increase agricultural production must _____ if food shortage is to be avoided.
    A. be made　　　B. make　　　C. have made　　　D. have been made

15. I assure you that the matter _____ as quickly as possible. Have a little patience.
    A. has been attended to
    C. is attended to
    B. will be attended to
    D. has attended to

16. I'll take down your name and address in case you _____ as a witness.
    A. are needed　　B. have needed　　C. need　　　D. were needed

17. Men and women _____ equal wages for equal jobs in China.
    A. are paid　　　B. paid　　　C. being paid　　　D. to be paid

18. If one _____ by vanity, he will be very particular about others' clothing and appearance.
    A. overcomes
    C. is overcome
    B. will be overcome
    D. has overcome

19. Don't be late. I hate _____ waiting for a long time.
    A. being keeping　　B. be kept　　C. to be kept　　D. be keeping

20. Most environmental problems exist because adequate measures for preventing them _____ in the past.
    A. was not taken　　B. were not taken　　C. didn't take　　　D. haven't taken

21. People whose property _____ should report to the police.
    A. had stolen
    C. has been stolen
    B. is being stolen
    D. had been stolen

22. By promoting more even income distribution in a developing country, a lower birth rate will _____.
    A. be achieved
    C. have been achieved
    B. achieve
    D. be achieving

23. He _____ the leader of the Model Group in our factory.
    A. has just been appointed
    C. just appointed
    B. has just appointed
    D. has just being appointed

24. He _____ to return earlier than 3 o'clock.
    A. was not expected
    C. not to be expected
    B. did not expect
    D. was not expect

25. We should keep ourselves _____ of the latest developments.

    A. informing   B. informed   C. to inform   D. inform

26. We got down to business as soon as we _____ each other.

    A. had introduced to   B. had been introduced to

    C. had introduced by   D. had been introduced by

27. Besides _____ , he had to pay back all the money he had received from bribes.

    A. jailing   B. being jailed   C. to be jailed   D. jailed

28. The riot is said _____ by the government's negligence of the people's welfare.

    A. to have been caused   B. being caused

    C. to be caused   D. to cause

29. Large sums of money _____ each year in painting the steelwork of bridges, ships, and other exposed structures.

    A. have spent   B. have to be spent

    C. have to spend   D. have to be spending

30. I found that my cheating in yesterday's English test _____ to my parents that very evening.

    A. was reported   B. had been reported

    C. had reported   D. was being reported

β Error Correction

1. The book is said to have translated into many languages.

2. A microphone enables a soft tone to amplify, thus making possible the gentle renditions of romantic love songs in a large hall.

3. The old woman was glad to have being given a separate room when she was in hospital.

4. The St. Lawrence Seaway, running between British Columbia and New York, completed by the United States and Canada in 1959.

5. These children have never exposed to Western culture.

6. All the drawers had been looked through and still the letter didn't find.

7. There are some important safety rules that must follow in case of an emergency or a sudden illness.

8. Great changes have been taken place in China since 1978.

9. He went in silently without seeing by anyone.

10. After the box was opened, we found that nothing had broken.

11. It has calculated that the earth's circumference around the equator is over forty miles longer than that around the poles.

12. All the leaves that had fallen swept away by the strong wind.

13. The change in which a new substance is formed calls a chemical change.

14. How long do you think the meeting will be lasted?

15. Even though she crippled by polio as a child, Wilma Rudolph won gold medals in the track and field events of the 1960 Rome Olympics.

II. Cloze Test

A Government 政府

Government is the political system by which a _____ (1) or community is administered and regulated.

Most of _____ (2) key words commonly used to describe governments, words _____ (3) as monarchy, oligarchy, and democracy, are of Greek _____ (4) Roman origin. They have been current for more _____ (5) 2,000 years and have not yet exhausted their _____ (6). This suggests that mankind has not changed very _____ (7) since they were coined; but such verbal and _____ (8) uniformity must not be allowed to hide the _____ (9) changes in society and politics that have occurred. _____ (10) earliest analytical use of the term monarchy occurred _____ (11) ancient Athens, chiefly in Plato's dialogues, but even _____ (12) Plato's time the word was not self-explanatory. There _____ (13) a king in Macedon and a king in Persia, _____ (14) the two societies, and therefore their institutions, _____ (15) radically different. To give real meaning to the _____ (16) monarchy in these two instances, it would be _____ (17) to investigate their actual political and historical contexts. _____ (18) general account of monarchy required then, and requires _____ (19), an inquiry as to what circumstances have predisposed _____ (20) to adopt monarchy, and what have led them to reject it. So it is with all political terms.

B Sociology 社会学

Sociology is a social science that studies _____ (1) societies, their interactions, and the processes that _____ (2) and change them. It does this by _____ (3) the dynamics of constituent parts of societies _____ (4) as institutions, communities, populations, and gender, racial, _____ (5) age groups. Sociology also studies social status _____ (6) stratification, social movements, and social change, as _____ (7) as societal disorder in the form of _____ (8), deviance, and revolution.

Social life overwhelmingly regulates _____ (9) behaviour of humans, largely because humans lack _____ (10) instincts that guide most animal behaviour. Humans _____ (11) depend on social institutions and organizations to _____ (12) their decisions and actions. Given the important _____ (13) organizations play in influencing human action, it _____ (14) sociology's task to discover how organizations affect _____ (15) behaviour of persons, how they are established, _____ (16) organizations interact with one another, how they _____ (17), and, ultimately, how they disappear. Among the _____ (18) basic organizational structures are economic, religious, educational, _____ (19) political institutions, as well as more specialized _____ (20) such as the family, the community, the military, peer groups, clubs, and volunteer associations.

III. Reading Comprehension

Passage One

The Federal Government
联邦政府

The Constitution

When America broke away from Britain in 1775, she did not adopt a British Constitution. The British have always had an unwritten constitution, whereas every item of the American Constitution is clearly written down and numbered, and can only be changed by a two-thirds majority vote of Congress.

Yet in their different ways, the American and British forms of government did have one thing in common. They were both democratic. As for American society, it was more democratic than British society, in that it paid less attention to class or wealth.

Political Parties

There are two major political parties in the USA, the Democratic Party and the Republican Party. The policies of the two parties are not basically opposed to one another. Inside both parties there moderates and right-wringers, though the Democrats still have the reputation of being somewhat more liberal than the Republicans. Voters are influenced by family traditions, but there are plenty of ordinary people who vote according to their hopes, fears and beliefs.

There are no other political parties that can compete with the two big parties, though there are occasionally independents who stand for the presidency and manage to collect quite a few votes. There are no left-wing parties. Most Americans are in favor of free enterprise, believing that it may one day help them fulfill the American Dream.

The President and Congress

The President of the USA has more power than any other president in the democratic world-except the French President. It is he who formulates foreign policy and prepares laws for the home front. He is leader of the nation and Commander-in-Chief of the Armed Forces. He represents the USA and, since the USA is a super power, the eyes of the whole world are on him. The fate of the world is in his hands, or so many people believe, and one careless, ill-prepared speech by him could precipitate a crises.

Actually, a great deal of the President's power is controlled by Congress, the American name for "parliament". It is Congress that declares war, not the President. Unlike the Prime Minister of Great Britain, or of Germany, he can make a treaty with a foreign power. But this treaty must be debated and agreed by Congress before it comes into force. The same control applies to laws at home. Congress has (on several occasions) refused to ratify treaties or given approval to laws proposed by the President. The USA is the only country, apart from France, where a president can rule with a parliament, the majority of whose members do not belong to his own political party.

Some Americans have the feeling that idealism has gone out of politics and that personal ambition and money have taken its place. The election campaign fro the Presidency is unique in the amount of money poured into it. The wooing of voters lasts for months. But before the campaign for the election of the President can begin, each political party has to choose its candidate for the Presidency. This can lead to some very close contests. Men aspiring to be elected as the party candidate employ top public relations and advertising men, who invent clever catch phrases and set about "selling" their man. There are whistle stop tours by train, by plane, by car. The candidate delivers countless speeches and shakes countless hands. This razzamatazz typifies American enthusiasm and extravagance.

Big money is necessary to support a presidential candidate's campaign and the candidate himself must be rich enough to pay his share. An attractive wife is an advantage, too. Money is also needed to become the Governor of a state, or a successful Senator, or member of the House of Representatives. Yet from this small group many excellent men have become President, and the same is true of members of Congress.

It is very unlikely that the President could ever become a dictator. Congress, the press and the people between them rule out such a possibility.

The Supreme Court

Perhaps the most effective safeguard of democracy is the Supreme Court, for one of its objects is to protect the individual against the government. It has the authority to cancel a law which it considers violates the Constitution. The Court sits for at least four days a week and any individual who has a grievance against the government can apply to it for help.

The Supreme Court goes way back to 1787, the days of the Founding Fathers, and is one of the cornerstones of American democracy. It gives judgement in disputes between States, or between a State and the Federal Government, and without invitation can declare a law made by Congress to be unconstitutional. The great Jefferson, who drew up the Declaration of Independence, saw to it, too, that there was a Bill of Rights which every American could thrust under the nose of anyone who tries to rob him of his freedom as a democratic citizen.

1. One thing in common between the American and British form of government is that they were both _____ .
   A. constitutional   B. unconstitutional
   C. democratic   D. interested in class and wealth
2. Every item of the American constitution is _____ .
   A. not numbered
   B. not written down

C. challenged by a 2/3 majority of Congress

D. clearly written down and numbered

3. American society was more democratic than British society, in that _____.

   A. it paid less attention to class and wealth

   B. it had more liberal parties

   C. it welcomed socialism as well as capitalism

   D. voters were never influenced by family traditions

4. The President represents the USA and one careless, and ill-prepared speech would _____.

   A. bring him an ill reputation

   B. deprive him of all the power he represents

   C. bring about a crisis in the world

   D. shock the world into the war

5. Which of the following can prevent the President from doing exactly what he likes?

   A. Congress.   B. The Armed Forces.

   C. The press and the people.   D. Congress, the press and the people.

Passage Two

Mass Protest Decries Bush Abortion Policies
群众抗议谴责布什的堕胎政策
by Deborah Zabarenko

WASHINGTON (Reuters) — Protesters crowded the National Mall on Sunday to show support for abortion rights and opposition to Bush administration policies on women's health issues in one of the biggest demonstrations in US history.

There was no official crowd count, but organizers claimed more than 1 million people participated.

Pink- and purple-shirted protesters raised signs reading "Fight the Radical Right", "Keep Abortion Legal" and "US Out Of My Uterus" and covered the Mall from the foot of Capitol Hill to the base of the Washington Monument.

Speakers ranged from actresses Whoopi Goldberg, Ashley Judd and Kathleen Turner to philanthropist Ted Turner, feminist icon Gloria Steinem and former Secretary of State Madeleine Albright.

Goldberg raised a wire coat hanger — a symbol of illegal abortions in the days before the Supreme Court's 1973 Roe vs. Wade ruling recognizing abortion rights — and told the crowd, "We are one vote away from going back to this!"

She was referring to the nine-member high court, which has frequently decided abortion-related cases on a five-four vote.

The abortion issue was the centerpiece of the march's broad protest against the policies of

President Bush, including his stance on funding international family planning. No US funds may be used for any family planning agency that mentions abortion to patients.

"Vote That Smirk Out of Office," was a characteristically political placard targeting Bush, but Dorothy Smith, 76, of Eldridge, Missouri, carried an emblem she made herself — a wire coat hanger draped with a sign reading "Never Again."

"I can remember when abortion was just as common as it is now, but it killed a lot of women," Smith said.

Major sponsors included stalwarts of the abortion rights movement — NARAL Pro-Choice America, Feminist Majority, National Organization for Women, Planned Parenthood Federation of America — as well as the American Civil Liberties Union, the Black Women's Health Imperative and the National Latina Institute for Reproductive Health.

Some 1,400 groups attended the event, including an international contingent with marchers from 57 countries. There were medical students who carried signs saying they planned to be the next generation of abortion providers, and there was a Texas group marching behind a banner that read, "Old Broads for Choice."

As the march wound from the Mall toward the White House and then turned onto Pennsylvania Avenue and toward Capitol Hill, abortion rights groups encountered antiabortion protesters.

These protesters carried posters showing photographs of fetuses at eight weeks gestation and signs reading "Abortion kills Babies."

March organizers claimed double the turnout of the last big abortion rights march in 1992, which drew 500,000, according to the US Park Police, who no longer gives official crowd counts. The biggest demonstration was an anti-Vietnam War rally in 1969, which drew 600,000. The largest gathering on the National Mall was the 1976 US bicentennial celebration.

Though the march was billed as nonpartisan and included a contingent called Republicans for Choice, much of the day's rhetoric was plainly aimed at Bush, a Republican who opposes abortion in most cases.

Democratic presidential candidate John Kerry vowed on Friday to champion abortion rights if elected. He received the endorsement of Planned Parenthood's Action Fund, the organization's political fund-raising arm.

Neither Bush nor Kerry attended the march, but US Sen. Hillary Rodham Clinton, a New York Democrat and former first lady, drew roars of approval when she exhorted the crowd to register to vote. Volunteers were on hand to register new voters.

Bush addressed an anti-abortion march in January, saying the effort to overturn the Supreme Court's 1973 Roe v. Wade ruling, which recognized a right to abortion, was "noble cause."

1. Which of the following is true according to the passage?

  A. Government officials estimated that more than one million people participated in the demonstration.

B. The police counted the number of people who participated in the demonstration as more than one million.

C. The organizers called on more than one million people to participate in the demonstration.

D. According to the organizers of the demonstration, there were more than one million people who took part in the demonstration.

2. Speakers at the demonstration included Gloria Steinem who _____.

   A. is a woman whose job is to design icons for computer software

   B. is a woman whom many female people admire

   C. is looked as a symbol for women's rights movement

   D. is looked as a person adored by those who are active in women's rights movement

3. By saying "We are one vote away from going back to this" Goldberg meant that _____.

   A. only one vote may lead us the situation after 1973 when abortion was considered as belonging to women's choice

   B. we are very close to the old situation before 1973 when abortion was considered as illegal

   C. we need one more vote to support Bush's policies concerning women's health

   D. we need one more vote to oppose Bush's anti-abortion policy

4. Which of the following is NOT correct according to the passage?

   A. The crowd consisted of people who were against Bush's anti-abortion policy.

   B. The crowd consisted of people both for and against Bush's anti-abortion policy.

   C. In the march there was a group of people from or supporting the Republican Party.

   D. The general message of the demonstration was opposing the Republican government's policies on women's health issues.

5. According to this passage, Bush's anti-abortion stance was most clearly shown _____.

   A. in the last paragraph   B. by the title of the passage
   C. in Dorothy Smith's words   D. in John Kerry's words

Passage Three

Rising Prices Cause House "Apartheid"
涨价导致房屋的"种族隔离"

The Government has admitted that soaring house prices have left people on average incomes, such as teachers and nurses, locked out of buying their first homes across large parts of southern England, including London and most of the South East.

A spokeswoman for the Deputy Prime Minister, John Prescott, admitted last night that there was now an effective "housing apartheid", with people in their own homes pulling further and further away from those yet to get on the property ladder.

With house prices rising at between 15 and 20 percent a year, incomes, which are rising at between 5 and 10 percent a year, cannot keep up.

"Increasing housing supply is a national priority. In large areas of the wider South East, house purchase remains out of reach for families with average household incomes," the official said.

A new report out tomorrow will reveal the full scale of the housing crisis. The study by Cambridge University for the housing charity Shelter reveals that the Government will need to spend £3. 5 billion a year to solve the housing problem.

More than 50,000 new homes are needed every year to help people on lower incomes to have their own homes. By 2014 a city the size of Leeds will need to be built.

Critics point out that, without the money, millions of people employed in the public sector will be unable to move to the South East to fill vacancies.

Without a new influx of staff, many hospitals and schools say that they will struggle to maintain standards. The Government is now expected to announce a package of measures in the Budget to try to help first-time buyers. The Treasury is considering raising the point at which people have to pay stamp duty, a tax paid on every house purchase.

The present threshold of £60,000 has remained unchanged since 1993, despite house prices increasing by 160 percent in that time.

Gordon Brown, the Chancellor, faces being accused of maintaining the threshold as a way of raising more tax because as house prices rise more and more people are dragged into paying the surcharge. More than 75 percent of all first-time buyers now pay the tax.

"The Government has to act," said Adam Sampson , the director of Shelter. The lack of affordable housing has a destabilising effect on the economy and its cost in human terms is massive.

"Successive governments have spoken about the growing housing crisis. It has now got to the point where it cannot be ignored any longer. Housing should be given the same priority as the other key areas of public life, health and education. "

The report says that more than three-quarters of all new homes are needed in the South of England, with about 20 percent in the North and the Midlands.

Shelter's figures on housing demand will form the basis of a Treasury review of housing to be published at the time of the Budget next week. The review, by Kate Barker, is likely to say that tens of thousands of new houses are needed and that planning restrictions should be relaxed so that housing developments can be built more easily.

She will also criticise a culture of nimbyism which has crept into many, particularly rural, towns. Many local communities block new housing even though it is desperately needed.

A study released this weekend by the Halifax revealed that first-time buyers cannot get on to the property ladder in 80 percent of towns and cities across the country. The bank said that areas were classed as "unaffordable" if first-time buyers needed to borrow more than 4. 27 times the local average salary to buy a home.

By that calculation, 100 percent of towns and cities in East Anglia were out of reach of first-time buyers, while 98 percent of towns and cities in the South West were unaffordable.

The Government is set to announce large amounts of extra funding for house building in the Budget. By 2006 the amount spent will have increased by £900 million, or 25 percent.

There will also be a £5 billion pot of money provided for affordable housing by 2006.

1. According to the passage, housing apartheid' refers to a situation where _____.

   A. houses are only built in specific places

   B. houses in some places become too expensive for people to buy

   C. black people and white people live in different houses in a place

   D. regulations are enforced on house pricing

2. What might NOT be the reason for the phenomenon that people on average incomes are unable to buy the houses?

   A. They have to pay high price stamp duty.

   B. Their incomes rise too slowly.

   C. House supply is decreasing.

   D. House prices are rising.

3. What may the government do to help first-time buyers?

   A. Allow them to buy houses at reduced prices.

   B. Raise the point at which people must pay stamp duty.

   C. Lower the price of stamp duty.

   D. Increase their incomes.

4. How many percent of new homes are needed in the south of England?

   A. About 20%.   B. More than 98%.   C. About 80%.   D. More than 45%.

5. We can learn from the passage that culture of nimbyism' means _____.

   A. treasuring the culture of one's own locality

   B. expending new houses in one's own locality

   C. welcoming the siting of developments in one's own locality

   D. objecting to the siting of developments in one's own locality

Passage Four

President George W. Bush
布什总统

George W. Bush is the 43rd President of the United States. He was sworn into office on January 20, 2001, re-elected on November 2, 2004, and sworn in for a second term on January 20, 2005. Prior to his Presidency, President Bush served for 6 years as the 46th Governor of the State of Texas, where he earned a reputation for bipartisanship and as a compassionate conservative who shaped public policy based on the principles of limited government, personal responsibility, strong families, and local control.

President Bush was born on July 6, 1946, in New Haven, Connecticut, and grew up in Midland and Houston, Texas. He received a bachelor's degree in history from Yale University in 1968, and then served as an F-102 fighter pilot in the Texas Air National Guard. President Bush received a Master of Business Administration from Harvard Business School in 1975. Following graduation, he moved back to Midland and began a career in the energy business. After working on his father's successful 1988 Presidential campaign, President Bush assembled the group of partners who purchased the Texas Rangers baseball franchise in 1989. On November 8, 1994, President Bush was elected Governor of Texas. He became the first Governor in Texas history to be elected to consecutive 4-year terms when he was re-elected on November 3, 1998.

Since becoming President of the United States in 2001, President Bush has worked with the Congress to create an ownership society and build a future of security, prosperity, and opportunity for all Americans. He signed into law tax relief that helps workers keep more of their hard-earned money, as well as the most comprehensive education reforms in a generation, the No Child Left Behind Act of 2001. This legislation is ushering in a new era of accountability, flexibility, local control, and more choices for parents, affirming our Nation's fundamental belief in the promise of every child. President Bush has also worked to improve healthcare and modernize Medicare, providing the first-ever prescription drug benefit for seniors; increase homeownership, especially among minorities; conserve our environment; and increase military strength, pay, and benefits. Because President Bush believes the strength of America lies in the hearts and souls of our citizens, he has supported programs that encourage individuals to help their neighbors in need.

On the morning of September 11, 2001, terrorists attacked our Nation. Since then, President Bush has taken unprecedented steps to protect our homeland and create a world free from terror. He is grateful for the service and sacrifice of our brave men and women in uniform and their families. The President is confident that by helping build free and prosperous societies, our Nation and our friends and allies will succeed in making America more secure and the world more peaceful.

President Bush is married to Laura Welch Bush, a former teacher and librarian, and they have twin daughters, Barbara and Jenna. The Bush family also includes two dogs, Barney and Miss Beazley, and a cat, Willie.

〜〜〜〜〜〜〜〜〜〜〜〜〜〜〜〜〜〜〜〜〜〜〜〜〜〜〜〜

1. George W. Bush earned a reputation for _____.
   A. involving two political parties in his administration
   B. representing two political parties
   C. working for the interests of two political parties
   D. supporting two political parties
2. As Governor of the State of Texas, George W. Bush shaped public policy NOT on the basis of which of the following principles?
   A. limited government   B. personal responsibility
   C. strong families   D. fight against terrorism

3. After George W. Bush, Sr. 's success in 1988 Presidential campaign, the junior gathered the group of partners _____ .

    A. to start the preparations for his own campaign for US presidency

    B. to buy the Texas Rangers baseball franchise

    C. to begin a career in the energy business

    D. to study for a Master of Business Administration

4. So far, George W. Bush, as US President, has been building a future of _____ for all Americans.

    A. ownership, riches, and possibility

    B. more money, less work, and no tax

    C. safety, wealth, and chance

    D. education, employment, and opportunity

5. George W. Bush firmly believes that the strength of America lies in _____ .

    A. the US armed forces   B. the struggle against terrorism

    C. the wealth of the United States   D. the American people

第六单元 语 气

I. Grammar: Mood

Ⓐ Multiple Choices

1. If you had done as I told you, this _____.
   A. should have not happened
   B. would not have happened
   C. did not happen
   D. had not happened

2. _____ no friction between the surface of the road and our feet, we could not walk at all.
   A. If there was
   B. Were there
   C. Was there
   D. There was

3. Henry _____ a rich man today if he had been more careful about his investment in the past.
   A. would be
   B. is
   C. will be
   D. would have been

4. She would go and inform him if she _____ his address.
   A. know
   B. had known
   C. knew
   D. would have known

5. It was recommended that passengers _____ smoke during the flight.
   A. not
   B. could not
   C. need not
   D. would not

6. _____ you were busy, I wouldn't have bothered you with my questions.
   A. If I realized
   B. I realized that
   C. Had I realized
   D. As I realized

7. Without electronic computers, much of today's advanced technology _____ achieved.
   A. will not have been
   B. have not been
   C. would not have been
   D. had not been

8. If you had been more careful in typing the report, you _____ to do it over again.
   A. did not have
   B. would not have
   C. had not have
   D. would not have had

9. They requested that we _____ them a sample of the product.
   A. sent
   B. to send
   C. send
   D. be sent

10. Last week my mother urged that I _____ more attention to my health.
    A. paying
    B. pay
    C. paid
    D. could pay

11. If you had spoken more clearly, you _____.
    A. would understand
    B. would be understood
    C. would have been understood
    D. would have understood

12. _____ I realized the consequences, I would never have intended to get involved.

    A. If   B. When   C. Had   D. Unless

13. John insisted that he _____ everything he could to make sure of Mary's happiness.

    A. do   B. does   C. did   D. must do

14. The sun rises in the east and sets in the west, so it seems as if the sun _____ round the earth.

    A. were circling   B. circles   C. is circling   D. be circling

15. It is high time that the government _____ measures to protect the rare birds and animals.

    A. takes   B. took   C. has taken   D. would take

16. Mary couldn't have received my letter; otherwise she _____ before now.

    A. would have replied   B. has replied

    C. must have replied   D. had replied

17. The lawyer demanded that the man _____ everything about the case.

    A. tell   B. tells   C. can tell   D. must tell

18. It is our wish that she _____ what she likes.

    A. take   B. takes   C. will take   D. can take

19. The professor recommended in his last lecture that English learners _____ on the lookout for tenses.

    A. will be   B. are   C. should be   D. must be

20. Without your timely advice and help, we _____ so much.

    A. will never achieve   B. could hardly achieve

    C. can't have achieved   D. wouldn't have achieved

21. There is a real possibility that these animals could be frightened, _____ a sudden loud noise.

    A. being there   B. should there be

    C. there was   D. there having been

22. If I had hurried, I _____ the plane.

    A. could catch   B. would catch

    C. should catch   D. would have caught

23. A safety analysis _____ the target as a potential danger. Unfortunately, it was never done.

    A. would identify   B. will identify

    C. would have identified   D. will have identified

24. Yesterday the manager insisted that the contract _____ signed as soon as possible.

    A. had   B. have   C. have been   D. be

25. What do you think of his proposal that some measures _____ to improve the working conditions?

    A. would be taken   B. be taken

    C. will be taken   D. will have to be taken

26. The millions of calculations, had they been done by hand, _____ all practical value by the time they were finished.
    A. could lose
    B. would have lost
    C. might lose
    D. ought to have lost

27. If he had told me earlier, I _____ like that.
    A. would not have done
    B. would not do
    C. would do
    D. will not do

28. That man must have the strength of a hippopotamus, or he never _____ that great beast.
    A. could have vanquished
    B. would vanquish
    C. should have vanquished
    D. had vanquished

29. _____ he here, he _____ his best to help you.
    A. Were... would try
    B. Were... would have tried
    C. If... would try
    D. Had been... would have tried

30. _____ any trouble with the boiler, the automatic controlling unit will cut off the fuel oil supply.
    A. There should be
    B. If there had been
    C. Should there be
    D. If there was

β Error Correction

1. It is appropriate that some time devoted to a thorough study of the result of the experiment.

2. I proposed that their offer could be accepted.

3. If I was you, I would not take part in the game.

4. It's time we go to the theater.

5. I teasingly suggested to my wife that she might get the recipe of the delicious cream puffs from her sister, a cooking talent.

6. If the police arrived earlier, they would have seen the accident.

7. So great was the influence of Thomas Paine on his time that John Adams suggested that the era was called "The Age of Paine".

8. I feel as if I am going to fall.

9. The post requires that the applicant is bilingual.

10. Environmental scientists are concerned that if industrial pollution was to continue without effective measures, the Earth's surface would warm up to a dangerous degree in the next few centuries.

11. Women have long been neglected, or else they would make a lot more achievements to the country in all fields.

12. It is insisted that he must take quick action to put this right.

13. If only he is here with me at present.

14. I advised he went at once.

15. I had known about his coming, I would have met him at the station.

II. Cloze Test

A Bush's Legacy (I) 布什的遗产 (I)

President Bush arrived in Washington and forged ahead with an ambitious agenda- _____ (1) tax cuts, vast changes in federal social programs, expansions of executive power and _____ (2) broad remaking of energy and education policies.

Claiming a mandate by simply declaring _____ (3) existence, his early successes dazzled his critics. With guru Karl Rove directing the _____ (4), Bush won a stunning series of political victories.

He muscled his agenda through _____ (5) friendly Congress, and gained seats for his party in the 2002 midterm elections. _____ (6) biggest triumph came in 2004, when he won a second term despite a _____ (7) unpopular war.

The "permanent" Republican majority he and Rove envisioned even seemed attainable _____ (8) Bush plunged himself into his most ambitious legislative effort yet: a partial privatization _____ (9) Social Security.

But the president who boasted about "political capital" in the heady _____ (10) after his re-election now faces the worst of political fates as he enters _____ (11) final year in office: borderline irrelevance.

The president's second term has _____ (12) defined by legislative paralysis, marked by record-low approval ratings, presidential candidates who are _____ (13) from his shadow, and a lingering war that's sapping his remaining reservoirs of _____ (14).

As he enters his final year in office with the war continuing, Republican _____ (15) for president bolting from his shadow, and his party back in the minority _____ (16) Congress, he is politically weakened, an early entry into lame-duck status.

And the _____ (17) Washington atmosphere he hoped to cure is just as nasty as it was _____ (18) he came to office seven years ago.

"He's left our political institutions much _____ (19) troubled than they were before," said Thomas E. Mann, a senior fellow at _____ (20) Brookings Institution, a Washington-based think tank. "He didn't create the ideological polarization, but he magnified it."

B Bush's Legacy (II) 布什的遗产 (II)

President Bush's push to oust Saddam Hussein _____ (1) power soon became more than a foreign-policy initiative; the _____ (2) and his allies used it as a wedge issue _____ (3) Democrats in the run-up to the 2002 elections.

"After 9/11, he _____ (4) a country that said, 'We're ready to follow,'" _____ (5) Rep. Rahm Emanual, D-Ill., a former top aide to President Bill _____ (6) and now a member of the House Democratic leadership. "There _____ (7) so much we could have done. But he said, 'Go shopping', _____ (8) then he divided the nation."

The hyper-political push for _____ (9) cost him the support of Democrats; there would be no _____ (10) big bipartisan successes for him to celebrate, such as his _____ (11) education law, No Child Left Behind.

Republicans stayed with him, _____ (12), and while they controlled Congress, that was often enough. It _____ (13) him politically potent through the 2002 and 2004 campaigns.

But _____ (14) spending programs and other breaks with conservative dogma hurt the _____ (15) standing inside the GOP, and he never really worked the Washingtongame to _____ (16) relationships with members of Congress.

In his _____ (17) term, Democrats scuttled Social Security reform even before the president _____ (18) file a bill. Opposition to Bush became their organizing principle — the formula they rode to success in 2006, _____ (19) the botched federal response to Hurricane Katrina and a continuing war left _____ (20) as damaged goods.

III. Reading Comprehension

Passage One

Stay the Course on Terror War
坚持反恐战争的道路

President Bush urged US allies Tuesday to remain committed to the reconstruction of Iraq, vowing that terrorist attacks like last week's bombings in Spain "will never shake the will of the United States."

"It's essential that we remain side-by-side with the Iraqi people as they begin the process of self-government," Bush said in a White House appearance with Dutch Prime Minister Jan Peter Balkenende.

Bush's comments come one year after the US-led invasion of Iraq and at a time when his handling of the war on terror is being questioned by many Democrats, particularly Sen. John Kerry, the presumed Democratic presidential nominee.

"They'll kill innocent people to try to shake our will," Bush said of terrorists. "That's what they want to do. They'll never shake the will of the United States. We understand the stakes."

The administration has cast the toppling of the regime of former Iraqi President Saddam Hussein as part of the broader war on terror. Bush has generally enjoyed high marks from the American public for his leadership on national security following the terrorist attacks of September

11, 2001.

But Democrats have grown increasingly vocal in their criticism of Bush's approach to the war on terror, saying he has alienated allies abroad and failed to match his often tough rhetoric with support for first responders, such as firefighters, at home and equipment for soldiers in the field.

Typical was a comment Monday from Kerry, when he addressed one firefighters' union that has endorsed his bid for the presidency.

"I do not fault George Bush for doing too much in the war on terror," Kerry said. "I believe he's done too little."

The administration has refuted the charges. Administration figures point out that about three dozen nations have contributed in some fashion to the reconstruction of Iraq. And Bush-Cheney campaign officials say it's Kerry — not Bush — who has failed to provide support for homeland security through various Senate votes. Kerry said the Republican campaign is taking a selective and misleading review of his votes.

"I'm not going to worry about them misleading because we're going to keep pounding away at the truth over the next few months," Kerry said at a campaign event in West Virginia on Tuesday, talking about the administration's record on several fronts.

But the challenge for Bush on the terror war is not just coming from the US campaign trail.

In the aftermath of last week's bombings of commuter trains in Madrid, Spanish voters ousted the Popular Party of Bush ally Jose Maria Aznar in favor of the Socialists, who opposed the US-led invasion of Iraq last March. Socialist leader Jose Luis Rodriguez Zapatero said Monday he wants to pull Spanish troops out of Iraq unless the United Nations takes on greater role there.

Asked how he would respond to Dutch citizens who have called for Balkenende to withdraw that country's troops, Bush said, "I would ask them to think about the Iraqi citizens who don't want people to withdraw because they want to be free."

About 1,100 Dutch troops are stationed in southern Iraq, part of the coalition that has occupied the country since the US-led invasion last March. Balkenende said his government has yet to discuss whether Dutch troops would remain in Iraq beyond the end of June, when the United States plans to hand over power to a new Iraqi government.

Bush said the al Qaeda terrorist network — a leading suspect in the Madrid bombings, which killed 201 people — hopes to stop the spread of freedom and democracy in the Middle East.

"Al Qaeda wants us out of Iraq because al Qaeda wants to use Iraq as an example of defeating freedom and democracy," he said.

1. This news report implies that _____.

    A. the United States itself is divided in opinion regarding its relationship with its allies

    B. George Bush and John Kerry were in serous dispute concerning the process of self-government in Iraq

    C. George Bush has not done enough to prevent terrorist attacks

    D. the Bush administration is under pressure both at home and abroad

2. Which of the following is a factor that contributes to Bush's popularity among the American public?

   A. Bush started the Iraqi war resolutely, supported by allies.

   B. Bush insisted that the Iraqi war was part of the war against terrorism.

   C. Bush has taken a tough line on national security issues.

   D. Bush maintained that the United States would win the Iraqi war.

3. Which of the following is NOT a criticism of the Bush Administration from the Democrats?

   A. Only thirty plus nations have contributed to the reconstruction of Iraq.

   B. The United States has been separating itself from the ally nations.

   C. The Administration has not done enough to support homeland security.

   D. The Administration has not kept its promise of giving sufficient support to the soldiers in the battlefield.

4. It can be inferred from the passage that _____.

   A. the Republicans are misleading the Senate votes

   B. the Democrats enjoy more seats in the Senate than Republicans

   C. Kerry is not refuting Bush effectively

   D. Bush is losing West Virginia in his presidential campaign

5. The train bombings in Madrid may have _____.

   A. caused the Spanish Popular party to lose its power to the Socialists

   B. led to the Dutch citizens to urge the Dutch government to withdraw troops out of Iraq

   C. shaken people's confidence in Bush

   D. been plotted by Al Qaeda

Passage Two

Hillary Rodham Clinton
希拉里·罗德姆·克林顿

During the 1992 presidential campaign, Hillary Rodham Clinton observed, "Our lives are a mixture of different roles. Most of us are doing the best we can to find whatever the right balance is… For me, that balance is family, work, and service."

Hillary Diane Rodham, Dorothy and Hugh Rodham's first child, was born on October 26, 1947. Two brothers, Hugh and Tony, soon followed. Hillary's childhood in Park Ridge, Illinois, was happy and disciplined. She loved sports and her church, and was a member of the National Honor Society, and a student leader. Her parents encouraged her to study hard and to pursue any career that interested her.

As an undergraduate at Wellesley College, Hillary mixed academic excellence with school government. Speaking at graduation, she said, "The challenge now is to practice politics as the art of making what appears to be impossible, possible."

In 1969, Hillary entered Yale Law School, where she served on the Board of Editors of Yale Law Review and Social Action, interned with children's advocate Marian Wright Edelman, and met Bill Clinton. The President often recalls how they met in the library when she strode up to him and said, "If you're going to keep staring at me, I might as well introduce myself." The two were soon inseparable — partners in moot court, political campaigns, and matters of the heart.

After graduation, Hillary advised the Children's Defense Fund in Cambridge and joined the impeachment inquiry staff advising the Judiciary Committee of the House of Representatives. After completing those responsibilities, she "followed her heart to Arkansas," where Bill had begun his political career.

They married in 1975. She joined the faculty of the University of Arkansas Law School in 1975 and the Rose Law Firm in 1976. In 1978, President Jimmy Carter appointed her to the board of the Legal Services Corporation, and Bill Clinton became governor of Arkansas. Their daughter, Chelsea, was born in 1980.

Hillary served as Arkansas's First Lady for 12 years, balancing family, law, and public service. She chaired the Arkansas Educational Standards Committee, co-founded the Arkansas Advocates for Children and Families, and served on the boards of the Arkansas Children's Hospital, Legal Services, and the Children's Defense Fund.

As the nation's First Lady, Hillary continued to balance public service with private life. Her active role began in 1993 when the President asked her to chair the Task Force on National Health Care Reform. She continued to be a leading advocate for expanding health insurance coverage, ensuring children are properly immunized, and raising public awareness of health issues. She wrote a weekly newspaper column entitled "Talking It Over," which focused on her experiences as First Lady and her observations of women, children, and families she has met around the world. Her 1996 book *It Takes a Village and Other Lessons Children Teach Us* was a best seller, and she received a Grammy Award for her recording of it.

As First Lady, her public involvement with many activities sometimes led to controversy. Undeterred by critics, Hillary won many admirers for her staunch support for women around the world and her commitment to children's issues.

She was elected United States Senator from New York on November 7, 2000. She is the first First Lady elected to the United States Senate and the first woman elected statewide in New York.

1. On the eve of becoming the First Lady of the United States, Hillary Rodham Clinton began to take service into consideration. Here the word "service" means _____.
   A. work in the army, navy or the air force
   B. work or duty done for the country
   C. work in any of the government departments
   D. work in the President's home
2. In 1969, Hillary Rodham Clinton entered Yale Law School, where she worked as _____.
   A. Ph. D. student   B. wife of Bill Clinton
   C. editor and intern   D. secretary

3. Hillary Rodham Clinton went to Arkansas for the purposes of becoming _____.

    A. a follower of Bill Clinton

    B. an advisor for the Children's Defense Fund

    C. an editor of a magazine

    D. a government official

4. Hillary Rodham Clinton got her first government appointment in the _____ Administration.

    A. Nixon   B. Carter   C. Clinton   D. Bush

5. Which of the following is NOT the task that Hillary Rodham Clinton was involved in as chair of the Task Force on National Health Care Reform?

    A. expanding health insurance coverage

    B. ensuring children's immunization

    C. raising public awareness of health issues

    D. writing a best seller

Passage Three

Ethics Office Backs Interior Official
民族部支持内政部的官员

    The Office of Government Ethics said the Interior Department's No. 2 official, Steven Griles, did not appear to violate ethics rules by arranging meetings between Interior officials and his former lobbying clients and partners.

    The office, after reviewing an 18-month investigation by the Interior Department's inspector general, said it found no ethics violations by Griles in the department's awarding of more than $1.6 million i contracts in 2001 and 2002 to Advanced Power Technologies Inc. , a former client.

    Interior Department Inspector General Earl Devaney said Griles' behavior is the latest case of an Interior official falling to consider perceived impropriety in his actions. He also called the department's underfunded ethics office "a train wreck waiting to happen."

    Interior Secretary Gale Norton and Republicans in Congress said the report clears Griles of any wrongdoing. Griles is gratified by the finding that he had "adhered to ethics laws and rules."

    "I am glad this matter is behind me," he said.

    Sen. Joe Lieberman, D-Conn. , called Devaney's report a case of the "foxes guarding the foxes," saying the questionable conduct and special treatment given to Griles' former clients "cannot help but leave a sour taste in the mouth of anyone who believes in the fairness of government."

    Environmentalists had alleged that Griles helped former clients land government contracts, intervened in an environmental study of coalbed methane development in Wyoming, and held a dinner for senior department officials at the home of his former lobbying partner.

    Two matters — the coalbed methane analysis and the Interior Department dinner — were referred to Norton by the Office of Government Ethics for possible action. Norton said they had been adequately addressed.

"This closes the issue," Norton said in a statement.

Kristen Sykes of Friends of the Earth disagreed and said Griles should be fired.

"It uncovers regular and consistent breaches of Griles' ethics agreements and , more importantly, blatant violations of the public's trust," she said. "If this White House is serious about ethics and accountability, Mr. Griles should be dismissed immediately."

Devaney did not draw conclusions in his report, but said in a letter to the department that regardless of whether Griles broke the law, the appearance of wrongdoing erodes public trust.

"This is the only one in a series of cases in which we have observed an institutional failure to consider the appearance of a particular course of conduct," he wrote. "It is my hope, however, that this may be the case that changes the ethical culture in the department."

Last month, Devaney cleared the department's former top lawyer, Bill Myers, of allegations that his official actions benefited former lobbying clients. An investigation is under way into whether Bureau of Land Management Director Kathleen Clarke violated ethics rules by participating in meetings regarding a land exchange in Utah, where she was the state's director of natural resources.

Griles continues to receive $284,000 a year as part of a four-year severance package from his former lobbying firm.

In April 2002, the Environmental Protection Agency was about to object to an environmental study of coalbed methane drilling in Wyoming when Griles intervened. In a phone call and letter, he urged EPA to resolve its differences to keep the project on track. At least six of Griles's former clients had interest in the project.

Devaney also found that Interior Department officials sought out projects to award to one of Griles' former clients, Advanced Power Technologies, Inc. , rather than letting APTI compete for existing projects.

After joining the Interior Department, Griles held a dinner party for senior department officials at the home of his former lobbying partner, Marc Himmelstein. Assistant Secretary Rebecca Watson, told Devaney she believed it was improper and could give the appearance of favoritism. Griles said it was a social event that he would have hosted at his home if he had space.

Devaney said ethics issues can arise with any appointee, but neglect and a lack of funding have left the Interior Department's enthics office unable to shepherd officials through the ethics minefield.

1. Which of the following is NOT true of Griles?
    A. Griles arranged for official from his office to meet his former clients.
    B. Griles was investigated by Earl Devaney.
    C. Griles's Interior Department favored Advanced Power Technologies Inc. in big contracts.
    D. Griles improperly violated ethic codes.

2. The news report indicates that Earl Devaney _____.

    A. made an eighteen-month investigation into Griles's case

    B. referred to Griles's case "a train wreck"

    C. accused the Interior Department of funding ethics office secretly

    D. did not act in Griles's favor

3. By referring to Devaney's report as a case of the "foxes guarding the foxes," Joe Lieberman most probably meant that _____.

    A. the report was very well phrased

    B. Devaney made a very complicated report

    C. the report deceitfully pictured an already unjust case

    D. he was doubtful of the fairness of government

4. The 2002 Wyoming coalbed methane drilling case is cited to _____.

    A. clear Griles of wrongdoing in it

    B. keep the drilling project going

    C. show Griles's innocence in all related allegations

    D. display Griles's inappropriate behavior, if not law-breaking

5. What, according to Devaney, seemed to be the causes of ethics problems with the Interior Department?

    A. Seeking out projects for former clients.

    B. Holding dinner parties at the home of former lobbying partners.

    C. Practicing favoritism.

    D. Having insufficient funding.

Passage Four

Legislation, Lawsuits Cover Both Sides on Same-sex Marriage
法律，在同性婚姻问题上诉讼两边不得罪

In courtrooms and state capitols nationwide, opponents and supporters of gay marriage have embarked on a collision course, pursuing lawsuits and legislation so deeply at odds that prolonged legal chaos is likely.

One plausible result: a nation divided, at least briefly, between a handful of states recognizing gay marriage and a majority which do not.

The most clear-cut option for averting such chaos is a federal constitutional amendment banning gay marriage. However, despite support from President Bush, the amendment is given little chance of winning the needed two-thirds support in both the House and Senate this year.

Without it, experts say, the rival sides are likely to litigate so relentlessly that the US Supreme Court will eventually be compelled to intercede and clarify whether a legal same-sex union in one state must be recognized in other states.

"It's going to be complicated for many years — we're going to have some free-marriages states, and some that are not," said Matt Foreman, executive director of the National Gay and Lesbian Task Force.

"This is not a new situation in our country," Foreman added. "We have had a hodgepodge of laws on different social issues. Invariably, we come to widespread consensus, and that's going to happen to this issue."

For now, though, consensus seems distant as two contrasting legal offensives take shape.

On one hand, courts in five relatively liberal states — California, New Jersey, New York, Oregon and Washington — are being asked to consider whether same-sex marriages should be allowed.

In each of these states, local officials have recently performed gay marriages. Gay-rights supporters predict the supreme courts in at least a couple of the states will join Massachusetts' Supreme Judicial Court in authorizing such marriages.

Meanwhile, legislators in many states are moving to amend their constitutions to toughen existing bans on gay marriage and explicitly deny recognition to same-sex unions forged elsewhere.

Four states — Alaska, Hawaii, Nebraska and Nevada — already have such constitutional amendments. Similar measures are either certain or likely to go before voters in several other states in November or thereafter, including Alabama, Arkansas, Mississippi, Utah and Wisconsin.

In 10 other legislatures, proposed constitutional amendments are pending — their fate not yet certain.

Matt Daniels, who as head of the Alliance for Marriage helped draft the proposed federal constitutional amendment, sees the developments in state legislatures as proof of strong grass-roots opposition to gay marriage.

"As the courts push the envelope, public opinion moves in our direction," he said, "It's a great national referendum... on whether we as a society are going to send a message through our laws that there's something uniquely special about marriage between a man and a woman."

However, Daniels is convinced that without an amendment putting that definition in the US Constitution, the courts will eventually strike down state down state laws banning gay marriage, as well as the federal Defense of Marriage Act. That measure, signed by President Clinton in 1996, allows states to refuse to honor same-sex unions performed elsewhere, and denies federal recognition to such unions.

Daniels said the proposed federal amendment, if it did clear Congress, would easily win the required ratification by at least 38 state legislatures.

He acknowledged that the measure may have difficulty getting two-thirds backing in the current Senate, where few Democrats support it. But he predicted that pressure on politicians to approve the amendment will increase, once gay couples married in Massachusetts or elsewhere successfully sue to have their marriage honored in other states.

"When the lawsuits start to export what happens in Massachusetts, you will have a political powder keg for politicians who refuse to pay heed to public opinion," Daniels said. "This will change the political landscape. "

William Reppy, a Duke University law professor, agreed that a challenge to the non-recognition of gay marriages across state lines will be critical — perhaps what ultimately decides the issue.

"There will be a split of authority — one state court will say it's valid, another will say it isn't," Reppy predicted. "Then the US Supreme Court would have their hand forced, and hear the case. They don't let splits of authority run rampant around the country for very long. "

〜〜〜〜〜〜〜〜〜〜〜〜〜〜〜〜〜〜

1. Which of the following is NOT true of the current state of legalization of gay marriage?
   A. It might be a long time before the matter could be settled.
   B. There are more states that do not support gay marriage than those that do.
   C. The nation might be separated into two different nations.
   D. Banning gay marriage constitutionally is highly unlikely to happen currently.

2. According to Foreman, the gay marriage issue _____ .
   A. will remain unsettled like many other social issues
   B. will be settled by way of constitutional amendments
   C. will finally be settled with a public majority reaching consensus
   D. has existed for a long time

3. Which of the following states might legalize gay marriage in the near future?
   A. California, New Jersey, New York, Orgeon and Washington.
   B. Alaska, Hawaii, Nebraska and Nevada.
   C. Alabama, Arkansas, Mississippi, Utah and Wisconsin.
   D. 10 other states that are not mentioned above.

4. Which of the following statement is true of Matt Daniels?
   A. He is one of the drafters of the constitutional amendment to support intersexual marriage.
   B. He is optimistic about a legal ban on gay marriage.
   C. He thinks that intersexual marriage is a unique constitutional proposition.
   D. He believes that eventually the states will gain the upper hand in approving of gay marriage.

5. According to Matt Deniels, the spread of lawsuits from Massachusetts to other states may lead to _____ .
   A. a split of authority in the gay marriage issue
   B. the US Supreme Court involvement in the gay marriage issue
   C. a political reform in the country
   D. pressure on politicians for them to attend to public opinion

第七单元 介 词

I. Grammar: Preposition

A Multiple Choices

1. John is no match _____ his younger brother at table tennis.
   A. to   B. at   C. for   D. on

2. The girl led the blind women _____ the arm to the other side of the road.
   A. by   B. on   C. to   D. with

3. He finished the work _____ the cost of his health.
   A. at   B. on   C. with   D. in

4. _____ the few who have failed in their exam, all the students in the hall are in very high spirits.
   A. Apart from   B. Despite   C. Due to   D. But for

5. _____ his cold, he came first in the athletics meet.
   A. Regardless   B. In spite   C. With regard of   D. In spite of

6. A teacher should always be considerate _____ the welfare of his pupils.
   A. in   B. to   C. of   D. at

7. Scientists have already found problems that associated _____ living in the ocean are nearly the same as those of living in outerspace.
   A. to   B. of   C. with   D. at

8. Whatever happened, our people will always stand _____ you.
   A. by   B. for   C. in   D. over

9. If anything should happen _____ her, let me know at once.
   A. to   B. on   C. in   D. with

10. Finding a job in such a big company has always been _____ his wildest dreams.
    A. under   B. over   C. above   D. beyond

11. We should put our disputes aside before the committee and abide _____ its decisions.
    A. to   B. in   C. by   D. with

12. Unless you sign a contract with the insurance company for your goods, you are not entitled _____ a repayment for the goods damaged in delivery.
    A. to   B. with   C. for   D. on

13. How can you fight your cancer if you cannot look it _____ the face.

    A. on   B. by   C. in   D. from

14. It might be a good idea just to skim _____ the important papers to get the main issues.

    A. along   B. off   C. from   D. over

15. "Good-bye and good luck!" _____ these words, he turned and got on the train.

    A. With   B. Of   C. By   D. On

16. All of them were shaking _____ laughter.

    A. over   B. through   C. with   D. by

17. Although we don't feel satisfied with the election results, we have to become reconciled _____ the decision made by our fellow countrymen.

    A. for   B. on   C. to   D. in

18. After the lecture the students shook hands with the visiting professor _____ turn.

    A. with   B. in   C. by   D. after

19. They asked _____ your health in their last letter.

    A. about   B. on   C. after   D. of

20. We should call _____ respect for the blue-collar workers.

    A. for   B. at   C. on   D. off

21. He is the sort of person who can go _____ any group.

    A. among   B. between   C. within   D. with

22. Contrary _____ what people generally believe, men, not women, need encouragement more.

    A. upon   B. beside   C. to   D. at

23. _____ the English examination, I would have gone to the concert last Sunday.

    A. In spite of   B. But for   C. Because of   D. As for

24. They are paid _____ the hour.

    A. for   B. to   C. by   D. on

25. Three weeks later, the police seemed to have given up _____ despair.

    A. out   B. in   C. on   D. from

26. The road accident resulted _____ five deaths.

    A. in   B. to   C. for   D. about

27. It is believed that today's pop music can serve as a creative force _____ stimulating the thinking of its listeners.

    A. by   B. with   C. at   D. on

28. _____ everybody's disappointment, the football match was put off.

    A. To   B. In   C. With   D. For

29. CEO stands _____ Chief Executive Officer.

    A. at   B. to   C. for   D. on

30. He reached _____ his cigarettes.

    A. to   B. out   C. down   D. for

β Error Correction

1. She buried her face in the flowers drinking upon the fragrance.

2. Having been robbed of economic importance, those states are not likely to count on very much in international political terms.

3. The protons in a nucleus being equal with the electrons outside, the atom is electrically neutral.

4. I was told to stay away out the dangerous instruments.

5. An important factor in a market-oriented economy is the mechanism of which consumer demands can be expressed and responded to by producers.

6. With help from all parts of the country, the people in the flooded area managed to get over that harsh winter.

7. Reading between the lines, I should say the scientists are disappointed for the outcome of the research project, though they will not openly admit it.

8. The boy had a bad fall. Will somebody send along a doctor?

9. You cannot say that the desire for material advantage is the basic motive in human behaviors; there are many exceptions for this.

10. He caught the thief with the collar and dragged him to the nearest police station.

11. You may be able to cheat some people for a time, but you won't succeed on fooling them forever.

12. The shopkeeper gave me a 100-yuan note instead of a 10-yuan note from mistake.

13. It was said that his disease was out cure.

14. The social separation among whites and blacks in the south was so great that it was not easy to establish ordinary personal relations across such a barrier.

15. When President Kennedy spoke in Berlin from behalf of the American people, he was received with a show of enormous enthusiasm.

II. Cloze Test

A A Recent Etymology of the Word "Culture" "文化" 一词的新词源

Look in an old dictionary — say, a pre-1960 Webster's — and you'll likely find a definition of culture _____ (1) looks something like this: "1. The cultivation of soil. 2. The raising, improvement, or development of some plant, animal _____ (2) product." This use of the word has its roots in the ancient Latin word cultura, "cultivation" or "tending," and _____ (3) entrance into the English language had begun by the year 1430. By the time the Webster's definition above was _____ (4), another definition had begun to take precedence over the old Latin denotation; culture was coming to mean "the training, _____ (5), and refinement of mind, tastes, and manners" (Oxford English Dictionary). The OED traces this definition, which today we associate _____ (6) the phrase "high culture," back as far as 1805; by the middle of the 20th century, it was _____ (7) becoming the word's primary definition.

However, if you try a more modern source, like the American Heritage English Dictionary, _____ (8) find a primary definition of culture which is substantially different than either of the two given above: "The totality _____ (9) socially transmitted behavior patterns, arts, beliefs, institutions, and all other products of human work and thought." Why such a _____ (10), and in such a (relatively) short period of time? Well, in the past 40 years, the use of the _____ (11) "culture" has been heavily influenced by the academic fields of sociology and cultural anthropology. These fields have gradually brought _____ (12) was once a minor definition of culture (the last of eight definitions given in the old 1958 Webster's quoted _____ (13)) into the mainstream.

It is easy to imagine how the US society which was so focused on "socially transmitted _____ (14) patterns" in the sixties would come to need a word to describe the object of its interest. The civil _____ (15) movement during this era brought everyone's attention to bear on cultural differences within US society, while the Vietnam War _____ (16) to emphasize the position of the US culture in relation to other world cultures.

Over time, these new uses _____ (17) the word culture have eclipsed its older meanings, those associated with cultivation of the land and the production of _____ (18). You might say that an aspect of US culture over the past 40 years is its fascination with the _____ (19) of culture itself — a fascination which has brought about many changes in the way we speak and the _____ (20) of words which we commonly use.

ß The Culture Debate in the US: Whose Culture Is This, Anyway?
美国的文化辩论：究竟是谁的文化？

Part of the debate about culture revolves around issues of perspective and ownership. Within a nation such _____ (1) the United States — a nation whose cultural heritage includes elements from every corner of the world — _____ (2) are a great many perspectives coexisting and intertwining in the cultural fabric. When we all ask _____ (3) as individuals, "what belongs to me, to my culture?" we are rewarded with a spectacular variety of _____ (4); in this way, different perspectives and ownership of different cultural traditions enriches everyone. But when we ask "_____ (5) belongs to us, to our culture?" we ask a much harder question. Do the people of the _____ (6) States, or of any culturally complex human society, necessarily share common cultural elements? If so, who gets _____ (7) decide what those elements are?

This debate is a crucial one in many cultures throughout the world _____ (8). In the US, the debate promises to impact the way we educate our children — that is, _____ (9) manner and shape in which culture reproduces itself — and the way we write our laws. In _____ (10) countries, equally crucial issues are at stake.

For many people, what is at stake is the character _____ (11) US national identity. Hirsch argues that this identity needs to become less culturally fragmented; others, like Walker, _____ (12) that the national character gets its strength from cultural diversity, from the freedom (at home and in _____ (13)) to celebrate, honor, and reproduce different cultural traditions. Those who take this latter view follow the reasoning _____ (14) Shweder, arguing that we need to accept that there are multiple valid cultural perspectives and that two _____ (15) perspectives can both be valid even though they might contradict one another.

Recognize that the position you _____ (16) in this debate about culture — whatever position you take — is a political one with implications _____ (17) what we should value, what we should praise, what we should accept, what we should teach. When _____ (18) reflect on this debate, when you contribute your own voice to the discussion, try to be _____ (19) of the implications that follow from your position. When you listen to the voices of others, try to _____ (20) with awareness, deciding for yourself what is at stake and how their positions relate to your own.

III. Reading Comprehension

Passage One

Chinese Buddhist Music Catches Audience in HK
中华佛教音乐吸引香港听众

The Hong Kong Cultural Center in Victoria Bay was packed on Thursday night, and loud applause periodically echoed through the neon lit sky. It was not rock music nor was it pop — it was traditional Chinese Buddhist music that made an instant hit in the modern metropolis.

Hong Kong is the fourth leg of the Buddhist music performance tour by a troupe consisting of more than 130 monks from the Chinese mainland and Taiwan. And this is also the first time monks from across the Taiwan Strait had jointly set up a troupe to perform on global stages.

Crowds of Hong King residents were lining up at the local port waiting to welcome members of the troupe who were sailing in from Macao, where they had just ended another successful performance on Wednesday night.

The monks returned the enthusiasm of the residents with a powerful performance. Almost without sleep, the monks drove to the concert hall preparing the stage and doing the rehearsals.

Buddhist music, which originated from ancient India, found its way into China some 2,000 years ago, and after absorbing elements of traditional Chinese folk music, court music and other religious music, a unique form which is now called Chinese Buddhist music came into being.

The monks of the troupe come from prestigious Buddhist temples including Fo Guang Shan

Temple in Taiwan, Shaolin Temple in central Henan Province, Labrang Temple in northwestern Gansu Province, and General Temple in southwestern Yunnan Province, representing the three branches of Buddhism in China, namely Chinese Buddhism, Tibetan Buddhism and Pali Buddhism.

The wind sweeping across the Victoria Bay was cool, but the atmosphere in the concert hall was hot. The audience was mesmerized by the great variety of genres of Chinese Buddhist music.

"It's great to see so many genres of Chinese Buddhist music performed on the same stage," said a female bank employee surnamed Chang, "It's so fascinating," she said.

Calling it a happy event in Hong Kong, the Venerable Kwok Kuang, president of the Hong Kong Buddhist Association, said that the concert served as a prelude to the display, in Hong Kong on May 26, of a relic from Famen Temple preserved in Xi'an, capital of northwest China's Shaanxi Province.

He said that Buddhism and Buddhist music in the Chinese mainland, Taiwan and Hong Kong had the same roots, and through the performance by monks from across the Taiwan Strait, the traditional religious art would be further developed and bring more happiness to the Chinese.

Co-sponsored by the Chinese Buddhism Association of China and Fo Guang Shan Temple in Taiwan, the troupe was formed in February this year and has since staged four successful performances in Taiwan and Macao, and will move on to Los Angeles and San Francisco in the US and Vancouver of Canada from Friday.

Hailing the joint performance as a major event in the history of Buddhism, Hsin Ting, deputy chief of the troupe and abbot of Fo Guang Shan, said that both the monks and the support staff had been working together very harmoniously ever since the formation of the troupe, indicating their inherited strong ties.

"I hope the troupe's tour to North America will help the world community better understand Chinese traditional culture, especially the harmonious relationships among the people across the Taiwan Strait," he said.

〜〜〜〜〜〜〜〜〜〜〜〜〜〜〜〜〜〜〜〜〜〜〜〜〜〜

1. How was the Chinese Buddhist music troupe received in Hong Kong?

    A. It was welcomed like any other rock or pop music bands.

    B. It was not as welcome as rock or pop music bands.

    C. It was so welcome that it would visit Hong Kong for the fourth time.

    D. It caused a great sensation among the local people.

2. What, according to the author, is the significance of the troupe's visit to Hong Kong?

    A. It signifies a beginning of strengthening cultural exchanges across the Taiwan Straits.

    B. It marks a beginning of reunification of the mainland and Taiwan.

    C. It marks a successful religious cross-Strait exchange and cooperation at a global level.

    D. It signifies that Taiwan and the mainland are of one country.

3. The different genres of Buddhist music performed on stage represent _____.

    A. a long history of Chinese Buddhism

    B. a richness of Chinese Buddhist music

C. many different temples across China

D. the three branches of Buddhism in China

4. Which of the following is NOT mentioned in the passage?

A. The troupe will offer three more performances after the Hong Kong event.

B. There will be another religious activity in Hong Kong after the music performance.

C. The troupe will continue its tour to North America.

D. The troupe is about four months old.

5. Hsin Ting and Fo Guang Shan attributed the success of the performance to _____ .

A. the good relationship between the monks and the support staff

B. the strong traditional ties that ensured the harmonious work for the performance

C. the long Chinese traditional culture

D. the long history of Buddhism in China

Passage Two

Meet the Bauls
遇见鲍尔人

Most Westerners, if they know the Bauls at all, remember the non sequitur of a couple of members of this Bengali sect standing next to Bob Dylan on the cover of Dylan's milestone album "John Wesley Harding." The story goes that Dylan was depressed, and his foster-father/ manager, Albert Grossman, arranged for the seer-singers to visit Woodstock to cheer up our poet laureate.

Apocryphal? I would agree, if my introduction to the Bauls weren't remarkably similar.

I'd gone to India as a recent recruit of The Dharma Bums, a group that had been invited to play the World Festival of Sacred Music in May. Unaccustomed to international travel, I got to the concert site in Bangalore dazed, sick, and terrified.

I came thoroughly awake at sound check. It's fear that does it. Peering out at 800 empty seats at the local college auditorium, fighting with squealing mikes, a smattering of hangers-on understandably unimpressed with the wretched sounds coming from our throats. When the concert began, I settled in to my seat to suffer the humiliation of watching a whole show of spiritually advanced musicians make contact with a highest being — before we came out and sucked.

Then four men dressed in flowing golden-orange gowns sauntered onstage, smiling. They sat, acknowledging applause. The oldest and straightest was blind.

The Bauls call themselves spiritual anarchists because they declare themselves to be Hindus and true Moslems — acknowledging no contradiction. Their home base is Calcutta, the Indian city famous for its "black hole," where everything is cut to the bone, spirituality included.

Seven months a year, the Bauls wander as musician mendicants, accepting alms for song. The remainder of the year, they return to their families and resume their "day job" of walking the cars of the hell-trains of Calcutta, performing their bloodless open-heart surgery for half-rupees and blessings.

The first of the four — the wasted remains of a handsome man — stood, commencing to wail and slowly, on bell-jangling feet, to dance. At the end of a long, thin arm he thumbed a one-stringed harp's single note, his voice so filled with mournful joy that tears instantaneously began to splash my cheek. He seemed to cry out: "All you see before you is yours Lord, do with me what you will." A single tooth flashed against the scarlet hole of this mouth, ecstasy-laced red eyes pinched shut, then opened again to pilot bare feet to a resting place. As he sat, we rained applause.

A smaller, more powerful black swan of a man stands. His voice, unlike his comrade's, is virile and revved up to matinee-idol pitch. The black swan plucks out a wobbling volley, then points his pick hand straight at a member of the audience. What proceeds is a wedding of power and passion as might have caused Otis Redding to reconsider his singing career. Our applause is thunderous. He makes the prayer sign at chest, and sits.

Up rises Oedipus at Colonnus, his eyes shameless wounds, never to heal; the fourth Baul, a young drummer, takes the elbow of this guru he walks beside every day, his master now singing and smiling. With each step, the blind man comments with even greater vigor at another even more extraordinary development in this, his dialogue with God. The guide prods him to the edge of the stage; once there, Oedipus raises both his hands and commences to crow for joy, connecting with such power as we, the audience, cry out to tell him where we are and to thank him, almost as a lover cries in gratitude. Hearing this, he redoubles his effort. At the very edge of the huge stage, the other three are bent, whipping up a small storm of accompaniment. Oedipus suddenly twists his head halfway between heaven and earth, and straight into the hot stage lights he peers as three shrill notes shoot from his small, misshapen mouth, making it all stop. He is with God already; what remains here with us is merely a witness to the beyond.

What else matters? Certainly not our performance. My only ambition at present is to be nearer the Bauls.

〜〜〜〜〜〜〜〜〜〜〜〜〜〜〜〜〜〜〜〜〜〜〜〜〜〜〜〜〜〜〜〜

1. It seems that the mention of Bob Dylan serves as an introduction _____.

    A. of the Bauls   B. of a musical genre

    C. to the album "John Wesley Harding"   D. to western music

2. How did the author feel about their rehearsal sound check?

    A. He was dazed, sick and terrified.

    B. He was totally unimpressed with the local college auditorium.

    C. He feared that their performance would be a failure.

    D. He was disappointed with the poor turn-out of audience.

3. What did the author think of the Bauls's performance?

    A. He felt completely humiliated by their performance lacking in spirit.

    B. He felt their performance rose to a superbly high spiritual level that his own band couldn't attain.

C. The Bauls's performance was blindly apocryphal.

D. The Bauls's performance was a great attraction to the local people.

4. It can be deduced that, for most time of the year, the Bauls _____.

A. live an exciting life in Calcutta

B. live a squalid, from-hand-to-mouth life

C. wander among the cars and train on the streets

D. offer their performances as blessings for the poor

5. The four men's performance on stage can be described as _____.

A. spiritual and bloodless   B. random and willful

C. shabby and shameful   D. soulful and exhilarating

Passage Three

What We Do
我们做的事情

The Humour Foundation is a national charity established in 1997 to promote the health benefits of humour. Clown Doctors are the core project, and children are the focus. Clown Doctor programs are established in all major children's hospitals around Australia and some general hospitals and hospices. Clowns have also visited east Timor and Afghanistan. LaughterWorks provides speakers and workshop presenters on humour and health to the health and welfare sector. International research has demonstrated the health benefits of humour.

Clown Doctors attend to the psycho-social needs of the hospitalised child. They parody the hospital routine to help children adapt to hospital. Clown Doctors distract children during painful or frightening procedures. They dispense doses of fun and laughter and help children forget for a moment that they are ill. Everyone benefits — patients, families and staff. Clown Doctors are highly skilled professionals that work in partnership with health professionals.

The Humour Foundation's core project is , touching the lives of over 85,000 people every year. The focus is children's hospitals, and Clown Doctors are now part of hospital life in all major children's hospitals around Australia.

"I am writing to thank you with all my heart for the fun, cheer and brightness you brought to me when I was in hospital for open heart surgery... I am thirty-seven years of age but felt just as excited as the kids no doubt are to see you. It was a terrific morale booster!"

Children are our focus, but adult patients benefit too. Humour is built around each person's interests and responses and participation is encouraged. Adults have just as much fun as the kids! Clown Doctors also play a role in palliative care. The aim is to provide ways of dealing with death, and paradoxically people frequently share their feelings. Clown Doctors take risks in balancing lightness with the profound. Caring clowning can speak the language of the heart and bring a sense of profound connection and consolation.

Doses of humour can help relieve stress, improve health and well-being. Laughter that is based on caring and empathy also creates bonds between people, is nourishing, helps develop resilience and helps people cope with difficult situations. By developing strategies to bring more laughter into your life, you can improve your focus and effectiveness, enhance your communication and creative problem solving and strengthen your relationships and overall health.

Put more laughter in your life, for *Aristotle* once said, "Laughter is a bodily exercise precious to health."

Smile often

Laugh every day

Laugh at yourself and at life

Lighten up-be playful and have fun

Tickle your funny bone and seek out opportunities to laugh

You don't have to be funny, just have fun

Develop a humorous perspective and look for the funny side

Use humour as a tool, not a weapon

The Humour Foundation is a charity dedicated to promoting the health benefits of humour. International research has found psychological and physiological advantages from doses of humour. Humour is an effective coping strategy. It can relieve fear and stress and aid recovery.

1. As a national charity, the Humour Foundation's major responsibility is _____.

    A. to recruit clowns

    B. to cure clowns of disease

    C. to employ clowns as baby sitters

    D. to take advantage of humour in treating patients

2. Which of the following do the Clown Doctors NOT do?

    A. to prescribe medicine

    B. to relieve children of pain or fright

    C. to provide children with fun and laughter

    D. to make children temporarily forget their illness

3. The italicized quotation is obviously part of a letter from _____.

    A. a parent of a patient   B. a clown

    C. a patient   D. a medical practitioner

4. The word *palliative* in the sentence "Clown Doctors also play a role in palliative care" is most probably in the meaning of _____.

    A. curing   B. healing   C. soothing   D. diagnosing

5. The main theme of this passage is to advise people _____.

    A. to believe that laughter is a cure-all

    B. to be optimistic in life

C. to seek help from clowns instead of doctors when ill

D. to be funny in life

Bringing More Humor and Laughter into Our Lives
在生活中带进更多的幽默和笑声

The sound of roaring laughter is far more contagious than any cough, sniffle, or sneeze. Humor and laughter can cause a domino effect of joy and amusement, as well as set off a number of positive physical effects. Humor and laughter strengthen our immune systems and help us recover from illness, as well as bring joy into our lives. The question is: how do we gain access to this priceless medicine?

A good hearty laugh can help

reduce stress

lower blood pressure

elevate mood

boost immune system

improve brain functioning

protect the heart

connect you to others

foster instant relaxation

make you feel good

Humor is a powerful emotional medicine that can lower stress, dissolve anger and unite families in troubled times. Mood is elevated by striving to find humor in difficult and frustrating situations. Laugh at yourselves and the situation helps reveal that small things are not the earth-shaking events they sometimes seem to be. Looking at a problem from a different perspective can make it seem less formidable and provide opportunities for greater objectivity and insight. Humor also helps us avoid loneliness by connecting with others who are attracted to genuine cheerfulness. And the good feeling that we get when we laugh can remain with us as an internal experience even after the laughter subsides.

Mental health professionals point out that humor can also teach perspective by helping patients to see reality rather than the distortion that supports their distress. Humor shifts the ways in which we think, and distress is greatly associated with the way we think. It is not situations that generate our stress, but it is the meaning we place on the situations. Humor adjusts the meaning of an event so that it is not so overwhelming.

Here are some additional things we can do to improve our mood, enjoyment of life and mental health.

Attempt to laugh at situations rather than bemoan them — this helps improve our disposition and the disposition of those around us.

Use cathartic laughter to release pent-up feelings of anger and frustration in socially acceptable ways.

Laugh as a means of reducing tension because laughter is often followed by a state of relaxation.

Lower anxiety by visualizing a humorous situation to replace the view of an anxiety-producing situation

Our work, marriage and family all need humor, celebrations, play and ritual as much as record-keeping and problem-solving. We should ask the questions "Do we laugh together?" as well as "Can we get through this hardship together?" Humor binds us together, lightens our burdens and helps us keep things in perspective. One of the things that saps our energy is the time, focus and effort we put into coping with life's problems including each other's limitations. Our families, our friends and our neighbors are not perfect and neither are our marriages, our kids or our in-laws. When we laugh together, it can bind us closer together instead of pulling us apart.

Remember that even in the most difficult of times, a laugh, or even simply a smile, can go a long way in helping us feel better.

Laughter is a birthright, a natural part of life. The part of the brain that connects to and facilitates laughter is among the first parts of the nervous system to come on line after birth. Infants begin smiling during the first weeks of life and laugh out loud within months of being born. Even if you did not grow up in a household where laughter was a common sound, you can learn to laugh at any stage of life.

1. Which of the following isn't laughter compared to?
   A. a contagious physical function   B. a domino effect
   C. an immune system   D. a medicine
2. What can't a good hearty laugh help do?
   A. reduce weight   B. connect you to others
   C. lower blood pressure   D. protect the heart
3. The good feeling derived from laughter can stay with us as _____ even after the laughter stops.
   A. an inner experience   B. a lifelong experience
   C. an outward experience   D. a mental reward
4. According to the passage, stress we experience in life results from _____.
   A. the way we think
   B. the situations we are in
   C. the mental problems we suffer from
   D. the way we understand our situations
5. Which of the following statements is NOT right?
   A. Laughter is a natural part of life.
   B. Human beings are not born to be able to laugh.
   C. Human beings can learn to laugh at any time of life.
   D. Laughter is a kind of medicine, so to speak.

第八单元　关系从句

．．．．．．．．．．．．．．．　**I. Grammar: Relative Clauses**　．．．．．．．．．．．．．．．

A **Multiple Choices**

1. Where is the article _____ you quoted this line?

   A. where   B. which   C. from where   D. from which

2. The weather turned out to be very bad, _____ was more than we could expect.

   A. what   B. which   C. that   D. it

3. The famous writer _____ you talked is writing another novel.

   A. about whom   B. about who   C. whom   D. who

4. The course normally attracts 50 students per year, _____ up to half are from overseas.

   A. in which   B. for whom   C. with which   D. of whom

5. The Oregon Trail went through the South Pass, _____ gold was discovered in 1842.

   A. where   B. which   C. that   D. when

6. Opposite the square is a very tall building, _____ top is well above the tops of the others.

   A. its   B. whose   C. which   D. that

7. The medicine has many functions, _____ are unknown to us.

   A. some of which   B. that some of them

   C. of which some of them   D. which of them

8. The winner of the Nobel Prize in physics dedicated the honor to his high school physics teacher, _____ had been an inspiration during his early years.

   A. who   B. whom   C. which   D. that

9. _____ is announced in today's papers, the Shanghai Export Commodities Fair is also open on this Sunday.

   A. That   B. Which   C. As   D. It

10. The voters were overwhelmingly against the candidate _____ proposals called for higher taxes.

    A. who   B. whose   C. whom   D. which

11. All _____ is needed is a continuous supply of fuel oil.

    A. what   B. that   C. which   D. this

12. Author Edith Wharton thoroughly understood the society _____ she had grown up.

    A. in which   B. which   C. in that   D. that

13. Mr. Jason Matthews, _____ collection of pictures a valuable Rembrand was given to the nation, died last night.

    A. from whom   B. from whose   C. from which   D. from what

14. The knee is the joint _____ the thigh bone meets the large bone of the lower leg.

    A. when   B. where   C. that   D. which

15. I hope that the little _____ I've been able to do has been of some use.

    A. which   B. what   C. whose   D. that

16. Some of the musical pieces for _____ Isadora Duncan choreographed dances were waltzes and mazurkas by Chopin.

    A. whom   B. that   C. which   D. what

17. He is regarded by all as a genius, _____ the important discovery was made.

    A. who   B. whom   C. about whom   D. by whom

18. Let's discuss only such questions _____ concerned everyone of us.

    A. what   B. that   C. as   D. and

19. Helen was much kinder to her younger child than she was to the others, _____, of course, made the others jealous.

    A. it   B. that   C. what   D. which

20. We will put off the picnic until next month _____ the weather may be better.

    A. where   B. that   C. when   D. which

21. No plant can possibly exist on the moon because there is no water, _____ is indispensable to life.

    A. that   B. which   C. it   D. of which

22. The award was won by Dennis Johnson, _____ the coach highly respects.

    A. who   B. whom   C. which   D. that

23. The two elements _____ water is made are the gases of oxygen and hydrogen.

    A. that   B. which   C. of which   D. with which

24. The residents, _____ had been damaged by the flood, were given help by the Red Cross.

    A. all their homes   B. all whose homes

    C. all of whose homes   D. all of their homes

25. After he has written his paper, he found some additional material _____ he should have included.

    A. that   B. of which   C. in which   D. whom

26. The two elements _____ water is made are oxygen and hydrogen.

    A. that   B. which   C. of which   D. with which

27. Besides the electrons, an atom also contains positive electrical particles _____ total charge must be equal to that of the electrons.

    A. which   B. that   C. whose   D. of which

28. Florida, _____ is reported, attracts 800 thousand tourists every year.

    A. which   B. as   C. where   D. who

29. The earth, _____ is the fifth largest planet in the solar system, is the third planet from the sun.

    A. who   B. whom   C. which   D. that

30. We've tested three hundred types of boots, none of _____ is completely waterproof.

    A. which   B. that   C. what   D. them

B Error Correction

1. This colorless gas is called oxygen, who fires burn much better.

2. The detectives were finally able to arrest the man whom finger prints had been found on the table.

3. My neighbors on either side of me have painted their houses, that of course makes my house look shabbier than it really is.

4. The symbols of mathematics which we are most familiar are the signs of addition, subtraction, multiplication, division and equality.

5. Beer is the most popular drink among male drinkers which overall consumption is significantly higher than that of women.

6. The explosion of a hydrogen bomb is the result of uncontrolled nuclear fusion. It is the most terrible weapon of war which man has invented.

7. The hours when the children spend in their one-way relationship with television people, undoubtedly affect their relationships with real-life people.

8. The veterinarian has examined several dogs, two of them are believed to be developing rabies.

9. The company where we visited the day before yesterday is not far from here.

10. The author wrote about the people and places which he had visited.

11. The period during when people learned to smelt iron is called the Iron Age.

12. Caves and hollow trees are not the only places that bats live.

13. Mountain Everest, the peak where is hardly seen, is the highest mountain in the world.

14. The Latin class had twenty students, most of which had had much better language training than I.

15. The Tartar chief controls a thousand men, all of which must obey his orders in both war and peace.

II. Cloze Test

A Every Object Tells a Story 凡事皆有戏

    Everyone has a particular object to which they attach a special meaning or story. Every Object Tells A _____ (1) is a participative website that enables people to explore the stories and meanings behind collections of museum objects. _____（2）to the site can create their own stories and share their own interpretations and objects online.

The project _____（3）on the art of storytelling and involves four regional museums, in partnership with Channel 4 and Ultralab, a _____（4）technology research centre at Anglia Polytechnic University. It will be led by the Victoria and Albert Museum. It _____（5）the personal meanings and histories behind objects to get people to look at them in new ways. It _____（6）designed to inspire them to create their own stories and share their interpretations and objects of personal significance _____（7）a growing online community.

Video, audio, text and pictures combine on the site to offer an enticing, accessible _____（8）into the content. Users can choose to browse the hundreds of objects featured, or they can search for _____（9）particular theme or person. They can decide on the level of information they want on an object, from _____（10）stories conveyed through text and pictures, to the richer experience offered by accompanying video and audio. They will _____（11）encouraged to add their own interpretation or object to the collection, by uploading text, images, video or audio _____（12）the site or by sending text and images from a mobile phone. In so doing, they will be _____（13）to the website's content and illustrating how a single object can convey different meanings to different people.

The _____（14）stories and wonderful objects will appeal to a broad audience. The project has specific relevance to all key _____（15）of the National Curriculum in English and literacy. Outreach sessions in regional partner museums will encourage people to _____（16）involved in the project locally and a video booth will travel around England, visiting shopping centres, libraries, bus _____（17）and the like, to enable people to capture their object and story in a short video. This will _____（18）be uploaded onto the site.

In addition to the national and local publicity given to the project, Channel 4 _____（19）promote the website from a number of its programmes, ensuring a wide appeal and providing an added _____（20）for people to contribute their content.

Ⓑ Customs of Bulgaria: Marriage and Family 保加利亚习俗：婚姻与家庭

The average age for women to marry is between 18 and 25. 25 tend to _____（1）when somewhat older. A church wedding often _____（2）the legal civil ceremony, and a large reception, which often involves _____（3）music and dancing, is held in the evening. Wedding traditions include _____（4）money on the bride's dress to represent future prosperity, the groom _____（5）the bride at her home, and the couple pulling on opposite _____（6）of a loaf of bread — whoever gets the largest piece will be _____（7）boss of the family. Honeymoons are a new tradition.

The principle _____（8）mutual support is valued in the Bulgarian family. The elderly are _____（9）cared for by their adult children. Unmarried adults live with their _____（10）and many newly married couples live with one set of parents _____（11）they are able to get housing of their own. Most families _____（12）urban areas live in apartments, which are in short supply, while _____ (13) in rural areas usually have their own houses. Many village houses _____ (14) owned by families who live in urban areas, who use them _____ (15) summer and weekend retreats, or for retired parents.

Most families in _____ (16) areas do not have more than two children, while families in _____ (17) areas tend to be larger. Grandparents play an important role in _____ (18) care, particularly in urban areas, where most women work outside the _____ (19). Men of the younger generation have begun to help with household _____ (20), once considered only women's responsibility.

III. Reading Comprehension

Passage One

When Dance Speaks the Unspoken and No Language Is Required
当舞蹈说出没有说出的话，就无需语言了

A complete dancer today, is well trained in more than one discipline. The European dance scene has seen a rebirth of the influence of Spanish dance with the fusion of Flamenco and Classical Spanish Dance with other styles. The excitements of these fusions are very present in the Bay Area, which is America's hotbed of Flamenco.

This heat wave of creation, arrived last summer in Walnut Creek with the premiere concert season of Carolina Lugo's Brisas de Espa — a Flamenco Dance Company. Carolina's company not only presents the powerful intense energy of solo flamenco but the grace and joy of classical dances. She herself was trained in classical Spanish dance, which is a world apart from the introverted nature of flamenco, with its familiar roots of the earth. What ballet gives to both her traditions, is the physical strength of movement that seeks light and takes to the air. Perhaps, where these very different traditions flow within her blood we have the true creative force of Ms. Lugo's work. Each tradition is like a river joining to form an even more powerful force with its own life. During a rehearsal in preparation for Brisas appearance with the Eagles, Clint Black, and Bruce Hornsby at the benefit concert for Tony La Russa's Animal Rescue Foundation, Carolina explained her intense passion for dance. When a dancer is on stage, it goes without saying, they must be one with the music. Without this connection to the music, movement, and yourself, a dancer is only counting steps and performing routines. The heart of the dancer's work is to embrace the audience with the depth of our lives and the fiery sensuality of dancing. The magic of performing is for the dancers and the audience to experience our fierce pride, love, happiness and tears. The art of Flamenco is the completeness of being, which the Gypsies of

Spain refer to as "duende", the possession of the sole. This quality, when it present, casts a spell over the audience and everyone becomes involved.

The gift of the modern age is that with the speed of travel and communications we are able to emerge in the changes of the world's cultures. International artist Manuel Manolo Betanzos will be returning from a world tour for a month of performances and dance workshops with the company. Carolina believes that Manolo's fused style of dance makes him one of Spain's best dancers. He was trained in the earthy traditions of flamenco and the elegance of classical Spanish dance by many of the greatest maestros in Spain. His commanding presence on stage last summer earned him the admiration of local dance fans. Pepe Haro also from Spain will join the company as guest guitarist. His playing and musical arrangements bring power to every chord, shading and singing melodic line and above all, a rich rhythmic pulse.

Exploring the emotions and feelings of flamenco has been a profound journey for Carolina. She was recently awarded a grand from the Diablo Regional Arts Association to further her own exploration of dance fusion and will collaborate for this year's performance with Brazilian Samba Queen, Katia Vaz. Carolina will present the World Premier of Dance Without Borders (Bailes Sin Fronteras). She promises that this work will be a moment, when dance speaks the unspoken and no language is required, only the passion to dance free of limitations. Both Spanish and Brazilian music and dance are diverse and represent a vast m lange of cultural similarities and differences. The emotions of life are the fundamental pieces of both dance traditions. Carolina and Katia, will be joined by Carolina Acea, daughter of Carolina an American original whose style has been influenced by both traditions. The music will be sung both in Spanish and Portuguese by Roberto Zamora and Patricia Velasquez. Carolina explains that the artistic essence of both Flamenco and Samba is their expression of a gamut of feelings about life, embodied with an attitude.

1. The performances by Carolina's company are described as _____.
   A. a mixture of different dances   B. a creation on the dance scene
   C. a rebirth of mixed disciplines   D. a hotbed of Flamenco
2. The author thinks that flamenco and classical Spanish dances _____.
   A. are of an introverted and extroverted nature respectively
   B. are of different origins
   C. are totally different
   D. have learned a lot from ballet
3. Which of the following does NOT represent Ms. Lugo's views on dance?
   A. Merging oneself into the music and movement while dancing.
   B. Concentrating yourself on the music while dancing.
   C. Involving the audience in your emotions while dancing.
   D. Creating an experience of fierce pride, love and happiness and tears.
4. The so-called "gift of the modern age" is present in _____.
   A. the great artist' joining the company for performance at ease
   B. traveling by air and communicating through the Internet

C. the fast changing of world's cultures

D. the emergence international artists one after another

5. Which of the following is true of Flamenco and Samba?

A. They are both of the same origin.

B. Both dances are centered on the emotional life of ordinary people.

C. Both dances share similar cultural origins.

D. They may merge into each other easily.

Passage Two

Running a School Book Stall
开办学校书店

I assume that the desirability of a school book stall needs no urging. Many schools sell food and toys. If we do not sell books it is surely strange? Many schools serve areas where book shops do not exist and the only books brought before children for buying are the dubious selections of supermarkets. Moreover even in communities where a good book shop is available the guidance which can be given at the book stall is valuable, as we soon found.

Essentially the school book stall is an extension of the encouragement and guidance in private reading which is part of the work of the English teacher. The first essential then, in setting up shop is a teacher particularly interested in children reading and in building up as wide as possible a knowledge of books to suit the school's range of pupils.

Given the teacher, the next requirement is a bookseller willing to supply you. In some cases you will be able to obtain your books on credit, paying as you sell, but if the school can find a sum to purchase its stock, or at least a part of it, this is a great help.

Having found your supplier you then approach the Publisher's Association for a Book Agent's licence. The licence entitles you to a discount on your purchase through your chosen supplier, the usual discount being 10% with service. Service usually consists of delivery and a sale or return arrangement, the latter essential in allowing you to be enterprising and experimental in your stock. Without service a slightly higher discount is given but the former arrangement is clearly preferable.

The biggest, indeed the only considerable, cost in running the book stall is the occasional theft of a book and this may well vary from school to school but the presence of the teacher and the alertness of the assistants is largely deterrent, and the discount should cover this and any other smaller expenses. Browsing is essential. The books must be handled. You cannot keep them safe and immaculate behind glass.

For equipment the only essentials are some tables on which to display the books and a cupboard to store them in. Incidentally an arrangement of books with covers rather than spines visible seems to be vastly more attractive and accessible to children who have not the habit of browsing. A single way out past the cash desk is helpful to security and we record details of each purchase including the age of the buyer both for reordering and as interesting information on reading habits.

Initially we stocked two hundred titles and the selection has grown to close on a thousand. It is convenient if cash or credit allows you to have duplicate copies of popular titles. What is stocked must depend on the teacher in charge. What you are prepared to sell in the cause of encouraging interest in reading will obviously be an individual judgment. Sales for their own sake are in the school context obviously purposeful and the teacher needs to be able to explain to interested parents why he thought a given book valuable for a certain child.

There are always more offers of help from pupils than we can accept. The assistants serve, recommend, order, make posters and arrange displays. Some of the least able pupils have worked devotedly at the book stall.

Publicity is vital. We have two display cases on the school approach containing forty books changed fortnightly and they arouse a lot of interest. Teachers' recommendations, book lists, beginnings of stories read to classes, do much. Some classes buy a book a week between them. The book stall is always open on such occasions as Parent's Evenings.

We open twice a week in the lunch hour and we sell twenty to forty books a week, commercially not much but in our opinion well worth the effort.

〜〜〜〜〜〜〜〜〜〜〜〜〜〜〜〜〜〜〜〜〜〜

1. The writer implies that the reason why a school needs a book stall is _____.
   A. because children always choose the wrong books
   B. children find it difficult to choose books in a supermarket
   C. because children only like strange books
   D. children find it difficult to choose the right books
2. According to the passage the teacher who runs a book stall should be _____.
   A. interested in reading children's books
   B. interested in children's ability to read
   C. interested in reading to children
   D. interested in writing children's books
3. To what does "this may well vary" refer?
   A. The expenditure on books   B. The number of books stolen
   C. The vigilance of the assistants   D. The number of books stocked
4. What is one of the ways of discovering the books that children prefer?
   A. by observing the children as they leave
   B. by recording the children's ages
   C. by noting which children buy books
   D. by noting which books children buy
5. The school makes it possible for the children to know what books are available by _____.
   A. rearranging all of the books every two weeks
   B. arranging fortnightly visits to the book stall

C. exhibiting books to advantage

D. holding regular exhibitions of books

Passage Three

Uffizi Tries to Outdo Louvre
Uffizi 试图胜过卢浮宫

Italy is to try to turn the Uffizi gallery in Florence into Europe's premier art museum, with an ambitious 56m euro scheme to double its exhibition space.

Giuliano Urbani, Italy's culture minister, said the enlarged gallery would surpass "even the Louvre".

By the time work is completed, visitors to the extensively remodeled Uffizi will be able to see 800 new works, including many now confined to the gallery's storerooms for lack of space.

The project — the outcome of nine months of intensive work by a team of architects, engineers and technicians — is a centrepiece of the cultural policy of Silvio Berlusconi's government.

With refurbishment plans also afoot for the Accademia in Venice and the Brera in Milan, Italy is bent on securing its share of a market for cultural tourism that is threatened not just by the Louvre, but also by the "art triangle" of Madrid, which takes in the Prado, the Thyssen collection and the Reina Sofia museum of art.

Schemes for the expansion of the Uffizi's exhibition space stretch back almost 60 years. The latest was mooted in the mid-1990s.

But the one adopted by the present Italian government has reached a far more advanced stage than any of its forerunners. Roberto Cecchi, the government official in charge of the project, said yesterday that all that remained to do was to tender for contracts.

The first changes will be seen as early as next week when a collection of pictures by Caravaggio and his school, including the artist's Bacchus, currently crammed into a tiny room on the second floor, is to be moved to more expansive premises on the first.

Mr. Cecchi said the biggest problem faced by his team was "inserting a museum into a building that is itself a monument". The horseshoe-shaped Palazzo degli Uffizi, began in 1560, was designed by the artist and historian Giorgio Vasari.

The latest plans are bound to stir controversy, involving as they do the creation of new stairwells and lifts in the heart of the building. There has already been an outcry over one proposed element, a seven-storey, canopy-like structure for a new exit by the Japanese architect Arata lsozaki.

But Mr. Urbani said in Florence on Tuesday that part of the scheme was "subject to further evaluation".

At the heart of the plan is the opening up of the first floor of the vast building, which for decades was occupied by the local branch of the national archives.

This will allow visitors to follow a more extensive, and ordered, itinerary that would turn the Uffizi into what Antonio Paolucci, Tuscany's top art official, called "a textbook of art history".

As at present, visitors will be channelled to the second floor, where they will be able to study early works by Cimabue and Giotto before moving on to admire the gallery's extraordinary collection of Renaissance masterpieces, including Botticelli's Primavera.

But most of what was painted after 1500 is to be moved down a storey to new exhibition space, and on the ground floor there will be a more extensive collection than at present of modern art. The overall increase in exhibition space will be from 6,000sq metres to almost 13,000.

Asked if the expansion might not increase the risk of inducing Stendhal's syndrome — the disorientation, noted by the French novelist, in those who encounter dozens of Italian Renaissance masterpieces — Mr. Cecchi replied fatalistically, "Yes. It'll double it".

1. Which of the following is true of Uffizi?

   A. It is threatened by the Louvre and the "art triangle" of Madrid.

   B. It is going to be remodeled by transforming its storerooms into showrooms.

   C. It involves a maintenance fee of 56m euro.

   D. It is a major attraction for Italy's cultural tourism.

2. The fact that a group of architects, engineers and technicians spent nine months on the project shows that _____.

   A. it was a large-scale project involving collaboration of experts from various fields

   B. it was completed at amazing speed

   C. the government attached great importance to the project

   D. the government was following the correct cultural policy

3. The passage indicates that the project will be carried out _____.

   A. by first moving all important pictures out of the building

   B. as economically as possible

   C. on a "refurbishing without interfering normal business" basis

   D. by involving many contractors

4. The outcry over a proposed element shows that _____.

   A. the public fully supported the Japanese architect for his design of a new exit

   B. people are very sensitive to the project

   C. people had profound respect for Giorgio Vasari

   D. many people wished to keep the original artistic value of Uffizi

5. What is attractive about the project, when completed, is that it will _____.

   A. increase Stendhal's syndrome in visitors

   B. no longer contain national archives on the ground floor of Uffizi

   C. provide a systematic survey of art history

   D. enable the display of works of several Renaissance painters

Passage Four

Skin Care
护肤

The eyes are described as the windows of the soul, the mouth as the courier of thought, and the nose as the servant of olfaction. The skin is just the frame to the picture. Unfortunately, many judge themselves according to this frame. They could either have feelings of content or censure of their own physical features. Good health and self-esteem go hand-in-hand during the process of exercising and establishing good health habits. The skin's clarity of acne, wrinkles, and sunburns is merely assistance to their stature of confidence. Having healthy skin is a step to confidence. Becoming worry-free of appearances is practicing good sleeping, eating, and drinking habits that lead to the success of a healthy looking person. Adolescents need about 8 – 10 hours of sleep a night, and adults need less than that. However, the body needs to rest and save energy for ongoing activities. Eating properly from the four basic food groups maintains the balance of proteins and nutrients. Fluid consumption of water is more recommended by doctors than the choice of soft drinks that are out on the market. Water provides plenty of water that is the key to have that fresh natural look. When actress, Rebecca Gayheart, (the commercial model of Noxema) was interviewed by Shape magazine in the 1998 November issue, she said, "My beauty routine is basically plenty of sleep and lots of water." Exercising regularly will circulate blood and keep skin firm and toned. Getting involved in an activity that a person enjoys, and they are most likely to be happy and look more healthy. Having to be the largest organ of the human body, the skin's main function is to protect the body from microbes. Because of the large coverage of the skin over the body, it would be encouraged to take care of its texture and form. Many desire healthy looking skin that is smooth and firm. The attraction for this desire makes the market place booming with industry in order to fulfil the consumers' desire. Viewers at home can be guaranteed to see some type of commercial advertisement on TV that focuses on the integument and appendages of hair, make-up, lotions, or nail products. Keeping the face clear promotes good self-esteem and confidence to one's appearance. Good skin can save time from make-up. When a girl wants to step out for a night of the town, the pimples and blemishes on her face will be the last thing that she will be conscious of. Little things can be erupted from something so miniscule. The first thing to combat would be the pores. Pores are what allows the skin to breathe. If pores were to be blocked by dirt, oil, or make-up, unwanted acne would take place. Avoid wearing make-up to sleep and touching the face when hands are dirty. Pores can be kept clean if washed daily, by using a soft facial cleanser versus the usage of deodorant soaps. Whenever heading for the pool or a day out in the sun, never forget to protect your skin from hazardous Ultraviolet (UV) rays. By overexposure to Ultraviolet rays, you're more likely to develop cancer. Through the appliance of sunscreen upon the exposed skin, and underneath make-up we can decrease the odds are more likely to be in your favor. Do not go out and tan, because that ruins the outer membranes. The high percentage of risk upon skin cancer is a large fear.

~~~~~~~~~~~~~~~~~~~~~~~~~~~~~~~~~~~~~

1. As the author says, many people tend to _____ because of their skin.
   A. feel contented or frustrated B. feel indifferent
   C. feel always confident D. feel always fearful

2. If you'd like to be free from worries about your appearances, you have to _____.
   A. sleep as long as you want B. eat whatever you are mad about
   C. drink more soft drinks D. establish good habits in life

3. In "the skin's main function is to protect the body from microbes", the word "microbe" is most likely in the meaning of _____.
   A. insect B. bacterium C. sun beam D. dirt

4. According to the passage, people are advised to wear make-up _____.
   A. 24 hours a day
   B. only during the sleeping time
   C. not while sleeping
   D. neither during the daytime nor during the nighttime

5. It could be inferred that people apply sunscreen upon the exposed skin when outdoors because they want to _____.
   A. be healthy looking B. protect the pores of the skin
   C. become more sun-tanned D. reduce the possibility of skin cancer

第九单元　过去及现在分词

········· **I. Grammar: Past and Present Participles** ·········

A Multiple Choices

1. _____ with his report, the boss told John to write it all over again.
   A. Not to satisfy
   B. Not being satisfied
   C. Not Having satisfied
   D. Not satisfying

2. All the tickets _____ out, we went away disappointed.
   A. being sold   B. be sold   C. having been sold   D. were sold

3. The University of California, _____ in 1868, is administrated by a president and governed by a twenty-four-member board of regents.
   A. founded
   B. has been founded
   C. to have been founded
   D. was founded

4. Characteristics of Op Art are the carefully _____ hues and geometric patterns that create optical illusions.
   A. arranging   B. arranged   C. being arranged   D. arrange

5. Greatly _____ by his words, she jumped into the cold water again.
   A. encouraged
   B. encouraging
   C. to be encouraged
   D. to encourage

6. Besides their sharing traditional male roles, women also play roles entirely different from those _____ by men.
   A. playing   B. be played   C. having played   D. being played

7. The poison, _____ in a small quantity, will be a medicine.
   A. use   B. using   C. used   D. is used

8. Yellowstone National Park, _____ in 1873, is the first national park in the world.
   A. founded
   B. founding
   C. having been founded
   D. being founded

9. In the 1850's Harriet Beecher Stowe's *Uncle Tom's Cabin* became the best seller of the generation, _____ a host of initiators.
   A. inspiring   B. inspired   C. inspired by   D. to inspire

10. Why do you stand and watch the milk _____ over?

    A. boiling   B. boiled   C. to boil   D. being boiled

11. At present we have to get most of the energy _____ in industry by burning coal or oil.

    A. used   B. use   C. using   D. uses

12. _____ under a microscope, a fresh snowflake has a delicate six-pointed shape.

    A. Seen   B. Sees   C. Seeing   D. To see

13. The number of people _____ the meeting was smaller than we had expected.

    A. attend   B. attending   C. attended   D. being attended

14. _____ many other countries, the United States has developed into a modern country in a relatively short time.

    A. Being compared with   B. To compare with

    C. Compared with   D. Comparing with

15. Scientists still cannot find any _____ link between intelligence and the quantity or quality of brain cells.

    A. convince   B. to convince   C. convinced   D. convincing

16. Jacob Lawrence executed many cycles of paintings _____ significant social themes.

    A. expressed   B. expressing   C. express   D. expression of

17. _____ their final medical check, the astronauts boarded their spacecraft.

    A. Receiving   B. Having received

    C. Received   D. Having been received

18. The advantages of computerized typing and editing are now _____ to all the written language of the world.

    A. extend   B. extending   C. being extended   D. being extending

19. _____, the inhabitants fled.

    A. The city taken   B. The city having been taken

    C. Having taken the city   D. The city being taken

20. Contrast may make something appear more beautiful than it is when _____ alone.

    A. seen   B. is seen   C. to be seen   D. having been seen

21. Commercial banks make most of their income from interest _____ on loans and investments in stocks and bonds.

    A. earn   B. earned   C. to earn   D. was earned

22. The young man was found _____ half unconscious under the tree.

    A. to lie   B. to have lain   C. lying   D. being lain

23. When _____ at the door, she was given a warm welcome.

    A. appear   B. appeared   C. appearing   D. to appear

24. When _____ about substances, the scientists find it convenient to classify them into solid, liquid and gas.

    A. thought   B. to think   C. thinking   D. having thought

25. _____ in the election, he went back to his native town.

    A. To be defeated   B. Defeated   C. Being defeated   D. Defeating

26. Closed plane figures like the square or the equilateral triangle can be grouped into a class ____ ____ polygons.

    A. called   B. to call   C. is called   D. called as

27. It is easy to blame the decline of conversation on the pace of modern life and on the vague changes _____ place in our ever-changing world.

    A. taking   B. to take   C. take   D. taken

28. Corn originated in the New World and thus was not known in Europe until Columbus found it _____ in Cuba.

    A. being cultivated   B. been cultivated

    C. having cultivated   D. cultivating

29. On his return from his college, he found the house _____.

    A. deserting   B. desert   C. deserted   D. to be deserted

30. I woke up in the night and heard water _____ through the ceiling.

    A. dripping   B. to drip   C. being dripped   D. drip from

β Error Correction

1. Believed the earth to be flat, many feared that Columbus would fall off the edge of the earth.

2. Seeing from space, our earth, with water covering over 70% of its surface, appears as a "blue planet".

3. So many representatives were absent, the conference had to be postponed.

4. The pancreas is an organ involving in the digestion of food and in the regulation of the sugar level in the blood stream.

5. Have the highest marks in his class, he was offered a scholarship by the college.

6. The material adding to steel increases the metal's hardness.

7. Commercial banks make most of their income from interest earning on loans and investments in stocks and bonds.

8. If keeping in the fridge, the fruit can remain fresh for more than a week.

9. Because its leaves remain green long after picking, rosemary became associated with the idea of remembrance.

10. We can supplement our own ideas with information and data gathering from our reading, our observation, and so forth.

11. Closed plane like the square or the equilateral triangle can be grouped into a class is called polygons.

12. The actual quantity of folic acid is required in the daily diet is not known.

13. They were pushed into the battle unpreparing.

14. Having eaten the cherry pie, I struck several pits and nearly broke a tooth.

15. The boiling-range cuts may vary depended on the type of crude oil and processing scheme to be employed.

II. Cloze Test

A Arrernte Language 阿兰达语

The Arrernte region is large and traditional, there are many different _____ (1) areas within it, each with their own dialect. Language is strongly _____ (2) with family membership and the relationships to land and Dreamings that _____ (3) with this. Identifying as a speaker of a particular language or _____ (4) can be very important for Arrernte people in a way that _____ (5) beyond just the actual language. It is a way of expressing _____ (6) in a particular family, or association to particular country. The differences _____ (7) dialects, even when they are only small differences, are often very _____ (8) to speakers.

The coming together of speakers of different dialects of _____ (9) in Alice Springs, in government and mission settlements, and on cattle _____ (10), has also resulted in some confusion about the traditional dialect distinctions _____ (11) the area. There have been quite large changes in some dialects _____ (12) older generations to younger, and there are many words that only _____ (13) oldest speakers now know. Arrernte people still know the different family _____ (14), but it is sometimes less clear which ones a particular word _____ (15) in.

From time immemorial — that is, as far back as _____ (16) go — the boundaries of the tribes have been where they _____ (17) now fixed. Within them their ancestors roamed about, hunting and performing _____ (18) ceremonies just as their living descendants do at the present day. _____ (19) has never apparently been the least attempt made by one tribe _____ (20) encroach upon the territory of another.

B Public Education in the United States 美国的公立教育

The national system of formal education in the United States developed in the 19th century. It _____ (1) from educational systems of other Western societies in three fundamental respects. First, Americans were more inclined _____ (2) regard education as a solution to various social problems. Second, because they had this confidence in _____ (3) power of education, Americans provided more years of schooling for a larger percentage of the population _____ (4) other countries. Third, educational institutions were primarily governed by local authorities rather than by federal ones. _____ (5) most notable characteristic of the American education system is the large number of people it serves. _____ (6) 2002, 86 percent of Americans between age 25 and 29 had graduated from high school, 58 _____ (7) had completed at least some college, and 29 percent had earned at least a bachelor's degree. _____ (8) access to college education is an important priority for US government.

After the American Revolution (1775 – 1783), the _____ (9) of the United States argued that education was essential for the prosperity and survival _____ (10) the new nation. Thomas Jefferson, author of the Declaration of Independence, proposed that Americans give a _____ (11) priority to a "crusade against ignorance". Jefferson was the first American leader to suggest creating a _____ (12) of free schools for all persons that would be publicly supported through taxes. His plans for _____ (13) educational and for publicly funded schools formed the basis of educational systems developed in the 19th _____ (14).

Until the 1840s American education was not a system at all, but a disjointed collection of _____ (15), regional, and usually private institutions. The extent of schooling and the type of education available depended _____ (16) the resources and values of the particular town or city, on the activities of religious groups _____ (17) to further their ends through schools and colleges, and on many other private groups — such _____ (18) philanthropic associations and trade organizations — that created different types of schools for different reasons. Most _____ (19) only provided educational opportunities for boys from wealthy families. Public governing bodies were rarely involved in _____ (20) financing or control of schools.

III. Reading Comprehension

Passage One

Girl Meets Game
姑娘玩游戏
by Lev Grossman

I love video games. I played my first one when I was 7. I feel lucky to be part of the first generation of gamers. I also get to be a first-generation-gamer parent; my parents regarded games with a primitive, chimplike suspicion, but my daughter Lily will have a parent who understands them and plays alongside her. A cool parent.

But when Lily played her first game a few weeks ago, at the age of 3, I found myself wondering something I never thought I would wonder: How cool a parent should I be? Lily has always been interested in the Web. A couple of weeks ago, we found a Flash game on a Teletubbies site involving five brown bunnies that need to be placed in their correct bunny-shaped holes. To my amazement, Lily shooed my hands away from the track pad and started slowly nudging bunnies toward burrows. When the fifth bunny hit home — and an unseen Tinky Winky shouted, "Yaaaaaay!" — every neuron in my daughter's brain seemed to fire at once. Her skull practically glowed. She climbed off the chair and did a dance. Then she climbed back up onto the chair and said, "Daddy? You can go now."

My feelings about this are conflicted. I'm not disappointed that Lily is learning to entertain herself, because I've been entertaining her for 3 years and could use a break in which to perform some basic personal hygiene. All the same, I'm confused about what games mean to a person that tiny. After all, video games didn't really exist when I was 3.

The most obvious questions are the easiest. Because I'm not psychotic, I would never allow my daughter to play — or see or know about — any game involving violence. When she plays the bunny game, Lily is learning about computers and refining her hand-eye coordination. So that's all good, right? Just to make sure, I called Susan Gregory Thomas, author of Buy Buy Baby, a scorching investigative study of how corporations target underage consumers. She also happens to be the most technologically aware mom I know. Or, as I now call her, Susie Joykiller.

Hand-eye coordination? Maybe. But she pointed out that kids that age — with their delicate, still developing carpal tunnels — are especially vulnerable to repetitive stress injury. O. K. , but here's something else: Lily gets frustrated easily, and the game rewards her for sticking with a problem till she solves it. "Maybe she could get the same kind of thing from trying to make a cake?" Thomas asked. "There are lots of other things to solve that have a much richer protocol. " I get it: that's what the real world is for.

There is a paucity of quality clinical data on little children and games, and Thomas explains that video games often depend on analogies and symbols that kids may not understand in the way we think they do. "Very young children are astonishingly concrete thinkers. If you look at a screen and understand that everything that happens on a computer is a metaphor for something real in life, it becomes very, very murky as to what they're actually getting out of this. " There are also troubling commercial aspects to a lot of games for preschoolers: they're basically ads for branded characters like Dora the Explorer and Ariel the mermaid. And Thomas points out-in the nicest way possible — how pathetic it is that I want people to think I'm a cool dad.

There's a lot more to think about than I thought there was. I'm still happy that Lily likes games, but I've resolved to limit her playing time, and I'm not going to let her play alone, personal hygiene be damned. She and I won't always be able to play games together, after all; far too soon she'll be far too cool to hang out with me. But for now, maybe it's a good idea for Daddy to stick around.

〜〜〜〜〜〜〜〜〜〜〜〜〜〜〜〜〜〜〜〜〜〜〜〜〜〜

1. Why does the author consider himself as a cool parent?
   A. He understands his daughter and plays video games alongside her.
   B. He has a daughter who can play video games at the age of three.
   C. He teaches her daughter to play video games and then plays with her.
   D. He feels lucky to be part of the first generation of gamers.

2. From the second paragraph we know that _____.
   A. with the help of her father, Lily finally arranged the five rabbits in the correct way so that they formed rabbit-shaped holes

B. when Lily succeeded in putting the five bunnies in the right place, she felt the game was very easy and simply continued to play with it

C. winning the game, Lily was so excited and confident of herself that she asked her father to let her play all by herself

D. when the fifth bunny bumped into the door of the home and an unseen Tinky Winky shouted "Yaaaaaay!", Lily was greatly amused

3. Which of the following is NOT the reason for the author's worry about his daughter's playing video games?

A. Many video games involved violence harmful to children.

B. His young daughter's carpal tunnels were delicate and easy to be injured by repetitive movement in playing video games.

C. As an exceptionally concrete thinker, his daughter could not understand analogies and symbols used by video games.

D. Some ads for branded characters were not well designed for young children.

4. How do you understand the latter part of Paragraph Five?

A. The game is beneficial for it encourages the player to persist in a problem till he succeeds.

B. Apart from video games, there are many other things for children to be engaged in.

C. If children learn to do correctly in games, they will be likely to perform well in the real world.

D. The real world is not so simple as games, and to succeed in life one needs to abide by more rules than in games.

5. What will the author do with his daughter at the present stage?

A. He is determined to limit her time playing video games.

B. He has decided not to allow her to play video games anymore.

C. He will make sure not to leave her alone when she plays video games.

D. He will first of all make sure she is clean before she can play video games.

Passage Two

An Oil Giant's Green Dream
石油大亨的绿色梦想
by Bryan Walsh

If you filled your tank with gasoline today, or warmed your home with natural gas, there's a decent chance you sent some money to Abu Dhabi. The capital of the United Arab Emirates (UAE) is blessed with fossil fuels, including the fourth-biggest reserves of oil in the world. Selling that petroleum at record prices has helped Abu Dhabi achieve the highest per-capita GDP in the world — wealth that's visible in every luxury hotel rising from the desert or spotless Mercedes prowling the streets. All those fossil fuels also mean that Abu Dhabi citizens have among the biggest carbon footprints in the world, and the emirate's exports are a big, if indirect, contribution to global climate change.

So it might come as a surprise to learn that Abu Dhabi is this week hosting the world's first Future Energy Summit, a three-day gathering of more than 4,000 entrepreneurs, analysts and officials from the alternative energy world, including heavyweights like green designer William McDonough and Icelandic President Olafur Grimsson. (Also present was Prince Charles, who gave a speech via hologram.)

But if the idea of an Arab oil power like Abu Dhabi supporting fossil fuel alternatives sounds a bit like a heroin dealer trying to sell methadone, think again. Virtually alone among its Persian Gulf neighbors, Abu Dhabi has embarked on a serious program in alternative energy research, backed with oil money. In 2006 it launched the Masdar Initiative (the name means "source" in Arabic), a multi-pronged scheme that includes a collaborative research institute with the Massachusetts Institute of Technology, support for solar and other kinds of green power within the city itself and a clean energy investment fund worth $250 million. The idea behind Masdar — which organized the Future Energy Summit — is a radical one: prepare Abu Dhabi and the UAE to move beyond fossil fuels. "The UAE wants to be more than just an oil-producing country," says Marc Stuart, the co-founder of the carbon-trading firm EcoSecurities.

That will take money, but thanks to record oil prices, money is one thing Abu Dhabi does not lack. At the summit's opening conference, Abu Dhabi's Crown Prince Sheikh Mohammad bin Zayed Al Nahaya announced that the government would channel an additional $15 billion to the Masdar Initiative. Although the money comes with no time frame, and officials wouldn't say exactly where the funding will go, Masdar also announced that it would join Rio Tinto and British Petroleum to build the world's first hydrogen power plant, a 500-megawatt operation that would cost at least $2 billion.

These are bold plans — especially for a city that had little green experience until recently — but for Abu Dhabi, investing in alternative power is a way to remain a world energy center in the event that concerns over climate change cut into the demand for fossil fuels. "We have a long tradition as a global energy leader and we have the financial resources to develop new fields of energy," said Sultan Ahmed Al Jaber, Masdar's CEO. "Leadership entails responsibility."

As the summit's hosts were only too eager to emphasize, when they weren't announcing a new hydrogen plant, almost every projection of energy use over the next several decades says that fossil fuels aren't going anywhere. Abu Dhabi will develop hundreds of megawatts of clean solar power, but it will export far more polluting power in oil — because the world will need it and there is nothing else feasible to replace it. "The World Future Energy Summit is nothing less than the future of the world itself," said Jonathan Porritt, founder of the UK sustainability organization Forum for the Future, one of the few speakers at the conference to call for a rapid reduction in fossil fuels. Green dreams are nice, but we need a green reality soon.

1. The oil giant in this passage refers to _____.

   A. the United States of America

   B. Abu Dhabi, the capital of the United Arab Emirates

   C. Mercedes

   D. William McDonough

2. The oil giant's green dream includes the following EXCEPT _____.

   A. to use solar power and other clean energies to replace fossil fuels

   B. to make Abu Dhabi and the UAE move beyond petroleum

   C. to engage in program in alternative energy research

   D. to remain a world energy center in case concerns over climate change reduce the demand for fossil fuels

3. Which of the following is the organizer of the Future Energy Summit?

   A. Masdar   B. UAE   C. Marc Stuart   D. Abu Dhabi

4. The first sentence of the third paragraph implies that _____.

   A. it's wrong to think Abu Dhabi will probably support fossil fuel alternatives

   B. it's wrong to think it improbable for Abu Dhabi to support fossil fuel alternatives

   C. to think of Abu Dhabi supporting fossil fuel alternatives is like to think of a drug dealer trying to sell methadone

   D. if you think Abu Dhabi is likely to sell methadone, you should think again

5. Why will Abu Dhabi still export oil since it entails polluting power?

   A. The world needs oil and there is nothing else feasible to replace it.

   B. Abu Dhabi has enough alternative fuels for its own use.

   C. By exporting oil, Abu Dhabi can achieve the highest per-capita GDP in the world.

   D. Abu Dhabi doesn't want to pollute itself and UAE anymore.

Passage Three

Promoting Local Control and Choice for Public Schools in California
促进对加州当地学校的控制与选择

Steve Poizner is passionate about educational reform. Running for the California State Assembly in the 21st district to represent Silicon Valley, the 47-year-old candidate says access to excellent public schools is a "fundamental civil right."

"It's so critical for students to exit the school system with skills to allow them to survive in this complex world," says Poizner. "Especially schools in low income areas, kids are not getting well served and equipped for higher education or the job market. There is no bigger civil rights issue or economic issue."

The high-tech business executive from Los Gatos, who also has a year of public school teaching and a White House fellowship on his resume, will face one of four Democrats vying for the State Assembly seat in this solidly Democratic district.

Poizner knows winning is an uphill battle, but he is working to build a grassroots effort that reaches across party lines. Positioning himself as a moderate Republican, Poizner focuses his message on solving the state's economic and educational problems, not partisanship. He hopes his agenda appeals to this highly educated district, where two-thirds of voters have college degrees.

Education is a hot-button issue here, where the state's school system is under enormous strain. "California used to have one of the top-notch public school systems in the country," says Poizner. "Now it is one of the worst." More than three-fourths of California's 4th and 8th graders aren't proficient in reading and writing. Students scored so poorly on the state's High School Exit Exam that the test had to be postponed until 2006.

With six million public school students in California, Poizner contends that the system is too massive to be fixed from the top down. "When you look at the structural challenges, you wonder why the legislature would want to micromanage something so complex and apply rules uniformly across all 1,000 school districts," he says. "I'm a huge proponent of local control. When you return power and control, you can tailor programs to meet the needs of local conditions."

Other educational issue on his platform:

· Recruit and retain top-notch teachers and principals
· Increase teacher pay and strengthen academic accountability
· Provide teachers with better working conditions and students a better learning environment
· Empower schools with the resources and flexibility they need
· Reduce the bureaucracy clogging California's educational system and reinvest the savings in under-funded areas, such as per-pupil spending on textbooks.
· Ensure consistency in school testing
· Support successful models of innovation and public school choice, including an expansion of California's charter school movement.

Poizner received his MBA. from the Stanford University Graduate School of Business in 1980 and his B. S. in Electrical Engineering from the University of Texas in 1978. Poizner's interest in educational reform is not something he latched onto as a candidate. He has long been an advocate for school choice and worked in the charter school movement. Charter schools are independent public schools, designed and run by educators, parents, community leaders and educational entrepreneurs. They operate free from the traditional bureaucracy of public schools.

In addition to founding two technology companies in California, Poizner formed a charitable foundation in 2000 focused on improving the quality of public education and donated $2 million to boost inner-city schools. He has been involved with groups in California that pushed for reform, such as EdVoice, Aspire Public Schools and the New Schools Venture Fund.

In 2002, Poizner wanted to get a first-hand look at the public school system so he taught 12th grade American government in an east San Jose public school for a year. "It's a rough area. I was there in the trenches every day. It was quite a challenge," he says. Poizner was overwhelmed by the amount of problems the kids faced, such as gang violence. "It was a real eye opener," he says. "From that experience, I developed a strong appreciation for the work good teachers do each and every day. "

❧❧❧❧❧❧❧❧❧❧❧❧❧❧❧❧❧❧❧❧

1. Which of the following is NOT Steve Poizner's point of view?

    A. A candidate running for State Assembly must put educational reform on the top agenda.

    B. All students should enjoy access to excellent public schools.

    C. School graduates are not competitive enough for higher education or the job market.

    D. Receiving excellent education is the most important civil rights and economic issues.

2. Winning for Poizner is an uphill battle, because _____.

    A. he is a highly educated district

    B. he will face four Democrats in the campaign

    C. he is a Democrat-dominated district

    D. only a moderate number of Republicans support him

3. The passage indicates that Poizner is a proponent for _____.

    A. solving the educational problems through legislature

    B. dealing with the educational problems by satisfying local needs

    C. top-down approaches

    D. dismantling legislature

4. Which of the following is NOT a proposal put forward by Poizner?

    A. Maintaining an excellent staff.

    B. Establishing a school atmosphere conducive to maximizing teaching effectiveness.

    C. Preventing schools from having too many tests.

    D. Emphasizing the influence of model schools.

5. It can be concluded that Poizner's proposition of improving education _____.

    A. arises from his personal interest involved in educational reforms

    B. arises from his educational background and experience

    C. is based on his wish to beat Democrat rivals

    D. is based on the Republican ideology

Passage Four

Charter School Class Gets a First-hand Social Studies Lesson
注册学校的班级获得第一手的社会研究课

Just a typical day in sixth grade social studies. Only it's a double period, usually reserved for reading or math. And it's in the science classroom, which has more space. The American and New York State flags are flanking the chalkboard, the school banner hanging above them, klieg lights shining on them from the back.

Oh, and there's a substitute teacher — Gov. George E. Pataki.

"Can someone tell me the three different branches of government?" he asked the scholars of Bronx Preparatory Charter School, on Webster Avenue in the Morrisania section.

They could. Their teacher, John Stassen, had done a special lesson on exactly that the day before. They knew who heads the executive branch, too, and the name of the nation's highest court, and what percentage of the Legislature it takes to override an executive's veto. But Mr. Pataki stumped them on how many houses form the legislative branch. "We haven't gotten to that," Mr. Stassen said.

Governor Pataki, a prime advocate of 1998 state legislation creating charter schools, which are publicly financed but free of state regulation, swooped into Bronx Prep yesterday and was greeted with gleaming hallways and singing children.

As a start-up school in its first year, Bronx Prep has been besieged with visitors — donors, state evaluators, entrepreneurs planning their own schools, potential employees, potential students, and a reporter and photographer chronicling its progress for this newspaper. (The mayor showed up in the fall.) Mostly they sit in the back, watching business as usual. But for the governor, well, a school puts on a show.

The principal, Marina Bernard Damiba, turned over the math class she teaches to Laura Barfield, the writing teacher, leaving herself free to stand on a chair and hang the school banner. Two artistic students were recruited to write "Welcome Governor Pataki" and "Thank you for our charter school" on the boards in the science room. A parent volunteer in a lavender dress and matching loafers came to shake hands.

Mr. Pataki arrived around 11 a. m. , joining several public officials and a dozen advance men and security people. In Tara Kelley's sixth-grade reading class, two students recited poems. In fifth-grade math, being taught by the sixth-grade teacher because Mrs. Damiba was leading the tour, the youngsters burst into their signature raplike chants of the multiplication tables.

"Could you keep up with the nines?" the governor asked a colleague as they shuffled to the next room, where fifth graders sang another diffy, pronouncing themselves "ready to read."

In Mr. Stassen's class, the cameras snapped as Mr. Pataki took questions from the students: Why did he want charter schools? Has he vetoed any laws? What does he do every day?

"Would you consider being president?" asked Thelma Perez.

"Thelma, I am very happy being governor of this state," Mr. Pataki said. "We'll just leave it at that."

There was the ceremonial exchange of gifts — the governor got a Bronx Prep polo shirt and $50 honorary Scholar Dollars, which students earn for good behavior; he gave the school a framed copy of the charter law, and a pen. On the way out, the school's director, Kristin Kearns Jordan, slid in a plea for tax legislation that would make it easier for young schools to finance buildings. By 12:15, after a brief news conference, two aides carried the flags down the steps and out the door.

"They left already?" Maria Ortiz, the administrative assistant, asked with a sigh of relief. "Everybody?"

And then she rang the little cow bell, signaling lunch.

1. Which of the following is NOT true of Bronx Prep?

    A. It is a charter school financed by public funds.

    B. It employs Governor Pataki as its substitute social studies teacher.

    C. It locates in New York State.

    D. Its students have little idea about the Senate and the House of Representatives.

2. The fact that John Stassen had done a special lesson the day before probably shows that _____ .

    A. social studies is one of the most important subjects in the school

    B. the school wants to get more support from the governor

    C. the school could not afford to loose face in front of the governor

    D. thorough preparation has been done to welcome the governor

3. The fact that Bronx Prep has been besieged with visitors indicates that _____ .

    A. charter schools are very popular with the public

    B. Bronx Prep is the first of its kind established under the 1998 state legislation

    C. Governor Pataki gives full support to the school

    D. Different people have different ideas about the school

4. The governor's visit to the school can best be described as _____ .

    A. a hands-on social studies class to school pupils

    B. a disruption to the school routine

    C. an unexpected exciting event

    D. a tiring, extravagant social event to both the teachers and the governor

5. The author's attitude can best be described as _____ .

    A. critical   B. sarcastic   C. ironic   D. objective

第十单元　状语从句

········· **I. Grammar: Adverbial Clauses** ·········

A **Multiple Choices**

1. On a rainy day I was driving north through Vermont _____ I noticed a young man holding up a sign reading "Boston".

   A. which   B. where   C. when   D. that

2. The senior librarian at the circulation desk promised to get the book for me _____ she could remember who last borrowed it.

   A. ever since   B. much as   C. even though   D. only if

3. Water, _____ it is given enough time, will dissolve almost any substance.

   A. thus   B. as long as   C. unless   D. in case

4. A man escaped from the prison last night. It was a long time _____ the guards discovered what had happened.

   A. before   B. until   C. since   D. when

5. They had to sell their house _____ they could pay off their father's gambling debts.

   A. whenever   B. so that   C. unless   D. since

6. The WTO could not live up to its name _____ it had not included a country that is home to one fifth of mankind.

   A. even   B. while   C. if   D. even though

7. It is a gripping story and one can't put it down _____ one has finished reading it.

   A. after   B. when   C. since   D. until

8. I didn't realize she was a famous film star _____ she took off her dark glasses.

   A. for fear   B. until   C. because   D. as

9. _____ everyone could hear the news, we turned the radio up to the maximum volume.

   A. Now that   B. In order that   C. That   D. In order to

10. Doing your homework is a sure way to improve your test scores, and this is especially true _____ it comes to classroom tests.

    A. before   B. as   C. since   D. when

11. Human behavior is mostly a product of learning, _____ the behavior of animal depends mainly on instinct.

    A. while   B. so   C. unless   D. that

12. We have received so many letters for our pen-friends' column, and it may be some time _____ we can publish your letter.

    A. after   B. when   C. before   D. while

13. The silkworm is an animal of such acute and delicate sensation _____ too much care cannot be taken to keep its habitation clean.

    A. that   B. so   C. as   D. so that

14. _____ your son is well again, you no longer have anything to worry about.

    A. Even   B. Though   C. Whether   D. Now that

15. _____ the sun is gaseous throughout its entire structure, it appears to have a definite surface when viewed with a suitable filter.

    A. Even   B. Because   C. So   D. Although

16. Some children are mad about video games. They just can't tear themselves away from them _____ they start.

    A. since   B. once   C. even if   D. as

17. I'm afraid that you are not spending as much time preparing your lessons _____ you should.

    A. if   B. whether   C. when   D. as

18. The engineers are going through with their highway project, _____ the expenses have risen.

    A. just because   B. even though   C. now that   D. as though

19. Do not shout or play your radio too loud _____ there's nobody around.

    A. now that   B. or   C. as if   D. so that

20. _____ the United States exports some textile products, it imports as well.

    A. Although   B. As if   C. Until   D. Now that

21. All gases and most liquids and solids expand _____ they are heated.

    A. so   B. though   C. when   D. in case

22. You should make it a rule to leave things _____ you can find them again.

    A. when   B. where   C. then   D. there

23. Pure naphtha is highly explosive _____ it is exposed to an open flame.

    A. if   B. before   C. wherever   D. so that

24. Gorillas are often quiet _____ they are able to make about twenty different sounds.

    A. when   B. otherwise   C. because of   D. even though

25. Farmers call the grosbeak the "potato-bird" _____ it eats potato beetles.

    A. although   B. why   C. in case   D. because

26. _____ she has a good sense of balance, she can't dance well.

    A. In spite of   B. Despite   C. For all that   D. No matter

27. I promised to meet him there in a month, _____ I was sufficiently recovered to do so.

    A. though   B. since   C. while   D. provided

28. In my opinion, parents do not owe their children an inheritance, _____ how much money they have.

    A. even if   B. although   C. no matter   D. whatever

29. Some women volunteered to do some social services, _____ they wanted to be useful outside their house.

    A. where   B. because   C. in case   D. so that

30. The problem is that, _____ children who are given cow's milk from birth benefit greatly from it, those who have never drunk it by a certain age are not able to tolerate it.

    A. because   B. provided   C. whereas   D. though

ß Error Correction

1. Although you've got a chance, you might as well make full use of it.

2. Since you can see, we've got five different types of recorders on show here.

3. It will not be long since man can harness the solar energy and make it serve mankind.

4. I think our boat can pass that treacherous water until cautiously handled.

5. Scarcely had he closed his eyes after somebody started knocking at the door.

6. If these difficulties can be overcome, further improvement can hardly be made.

7. Young scientists cannot realize too soon that existing scientific knowledge is not nearly so complete, certain and unalterable for many textbooks seem to imply.

8. Unless he arranges everything properly, he can have a more comfortable time.

9. Scientists have recently argued that Einstein's contributions to physics and mathematics are less important as Newton's.

10. Advertising is distinguished from other forms of communications so that the advertiser pays for the message to be delivered.

11. We should do our utmost otherwise we can fulfil the task in time.

12. Batteries must be kept in dry places even if there should be a leakage of electricity.

13. The volume of the gas becomes greater whether the temperature is increased.

14. Once it is not the largest of the world's oceans, the Atlantic has by far the largest drainage area.

15. Dried leaves continue to hang on the branches of some deciduous trees because the new leaves appear.

II. Cloze Test

A Obesity Grows Despite Diets to Curb It（Ⅰ）节食对肥胖无能为力（Ⅰ）

Americans are getting morbidly fatter even as they speed up their efforts to lose weight.

The American Heart Association hosted a panel Friday to try to unearth what Americans eat and what, exactly, is contributing to the rising tide of obesity.

Spurred by the aggressive marketing of diets that promote fat over carbohydrates, researchers _____ (1) the Mayo Clinic decided to see if these campaigns were affecting what people _____ (2) eating. After surveying 1,200 residents of Olmstead County, Minn., the answer was a _____ (3) yes. Between 1999 and 2003, a larger proportion of calories were coming from _____ (4), saturated fat, and dietary cholesterol.

"The findings reverse some of the trends seen _____ (5) the past 20 years," says lead author Dr. Randal J. Thomas. Thomas adds _____ (6) these findings "suggest that there are some tough times ahead with respect to _____ (7) disease."

While the popularity of low-carb, high-fat diets may indeed be behind some _____ (8) these changes, Thomas says many other factors could also be contributing.

Another study _____ (9) a number of characteristics that seemed to be related to consuming larger portion _____ (10) among a group of postmenopausal women with type 2 diabetes who were trying _____ (11) follow the Mediterranean diet. This group has a high risk of developing coronary _____ (12) disease.

Women with higher incomes, education levels, and body weight and a lower _____ (13) tended to eat larger sizes. Also, larger portion sizes were linked to lower _____ (14) of physical activity, higher "bad" cholesterol, less ability to manage stress, greater depression, _____ (15) higher blood pressure.

Researcher Kristie J. Lancaster of New York University found important _____ (16) between ethnic subgroups of African-Americans who are usually lumped together in terms of _____ (17). Non-Hispanic blacks who were born in the United States had a higher 10-year _____ (18) of developing coronary heart disease (CHD) than those born outside the United States. _____ (19) born in the United States also had a higher proportion of calories from _____ (20) and saturated fat and ate fewer fruits, vegetables and legumes. They were also more likely to smoke.

"All black groups need to improve in diet and CHD risk," Lancaster says, "but, in particular, African-Americans have greater needs when it comes to diet and CHD risk, so we need more investigation of these groups."

Ⓑ Obesity Grows Despite Diets to Curb It (Ⅱ) 节食对肥胖无能为力 (Ⅱ)

A national survey of 6,739 adults found that about half felt that "dinner _____ (1) not right without meat." Meat, of course, tends to have more fat, and _____ (2) who consume more meat tend to be heavier. Less than a third of _____ (3) respondents (29 percent) felt they ate enough fruits and vegetables according to the _____ (4) recommended guidelines.

"This information could be used in the development of nutritional information _____ (5) healthy eating," says Alison Jane Rigby of Stanford University.

Finally, another study looked _____ (6) 4,000 participants in four countries — China, Japan, the United Kingdom and the _____ (7) States — to find associations between weight and dietary intake.

"We looked at _____ (8) who were winning the game of weight control," says Linda Van Horn _____ (9) Northwestern University. "Lo and behold, what we did find is that, without exception, a _____ (10) complex-carbohydrate, high-fiber, high-vegetable diet was associated with a low body mass index."

High _____ (11), especially high animal protein, diets were associated with a greater body mass index. "_____ (12) association between dietary patterns that are associated with lower body weight are consistent _____ (13) those the American Heart Association has recommended for years," Van Horn says.

The _____ (14) weight loss message, as AHA spokesman Dr. Robert H. Eckel put it, is _____ (15), very simple but difficult to implement.

That message is: take in less than _____ (16) give out. "It has to be a matter of energy balance," Van Horn _____ (17). "In our study, the healthiest people were eating the most calories but had _____ (18) leanest body mass index, but the point is to be physically active. That _____ (19) you the discretion to have additional calories. You can get away with more _____ (20) as long as you're burning them off."

III. Reading Comprehension

Passage One

Counseling Cheers Depressed Heart Attack Patients
咨询让压抑的心力衰竭病人振作起来

Psychological counseling can help heart attack patients deal with the depression they often experience, but it doesn't improve survival or reduce the odds of a second attack, says a new study.

Researchers reached those conclusions after following up nearly 2,500 heart attack patients from 73 hospitals for an average of 29 months. They publish their findings in the June 18 issue of the *Journal of the American Medical Association*.

The Enhancing Recovery in Coronary Heart Disease Patients trial, funded by the National Heart, Lung, and Blood Institute, was conducted from late 1996 through April 2001. The patients, average age 61, were assigned to a "usual care" group or an intervention group.

Three-quarters of the subjects had depression, with the other quarter suffering from what they perceived as low social support. Both conditions are associated with higher death rates and subsequent heart problems in cardiac patients, previous studies have found.

And depression in heart attack patients is common, as the researchers note in their report. About 20 percent have severe depression and another 27 percent have minor depression.

So the researchers set out to find whether treating that depression and improving perceived social support — the patient's felling that he could turn to many loved ones for help — would reduce the death rate from heart attack and decrease the risk of having a repeat attack.

Those in the intervention group, besides receiving the same care as the "usual care" group, also got weekly individual counseling sessions, sometimes supplemented by group sessions, designed to help them stop negative thoughts and reduce stress. Antidepressants were prescribed to those who needed them in both groups, with 20 percent of the usual care and 28 percent of the intervention group using antidepressants by the study's end.

"There was significant improvement in depression after six months of counseling," says Susan M. Czajkowski, a researcher at the National Heart, Lung, and Blood Institute and project officer of the study. The patients' perception of their social support improved, too.

But at the end of the follow-up, 75.9 percent of the usual care group survived, versus 75.8 percent of those who got counseling.

"We are going back and taking a good in-depth look at the data," Czajkowski says. The lack of benefit on survival and subsequent heart attack was not expected, she says.

Why did the usual care group do better than expected? "We suspect that the patients in the usual care group may have gotten some counseling on their own, or their doctors may have referred them," Czajkowski says. And, she notes, the rate of antidepressant use was fairly similar between the two groups.

But the improvement in depression and social functioning in those who got counseling shouldn't be downplayed, she says. "Even though there was no difference in survival, we did make a difference in terms of the depression and their social functioning," she says.

The study, the largest controlled trial of psychotherapy for heart patients, is an accomplishment in itself, says Nancy Frasure-Smith, a professor of psychiatry at McGill University and the Montreal Heart Institute who co-authored an editorial accompanying the study.

"We may never know whether treating depression can affect the cardiac prognosis," she says. "That isn't as important as encouraging trials to improve the treatment of depression."

While many doctors know to be on the lookout for depression in heart attack patients, Czajkowski advises patients or their loved ones to be aware of the signs of depression and ask for help. Those symptoms include a downcast mood for two weeks or more, loss of energy, feelings of worthlessness and a loss of appetite.

1. The researchers _____ and started so tudy problems associated with depression and lack of social support.

   A. drew on previous findings and their own experiences

   B. believed counseling could help improve survival rate in cardiac patients

C. were encouraged by the *Journal of the American Medical Association*

D. got support from two groups of patients

2. The hypothesis for doing the research was that _____.

A. heart attack-induced deaths and suffering a second attack are related to depression and lack of social support

B. doing it would surely help understand heart disease-related issues

C. depression and social support were sure to have nothing to do with heart problems

D. "usual care" and intervention were two sides of the same treatment strategy

3. Which of the following is NOT true of the "intervention group"?

A. Individual and group counseling sessions were provided to the patients as needed.

B. The patients received the same care as the "usual group".

C. The patients suffered less depression than the "usual group" after half a year's treatment.

D. The patients felt that they were obtaining more social support than before.

4. The passage indicates that Czajkowski had expected that _____.

A. both groups would have an equal percentage in survival rate

B. nothing would go wrong with the data

C. the research would reveal the difference betwwen self-counseling and external counseling

D. the "intervention group" would do better in survival rate after the follow-up

5. Providing counseling to heart patients is by no means unimportant because _____.

A. it somewhat improves survival rate in heart patients

B. it encourages and improves treatment of the disease

C. it improves the quality of life in patients in terms of depression and counseling's social functioning

D. it cautions both patients and their families to guard against depression

Passage Two

Drug Helps Smokers Quit and Lose Weight
药物帮助抽烟者戒烟和减肥

For all those smokers who want to quit but haven't because they're afraid of packing on the pounds, researchers have exciting news.

A new drug called rimonabant helped smokers kick the habit and even lose a little weight in the process, according to a presentation made this week at the American College of Cardiology's annual meeting in New Orleans.

"It is early, but our findings are very promising," says co-researcher Dr. Lowell Dale, associate director of the Mayo Clinic Nicotine Dependence Center in Rochester, Minn. "This medication really appears to have the potential to assist in stopping smoking and controlling weight while stopping, which could significantly reduce the risk of cardiovascular disease."

The findings were announced just before a study in the March 10 issue of the *Journal of the American Medical Association* reported that smoking, obesity and a sedentary lifestyle are responsible for more than 800,000 deaths in the United States every year. Tobacco, according to the report, is the biggest killer, causing 435,000 deaths.

"To have a drug which could get to two of the major lifestyle problems associated with heart and vascular disease would just be incredible," says cardiologist Dr. Stephen Siegel of New York University Medical Center.

Dr. LaMar McGinnis, a senior medical consultant with the American Cancer Society, agrees. "If this drug does have minimal side effects and consequences, then the benefits could be enormous."

"We are excited about the potential for this, but we are in a wait-and-see mode," he adds, noting that more research, particularly long-term studies, needs to be done.

The current study followed 787 smokers who were "motivated" to stop smoking, according to Dale. They'd been smoking for 11 to 24 years and averaged 23 cigarettes a day.

One-third of the group was given a placebo, another third received 5 milligrams daily of rimonabant, and the final third received 20 milligrams of rimonabant once a day.

Treatment started two weeks prior to the volunteers' quit day, and continued for eight weeks. The participants couldn't use any additional measures to stop smoking — such as nicotine replacement, antidepressants or behavioral therapy — during the clinical trial and in the three months leading up to the trial.

Almost 28 percent of those taking 20 milligrams of rimonabant were able to stop smoking during the study period. By comparison, only 15.6 percent of those taking the low dose of rimonabant were successful in their quit attempt, and 16.1 percent of those taking a placebo stopped smoking.

What's more, those on the high dose of rimonabant managed to lose slightly more than half a pound during the study period, while those given a placebo gained 2.5 pounds.

Side effects appeared to be minimal. The most common, according to Dale, was nausea.

Rimonabant is the first in a new class of drugs that target the Endo Cannabinoid system, which is located in the brain and other areas of the body. Dale says this system is stimulated by nicotine and possibly by overeating. When it's stimulated, dopamine — a neurotransmitter — is released, causing feelings of pleasure, which reinforces the behavior, he says.

"This drug blocks this system, so that when people eat or smoke, they don't get the same response, which tends to decrease the behavior," Dale explains.

He says there are two more clinical trials in progress, and a year-long trial to assess the long-term effects of the medication is planned. He says he believes the manufacturer of rimonabant will likely begin the US Food and Drug Administration approval process by the end of this year or early next year.

At the same conference, Canadian researchers reported on a trial of more than 1,000 people with body mass indexes (BMIs) over 27. A BMI above 24 is considered overweight. Those who took 20 milligrams daily of rimonabant lost an average of 20 pounds and more than three inches off their waist circumference. They also lowered their cholesterol levels by 25 percent and their triglyceride levels by 15 percent, the study found.

Siegel says his big concern about rimonabant is that you may need to stay on it indefinitely, particularly if you're taking it for overeating.

"The long and short of it is that this drug is extremely enticing and thought-provoking in therms of the actual drug, and in terms of how some of our dependencies develop," says Siegel.

1. "Packing on the pounds" in the first sentence means _____.
   A. saving money　　　　　　　　　　　B. ending up in a police station
   C. costing extra money　　　　　　　　D. increasing weight

2. What might be the "two major lifestyle problems" that Dr. Stephen Siegel mentioned?
   A. Cardiovascular disease and smoking.　　B. Smoking and obesity.
   C. Smoking and a sedentary lifestyle.　　　D. Heart and vascular disease.

3. The passage indicates that _____.
   A. a daily intake of 5mg of rimonabant is not so effective as taking placebo
   B. the more rimonabant you take, the more chances of quitting smoking there is
   C. the longer you take rimonabant, the more effective it is
   D. taking additional measures while taking rimonabant can reduce the effectiveness of the drug

4. The mechanism of the efficacy of rimonabant is that _____.
   A. it eliminates the Endo Cannabinoid system
   B. it prevents the Endo Cannabinoid system from being stimulated
   C. it stops nicotine from causing dopamine to be released
   D. it helps reinforce people's feeling of pleasure

5. One possible side effect of rimonabant is that it _____.
   A. might reduce the cholesterol and triglyceride levels in patients
   B. reduces the patients' waist circumference
   C. may cause addiction to it
   D. may be thought-provoking

Passage Three

Immune Therapy May Help Some Heart Failure Patients
免疫疗法也许能拯救有些心力衰竭的病人
by Amanda Gardner

Some patients with heart failure may stand to benefit from therapy which modifies the body's immune response.

A study in the Jan. 19 issue of *The Lancet* found that patients with no history of heart attacks, as well as those in a milder stage of heart failure, had a reduced rate of death and of subsequent hospitalizations with such a treatment.

But the novel therapy is far from hitting hospitals or doctors' offices any time soon, experts said.

"It had absolutely no improvement in the general study population," noted Dr. Norbert Moskovits, director of the Heart Failure Program at Maimonides Medical Center in New York City. "The subgroup analysis is more or less a way to come up with a new study. If they show improvements in certain subgroups then next time they can look at that in a larger trial. You cannot draw any conclusions from this, really. It was a very good trial and it still showed nothing."

According to the American Heart Association, some five million Americans have heart failure. "There are half a million new cases each year. It is the number one discharge diagnosis for Medicare patients," Moskovits said. "It's a huge problem, and that's why everyone is looking for a new angle."

Heart failure is commonly treated with drugs, including ACE (angiotensin converting enzyme) inhibitors, beta blockers and diuretics. "Most improve patient survival, symptoms and lifestyle," Moskovits said.

Some experts believe that inflammation plays a role in chronic heart failure. Logic would dictate, then, that interfering with the immune system and related inflammatory processes could impact the course of the disease.

But interventions that have targeted specific inflammatory cytokines (signaling chemicals central to the immune system) have not met with much success.

This has led scientists to hypothesize that affecting the immune system more generally might have a benefit.

This study involved more than 2,400 heart failure patients who were randomly assigned to receive non-specific immunomodulation therapy (IMT) or a placebo. They also had left ventricular systolic dysfunction and had undergone hospitalization for heart failure or IV drug therapy in an outpatient setting within the past 12 months.

In this case, IMT involved taking blood from patients with congestive heart failure, exposing the blood to oxidative stress for 20 minutes, then injecting the blood back into the muscle on days 1, 2 and 14, and then every 28 days for at least 22 weeks.

"Certain blood cells in these samples were more or less killed off and, by injecting them, you attenuate the immune response," Moskovits explained. "It's a very cumbersome process."

But after a mean follow-up of more than 10 months, patients in the IMT group showed only an 8 percent reduction in risk of death or hospitalization, which essentially translates into no difference.

However, the results were more impressive in two subgroups of participants: Those with no previous history of heart attack had a 26 percent reduction in risk while those classified with New York Heart Association functional class II heart failure-meaning they had only slight or mild limitations in their activities — had a 39 percent reduction in risk.

Both of these subgroups were younger and had less severe disease than the entire group of participants.

There was also a trend toward a lowering in C-reactive protein (CRP) concentrations in the IMT arm. CRP is a marker of inflammation and this finding, the authors said, indicates that the concept of treating heart failure with immunomodulation is not yet dead.

But long-term effects also need to be investigated. "By attenuating the immune response, do you subject patients to a higher risk for infections, for cancer?" Moskovits asked. "There are a lot of questions."

Moskovits also pointed out that many therapies for heart failure are counterintuitive. Beta blockers, for instance, were thought for many years to be contraindicated for heart failure. Similarly, a medication to improve heart muscle function in heart failure patients ended up worsening their survival.

1. What experts said in the third paragraph means that _____ .
   A. the new therapy will soon be put in practice for the majority of heart failure patients
   B. the new therapy is not likely to be put in practice for its ineffectiveness for the majority of heart failure patients
   C. there might be quite a long time before the new therapy can be used in hospitals or doctors' offices
   D. some time later the new therapy will be so effective that hospitals or doctors' offices will be struck

2. According to Dr. Norbert, if there is improvement in the subgroups in trial, _____ .
   A. the new therapy will then be introduced in hospitals or doctors' offices.
   B. there will be a trial on a larger extent to see weather the same effect can be found
   C. it can be concluded that the trail is good although it showed nothing
   D. no conclusions can be drawn for heart failure patients in general

3. How many kinds of medicines are mentioned in the passage as commonly used to treat heart failure?
   A. none   B. one   C. two   D. three

4. What is the most important step of the immunomodulation therapy?
   A. To take blood from the patient with congestive heart failure.
   B. To expose the blood to oxidative stress for 20 minutes.
   C. To inject the blood back into the patient.
   D. To treat the patient with drugs.

5. The author's attitude towards the new therapy is _____ .
   A. generally positive   B. generally negative
   C. reserved positive   D. not expressed

Passage Four

A Surgical Cure for Diabetes
外科手术治疗糖尿病
by Johnson Carlak

A new study gives the strongest evidence yet that obesity surgery can cure diabetes. Patients who had surgery to reduce the size of their stomachs were five times more likely to see their diabetes disappear over the next two years than were patients who had standard diabetes care, according to Australian researchers.

Most of the surgery patients were able to stop taking diabetes drugs and achieve normal blood tests.

"It's the best therapy for diabetes that we have today, and it's very low risk," said the study's lead author, Dr. John Dixon of Monash University Medical School in Melbourne, Australia.

The patients had stomach band surgery, a procedure more common in Australia than in the United States, where gastric bypass surgery, or stomach stapling, predominates.

Gastric bypass is even more effective against diabetes, achieving remission in a matter of days or a month, said Dr. David Cummings, who wrote an accompanying editorial in the journal but was not involved in the study.

"We have traditionally considered diabetes to be a chronic, progressive disease," said Cummings of the University of Washington in Seattle. "But these operations really do represent a realistic hope for curing most patients."

Diabetes experts who read the study said surgery should be considered for some obese patients, but more research is needed to see how long results last and which patients benefit most. Surgery risks should be weighed against diabetes drug side effects and the long-term risks of diabetes itself, they said.

Experts generally agree that weight-loss surgery would never be appropriate for diabetics who are not obese, and current federal guidelines restrict the surgery to obese people.

The diabetes benefits of weight-loss surgery were known, but the Australian study in Wednesday's Journal of the American Medical Association is the first of its kind to compare diabetes in patients randomly assigned to surgery or standard care. Scientists consider randomized studies to yield the highest-quality evidence.

The study involved 55 patients, so experts will be looking for results of larger experiments under way.

"Few studies really qualify as being a landmark study. This one is," said Dr. Philip Schauer, who was not involved in the Australian research but leads a Cleveland Clinic study that is recruiting 150 obese people with diabetes to compare two types of surgery and standard medical care.

"This opens an entirely new way of thinking about diabetes."

Obesity is a major risk factor for diabetes, and researchers are furiously pursuing reasons for the link as rates for both climb. What's known is that excess fat can cause the body's normal response to insulin to go haywire. Researchers are investigating insulin-regulating hormones released by fat and the role of fatty acids in the blood.

In the Australian study, all the patients were obese and had been diagnosed with type 2 diabetes during the past two years. Their average age was 47. Half the patients underwent a type of surgery called laparoscopic gastric banding, where an adjustable silicone cuff is installed around the upper stomach, limiting how much a person can eat.

Both groups lost weight over two years; the surgery patients lost 46 pounds on average, while the standard-care patients lost an average of 3 pounds.

Blood tests showed diabetes remission in 22 of the 29 surgery patients after two years. In the standard-care group, only four of the 26 patients achieved that goal. The patients who lost the most weight were the most likely to eliminate their diabetes.

Both patient groups learned about low-fat, high-fiber diets and were encouraged to exercise. Both groups could meet with a health professional every six weeks for two years.

In the United States, surgeons perform more than 100,000 obesity surgeries each year.

The American Diabetes Association is interested in the findings. The group revises its recommendations each fall, taking new research into account.

"There is a growing body of evidence that bariatric surgery is an effective tool for managing diabetes," said Dr. John Buse of the University of North Carolina School of Medicine in Chapel Hill, the association's president for medicine and science.

"It's just a question of how effective is it, for what spectrum of patients, over what period of time and at what cost? Not all those questions have been answered yet."

1. Which of the following is true according to the passage?
   A. Stomach band surgery is more familiar to people in the United States.
   B. Stomach stapling is more familiar to people in the United States.
   C. Stomach stapling is more familiar to people in Australia.
   D. Gastric bypass surgery is more familiar to people in Australia.

2. Which of the following is NOT true according to the passage?
   A. Surgical operation has some risks for patients.
   B. Surgical operation is preferred if its risks are smaller than drug side effects and the risks of diabetes itself.
   C. Surgical operation should be only considered for some obese patients.
   D. Surgical operation is applicable to patients with diabetes, whether they have obesity or not.

3. The new study is thought to yield high-quality evidence because _____.
   A. it used random selection in terms of patients to receive surgery or standard medical care
   B. it showed that reducing weight is beneficial to diabetes cases
   C. it was elaborately planned and carefully conducted by researchers and surgeons
   D. it has been published in the Journal of the American Medical Association

4. According to the passage, why obesity is dangerous for diabetes?

    A. Excess fat can regulate the body's response to insulin growth.

    B. Excess fat can cause the body's response to insulin to become irregular.

    C. Fat will release a kind of hormone which will stimulate the growth of insulin.

    D. Fatty acids in the blood are likely to increase the growth of insulin.

5. The American Diabetes Association thinks in the following terms EXCEPT that _____.

    A. there are more and more evidences of the effectiveness of bariatric surgery for managing diabetes

    B. there are still questions concerning the surgical treatment of diabetes

    C. it is not known exactly how effective the surgical operation is

    D. the surgical operation can soon be used in clinical treatment in hospitals

第十一单元　情态动词

A Multiple Choices

1. The construction crew might _____ the bridge in time for the holiday traffic.

   A. finished   B. to finish   C. finish   D. finishing

2. The children should _____ "thank you" to you when you gave them their gifts.

   A. had said   B. to have said   C. have said   D. saying

3. If you have an aquarium, you _____ give your tropical fish too much food or they'll die.

   A. must/have to   B. must not   C. don't have to   D. might

4. You _____ quit your job until you find another one.

   A. had better not to   B. had better not

   C. would better not to   D. would better not

5. You _____ exert yourself. You're still not fully recovered from your surgery.

   A. must/have to   B. must not   C. don't have to   D. should

6. My room is a mess, but I _____ clean it before I go out tonight. I can do it in the morning.

   A. must/have to   B. must not   C. don't have to   D. ought

7. "_____ you hand me that pair of scissors, please?" "Certainly."

   A. May   B. Shall   C. Will   D. Should

8. "Larry drove all night to get here for his sister's wedding. He _____ exhausted by the time he arrived." "He was."

   A. ought to be   B. could be   C. must have been   D. will have been

9. "I locked myself out of my apartment. I didn't know what to do." "You _____ your roommate."

   A. could have called   B. may have called

   C. would have called   D. must have called

10. — Don't forget to come to my birthday party tomorrow.

    — I _____.

    A. don't   B. won't   C. can't   D. shouldn't

11. Research findings show we spend about two hours dreaming every night, no matter what we _____ during the day.

    A. should do   B. may do

    C. should have done   D. may have done

12. He painted his bedroom black. It looked dark and dreary. He _____ a different color.

    A. had to choose   B. should have chosen

    C. must have chosen   D. could have been choosing

13. You _____ him so closely; everybody has his private distance.

    A. couldn't have followed   B. mustn't have followed

    C. couldn't have been following   D. shouldn't have been following

14. Whenever my parents went out in the evening, I _____ the job of taking care of my younger brother.

    A. would get   B. should get   C. must have gotten   D. had better get

15. If you _____ me, I shall be grateful to you.

    A. helped   B. will help   C. are helping   D. will be helping

16. I can't find my wallet anywhere. I _____ it in the office.

    A. have left   B. must have left   C. could have left   D. should have left

17. "Why are you so sure that Ann didn't commit the crime she's been accused of committing?"

    "She _____ that crime because I was with her, and we were out of town on that day."

    A. may not have committed   B. wasn't supposed to commit

    C. committed   D. couldn't have committed

18. Many people who _____ like to lose weight have joined health clubs and nutrition centers.

    A. will   B. would   C. shall   D. are to

19. My pain _____ apparent the moment I walked into the room, for the first man I met asked sympathetically: "Are you feeling all right?"

    A. must be   B. had been   C. must have been   D. had to be

20. I _____ my examinations easily but I made too many stupid mistakes.

    A. can pass   B. could have passed

    C. must pass   D. can have passed

21. I don't know where Bill has put the matches. But I don't think he _____ them away.

    A. should have thrown   B. must throw

    C. can't have thrown   D. can have thrown

22. The bridge was barely wide enough so that somebody _____ give way.

    A. had to   B. may   C. can   D. needs

23. I _____ to make an airline reservation, but I was so carried away by an interesting book that I forgot all about it.

    A. might call   B. must have called   C. could call   D. should have called

24. I _____ lose a dozen cherry trees than that you should tell me one lie.

    A. will rather   B. should rather   C. would rather   D. could rather

25. As it turned out to be a small house party, we _____ so formally.

    A. needn't dress up   B. didn't need have dressed up

    C. didn't need dress up   D. needn't have dressed up

26. It's a pity you've had to wait, sir. Now _____ see if we can solve your problem?

    A. can I   B. are we going to

    C. will we   D. shall we

27. I am so surprised that you _____ treat him as your close friend.

    A. should   B. could   C. must   D. might

28. After the well has been completed, the oil _____ up from the bottom of the hole to surface.

    A. has to bring   B. had to be brought

    C. had to bring   D. has to be brought

29. Minerals _____ as catalyst in oil formation.

    A. might be acted   B. may be acted

    C. might have been acted   D. may have acted

30. No matter how hard a solid _____ be, we can change its shape.

    A. should   B. must   C. may   D. does

B Error Correction

1. You don't need ask for his permission every time you want to leave the room.

2. Dares the King show himself in front of the rebels?

3. I can't find the grocery fish. Gail must take it with her when she went out.

4. "Will you mind taking me downtown on your way to work this morning?" "Not at all."

5. "You haven't eaten anything since yesterday afternoon. You will be really hungry!" "I am."

6. "I left a cookie on the table, but now it's gone. What happened to it?" "I don't know. One of the children may eat it."

7. From the tears in her eyes we may deduce that something sad can have occurred.

8. "Since we have to be there in a hurry, we would better take a taxi." "I agree."

9. I wonder why they haven't arrived yet. I told them how to get there but perhaps I should give them a map.

10. Oil and other chemicals should kill fish and make water bad for drinking.

11. The manager is furious. You ought to report the matter to the manager the day before yesterday.

12. You ought to come yesterday if you were really serious about your work.

13. You will not have poured water into sulphuric acid.

14. The vase we bought last month has broken already. We had far better bought the more expensive one.

15. He places the instrument carefully on the table lest it may fall down.

II. Cloze Test

A Current Trends in Business 商务界目前的趋势

Business activities are becoming increasingly global as numerous firms expand their operations into overseas markets. Multinational _____ (1) (MNCs), which operate in more than one country at once, typically move operations to wherever they can find _____ (2) least expensive labor pool able to do the work well. Production jobs requiring only basic or repetitive _____ (3) are usually the first to be moved abroad. MNCs can pay these workers a fraction of what _____ (4) would have to pay in a domestic division, and often work them longer and harder. Most US _____ (5) businesses keep the majority of their upper-level management, marketing, finance, and human resources divisions within the United _____ (6). They employ some lower-level managers and a vast number of their production workers in offices, factories, and _____ (7) in developing countries. MNCs based in the United States have moved many of their production operations to _____ (8) in Central and South America, China, India, and nations of Southeast Asia.

Mergers and acquisitions are also _____ (9) more common than in the past. In the United States, for example, America Online, Inc. (AOL) and _____ (10) Warner merged in 2000 to form AOL Time Warner, Inc., a massive corporation that brought together AOL's _____ (11) franchises, technology and infrastructure, and e-commerce capabilities with Time Warner's vast array of media, entertainment, and news _____ (12). Internationally, a growing number of mergers and acquisitions have been taking place, including Daimler Benz's acquisition of Chrysler to _____ (13) DaimlerChrysler AG and Ford Motor Company's acquisition of Volvo's automobile line.

With large mergers and _____ (14) development of new free markets around the world, major corporations now wield more economic and political power _____ (15) the governments under which they operate. In response, public pressure has increased for businesses to take on _____ (16) social responsibility and operate according to higher levels of ethics. Firms in developed nations now promote — and _____ (17) often required by law to observe — nondiscriminatory policies for the hiring, treatment, and pay of all employees. _____ (18) companies are also now more aware of the economic and social benefits of being active in local _____ (19) by sponsoring events and encouraging employees to serve on civic committees. Businesses will continue to adjust their _____ (20) according to the competing goals of earning profits and responding to public pressures for them to behave in ways that benefit society.

B Electronic Commerce 电子商业

Electronic Commerce, or e-commerce, is the exchange of goods and services by means of the Internet _____ (1) other computer networks. E-commerce follows the same basic principles as traditional commerce — that is, buyers and sellers _____ (2) together to exchange goods for money. But rather than conducting business in the traditional way — in stores _____ (3) other "brick and mortar" buildings or through mail order catalogs and telephone operators — in ecommerce buyers and _____ (4) transact business over networked computers.

E-commerce offers buyers convenience. They can visit the World Wide Web _____ (5) of multiple vendors 24 hours a day and seven days a week to compare prices and _____ (6) purchases, without having to leave their homes or offices. In some cases, consumers can immediately obtain _____ (7) product or service, such as an electronic book, a music file, or computer software, by downloading _____ (8) over the Internet.

For sellers, e-commerce offers a way to cut costs and expand their markets. _____ (9) do not need to build, staff, or maintain a store or print and distribute mail order _____ (10). Automated order tracking and billing systems cut additional labor costs, and if the product or service _____ (11) be downloaded, e-commerce firms have no distribution costs. Because they sell over the global Internet, sellers _____ (12) the potential to market their products or services globally and are not limited by the physical _____ (13) of a store. Internet technologies also permit sellers to track the interests and preferences of their _____ (14) with the customer's permission and then use this information to build and ongoing relationship _____ (15) the customer by customizing products and services to meet the customer's needs.

E-commerce also has some disadvantages, however. _____ (16) are reluctant to buy some products online. Online furniture businesses, for example, have failed for the _____ (17) part because customers want to test the comfort of an expensive item such as a sofa _____ (18) they purchase it. Many people also consider shopping a social experience. For instance, they may enjoy _____ (19) to a store or a shopping mall with friends or family, an experience that they cannot _____ (20) online. Consumers also need to be reassured that credit card transactions are secure and that their privacy is respected.

III. Reading Comprehension

Passage One

Globalization "Rethink" Urged
国际化的 "反思"
by Megan McCloskey

People, not markets, should be the focus of globalization, according to a report released yesterday by the International Labor Organization.

"We believe the dominant perspective on globalization must shift from a narrow preoccupation with markets to a broader preoccupation with people," said President Tarja Halonen of Finland and President Benjamin William Mkapa of Tanzania, co-chairpersons of the commission that conducted the study.

The ILO commissioned 26 political, labor and economic leaders to survey opinions in countries and prepare proposals to better address globalization issues. The results are outlined in the report, "A Fair Globalization: Creating Opportunities for All."

"The future of our countries, and the destiny of our globe, demand that we all rethink globalization," Mrs. Halonen and Mr. Mkapa said.

The commission says the social dynamics of globalization often are disregarded by governments and institutions and that steps need to be taken to incorporate social issues into the public debate.

But Bill Murray, spokesman for the International Monetary Fund, argued that social development has been considered by the IMF and in documents such as the United Nations Millennium Declaration, a broad mission statement issued by the world body to mark the new millennium.

"It's been pretty clear in recent years that social development takes a prominent role," he said.

The ILO report said there is a need for international organizations dealing with development to coordinate their policies. The separate agendas of the organizations sometimes undermine each other, it said.

The authors said the United Nations is best equipped to handle that coordination.

Globalization is occurring without proper governance to guide it, the report said. It recommends a globalization forum that would bring together the major actors, such as the IMF, the World Bank and the United Nations among others, to formulate policy initiatives. This forum also would produce a "State of Globalization" annual review.

"There is a rather great disjunct between the institutions created after World War II and the needs for the future," said John Sewell, a senior scholar at the Woodrow Wilson International Center for Scholars.

Mr. Sewell said political leaders hold the key to reaching a global consensus on social issues. "Those institutions are really the property of their members. Until the heads of government decide they want to do things, it's hard for them to do it themselves."

International organizations need to better reflect the needs and voices of the small nations who typically lack influence in the global sphere, the report said. One reason for the lack of global governance is the disparity in power, which typically is shared only among the developed nations.

U. N. Secretary-General Kofi Annan said in his report on the U. N. Millennium Declaration, "My own view is that member states need at least to take a hard look at the existing architecture of international institutions and to ask themselves whether it is adequate for the tasks we have set before us."

1. The need to rethink globalization comes from the fact that _____.

    A. emphasis has always been unduly laid on markets at the expense of people

    B. the future of the world is under great threat

    C. people are not treated equally

    D. 26 leaders were commissioned to survey globalization issues

2. Bill Murray disagreed with the ILO commission for _____.

    A. social development is not a responsibility of ILO

    B. the IMF has incorporated the social development issue into its work

    C. there is nothing more to do regarding social development

    D. social development is an on-going issue

3. The ILO report suggested that harmony across major international organizations was needed to _____.

    A. make the United Nations function at its best

    B. bring about necessary changes in global governance

    C. prevent inconsistency in their policy formulation

    D. coordinate the shift of emphasis from rich to poor countries

4. John Sewell indicated that _____.

    A. international organizations disagreed with each other greatly

    B. the United Nations institutions were not fulfilling their functions

    C. there was a need to reform the institutions with a view to future needs

    D. political leaders were unwilling to involve themselves in social issues

5. In his statement, Kofi Annan's expressed concern over _____.

    A. the inadequacy of work done by international institutions

    B. the current office premises for international institutions to carry out their jobs efficiently

    C. the feasibility of the ILO report

    D. the composition of the United Nations

Passage Two

Can Cash Create Goodwill in Iraq?
金钱能在伊拉克创造友善吗?
by Daniel Pepper

At the edge of a dirt crater 40 feet wide and 20 feet deep, Lieutenant Shawn Spainhour and Sheikh Dawood Rashid al-Shuhaib stare down in silence at the wreckage. In August 2007, the US military bombed the sheikh's house, obliterating it with a 500-lb. JDAM "bunker buster." The rest of the village was flattened by artillery. Spainhour, in full battle gear — flak jacket, helmet, knife, guns, boots, camouflage and radio — turns to the grief-stricken, 60-year-old Sheikh, who is wearing resplendent traditional Arabian dress, and asks his translator to tell him that "I sincerely apologize for everything that has happened here. " Spainhour pauses as they survey the damage. "It's the cost of war. " Literally. Coming along with the apology will be US dollars.

That's why the sheikh and Spainhour stroll through this former war zone together: to survey the extent of the damage. Spainhour and his commanding officer are trying to help the sheikh rebuild his village as part of the larger strategy to bring peace and reconciliation to their corner of Baghdad. It illustrates the paradigm shift that has been taking place for the US military across Iraq — trying to win over both former enemies and stave off potential new ones with the use of large sums of cash.

The trouble is that there is only so much cash available. The sheikh says his house will cost about 200 million Iraqi dinars, or about $150,000, to rebuild. Lt. Spainhour explains that big money is very hard to get, but that supplies and humanitarian assistance might be available. Spainhour's superior, Captain Douglas Willig, says the US military can offer about $1,000 per family for claims money; he can offer them micro-grants to start small businesses; and he has two construction packs for a school and a marketplace each worth about $20,000. "I want to help you help your village for the future," Willig tells the sheikh. "The most important thing is your coming to talk to us about your problems. " The sheikh and the 34 families of his village are likely to get a total of $100,000 in cash, grants, jobs and material.

According to Lt. Col. James Hutton, a US Army public affairs officer, in the fiscal year 2006 9,257 claims were filed in Iraq, of which 3,658 were paid, totaling $8,397,726. Fewer were filed in and paid out in 2007 — 7,103 and 2,896 respectively — but the total dollar amount was larger: $13,074,660. US officers praise the program, though it is impossible to say how many Iraqi hearts and minds have been appeased. It can take months for a claim to be paid and if a claim is filed after the US military unit involved is rotated out of Iraq, the odds are that the claim will never be awarded. In Iraq today, it is not uncommon for Iraqi civilians to beseech mid-ranking US officers for claims for damages done in 2003 or 2004.

In the case of Sheikh al-Shuhaib, he and the village's other families — all Shi'ite Muslims — had been kicked out in November 2006 by al-Qaeda fighters, who commandeered the sheikh's house, using it as their headquarters until they were routed by American firepower this past August. Now, after filing a claim with the US, he has come back to retake his property and to rebuild. The sheikh is confident that he will get the help he needs from the US: "I do trust [the Americans] helping me rebuilding my house and my village again, and they will do it. "

Sarah Holewinski, executive director for the Washington-based Campaign for Innocent Victims of Conflict (CIVIC), a group lobbying for fair and equal treatment for families of bystanders killed in conflict by the US military says: "The military has a big interest in getting it right. Right now, we see a good effort but not good implementation. Make sure payments are fair, make sure they're uniform from one family to another, make sure they're immediate following the bombs and bullets and make sure this is true whenever US troops head into combat — that's how you properly dignify deaths and injuries. Anything less diminishes the impact and cheapens the good intentions. " Senator Patrick Leahy, chairman of the Judiciary Committee, has drafted legislation with the input of CIVIC that would ensure a fair compensation program for civilians accidentally harmed by US forces in conflict. It is expected to be introduced later this year.

1. The phrase "to file claims" in the passage means _____.
   A. to blame someone who has misbehaved according to a document
   B. to arrange documents of claims in good order
   C. to demand that damages or something like that be paid
   D. to pay for claims

2. According to Lt. Col. James Hutton, how much claim money was paid in 2007?
   A. $2,896.　　　　B. $7,103.　　　　C. $3,658.　　　　D. $9,257.

3. Which of the following is true according to the passage?
   A. Having been paid the claims, many Iraqi people were appeased.
   B. It won't take long for a claim to be paid.
   C. Before leaving Iraq, the US troops involved will leave behind something to pay for the damages.
   D. It is probable that after the US troops leave Iraq, the claims will remain unpaid forever.

4. In November 2006, _____.
   A. Sheikh and the village's other families were forced out of their village by American soldiers
   B. Sheikh and the village's other families were forced out of their village by al-Qaeda fighters
   C. Al-Qaeda fighters occupied Sheikh's house which was later flattened by American firepower
   D. American troops defeated al-Qaeda fighters and then occupied Sheikh's village

5. The following can be inferred in the last paragraph EXCEPT that _____.
   A. damage compensations are not always fair for each family involved
   B. claims are not always paid in time
   C. American military is greatly interested in doing right things
   D. despite good intentions, the American military hasn't done a satisfactory job treating innocent victims of Iraqi people

Passage Three

A Princely Pioneer
皇室先驱
by Christopher Redman

Once upon a time there was a prince who unwisely confided to the media that while tending his beloved garden, he often talked to his plants. He also warned his future subjects about losing touch with their natural surroundings and their rich cultural heritage. But the people scoffed and said it was the fuddy-duddy Prince who was out of touch. And as for talking to his plants —

well, they shook their heads and remembered the madness of the Prince's forebear, King George III, who famously struck up a conversation with a tree that he had mistaken for the King of Prussia.

These days Britain's Prince of Wales is still considered a tad eccentric: after all, who in his right mind would have lost the love of the fairy-tale Princess Diana? But increasingly, Charles Philip Arthur George Windsor (who is not only Prince of Wales but also, inter alia, Duke of Cornwall, Lord of the Isles and Great Steward of Scotland) is winning applause for his not-so-crazy campaign to combat what he calls "the wanton destruction that has taken place... in the name of progress." For 30 years the Prince has been in the forefront of efforts to promote kinder, gentler farming methods; protect Britain's countryside from urban sprawl; improve city landscapes; and safeguard the nation's architectural heritage. And whereas he was once a lonely if plummy voice crying in the wilderness, the Prince has seen many of his once maverick opinions become mainstream.

Charles is not the first royal concerned about nature. Mad King George dabbled in botany when he wasn't losing his mind or the American colonies, and Charles' father, the Duke of Edinburgh, has long supported wildlife causes. But it is Charles who has become the crusader, with a vision of Britain that may border on the romantic but is in synch with Britons alarmed by what is happening to their green and pleasant land. He has the energy and dedication to get things done. "My problem," he has said, "is that I become carried away by enthusiasm to try and improve things, and also feel very strongly that the only way to progress is by setting examples and then hoping others will eventually follow."

An example people are following is organic farming, which Charles has adopted wholeheartedly on his own farmlands in the Duchy of Cornwall and surrounding his country home at Highgrove in western England. Charles once noted that when he decided to go organic, which means forswearing artificial fertilizers and pesticides, the experts were very polite, "but what they were saying about this latest demonstration of insanity once they were out of earshot can only be surmised." Today the experts have been confounded. The duchy's Home Farm near Highgrove is 100% organic and highly profitable and serves as a model for farmers around the country at a time when farm incomes are falling and organic produce is in high demand, fetching premium prices in shops and supermarkets.

"Seeing is believing" is one of Charles' favorite sayings, no doubt repeated when the US Secretary of Agriculture recently paid Highgrove a visit. And it's a safe bet that the American visitor received an earful on Charles' other farming concern: genetically modified crops. Once again the Prince has shown himself to be ahead of the curve. Back in December 1995 he pronounced himself "profoundly apprehensive" about the brave new world of genetically modified organisms and complained of the "confidence bordering on arrogance" with which they are promoted. The Prince practices what he preaches, and a sign by the lane leading up to his Home Farm announces that YOU ARE ENTERING A GMO-FREE ZONE. Charles' philosophy is simply expressed. "We should," he says, be adopting a "gentler, more considered approach, seeking always to work with the grain of nature in making better, more sustainable use of what we have."

~~~~~~~~~~~~~~~~~~~~~~~~~~~~~~~~~~

1. What is the main idea of the passage?
   A. Britain has exerted huge efforts to explore more sensible farming methods, with Prince Charles as an example.
   B. British royal family has long ago begun worrying about the way men treated nature now has Prince Charles as the pioneer to protect nature.
   C. Prince Charles sets an example for farmers to follow in organic farming and proves experts' disapproval to be wrong.
   D. Prince Charles seems to be an eccentric refusing things technologically advanced and probes ways to protect traditional, good-nature, and practical farming.

2. According to the last sentence in the second paragraph, Charles' view on the saving of nature was once regarded as _____.
   A. peculiar   B. independent   C. idealistic   D. sentimental

3. When he first decided to go organic, Charles said that the experts _____.
   A. politely showed their worries   B. thought that his view was mad
   C. were uncertain about his decision   D. insisted on their own opinions

4. What does the phrases in the last paragraph "profoundly apprehensive" possibly mean according to the passage?
   A. Greatly excited.   B. Deeply understanding.
   C. Deeply worried.   D. Very much encouraged.

5. In the author's opinion, the most important difference between Charles and his forebear in their concern about nature lies in the fact that Charles is _____.
   A. less eccentric   B. more romantic   C. action-driven   D. more energetic

Passage Four

Why Writers Attack Writers
相煎何所急
by Roger Rosenblatt

The small but insignificant world of media chitchat was fluttered last week by Renata Adler's new memoir that takes a brilliant flamethrower to the New Yorker magazine. Adler is a scrupulous, usefully unsettling critic, not to be yoked with casual hit men. She eviscerates so elegantly that her corpses remain standing. But her book and its overheated reception invoke the whole delightful genre of vengeful, venomous, and ultimately purposeless, literary assaults.

Recently John Irving attacked Tom Wolfe as being unreadable. Wolfe responded by attacking Irving as being washed up as a novelist, along with Norman Mailer and John Updike, who had attacked Wolfe earlier. So it has always gone. Truman Capote on Jack Kerouac: "That's not writing, it's typing." Gore Vidal on Capote: "He has made lying an art. A minor art." The novelist James Gould Cozzens, perhaps expressing sour grapes of wrath: "I cannot read 10 pages of Steinbeck without throwing up."

Jazz musicians say only the most adoring things about one another; actors, generally the same. Only writers claw and spit, even though nobody cares but other writers, and public opinion of the attackee is affected not at all. What drives this pointless sniping?

Often the reasons have to do with professional advancement. An unknown writer with no other means of getting noticed will attack someone to climb upward. Not long ago, a fellow wrote an ambitious op-ed piece in the Wall Street Journal attacking me as the worst writer in history. (I shall try to improve.) But even important writers will attack for success. James Baldwin admitted that he felt he had to "kill" Richard Wright in an essay, to supplant him.

The trouble with the genre is that it makes for wasteful digressions in a writer's career and is the antithesis of real, worthy writing itself. The aim of real writing is to make lives larger, more alert and, with luck, happier. Attack writing is personal and seeks to do personal injury; it shrivels up everything it touches.

It is also, by nature and intention, unfair and incomplete, and frequently irrational. Macaulay said of Socrates, "The more I read him, the less I wonder that they poisoned him" — which might have made sense if Socrates (whom we know only from Plato) had left anything to read. Charles Kingsley called Shelley "a lewd vegetarian" — an intriguing idea but difficult to picture.

And it creates a false sense of accomplishment. Friends of an attacker will always rush to congratulate him on the meanness of his attack, because they get a twofer: one writer has been belittled and another has looked like a jackass doing it.

On goes the dainty violence, nonetheless, for reasons that are somewhat understandable and forgivable, somewhat not. Writers tend to live in dank, airless cells of self-recrimination. Nothing is ever as good as it should be, and sometimes it is plain awful. Realizing what they have done, they hate themselves, frequently showing excellent judgment, and commit murder instead of suicide.

Who knows what terrible solitary stewing drove Hemingway to say of Wyndham Lewis that "his eyes had the look of an unsuccessful rapist."

A writer alone is almost as frightening a sight as a writer among others, especially at a book party. Paranoia fills the bloodstream. He grows certain that everyone is plotting against him, whereas no one is thinking about him at all. Unable to decide which is more humiliating, he goes for his verbal 45.

But I'm afraid the true reason is that a great many writers lack noble virtue. Their mode of warfare is the sneak attack; their shots are cowardly and cheap. A few years ago, a writer of movie scripts sucker-punched a journalist while he was sitting at a New York City restaurant and knocked him to the floor. People were shocked that he hadn't stabbed him in the back.

In fact, one reason writers become writers in the first place is to enable them to look more decent and honorable in print than they ever could in person. It's a bad lot on the whole — petty, nasty, bilious, suffused with envy and riddled with fear. Myself excluded, of course. And that fathead, Shakespeare.

1. Which of the following statements best reveals the implication of "She eviscerates so elegantly that her corpses remain standing" in the first paragraph?
    A. She exerts her critical views on other writers' work so carefully that her own fame remains unaffected.
    B. She is such a brilliant and welcomed critic that her fame will remain even after her death.
    C. Unlike other critics, she seldom permits her rivals any chance to attack her, so her corpses will stay intact.
    D. Her writings prove to be outstanding and able to endure any criticism.
2. Which of the following best explains the characteristics of attack writing, according to the passage?
    A. It is a traditional, delightful genre invoked by most writers in order to gain more popularity.
    B. It helps accomplish a writer's comprehensive skills needed for professional advancement.
    C. Although prevailing in the writers' world, it attracts no public attention from the general readers.
    D. It betrays the general goals of writing and aims at disgraceful offense against others.
3. Which set of adjectives can be used to describe writers in the author's opinion?
    A. Brilliant, scrupulous, venomous.   B. Stupid, ungenerous, cowardly.
    C. Purposeless, revengeful, venomous.   D. Jealous, bitter, disagreeable.
4. The article says that the genuine reason why writers attack writers is that _____
    A. many writers don't have an adequate moral standard.
    B. writers attack for professional advancement.
    C. this kind of attack is part of the literary tradition.
    D. people love to know the weakness of a famous writer.
5. What can we infer about the article from the ending sentence "And that fathead, Shakespeare"?
    A. Like the author himself, Shakespeare does not belong to the nasty group of most writers.
    B. Though a distinguished writer in English literature, Shakespeare could not be exempt from the unpleasant features of most writers.
    C. With this statement, the author managed to indicate that most writers are the same in terms of attacking one another with no exception of himself.
    D. The tradition of attacking one another among writers can be well traced back to the time of Shakespeare.

第十二单元　固定搭配

I. Grammar: Collocation

A Multiple Choices

1. After the big job was finished, the builder _____ the number of men working for him.

   A. cut down　　　　B. cut across　　　　C. cut off　　　　D. cut back

2. Advertisements are intended to _____ the best qualities of the product to the public.

   A. put down　　　　B. put across　　　　C. put away　　　　D. put aside

3. Eventually these feelings could be _____ no longer; there were outbreaks of violence everywhere.

   A. held forth　　　　B. held off　　　　C. held on　　　　D. held in

4. I have _____ the conclusion that it would be unwise to accept his proposal.

   A. come at　　　　B. come to　　　　C. come for　　　　D. come up

5. The plans for the building were _____ a few months ago.

   A. drawn on　　　　B. drawn back　　　　C. drawn out　　　　D. drawn up

6. The insurance company decided to _____ his driving record before insuring him.

   A. check out of　　　B. check on　　　　C. check in　　　　D. check over

7. In the next few years major changes will be _____ in China's industries.

   A. brought forward　　B. brought on　　　C. brought about　　D. brought up

8. It began to rain heavily when we were about to _____ for the station.

   A. set out　　　　B. set up　　　　C. set about　　　　D. set on

9. The president of the university _____ to be a young lady of about 35 years old.

   A. turned to　　　　B. turned over　　　　C. turned out　　　　D. turned back

10. Under the present system, state enterprises must _____ all profits to the government.

    A. turn down　　　　B. turn up　　　　C. turn out　　　　D. turn in

11. Important people don't often have much free time as their work _____ all their time.

    A. takes away　　　B. takes over　　　　C. takes up　　　　D. takes in

12. This popular sports car is now being _____ at the rate of a thousand a week.

    A. turned down　　　B. turned out　　　　C. turned in　　　　D. turned up

13. Generous public funding of basic science would _____ considerable benefits for the country's health, wealth and security.

    A. lead to   B. attribute to   C. devote to   D. subject to

14. His efforts to bring about the reconciliation between the two parties _____ as he had hoped.

    A. came off   B. came on   C. came around   D. came down

15. Difficulties and hardships have _____ the best qualities of the young geologists.

    A. brought out   B. brought about   C. brought forth   D. brought up

16. The inscription on the tombstone had been _____ by the weather and could scarcely be read.

    A. brought away   B. taken away   C. run away   D. worn away

17. Oil companies in the US are already beginning to feel the pressure. Refinery workers and petroleum equipment-manufacturing employees are being _____.

    A. laid out   B. laid off   C. laid down   D. laid aside

18. Because of the limitation of space, I had to _____ a lot of excellent materials.

    A. leave out   B. leave behind   C. leave alone   D. leave off

19. No ready technical data were available, but we managed to _____.

    A. go for   B. go off   C. go without   D. go through

20. The exploration team is determined to _____ the most dangerous circumstances.

    A. stand up   B. stand up for   C. stand up to   D. stand up with

21. We cannot always _____ the wind, and new windmills should be so designed that they can also be driven by water.

    A. hang on   B. hold on   C. count on   D. come on

22. One reason that led to the collapse of the country was that its leadership failed to _____ the development of world economy.

    A. come up with   B. put up with   C. catch up with   D. feed up with

23. He regretted to tell the Board of Directors that the deal had _____.

    A. fallen through   B. fallen away   C. fallen off   D. fallen to

24. Nobody knows how long and how seriously the shakiness in the financial system will _____ the economy.

    A. put down   B. settle down   C. drag down   D. knock down

25. Some electrical appliances are designed to _____ the ability of an electric current to heat wire.

    A. take advantage of   B. take advantage on
    C. take advantage to   D. take advantage over

26. There are many inconveniences that have to be _____ when you are camping.

    A. put up with   B. put up at   C. put up for   D. put up to

27. The composition is not very good. You should make attempt to _____.

    A. touch up   B. round off   C. touch on   D. round about

28. A film of oil is put between the metal surfaces so that they do not _____ each other.

    A. keep on   B. turn on   C. bear on   D. get on

29. Heat is _____ in the reaction; hence the reaction will become more nearly complete at comparatively low temperatures.

    A. knocked off   B. given off   C. passed off   D. marked off

30. They are _____ the development of science and technology.

    A. concerned to   B. concerned for   C. concerned with   D. concerned on

Ⓑ Error Correction

1. She wanted to break out from her husband and begin a new life.

2. The negotiations broke apart because neither side would compromise.

3. Very few experts come with completely new answers to the world's economic problems.

4. The teacher pointed about that it was dishonorable to do cheating at exams.

5. The problem of juvenile delinquency calls in the attention of the whole society.

6. All the evidence I have collected boils off to the fact that he is a shoplifter.

7. As the managing director dictated the letter, his secretary took on what he was saying in shorthand.

8. He always gives up to his wife's demands and does whatever she tells him to do.

9. Prices skyrocketed. It was difficult for the old couple to meet their ends with their pensions.

10. If he wants my vote, he'll have to make a stand on the question of East-West relations.

11. Chinese food is marvelous. I'm afraid I've put out a lot of weight during my stay here.

12. We must get everything ready for plowing and sowing before the rainy season sets out.

13. It is not easy to learn English well, but if you hang around, you will succeed in the end.

14. They are trying to put around all obstacles and difficulties to finish the task by the end of the month.

15. Many of his former associates turned out him when it became known how he had abused his position of trust.

II. Cloze Test

Ⓐ International Trade 国际贸易

    Accounts of barter of goods or of services among different peoples can be traced back almost as far as the record of human history. International trade, however, is specifically an exchange between members of different nations, and _____ (1) and explanations of such trade begin only with the _____ (2) of the modern nation-state at the close of the European Middle Ages. As political thinkers and philosophers _____ (3) to examine the nature and function of the nation, trade with other nations _____ (4) a particular topic of their inquiry. It is, accordingly, no surprise to find _____ (5) of the earliest attempts to describe the function of international trade within that _____ (6) nationalistic body of thought now known as "mercantilism." Mercantilist analysis, which reached the _____ (7) of its influence upon European thought in the 16th and 17th centuries, focused _____ (8) upon the welfare of the nation. It insisted that the acquisition of wealth, _____ (9) wealth in the form of gold, was of paramount importance for national policy. _____ (10) took the virtues of gold almost as an article of faith; consequently, they _____ (11) undertook to explain adequately why the pursuit of gold deserved such a high _____ (12) in their economic plans. The trade policy dictated by mercantilist philosophy was accordingly _____ (13): encourage exports, discourage imports, and take the proceeds of the resulting export surplus _____ (14) gold. Because of their nationalistic bent, mercantilist theorists either brushed aside or else _____ (15) not realize that, from an international viewpoint, this policy would necessarily prove self-defeating. _____ (16) nation that successfully gains an export surplus must ordinarily do so at the _____ (17) of one or more other nations that record a matching import surplus. Mercantilists' _____ (18) often were intellectually shallow, and indeed their trade policy may have been little _____ (19) than a rationalization of the interests of a rising merchant class that wanted _____ (20) markets-hence the emphasis on expanding exports — coupled with protection against competition in the form of imported goods. Yet mercantilist policies are by no means completely dead today.

B Marketing 市场营销

Marketing's principal function is to promote and facilitate exchange. Through _____ (1), individuals and groups obtain what they need and want by _____ (2) products and services with other parties. Such a process can _____ (3) only when there are at least two parties, each of _____ (4) has something to offer. In addition, exchange cannot occur unless _____ (5) parties are able to communicate about and to deliver what _____ (6) offer. Marketing is not a coercive process: all parties must _____ (7) free to accept or reject what others are offering. So _____ (8), marketing is distinguished from other modes of obtaining desired goods, _____ (9) as through self-production, begging, theft, or force.

Marketing is not _____ (10) to any particular type of economy, because goods must be _____ (11) and therefore marketed in all economies and societies except perhaps _____ (12) the most primitive. Furthermore, marketing is not a function that _____ (13) limited to profit-oriented business; even such institutions as hospitals, schools, _____ (14) museums engage in some forms of marketing. Within the broad _____ (15) of marketing, merchandising is concerned more specifically with promoting the _____ (16) of goods and services to consumers (i.e., retailing) and hence _____ (17) more characteristic of free-market economies.

Based on these criteria, marketing _____ (18) take a variety of forms: it can be a set _____ (19) functions, a department within an organization, a managerial process, a _____ (20) philosophy, and a social process.

III. Reading Comprehension

A Tale Of Three Cities
三城计

by Michael Elliott

They tend to be an optimistic lot, the bankers and business leaders, politicians and pundits, who every year make their way to the annual meeting of the World Economic Forum in Davos, Switzerland. Those who have power and influence often have much to be optimistic about, to be programmed to lift up their eyes to the hills — of which Davos has plenty — and see more prosperity coming their way.

This year's meeting, which starts on Jan. 23, might be a little different. Thoughts may be in the valley rather than the hills. A year ago, subprime had not entered the lexicon of the nightly news, and most Americans probably thought that "credit crunch" was a breakfast cereal. We all know better now. In the wake of the report that December's US unemployment rate had jumped to 5%, the highest level in two years, the Bush Administration and Congress, Republicans and Democrats, started falling over themselves trying to find a politically acceptable stimulus package. With a recession in the American economy looking to be imminent, the tireless locomotive of the global economy seems finally to have run out of puff.

How serious are the consequences likely to be? Much more could go wrong: a collapse of the dollar, or of US consumer confidence as house prices continue their fall. But on balance, the denizens of Davos would be well advised to keep up their sunny spirits. Taking the long view, the global economy is at a remarkable moment. Whatever the chance of a recession this year, the US has experienced what the economist and former Under Secretary of the Treasury for International Affairs John B. Taylor of Stanford University calls a "long boom" since the Fed started to squeeze inflation out of the system in 1979. For nearly 30 years, Taylor points out, the few downturns the US has suffered have, in historical terms, been both short and shallow. Even more extraordinary is the tale outside the US According to the World Bank's recent Global Economic Prospects report, global growth in 2007 was 3.6%, down a little from 3.9% in 2006. But among developing economies, growth was a remarkable 7.4%, the fifth successive year of an expansion of more than 5%. This isn't just the predictable tale of the rise of China and India; on the back of strong commodity prices (and relative peace), African economies, too, are performing better than they have for a generation.

How did the world come to this happy position? You can list the usual reasons: two decades of decent macroeconomic policymaking, the triumph of markets and the collapse of command economies, the dissemination of transforming technologies and tools such as the Internet, and open trading systems. All of these are the attributes that combine to form that much discussed phenomenon: globalization. But in this special report, we look at one overlooked aspect of a generation's worth of global growth: the extent to which New York City, London, and Hong Kong, three cities linked by a shared economic culture, have come to be both examples and explanations of globalization. Connected by long-haul jets and fiber-optic cable, and spaced neatly around the globe, the three cities have (by accident — nobody planned this) created a financial network that has been able to lubricate the global economy, and, critically, ease the entry into the modern world of China, the giant child of our century. Understand this network of cities — Nylonkong, we call it — and you understand our time.

Go back nearly 30 years, and few would have thought that any of the three cities were about to remake the world for the better. In September, 1982, the Hong Kong stock exchange lost a quarter of its value. At the same time, London and New York City were bywords of urban decay. In 1981, London saw some of the most bitter riots in a century. New York almost went bankrupt in 1975; by the early 1980s, its streets were potholed, filthy and dangerous. The city routinely had nearly 2,000 homicides a year. Last year, the number was just 494, the lowest since consistent record-keeping began in 1963.

1. What do you understand from the first two paragraphs?
   A. The bankers and business leaders, politicians and pundits are optimistic about the prospect of world economy.
   B. In Davos, Switzerland one can see a lot of hills.
   C. Prosperity can be looked forward to at the World Economic Forum every year, and this year is no exception.
   D. After years of economic prosperity in the world, a recession in US economy may lead to a sad situation in the global economy this year.
2. Which of the following does the word "Subprime" refer to in the second paragraph?
   A. Something common in the breakfast.
   B. Something far from the best.
   C. Credit crisis.
   D. A collapse of American consumer confidence.
3. What does NOT contribute to the globalization according to the passage?
   A. Correct macroeconomic policymaking.
   B. The collapse of command economies.
   C. The technologies and tools of transportation.
   D. The triumph of markets.
4. In the passage, "Nylonkong" refers to _____.
   A. New York City, London and Hong Kong
   B. an international institution with New York City, London and Hong Kong as its members

C. a kind of new synthetic material

D. a giant child of the century

5. Comparing the present economic situation in the world with that of 30 years ago, the author _____.

A. means to say that the world economy in the past was better than it is now

B. implies that the present world economy is better than it was in the past

C. means to criticize the present economic policies

D. emphasizes the challenges the world economy is facing today

Passage Two

Here Be Dragons
龙的故乡

by Jason Tedjasukmana

"Visitor-friendly" might not be the first description that comes to mind when talking about an island swarming with giant, carnivorous lizards. But Indonesia's Komodo, the entire area of which is a World Heritage Site and national park, is becoming just that, thanks to an array of new visitor facilities that make seeing the fabled Komodo dragons more enjoyable.

Komodo lies between the islands of Flores and Sumbawa. Overseas visitors typically take a 90-minute flight from Bali to Labuan Bajo in the western part of Flores, then charter a boat to Komodo — the closest you'll ever come to Jurassic Park.

More than 2,500 Komodo dragons still roam freely across the island, with some measuring up to 10 ft. (3 m) in length. There are 37 different types of reptile species besides, as well as 32 species of mammals. The waters off Komodo are diver heaven — home to more than 1,000 species of fish, 385 species of reef-building corals and six species of whales.

These kinds of natural assets have prompted the US-based Nature Conservancy (TNC), in partnership with the International Finance Corporation (a World Bank offshoot) and the local government, to develop Komodo into an ecotourism destination that will eventually become self-supporting, they hope, through visitor revenues. Some 17,000 visited the park in 2007 but TNC hopes to double that number over the next few years.

"We are trying to create tourism with a sense of responsibility," explains Marcus Matthews-Sawyer, director of tourism, marketing and communications at Putri Naga Komodo, a private-sector partnership set up in 2005 to manage the park. "This is a world-class destination that needs the right facilities to make it attractive to more than just adventure travelers."

The badly needed new additions include a visitor-reception building, decent toilets, a combined restaurant and retail outlet with great souvenirs, and information panels detailing the flora and fauna on the island. "Our vision is to position Komodo National Park as a World Heritage Site in Indonesia and the region as a whole," says Rili Djohani of TNC. "Hopefully, when people think ecotourism and nature, they will think of Komodo National Park."

Detailed information, including a guide to alternative transport arrangements, can be found at www. komodonationalpark. org. Do note that July and August is mating season, which makes it more difficult to catch a glimpse of the dragons — and even if you do spot one, a mating Komodo dragon is disturbed only at your dire peril.

~~~~~~

1. It is implied in the first paragraph that "visitor-friendly" _____.

   A. is just proper to be used to describe Indonesia's Komodo

   B. might not be the first description for Indonesia's Komodo

   C. is borrowed from "user-friendly" in information technology

   D. means that visitors are welcome to Indonesia's Komodo

2. Which of the following is the closest route for foreign visitors to come to Komodo?

   A. Go from Flores to Bali by air, and then go to Komodo by road.

   B. Go from Bali to Flores by air, and then go to Komodo by water.

   C. Go from Jurassic Park to Bali by water, and then go to Komodo by air.

   D. Go from Labuan Bajo to Bali by air, and then go to Komodo by water.

3. Visitors can see all of the following EXCEPT _____ in Komodo.

   A. Komodo dragons B. whales   C. mammals   D. divers

4. A few years later, hopefully, there might be _____ coming to Jurassic Park.

   A. 2,500 Komodo dragons   B. 1,000 species of fish

   C. about 34,000 tourists   D. all of the above

5. Which of the following is true according to the last paragraph of the passage?

   A. It is difficult to see Komodo dragons in whole summer.

   B. The mating season for Komodo dragons is likely to attract many tourists coming to Komodo.

   C. You will be in great danger if you disturb a mating Komodo dragon.

   D. Komodo dragons like to stay together at one spot.

Passage Three

A Partnership No More
断交

Such was Jamie Dimon's status within the financial services industry that the news of his hiring in March 2000 spurred an immediate 20% pop in Bank One's stock price, subsequently termed the "Jamie premium."

Dimon's reputation stemmed from his 17 years at Citigroup Inc. and its predecessor companies, where he served as second-in-command and heir apparent to chief executive Sandy Weill. The two became famous at predecessor Travelers Group for their ability to purchase under-performing companies and improve them. They capped off that process with a transforming merger with Citicorp in 1998.

A subsequent fallout with Weill left Dimon with time to mull his career options. Taking the Bank One lab following the departure of that company's long-time CEO, John B. McCoy, was a major career gamble. Bank One's myriad problems at the time included severe credit losses, a credit card unit hemorrhaging customers, a failed Internet strategy and a retail franchise languishing from under investment.

But Dimon invested $58 million of his own money in Bank One's then-seriously devalued stock, rolled up his sleeves and sat to work. He began with a management housecleaning. Three years later, virtually no senior executives remain from the McCoy Buffed. Most of the new team, not surprisingly, hails from Citigroup, although one notable exception was Austin R. Adams, former technology guru at Wachovia Corp.

Another casualty was the "Uncommon Partnership," a slogan used within Bank One during the McCoy era to describe the company's then-decentralized management and operational style. By granting acquired banks a high degree of autonomy, the Partnership was designed to encourage potential targets to join the Bank One family.

The downside of the Uncommon Partnership was operational inefficiency, which became more manifest as Bank One purchased ever-larger banks in the '90s. "It was kind of like a medieval map of Europe where the city states did not interact with each other," says analyst Brock Vandervliet, with Lehman Brothers in New York.

In addition to being expensive, this arrangement made it difficult for Bank One to carry out any company-wide product innovation or marketing. A lack of centralized credit controls also caused problems.

Recognizing these handicaps, McCoy began moving as early as 1995 to shift from a geographically based to a line-of-business management system. But all the "merger of equals" politics involved in the 1998 acquisition of First Chicago NBD Corp. delayed much of the systems integration. Until Adams took charge of the integration project in 2001, for example, the company still operated seven different deposit systems.

Dimon and his team have swept away the last of the managerial fiefdoms and finally moved the company to a one-hank model, with corporate-wide marketing and branding. Last year, for example, the credit card unit shed its "First USA" label and became known as Bank One Card Services. The company's 1,800 branches are currently being refurnished to give them more of a common look.

"I'm not an image fanatic that says we need to be branded in a certain consistent amid exact way everywhere, but there is a standard we should set for ourselves," says executive vice president and retail herb Charles W. Scharf.

Some vestiges of the Uncommon Partnership continue to linger in remote corners of the franchise, however. Scharf recalls visiting a south Chicago suburb last year and discovering some branches closed in the middle of the week — flouting the industry trend of extended hours. The local manager explained that bank branches in that town had always been closed on Wednesday. "Last time I checked, Wednesday was a normal business day for the public," says Scharf, who quickly changed the out-dated policy.

~~~~~~~~~~~~~~~~~~~~~~~~~~~~~~~~~~~~~~

1. How did Jamie Dimon attain his current reputation?

   A. He managed to bring up Bank One's stock price by 20%.

   B. He served at Citigroup Inc. and other famous companies for 17 years.

   C. He was second-in-command with Citigroup Inc.

   D. He had many years of executive experience as well as the ability to improve businesses.

2. Why did the author say that taking the Bank One lab was a major career gamble for Dimon?

   A. Because Sandy Weill, by leaving the company, put him in very difficult situations.

   B. Because John B. McCoy left Bank One at a time of the company reform.

   C. Because Citigroup Inc. just merged with Citicorp in 1998.

   D. Because the company was faced with numerous difficulties when he took over.

3. Which of the following is NOT true of Dimon in reforming the bank?

   A. He bought in big amount of the company's stock.

   B. He called up his managerial staff to appraise the company resources.

   C. He kept Austin R. Adams in his executive group.

   D. He dismantled the "Uncommon Partnership" system of management.

4. It can be concluded that McCoy _____.

   A. was not able to implement his plan of integrating the bank system

   B. was not successful in introducing the Uncommon Partnership management system

   C. was in favor of a democratic management system

   D. failed in his reform due to political influences

5. The last sentence of the paragraph is telling us that _____.

   A. Scharf is also an important person besides Dimon

   B. Scharf is always ready to accept public opinions and adjust the company policies

   C. Bank One has successfully implemented its new management system

   D. Bank One has adopted a democratic model of management style

Passage Four

Industrial Production Managers
工业生产经理

Nature of the Work: Industrial production managers coordinate the resources and activities required to produce millions of goods every year in the United States. Although their duties vary from plant to plant, industrial production managers share many of the same major responsibilities.

These responsibilities include production scheduling, staffing, procurement and maintenance of equipment, quality control, inventory control, and the coordination of production activities with those of other departments.

Working Conditions: Most industrial production managers divide their time between production areas and their offices. While in the production area, they must follow established health and safety practices and wear the required protective clothing and equipment. The time in the office, which often is located near production areas, usually is spent meeting with subordinates or other department managers, analyzing production data, and writing and reviewing reports.

Employment: Industrial production managers held about 255,000 jobs in 2000. Almost all are employed in manufacturing industries, including the industrial machinery and equipment, transportation equipment, electronic and electrical equipment, fabricated metal products, instruments and related products, and food and kindred products industries, or are self-employed. Production managers work in all parts of the country, but jobs are most plentiful in areas where manufacturing is concentrated.

Training: Because of the diversity of manufacturing operations and job requirements, there is no standard preparation for this occupation. However, a college degree is required, even for those who have worked their way up the ranks. Many industrial production managers have a college degree in business administration, management, industrial technology, or industrial engineering. Others have a master's degree in industrial management or business administration (MBA). Some are former production-line supervisors who have been promoted. Although many employers prefer candidates with a business or engineering background, some companies hire well-rounded liberal arts graduates.

Job Outlook: Employment of industrial production managers is expected to grow more slowly than the average for all occupations through 2010. However, a number of job openings will stem from the need to replace workers who transfer to other occupations or leave the labor force. Applicants with a college degree in industrial engineering, management, or business administration, and particularly those with an undergraduate engineering degree and a master's degree in business administration or industrial management, enjoy the best job prospects.

Earnings: Median annual earnings for industrial production managers were $61,660 in 2000. The middle 50 percent earned between $46,290 and $81,930. The lowest 10 percent earned less than $35,530, and the highest 10 percent earned more than $106,020.

Related Occupations: Industrial production managers oversee production staff and equipment, ensure that production goals and quality standards are being met, and implement company policies. Occupations requiring similar training and skills are engineers, management analysts, operations research analysts, and top executives.

1. The passage is mainly about _____.
    A. the procedures for industrial production
    B. the ways to raise working efficiency and productivity

C. the importance of coordination in production activities

D. the role of an industrial production manager

2. To meet the production quota, it is of importance that _____.

A. every machine be utilized to its fullest capability

B. problems be corrected at once whenever they arise

C. work shifts be arranged to yield the highest productivity

D. the optimal staffing and budgeting arrangement be made

3. Which of the following aspects is the focus of the fourth paragraph?

A. Quality control.

B. Inventory control.

C. Coordination of production activities.

D. The necessity to obtain the latest information.

4. The procurement department is in charge of _____.

A. purchasing the production materials

B. distributing the inventories in stock

C. controlling the quality of the products

D. making constant communication with other departments

5. What is the role of computers in the production process?

A. They control the techniques of production.

B. They keep each department well-informed.

C. They monitor the progress and status of work.

D. They transmit directions from the management to employees.

第十三单元 时 态

I. Grammar: Tense

A Multiple Choices

1. "Bob must be very wealthy."

   "Yes. He _____ more in one day than I do in a week."

   A. has been earned   B. had earned   C. earns   C. has earnings

2. She gave me that notebook on my birthday, and I _____ it in my drawer.

   A. have since kept   B. since kept   C. am since keeping D. had since kept

3. "It is good to see you again, Peter." "This has been our first chance to visit since _____ from Thailand."

   A. you return   B. you returned

   C. you have returned   D. returning

4. You _____ your books about.

   A. constantly leave   B. are constantly leaving

   C. constantly left   D. have constantly left

5. Even though they _____ for twenty years, the two neighbors are not very friendly.

   A. having been lived side by side   B. has been living side by side

   C. have been living side by side   D. having been living side by side

6. "My father will be here tomorrow." "Oh, I thought that he _____ today."

   A. was coming   B. is coming   C. will come   D. comes

7. "Was the driving pleasant when you vacationed in Mexico last summer?" "No, it _____ for four days when we arrived, so the roads were very muddy."

   A. was raining   B. would be raining C. had been raining D. have rained

8. "Was he studying for an examination?" "Yes, he's _____ it next week."

   A. doing   B. to take   C. making   D. to give

9. I would have gone to visit him in the hospital had it been all possible, but I _____ fully occupied the whole of last week.

   A. were   B. had been   C. have been   D. was

10. Great efforts to increase agricultural production must be made if food shortage _____ avoided.

    A. is to be   B. can be   C. will be   D. has been

11. They will have to decide what to do about the energy crisis before the oil _____.

    A. is run out   B. will be run out   C. runs out   D. will run out

12. You will hardly believe it, but this is the third time tonight someone _____ me.

    A. telephoned   B. has telephoned   C. telephones   D. should telephone

13. The company _____ a rise in salary for ages, but nothing has happened yet.

    A. is promised   B. is promising

    C. has been promising   D. promised

14. "The possibility of a flood was just reported over the radio." "I know. I heard about it. The river _____ the top of its bank."

    A. was reached   B. reaching   C. had been reachedD. has reached

15. It was not until then that I came to realize that knowledge _____ only from practice.

    A. had come   B. has come   C. came   D. comes

16. He _____, but I dived in and rescued him.

    A. was drowning   B. had drowned   C. drowned   D. had been drowned

17. It is reported that by the end of this month the output of cement in the factory _____ by about 10%.

    A. will have risen   B. has risen   C. will be rising   D. has been rising

18. "Did you expect Frank to come to the party?"

    "No, but I had hoped _____."

    A. him coming   B. that he comes   C. that he would come D. him to

19. The students _____ busily when Miss Brown went to get the book she _____ in the office.

    A. had written left   B. were writing has left

    C. had written had left   D. were writing had left

20. I _____ to send him a telegram to congratulate him on his marriage, but I didn't manage it.

    A. hope   B. hoped   C. have hoped   D. had hoped

21. "What were you doing when Anna phoned you?"

    "I had just finished my work and _____ to take a bath."

    A. starting   B. to start   C. have started   C. was starting

22. Throughout the United States, city residents now suffer from far more violence and juvenile delinquency than they _____ a decade ago.

    A. did   B. would do   C. had done   D. were doing

23. Instead of trying to imitate reality in their works, many artists of the early twentieth century _____ to reveal their feelings and ideas in abstract art.

    A. began   B. had begun   C. beginning   D. have begun

24. Today more and more people are becoming concerned about the way nature _____.

    A. ruins   B. is ruined   C. is being ruined   D. is ruining

25. When I last saw Mary, she _____ to her next class on the other side of the campus and didn't have time to talk.

    A. hurries   B. hurried   C. is hurrying   D. was hurrying

26. Irene _____ New Hampshire in 1976 and _____ in Virginia since then.

    A. left worked   B. has left has worked C. left has worked   D. has left worked

27. "Sarah left for Ohio this morning." "Oh, I thought she _____ until next week."

    A. won't be going   B. isn't going   C. wasn't going   D. hadn't been going

28. "Exams will start in a week." "I know, I _____ all next weekend."

    A. will be studying   B. study   C. studied   D. have been studying

29. "Are you going to the movies tonight?"

    "Yes. By then I _____ my work."

    A. finished   B. will finish   C. finish   D. will have finished

30. "Will you pay me now?" "I'll pay for the apples on the day you _____ them."

    A. will deliver   B. would deliver   C. delivered   D. deliver

β Error Correction

1. The conveniences that Americans desire reflected not so much a leisurely lifestyle as a busy lifestyle in which even minutes of time are too valuable to be wasted.

2. I decided to go to the library as soon as I finished what I did.

3. If city noises are not kept from increasing, people have to shout to be heard even at the dinner table 20 years from now.

4. If the population of the Earth goes on increasing at its present rate, by the middle of the 21st century, we will use up all the oil that drives our cars.

5. Biologists are predicting that they have been able to alter genes and control heredity.

6. The adult mosquito usually lives for about thirty days, although the life span varied widely with temperature, humidity, and other factors of the environment.

7. Maria Martinez, a Pueblo Indian, rediscovered the ancient art of pueblo black pottery and, by teaching the process to family and friends, develop a lucrative business.

8. I would like to go to visit that beautiful lake but I couldn't get in touch with you while I am now in Shanghai.

9. Oberlin College awards degrees to both sexes as early as 1837, but coeducation in American colleges did not spread until the second half of the century.

10. After the horse had threw the jockey several times, its owners decided it was best to withdraw it from the upcoming race.

11. As soon as they will finish the new administration building, our offices are going to be moved.

12. Almost every morning I receive cards inviting me to art exhibitions, and on the cards had been

photographs of the works exhibited.

13. After searching the house for evidence the police concluded that someone must have come in through the kitchen window and stole the silver while the family was asleep.

14. Long before humans launched the first artificial satellite into space, the Russian scientists have presented the possibilities of space colonization.

15. He was standing quietly when presently a young woman, who had been combing her hair and watched him, approached and asked him for directions.

II. Cloze Test

A Service Industry 服务业

Service industry is an industry in that part of the economy _____ (1) creates services rather than tangible objects. Economists divide all economic activity _____ (2) two broad categories, goods and services. Goods-producing industries are agriculture, mining, _____ (3), and construction; each of them creates some kind of tangible object. _____ (4) industries include everything else: banking, communications, wholesale and retail trade, all _____ (5) services such as engineering and medicine, nonprofit economic activity, all consumer _____ (6), and all government services, including defense and administration of justice.

The _____ (7) of the world economy devoted to services has been rising for hundreds of years, most _____ (8) since the beginning of the 20th century. _____ (9) services-dominated economy is characteristic of developed nations, while less developed nations _____ (10) to employ more people in "primary" activities such as agriculture. In the United States, for _____ (11), the service sector in 1929 accounted for _____ (12) 54 percent of the gross national product, whereas in 1978 service _____ (13) accounted for about 66 percent of the gross national product. This _____ (14) growth did not occur because goods production declined but rather because _____ (15) total gross national product increased nearly five fold, with most of _____ (16) increase attributable to services.

The simplest explanation for the growth of _____ (17) industries is that goods production has become increasingly mechanized. Because machines _____ (18) a smaller work force to produce more tangible goods, the service _____ (19) of distribution, management, finance, and sales become relatively more important. Growth _____ (20) the service sector also results from a large increase in government employment.

B Mining Safety 开矿安全

Mining is a hazardous occupation, and the safety of mine workers is an important _____ (1) of the industry. Statistics indicate _____ (2) surface mining is less hazardous than underground mining and that metal mining is less hazardous than coal mining. A study of the frequency and severity of accidents shows _____ (3) the nature of the operation. _____ (4) all underground mines, rock and roof falls, flooding, and inadequate ventilation are the greatest _____ (5). Large explosions are characteristic in coal mines, but more miners suffer accidents from the _____ (6) of explosives in metal mines.

A number of debilitating hazards exist that _____ (8) miners with the passage of time and that are related to the quality and _____ (9) of the environment in the mines. Dust produced during mining operations is generally injurious _____ (10) health and causes the lung disease known as black lung, or pneumoconiosis. Some fumes _____ (11) by incomplete dynamite explosions are extremely poisonous. Methane gas, emanating from coal strata, is _____ (12) hazardous although not poisonous in the concentrations usually encountered in mine air, and radiation _____ (13) be a hazard in uranium mines. A tight and active safety program is usually _____ (14) operation in every mine; where special care is taken to educate the miners in _____ (15) precautions and practices, accident rates are lower.

Some hazards are related to the local _____ (16) and the state of stress in the rocks in the mine. The mining operation _____ (17) in the shifting of loads on the strata, and in extreme cases such shifts may apply _____ (18) on a critical section of rock that exceed the strength of the _____ (19) and result in its sudden collapse. This phenomenon, which is known as a rockburst, _____ (20) particularly in deep mines, and research is under way to eliminate the danger.

III. Reading Comprehension

Passage One

The Greenhouse Effect
温室效应

The air we breathe keeps us alive in more ways than one. Without our atmosphere, average global temperature would be about minus 18℃ (minus 0.4 ℉) instead of the present 15℃ (59 ℉). All the incoming sunlight, with energy equivalent to about three 100-watt light bulbs per square yard, would strike Earth's surface, causing it to emit infrared waves like a giant radiator. That heat would simply travel unimpeded back out into the void.

Because of the atmosphere, however, only a fraction of that heat makes it directly back into space. The rest is trapped in the lower air layers, which contain a number of gases-water vapor, CO_2, methane, and others that absorb the outgoing infrared radiation. As those gases heat up, some of their warmth radiates back down to the surface. The entire process is called the greenhouse effect, and most of it is caused by the predominant greenhouse gas, water vapor.

With increased heating, more water evaporates from oceans, lakes, and soils. Because a warmer atmosphere can hold more water vapor, this creates a powerful feedback loop: The hotter it gets, the higher the water vapor content of the air, and thus the greater the greenhouse warming.

Human beings have little direct control over the volume of water in the atmosphere. But we produce other greenhouse gases that intensify the effect. The Intergovernmental Panel on Climate Change (IPCC) estimates that rising CO_2 emissions, mostly from burning fossil fuels, account for about 60 percent of the warming observed since 1850. Carbon dioxide concentration has been increasing about 0.3 percent a year, and it is now about 30 percent higher than it was before the Industrial Revolution. If current rates continue, it will rise to at least twice pre-industrial levels by about 2060 and by the end of the century could be four times as high. That is particularly worrisome because CO_2 lifetime is more than a hundred years in the atmosphere, compared with eight days for water vapor.

Methane, the principal ingredient of natural gas, has caused an estimated 15 percent of the warming in modern times. Generated by bacteria in rice fields, decomposing garbage, cattle ranching, and fossil fuel production, methane persists in the atmosphere for nearly a decade and is now about 2.5 times as prevalent as it was in the 16th century. Other major greenhouse gases include nitrous oxide produced by both agriculture and industry and various solvents and refrigerants like chlorofluorocarbons, or CFCs, which are now banned by international treaty because of their damaging effect on Earth's protective ozone layer.

The relentless accumulation of greenhouse gases has led the IPCC to project that in the next hundred years global average temperatures will rise by 1 to 3.5 degrees C. That may not seem like much. Yet the "little ice age," an anomalous cold snap that peaked from 1570 to 1730 and forced European farmers to abandon their fields, was caused by a change of only half a degree C.

But how credible are current projection? The computer models used to project greenhouse effects far into the future are still being improved to accommodate a rapidly growing fund of knowledge. And it is remarkably difficult to detect a definitive "signature" of human activity in the world's widely fluctuating climate record.

1. The main part of the heat caused by sunlight is absorbed by _____.
   A. the lower air layers
   B. a number of gases in the lower air layers
   C. the earth's surface
   D. water vapor

2. Paragraphs 4 and 5 deal with other greenhouse gases many make _____.
   A. by burning fossil fuels   B. by bacteria in rice fields
   C. by CO_2, methane, and nitrous oxide   D. both A and B

3. The word "relentless" in the first sentence of Paragraph 6 "The relentless accumulation of greenhouse gases has led the IPCC to project that" means _____.

A. without permission　B. without pity　　C. less severe　　D. less harmful

4. Which of the statements about volume of water in atmosphere is true?

A. Man has done a lot with it.　　　　B. Man has little direct control over it.

C. Man has taken measures for it.　　　D. Man has nothing to do with it.

5. What is the main idea of the last paragraph?

A. The computer models used to project greenhouse effects are not satisfactory.

B. The climate of the world has been changing.

C. Our present projection about Greenhouse Effect is somewhat undependable.

D. Human knowledge has been increasing very quickly.

Passage Four

Nike Third-quarter Earnings up 61 Percent
耐克第三季度盈利上升61%
by William McCall

Quarterly income surged 61 percent at Nike Inc. to ＄200.3 million, or 74 cents a share, on sales of ＄2.9 billion for the third quarter. The results easily passed Wall Street forecasts.

The athletic shoe and clothing giant earned ＄124.7 million for the same period in 2003, or 47 cents a share. Sales improved 21 percent from ＄2.4 billion for the third quarter last year.

Analysts surveyed by Thomson First Call had expected Beaverton, Ore. -based Nike to earn 67 cents per share.

Also Thursday, Nike reported a 10 percent jump in orders, with more than a third of that growth due to favorable currency exchange rates.

Orders for the US market, which have been flat for the past few years, were up 4.5 percent for the third quarter, while Europe grew by 11 percent and Asia jumped 23 percent, the company said.

Nike officials attributed the booming sales to economic recovery in the United States, increased consumer demand for high-priced basketball shoes, and major sports events tied to Nike products.

"I believe calendar 2004 has the potential to be the most exciting year in Nike's history," Nike president Mark Parker said on a conference call with analysts.

Parker noted that in six of the last seven Olympics years, Nike outperformed the Standard & Poor's index by an average of 21 percent.

During the third quarter, US sales increased 4 percent to ＄0.37 billion compared to ＄0.33 billion for the third quarter of 2003.

Nike Chairman Phil Knight said the results continue a pattern of steady growth over the past nine months.

Analysts said the improvement was impressive as Nike moved into 2004 with plans to spend heavily on major sports events, including the NCAA basketball tournament, World Cup soccer and the 2004 Olympics.

"They've got just a lot of big events coming up," said Jamelah Leddy, an analyst with McAdams Wright Ragen in Seattle.

Part of the increase was due to stronger demand for basketball shoes selling for ＄100 and up, an upscale market that had declined during the recession.

But she noted that one of the growth factors — exchange rates — was a market factor, not a result of management.

"The underlying business is growing but keep in mind how much is related to currency exchange," Leddy said.

Nike had announced earlier this month that it expected higher earnings than analysts had predicted, despite the bankruptcy of Footstar Corp., the third-largest US retailer for athletic shoes. The West Nyack, N. Y., company, which runs the Just For Feet and Footaction shoe chains, is a major vendor of Nike shoes but owed only ＄19.4 million, a relatively small amount in comparison to overall sales.

Nike shares rose 67 cents to close at ＄76.82 Tuesday on the New York StockExchange, before the results were released. The shares dropped 82 cents in the extended session.

1. The passage indicates that Wall Street forecasts were _____.
    A. too optimistic   B. accurate   C. pessimistic   D. conservative

2. How much more did Nike Inc. earn for the third quarter than for the same period last year?
    A. About ＄2.9 million.   B. About ＄2.4 million.
    C. About ＄500,000.   D. About ＄200 million.

3. Which of the following, according to a Nike report, is a contributing factor for the increase in orders?
    A. US dollar is revalued.
    B. US dollar is debased.
    C. Currency exchange rate is stable.
    D. Currency exchange rate is turbulent.

4. It can be inferred from the passage that a major way Nike increases its sales is _____.
    A. promoting US sales   B. maintaining a steady market
    C. sponsoring major sports events   D. pricing highly for its basketball shoes

5. Which of the following is NOT mentioned as a factor influencing Nike's business?
    A. Economic recovery.
    B. Favorable currency exchange rates.
    C. Proficient management.
    D. Increased demand for high-priced basketball shoes.

Passage Four

Australia Celebrates its First Century
澳大利亚庆祝自己的第一个百年
by David Hardy

Australians lived in six distinct colonies prior to 1901. These would later become Australian states: New South Wales, Victoria, Queensland, South Australia, Western Australia and Tasmania. These six colonies had their own laws, postal services, customs, defense and immigration, and there was a strong feeling for decades before 1901 that these issues would be more effectively and efficiently handled by a central government. People moved freely between the colonies and considered themselves Australians, but the colonies were not formally joined to each other in any way, and there were some significant differences in the ways that colonies handled issues. Because of these differences, and because of the development of regional identity, many Australians at the time wanted to protect their own interests and preserve their own identities. This made the federal model of government, providing a balance of power between the Central Government and the State Governments, the preferred model.

Shortly before the Federation of States, ten representatives from each colony met to write a Constitution, and in 1899 all colonies voted to join together to form a Federation of States, similar to the system of government in Switzerland. In 1900, Britain's Queen Victoria, Australia's Head of State at the time, signed the necessary papers, and all colonies, now States, joined as members of the Federation, to be known as the Commonwealth of Australia. On 1st January 1901, Australia came into existence as a nation.

After this, the Commonwealth Government took on the responsibilities of defense, immigration, postal services, trade and taxes, while the State Governments looked after schools, health services, roads and railways.

Elections for the new Commonwealth Parliament were held in March 1901, and on 9th May of that year the first Commonwealth Parliament was ceremonially opened at the Exhibition Building in Melbourne. The Parliament formally sat in the Victoria State Parliamentary building until it transferred to its permanent home in 1927, in the newly created national capital, Canberra.

Shortly after the formation of the Federation, the first Prime Minister of Australia (Australia's Head of Government), Edmund Barton, announced a national flag competition. There were five winners, including a 14-year-old schoolboy, Ivor Evans, with a similar design. Together, the five winners created the Australian flag, combining the British Union Jack, a six-pointed star under the Union Jack representing the six states of the Commonwealth of Australia, and to the right of the Union Jack, the Southern Cross constellation. Ivor Evans included the Southern Cross as it is "the brightest constellation in the Southern Hemisphere, representative of Australia's bright future as a leading nation." Australia's national anthem remained "God Save the Queen" until 1974, when the patriotic song "Advance Australia Fair" was chosen to replace it.

In 1901, Australia was already a culturally diverse society, composed of Australian aborigines, Torres Strait Islanders and immigrants drawn from all corners of the globe, especially at the time of Australia's Gold Rush in the mid-19th century. A Swedish newspaper started up in Melbourne in 1857, Polish Australians formed a Committee to support the Polish January Uprising against Russian domination in 1863, and the French set up the first Alliance Fran aise in Australia in 1890.

Today, over 23 percent of Australians were born in another country. Australian society is made up of traditions and ideas from many cultures, and has forged a new identity as a tolerant and vibrant multicultural society. Australian immigration policy is proudly non-discriminatory, and the policy of multiculturalism has been pursued enthusiastically by Australian Governments over the past two decades.

One hundred years on, Australia is one of the world's most successful, culturally diverse and democratic national communities. This has been built on a Federal framework, which brings together the values of Australian democracy, citizenship and participation.

1. The idea of establishing a central government appeared _____
   A. around 1901   B. in 1899
   C. for decades before 1901   D. as the British government proposed it
2. The following are all British EXCEPT _____.
   A. Union Jack   B. God Save the Queen
   C. the Southern Cross constellation   D. six colonies
3. After 1901, Australia _____.
   A. still regarded Queen Victoria as their Head of State
   B. remained as a colony of U. K. as Switzerland did
   C. had nothing to do with the British government
   D. broke away from U. K.
4. What the Australian national flag doesn't represent is _____.
   A. the bright future of Australia
   B. the spirit of independence
   C. the leading position of Australia in the south hemisphere
   D. the respect for the United Kingdom
5. Which of following statements is NOT true according to the passage?
   A. Australians wanted to preserve their own regional identities and didn't want a federal government.
   B. There is a change for Australian national anthem in the 1970's.
   C. One of the designers of Australian national flag was a young boy.
   D. The Commonwealth of Australia is a federal nation.

Passage Four

Amazon Research Raises Tough Questions
亚马逊雨林研究出现棘手的问题
by Michael Astor

Julio Tota stood atop a 195-foot steel tower in the heart of the Amazon rain forest, watching "rivers of air" flowing over an unbroken green canopy that stretched as far as the eye could see.

These billows of fog showed researcher Tota how greenhouse gases emitted by decaying organic material on the forest floor don't rise straight into the atmosphere, as scientists had supposed.

Instead, they hover and drift-confounding scientific efforts to unlock the secrets of the world's largest remaining tropical wilderness.

"What we've learned is the Amazon rain forest is much more fragile and much more complex than we had first imagined," Tota said. "My research is pretty specific. It's aimed at showing why all our measurements are probably off."

Tota is part of the Large Scale Biosphere-Atmosphere Experiment, a decade-old endeavor involving hundreds of scientists, led by Brazilians and with funding from NASA and the European Union. Their open-air "laboratories" are 15 such observation posts spread over an area of rain forest larger than Europe.

The project's goal is to make the best scientific arguments for why this vast rain forest-along with other endangered forests in Africa, southeast Asia and elsewhere is essential to combating global climate change.

But as the first phase of the $100 million experiment draws to a close, its researchers acknowledge that the data have raised more questions than answers.

Scientists can now say with certainty that the Amazon is neither the lungs of the Earth, nor the planet's air conditioner. Paradoxically, the forest's cooling vapors also trap heat, by reflecting it back toward Earth in much the same way greenhouse gases do.

But a key question remains unanswered: Does the Amazon work as a net carbon "sink," absorbing carbon dioxide, or is it adding more CO_2 to the atmosphere than it is subtracting, because of burning and other deforestation that have claimed an average 8,000 square miles — an area the size of Israel or New Jersey — each year of the past decade?

Scientists also can't predict every way in which continued destruction of the Amazon — for timber, for cattle ranching, for soybean farming — might affect global climate. But it will almost certainly lead to drier conditions over a wide area, since ground moisture taken up and evaporated through trees is recycled as rainfall.

Some computer simulations suggest deforestation could cause droughts as far afield as the US grain belt, apparently because chain reactions in the atmosphere would shift the Polar Jet Stream and the precipitation it brings.

These questions take on new urgency as global warming's effects become ever more apparent, and as forests fall at a nonstop pace. In one sign of growing concern, Brazil's national leadership met in emergency session on Jan. 24 to deal with a sudden surge in deforestation after a three-year slowdown.

New studies suggest the Amazon may be approaching a tipping point, at which the drier conditions caused by deforestation will reduce rainfall enough to transform the humid tropical forest into a giant savanna.

If preserving the 80 percent of the Amazon still standing would help offset some greenhouse emissions, destroying it would almost certainly accelerate global warming by releasing perhaps 100 billion tons of carbon into the atmosphere-equal to some 10 years' worth of total global emissions.

"If you cut down all the tropical forests in the world, you may increase CO_2 concentrations by 25 percent," said Brazilian climatologist Carlos Alberto Nobre. "It's important to keep the forests intact because we are in a global warming crisis and it's important not to reach a tipping point from which we can't come back."

Deforestation — both the burning and rotting of wood in the Amazon — already releases an estimated 400 million tons of carbon dioxide into the atmosphere every year, accounting for up to 80 percent of Brazil's greenhouse gases, boosting this country to sixth place or higher among emitter nations.

By contrast, each acre of rain forest that remains intact takes somewhere between 80 and 480 pounds of carbon out of the atmosphere each year through the process of photosynthesis.

1. From the first three paragraphs we know that _____.
   A. "rivers of air" is what scientists are mostly concerned about
   B. scientists had supposed that greenhouse gases emitted by the Amazon rain forest don't rise straight into the atmosphere
   C. there are "rivers of air" and billows of fog in the Amazon rain forest
   D. the billows of fog hovering and drifting above the top of trees produce problems for scientists and researchers to understand the Amazon rain forest
2. The purpose of Tota's research is to _____.
   A. know why it is difficult to make all the measurements of the Amazon rain forest
   B. know why the Amazon rain forest is much more fragile and complex than it was first imagined
   C. find out reasons for the disagreement between the calculations made and the facts learned
   D. find out a way to make more specific measurements
3. Some important questions facing scientists include the following EXCEPT _____.
   A. how continued destruction of the Amazon might affect global climate
   B. burning and other deforestation have claimed an average 8,000 square miles of forest land each year for the past 10 years

C. deforestation could cause droughts

D. whether the Amazon absorbs more carbon dioxide or adds more of it to the atmosphere

4. According to Brazilian climatologist Nobre, _____.

    A. cutting down all the tropical forests in the world may increase carbon dioxide concentration by 25 percent

    B. preserving the 80 percent of the Amazon would help offset some greenhouse emissions

    C. we are just at the tipping point from which we can't come back

    D. we should keep the tropical forests forever

5. It seems that _____ is/are one of the chief causes of global warming according to the passage.

    A. the precipitation brought by the chain reactions in the atmosphere

    B. the burning and rotting of wood in the Amazon

    C. the billows of fog over the Amazon rain forest

    D. the absorption of carbon dioxide of the atmosphere by trees

第十四单元 代词及其他

A Multiple Choices

1. They looked at _____ and hesitated to leave first.
   A. another one   B. one another   C. one other   D. each another

2. However, what he needs is to be fitted into a highly organized university system quite different from _____ at home.
   A. those   B. which   C. what   D. that

3. No agreement was reached in the discussion as neither side would give way to _____.
   A. the other   B. any other   C. another   D. other

4. He is not well known here, but he is _____ in his hometown.
   A. someone   B. somebody   C. anyone   D. anybody

5. We agreed to accept _____ they considered as the best tourist destination.
   A. whatever   B. whoever   C. whomever   D. whichever

6. There aren't any cupboards _____ utensils in the kitchen.
   A. but   B. and   C. any   D. or

7. My mother is interested in _____ I have told her.
   A. that   B. all that   C. all which   D. all what

8. The teacher asked _____ who had finished their homework to leave the classroom as quickly as they could.
   A. them   B. they   C. those   D. these

9. A good writer is _____ who can express the commonplace in an uncommon way.
   A. that   B. one   C. this   D. which

10. _____ I waved to him again and again did he see me.
    A. When   B. Till   C. Until   D. Not until

11. You can benefit from your study plan _____ you keep to it steadily.
    A. unless   B. but   C. as long as   D. nevertheless

12. You should respect _____ as you would like to be respected.
    A. other   B. others   C. the other   D. the others

13. To the finalists, _____ , the last high jump was the most important.

    A. he and I   B. him and I   C. he and me   D. him and me

14. Two suspects were found, but the police didn't arrest _____ of them.

    A. either   B. neither   C. any   D. none

15. Nearly _____ student enrolled in universities was over the age of eighteen.

    A. all   B. none   C. each   D. every

16. If the car is not Danny's, _____ can it be?

    A. who's else   B. whose else   C. whose else's   D. who else's

17. China is a wonderful place and there is _____ to see and enjoy.

    A. a lot of   B. many   C. much   D. many more

18. — How many students did you find in the playground?

    — _____ .

    A. None   B. No one   C. No body   D. Not one

19. He, hungry and tired, had no choice _____ to leave the heavy package behind.

    A. however   B. but   C. otherwise   D. nevertheless

20. Tall _____ it is, bamboo is very light.

    A. though   B. but   C. , as   D. so

21. It is a pity that _____ of her two husbands has been capable of understanding her.

    A. either   B. neither   C. both   D. each

22. It's years _____ they last met each other at the conference in Philadelphia.

    A. since   B. when   C. before   D. after

23. It is one thing to enjoy listening to good music, but it is quite _____ to perform skillfully yourself.

    A. another   B. any other   C. other thing   D. some other

24. Nearly two hundred people took part in the new medicine test. Only one in _____ kept on till the end.

    A. ten   B. tens   C. tenth   D. tenths

25. I will not go such a long way to visit the library _____ you drive me there.

    A. if   B. since   C. unless   D. when

26. When science, business, and art learn something of _____ goals, the world will have come closer to cultural harmony.

    A. one another's   B. each other's   C. one another   D. each other

27. — I need a black dress for the concert next week.

    — I am sure Emily will let you wear _____ .

    A. one of her   B. her   C. one of hers   D. her one

28. Children, hold the bottle with your right hand. Tommy, you're not correct. Please use your _____ hand.

    A. other   B. the other   C. another   D. the another

29. I know of no other person in the club who is as kindhearted as _____.

    A. he   B. him   C. his   D. himself

30. _____ is often the case, he lighted a cigar after dinner.

    A. It   B. That   C. As   D. What

β Error Correction

1. If you had some sense, you would not have left the door unlocked and the police would not have been here for the burglary.

2. Each man and woman must sign their full name before entering the examination room.

3. It is annoying to someone whose keys are missing.

4. TV is more popular than the other kinds of entertainment.

5. Let me give you two of the consequences of which I would guess that one will shock you while another may perhaps surprise you more favorably.

6. Our country has plenty of natural resources while their has far less than they need.

7. This is widely believed that the pull of gravity on a falling raindrop changes the drop's round shape into a teardrop shape.

8. The tall building was on a big fire which smoke filled the air.

9. We didn't arrive at the platform before the train began to move.

10. Most substances contract when they freeze so that the density of a substance's solid is higher than those of its liquid.

11. Wagner and Strauss were such good friends that they frequently exchanged gifts with the other.

12. That child of him is cleverer than the other children.

13. You have to hurry up if you want to buy something because there is hardly something left.

14. I can give every of you two weeks to write the outline of your papers.

15. The managing director refused to accept either of the four proposals made by the contractors.

II. Cloze Test

A Poultry Production 家禽生产

    Large-scale intensive meat _____ (1) poultry production is a waste of food resources. This is _____ (2) more protein has to be fed to animals _____ (3) the form of vegetable matter than can ever _____ (4) recovered in the form of meat. Much of the food value _____ (5) lost in the animal's process of digestion and cell replacement. _____ (6) the case of chicken, neither can one eat feathers, blood, feet _____ (7) head. In all, only about 44% of the live animal fits _____ (8) be eaten as meat.

    This means one _____ (9) to feed approximately 9 – 10 times as _____ (10) food value to the animal than one can consume _____ (11) the carcass. As a system _____ (12) feeding the hungry, the effects can prove disastrous. _____ (13) times of crisis, grain is the food of life.

_____ (14) the huge increase in poultry production _____ (15) Asia and Africa continues. Normally British or US firms are involved. _____ (16) instance, an American based multinational company _____ (17) this year announced its involvement in projects _____ (18) several African countries. Britain's largest suppliers of chickens, Ross Breeders, _____ (19) also involved in projects all _____ (20) the world.

β Natural Chemicals 天然化学剂

Though the public increasingly demands no-risk food, there is no _____ (1) thing. Bruce Ames, chair of the biochemistry department _____ (2) the University of California, points out that _____ (3) to 10% of a plant's weight is made up _____ (4) natural pesticides. He says: "_____ (5) plants do not have jaws or teeth to protect _____ (6) they employ chemical warfare." And many naturally produced chemicals, _____ (7) occurring in tiny amounts, prove in laboratory tests _____ (8) be strong carcinogens — _____ (9) substance which can _____ (10) cancer. Mushrooms might be banned _____ (11) they were judged by the same standards that _____ (12) to food additives. Declares Christina Stark, a nutritionist at Cornell University: "We've got _____ (13) worse natural chemicals in the food supply _____ (14) anything man-made."

Although Americans have _____ (15) reason to be terrified to sit down _____ (16) the dinner table, they have every reason _____ (17) demand significant improvements _____ (18) food and water safety. Though most people will withstand the small amounts of contaminants in food and water, at _____ (19) a few individuals will probably get cancer _____ (20) day because of what they eat and drink.

III. Reading Comprehension

Passage One

Female Farmers
女性农场主

In the United States, women in agriculture are not a new concept; women have farmed with their families for centuries. However, women farming either on their own or as true managing partners with their spouses are a growing phenomenon. Many women have now expanded their role from farm wife to that of farm manager and key decision-maker.

Recognition of the expanding role of women in agriculture comes at a critical juncture in American struggle to diversify agriculturally and renew its emphasis on rural development. Policies aimed at rural women typically have focused on their roles as farm wives and mothers who benefit from family nutrition and health programs, but effective agricultural and rural policies need to be based on current rural realities, reflecting women's economic contributions as well.

The latest census of agriculture reports that women own almost half of all the private agricultural land in the United States. Both the increase in independent female farmers and the amount of farmland owned by women signify an increasing role for women in agriculture.

Most female farmers in Kentucky reside on their farms (71.4 percent), yet more than half (60 percent) do not list farming as their principal occupation. On average, female farmers have spent approximately 20 years on their current farms. Their average age is 60.2 years, 6.8 years more than the average age of male farmers.

Most farms operated by women are fewer than 140 acres. Male farmers, who on the average operate much larger farms, own a smaller percentage (71.4 percent) of their farmland than female farmers do. Male farmers rent or lease almost 30 percent of their land.

Almost half of all female farmers operate crop farms: nearly half operate farms yielding tobacco, hay, and similar products. The remaining farms operated by women are concentrated in oilseed and grain farms, beef cattle operations, and aquaculture and other animal farms. When assessed by market value of agricultural products sold, farms operated by women in general have lower sales than those operated by men.

Role models are needed for women in agriculture. The opportunities and barriers that exist for them are challenges for educators, Extension personnel, and researchers interested in improving the economic and social conditions of agricultural communities and farm families. More information is needed on how women learn about agricultural practices and view those practices and about the contribution of women members to agricultural organizations.

The changing role of farm women has implications for Extension fieldwork. If women obtain more information about farm production and marketing in different ways than men do, Extension will need to offer some different educational programming, such as home study courses or programs targeted specifically to women farmers.

Ann Bell is a Scott County farmer who operates a farm along with other family members. Although the family manages some of the farm together, she is the sole decision-maker and manager of 5 acres and considers herself a full-time farmer. She always had an interest in farming, but did not find her way back to her vocation until she completed college.

"After trying to do every other job in the world I could find other than farming, I slowly got back to it," says Bell about her return to the farm. After someone suggested she should help start a farmers' market in her hometown, she decided to begin producing fruits and vegetables on her family's farm with her brother and her father.

"As much as I tried to get away from farming, I realized that's where I wanted to be. I realized I'd never be happy doing anything else," she says. Bell says the major challenges in farming for her are "to diversify and market to fit in with our (farm's) commodities and (to have) all of my family participating on the same land to make a living."

Today Bell grows and sells vegetables at the Lexington and Georgetown farmer's markets, at retail and wholesale markets, and to restaurants. She is involved in numerous agricultural groups and programs, including the Philip Morris Leadership Program (sponsored by the UK College of Agriculture for farm-business leaders), the Campaign for Sustainable Agriculture, and the Community Farm Alliance.

1. There is a new tendency that _____.

   A. farms operated by women are generally smaller than that by men

   B. role models are necessary for women farmers

   C. many women farmers have expanded their role on their farms

   D. women farmers have aimed at retail and wholesale markets

2. Which of the following is NOT true?

   A. Farms run by female farmers are smaller than farms run by male farmers.

   B. The farm ownership percentage of men farmers is higher than that of women farmers.

   C. Women farmers used to be considered as farm wives and mothers.

   D. The government should renew its emphasis on rural development.

3. Female farmers mainly produce _____.

   A. grain   B. vegetables   C. fruits   D. all of the above

4. Women farmers need some educational programming in order to _____.

   A. break down the barrier between them and male farmers

   B. complete their college education

   C. contribute more to the agriculture organization

   D. be the winner of farm production and marketing

5. More attention should be paid to _____.

   A. family nutrition and health program

   B. female farmers' economic and social condition

   C. the production of fruits and vegetables

   D. product prices of female farmers

Passage Two

Mad Cow Disease
疯牛病

What are the concerns over BSE?

BSE (bovine spongiform encephalopathy or mad cow disease) is a disease of cattle. It is believed to cause the human disease variant Creutzfeldt-Jacob disease (vCJD), which has no cure and is always fatal. The most likely route of transmission of the BSE agent to people is through consumption of contaminated food. BSE, once thought as only a UK problem, has now been identified in a number of continental European herds following increased testing procedures. The spread of BSE is linked to the inclusion of meat and bone meal from infected animals into cattle feedstock. It is likely that some of this infected feedstock has been exported globally.

Why can't we continue with the temporary suspension?

To protect the Australian public, the temporary suspension announced on 5 January built on the ban that Australia has had in place since 1996 on the importation of specified foods containing British beef following the links between BSE infected beef and vCJD. New measures will be implemented from 16 September 2001 and will apply to all countries seeking to export beef and beef products to Australia. The official veterinary authorities of countries supplying Australia with beef products will need to certify, to the satisfaction of the Australian Quarantine and Inspection Service (AQIS), that their cattle are BSE-free.

How will this requirement be enforced?

AQIS is requested to intercept all beef and beef products at Australia's borders to determine the country of origin of the products and of any beef ingredient. AQIS will handle applications to import beef and beef products according to the risk category of the country from which the beef ingredients in a product are sourced. Origin countries will be allocated to one of four categories, according to the level of risk:

Category A (certification required) — beef and beef products from these countries are regarded posing a negligible risk to human health.

Category B (certification required) — these countries, while not reporting cases of BSE, may have been exposed to high risk factors, such as the importation of high-risk meat and bone meal.

Category C (certification required) — countries in this category are known to have considerable exposure to BSE risk materials, but have not reported indigenous cases of BSE.

Category D — beef and beef products from countries in this category pose the highest level of risk and will be refused entry to Australia. These countries have reported cases of indigenous BSE in their herds.

Consignments of beef and beef products from Category D countries cannot be imported. Products from Category B and C countries can only be imported if the national authority can certify that the product is derived from animals not exposed to BSE risk and if specific risk materials have been excluded from the food chain.

AQIS will require official certificates supplied by the agreed Competent National Government Authority from countries placed in the A, B or C risk categories. The certification requirements will depend on the category.

Are any beef products exempt from these certification arrangements?

Yes. Milk and dairy products, gelatine, fats and tallows, collagen from bovine skins and hides are exempt. Current scientific opinion is that BSE cannot be transmitted through these products.

Will beef products already on supermarket shelves be removed if countries do not provide certification of BSE status by 16 September 2001?

AQIS has requested that retailers voluntarily withdraw beef and beef products from supermarkets from 16 September 2001 if the beef ingredients are sourced from any countries for which on certification of BSE-free status of BSE preventative measures have been obtained by this date. It will be working with manufacturers and retail organizations to identify these products.

1. Which of the following is NOT true?

    A. BSE is an equivalent of mad cow disease.

    B. Having BSE infected beef will lead to vCJD.

    C. Beef and beef products in Category A are free from BSE.

    D. BSE is a human disease variant.

2. We can't continue with the temporary suspension because _____.

    A. new measures will be implemented

    B. origin countries will be allocated to one of the four categories

    C. BSE can never be transmitted to humans

    D. the beef ingredients infected by BSE will be sterilized

3. The four categories represent _____.

    A. the level of import certification risk   B. the level of export certification risk

    C. the level of consumption certification risk D. the level of BSE infection risk

4. Which of the following is true?

    A. Beef products allocated in Category A can be imported without certification.

    B. Beef products allocated in Category B can be imported if they are certified as BSE free.

    C. Beef products allocated in Category C will be refused entry to Australia.

    D. Beef products allocated in Category D will be the most dangerous.

5. BSE can be transmitted through _____.

    A. hides   B. meat   C. milk powder   D. butter

Passage Three

Greens
绿色食品

Nothing sounds and tastes more like spring than greens. Greens are gaining popularity in the country. From May through June and then again from September through November, we can enjoy the freshness and flavor of locally grown greens. If you do not have a garden of your own, visit your local farmers' market, which generally offers, along with other fruits and vegetables, greens picked at the peak of the season.

We used to think of greens as a salad of iceberg lettuce. Today, greens run the gamut from iceberg lettuce to cooked collards and include beet and turnip tops, Swiss chard, chicory (curly endive), collards, dandelion and mustard greens, kale, endive, escarole, parsley, rape, spinach, and watercress. Common cooking greens include collards, kale, beet, mustard, and turnip greens. Many kinds of greens are available year-round.

Dark green leafy vegetables are packed with vitamins that promote health, and greens are a major source of vitamins A and C. Vitamin A is needed for vision, normal growth, reproduction, and a healthy immune system. One serving (1/2 cup) of greens can supply up to 50 percent of our daily need for Vitamin A. Vitamin C, also known as ascorbic acid, plays a vital role in fighting infection, keeping gums healthy, and healing wounds. A serving of greens can supply up to 30 percent of our daily need for Vitamin C. Both vitamins A and C are also antioxidants that may reduce the risk of chronic disease, and they both contain phytochemicals that fight disease.

Greens also provide about 20 percent of our daily need for calcium, and that can make them important for people with lactose intolerance. Greens are also low in calories — a half-cup serving contains 20 to 30 calories. These are good reasons to try to consume all the greens that come in from the garden or to buy plenty from the local farmers' market.

Regardless of the type of greens you choose, look for bright green leaves that are fresh, young, moist, and tender. Leaves that are injured, torn, dried, limp, or yellowed indicate poor quality and thus poor nutritional value. Avoid greens with coarse stems that may result in excess waste. Farmers' markets usually have a good selection of greens, allowing you to purchase enough for dinner or freeze for the same fresh taste in winter.

Store greens in the cold section of the refrigerator for no more than two to three days. After that, the flavor of some greens can become quite strong, and the leaves will be limp.

Wash greens well in lukewarm water or swirl them in lukewarm water in a large bowl (dirt will sink to the bottom of the bowl). Remove any roots, rough ribs, and the center stalk if it is large or fibrous. To use greens in salads, thoroughly drain and dry them. This allows the salad dressing to stick to the leaves. Mild-flavored greens such as chard, kale, or spinach should be steamed until barely tender. Strong-flavored greens such as collard, mustard, or turnip greens need longer cooking in a seasoned broth. To avoid bitterness, blanch strong-flavored greens before adding them to soups and stews.

Basic Green Salad: Wash and dry 1 bunch arugula, 1 small head radicchio, 1 small head Boston lettuce, and 12 ounces fresh spinach. Into a large salad bowl, tear the greens into bite-size pieces. Drizzle with desired dressing and serve immediately.

To cook: Add washed greens to a medium saucepan with 1/4 inch of water in the bottom of the pan. Salt if desired, using 1/2 teaspoon of salt for every pound of greens. Bring the water to a boil. Cover and cook until tender. For leafy greens, cook 1 to 3 minutes, until they are wilted. For other greens, cook until they are crisp-tender (about 5 to 10 minutes). Many seasonings and herbs are available that will enhance the flavor of greens without adding sodium. Try allspice, lemon, onion, nutmeg, or vinegar. Or, braise the greens by adding 1/4 cup of olive oil and 1 to 2 cloves of minced garlic to 1 pound of greens and then cook them an additional 20 minutes. (Do not use an aluminum pan when cooking greens. Natural acids in the greens may pit the aluminum pans.)

To freeze: Wash young tender green leaves thoroughly and cut off woody stems. Greens must be blanched before freezing, so blanch collards in water 3 minutes and all other greens 2 minutes. Cool, drain, and package, leaving 1/2-inch headspace. Seal, label, and freeze. Greens store well for up to one year.

1. The peak season of greens is _____.
   A. in April and August   B. from May to November
   C. from July to August   D. not in December
2. Which of the following is NOT true?
   A. People like to eat greens.
   B. You can buy fruits and vegetables at the farmers' market.
   C. Greens can't be eaten without cooking.
   D. You can get certain kind of greens year-round.
3. Greens provide us with _____.
   A. both vitamins A and C   B. calcium and high calories
   C. vitamins A, C and high calories D. vitamins A, C and calcium
4. People buy plenty of greens at the market because _____.
   A. they are nutritious
   B. there are many kinds of greens available
   C. they can fight disease with greens
   D. they are fresh
5. _____ belongs to strong-flavored greens.
   A. Onion   B. Mustard   C. Lemon   D. Garlic

Passage Four

Corn
玉米

Nothing is more delicious than the sweet corn picked at the peak of ripeness. Corn is low in fat and a good source of fiber and B vitamins. Research shows that if you follow a low-fat, high-fiber diet, you lower your risk of heart disease and certain cancers, giving you even more reason to consume all the corn from the garden or buy a plentiful supply from your local farmers' market.

Today, more than 200 varieties of corn are available. Yellow corn has large, full-flavored kernels. The kernels of white corn are small and sweet. The super-sweet varieties, while great to eat, are not suitable for canning because the natural sugar in the corn caramelizes and turns brown during processing. It is best to freeze super-sweet varieties in order to preserve them.

Look for ears with green shucks, moist stems, and silk ends that are free of decay. Kernels should be small, tender, plump, milky when pierced, and fill up all the spaces in an ear's rows. The good selection of corn available at farmers' markets will allow you to buy enough.

Since corn can absorb odors from foods such as green onions, avoid storing corn with other produce. Keep unshucked fresh corn in the refrigerator until ready to use, wrapped in damp paper towels and placed in a plastic bag. Corn's natural covering will prevent it from drying out. The typical shelf life of corn is four to six days, so refrigerate it for no more than two days. Each day corn is kept after picking reduces its just-picked fresh taste.

After shucking, fresh sweet corn can be steamed, boiled, oven-roasted, or grilled and then eaten off the cob by hand. Fresh corn kernels can be used to make corn soup or be added to other soups; used in salads, vegetable saut s, fritters, and relishes; creamed; or made into puddings or souffl s. A Creole version of creamed corn uses fresh red, green, and yellow peppers and fresh basil. Both peppers and basil are generally available from vendors at your local farmers' market.

If you love corn on the cob, corn salsas, chowders, and all the other wonderful ways to prepare corn when it is in season, you may be interested in trying a tool that removes corn kernels. It cuts kernels off the cob, allowing you to move the blade closer if you want creamier corn. Look for it during the summer season at your local cookware store.

When corn is picked, its sugar immediately begins to turn to starch, reducing the corn's natural sweetness. So, it's important to cook corn as soon as possible after you buy it.

To steam: Remove shucks and silk. Trim stem ends. Arrange ears on a rack and steam in a double boiler about 8 to 10 minutes or until tender. Or, stand ears in a tall pot with 1 inch of water in the bottom of the pot. Cover the pot with a tight-fitting lid and steam the corn for 5 minutes.

To microwave: Place the ears of corn, still in the shucks, in a single layer in the microwaver. Microwave on high for a period equal to 2 minutes times the number of ears, turning the ears halfway through cooking. Allow corn to rest several minutes before removing the shucks and silk.

To boil: Remove shucks and silk. Trim stem ends. Carefully place ears in a large pot of boiling water. Cook 2 to 4 minutes or until the kernels are tender.

To grill: Turn back the inner shucks and remove the silk. Sprinkle each ear with 2 tablespoons of water and nonfat seasonings such as salt, pepper, or herbs. Replace shucks and tie them shut. (Cooking corn in the shucks gives it an earthy, grassy flavor.) Place ears on a hot grill, turning often for 20 to 30 minutes. You can also remove the shucks and silk and wrap the ears in double-folded, heavy-duty aluminum foil. Before wrapping, sprinkle each ear with 2 tablespoons of water and seasonings such as salt, pepper, or herbs. Twist the ends of the foil.

Cook, turning once, about 10 to 15 minutes until done.

>>>

1. Which of the following is NOT true?

A. Low-fat, high-fiber diet keeps you away from certain diseases.

B. Fresh corn should be kept unshucked in the fridge.

C. Fresh taste will gradually reduce after picking.

D. In selecting corn you should use your ears to listen.

2. Super-sweet varieties cannot be canned because _____.

A. the sugar in them will turn them brown   B. they will be preserved

C. they're too large   D. they're full-flavored

3. Steam the shucked corn for _____ minutes.

A. 2 – 4   B. 8 – 10   C. 10 – 15   D. 20 – 30

4. In microwaving the corn, you should _____.

A. shuck the corn first

B. set the time period to 2 minutes

C. put the microwaver on a high place

D. not remove the shucks immediately after cooking

5. Grill the corn unshucked in order to _____.

A. doubly fold it   B. remove the silk

C. give it an earthy, grassy flavor   D. sprinkle water and seasonings

第十五单元 各种语法点

······ **I. Grammar: Miscellaneous Grammatical Points** ······

A) Multiple Choices

1. _____ break up rock, slowly wearing it away over millions of years.
   A. Ice, wind and running water which   B. Ice, wind and running water
   C. If ice, wind and running water   D. When ice, wind and running water

2. In 1983, the fossilized claw and bones _____ a dinosaur were found in Surrey, England.
   A. that   B. is   C. which is   D. of

3. You think that everyone should be equal, and this is _____ they disagree.
   A. how   B. which   C. when   D. where

4. Minoan civilization _____ rapidly after a huge volcanic eruption; Crete was eventually overrun with people from mainland Greece.
   A. declining   B. declined   C. was declined   D. to decline

5. We all think _____ that the football match has been cancelled.
   A. it a pity   B. it pity   C. what a pity   D. a pity is

6. As Mercury moves in its solar orbit, _____ its axis, an imaginary line that runs through its center.
   A. rotates it on   B. it rotates on C. on rotates it   D. rotates on it

7. Their keen senses of hearing and smell have made some types of dogs _____ in hunting and tracking and as security guards.
   A. as valuable   B. of the value   C. are valued   D. valuable

8. _____ as much as 1/4 of all timber harvested has not been used.
   A. That is estimated   B. It is estimated that
   C. There is estimated   D. It estimates that

9. Igneous rocks form _____ hot melted rock from inside the Earth cools and becomes solids.
   A. when   B. when does   C. and when   D. it is when

10. Early philosophers believed that the mind was divided into three faculties _____ as feeling, intellect, and will.
    A. to know   B. known   C. knowing   D. knew them

11. The ionosphere, _____ extremely thin air, lies above the stratosphere and extends upward some 650 miles.

    A. is a layer　　　　B. layer of　　　　C. has a layer of　　D. a layer where

12. The twelve constellations located along or near the ecliptic _____ the signs of the zodiac.

    A. are referred to as　　　　　　　　B. as referred to

    C. they are referred to　　　　　　　D. to which are referred

13. _____ our most recent memo indicates is _____ we haven't yet protected ourselves against the risk of the market.

    A. What that　　　B. What what　　　C. That what　　　D. That that

14. Food is to body _____ knowledge is to mind.

    A. what　　　　　B. as　　　　　　　C. which　　　　　D. how

15. In areas away from the poles, the size of glaciers decreases in summer because the rising temperature causes the lower parts _____.

    A. melt　　　　　B. are melting　　　C. melted　　　　　D. to melt

16. Of particular interest to visitors _____ the large number of bookstores that sell books in different languages.

    A. are　　　　　　B. is　　　　　　　C. were　　　　　　D. was

17. Such _____ the case, there were no grounds to justify your complaint.

    A. was　　　　　　B. were　　　　　　C. being　　　　　　D. had been

18. Lack of money means that the _____ of free clinics must be reduced.

    A. amount　　　　B. number　　　　　C. degree　　　　　D. quantity

19. Show me your ID card, _____?

    A. will you　　　　B. do you　　　　　C. shan't you　　　D. can't you

20. So small _____ that the most powerful microscopes cannot detect them.

    A. are these particles　　　　　　　B. were these particles

    C. these particles are　　　　　　　D. these particles were

21. Mary never dreams of _____ for her to be sent abroad very soon.

    A. there being a chance　　　　　　B. there to be a chance

    C. there be a chance　　　　　　　D. being a chance

22. The invention of telephone means _____ people could send messages a long way at great speed.

    A. what at last　　B. at last what　　C. that at last　　　D. at last that

23. _____ in an atmosphere of simple living was what her parents wished for.

    A. The girl was educated　　　　　　B. The girl educated

    C. The girl's being educated　　　　D. The girl to be educated

24. If he _____ tomorrow, I would give him the dictionary he needs.

    A. comes　　　　　B. should come　　　C. would come　　　D. will come

25. I wish our view _____.

    A. weren't so far apart　　　　　　　B. weren't so far away

     C. hadn't been so far away   D. aren't so far apart

26. He _____ abroad but he was suddenly taken ill.

     A. is to go   B. went to   C. was going   D. was to have gone

27. If there are a lot of interesting people and good food, we won't object to _____ to the welcome party.

     A. come   B. having come   C. coming   D. being come

28. The development of mechanical timepieces spurred the search for more accurate sundials _____.

     A. which to regulate them with   B. with which to regulate them

     C. to regulate them with which   D. which to regulate with them

29. Nancy hasn't begun working on her Ph. D. _____ working on her Master's.

     A. still because she is yet   B. yet as a result she is still

     C. yet because she is still   D. still while she is already

30. _____ that you win the prize, you will be notified by mail.

     A. In the event   C. In the event of   C. At all events   D. In any event

β Error Correction

1. Social reformer Frederick Douglass dedicated his life to work for the abolition of slavery and the fight for civil rights.

2. About 150 years ago, Charles Darwin shocked the world with his theory that humans were relativity to apes.

3. The ovaries of certain primates each container approximately three hundred thousand eggs which are released one by one over a span of about thirty years.

4. When a nucleus is not dividing, it consisting of a nuclear membrane, a nucleolus, and evenly distributed genetic materials.

5. Animals usually prepare for hibernation by eating large amount of food to build out stored fat in their bodies.

6. Traditionally, ethnographers and linguists have paid little attention to cultural interpretations giving to silence, or to the types of social contexts in which it tends to occur.

7. Although all humans age, the rate at which this inevitable process occurs is different each person.

8. How I wish to help the people whose kindness and gentleness have made my life worth to live.

9. Eclecticism is the practice of mixing elements dissimilar in style in single work of art.

10. One of Phillip Wheatley's earliest verses, composed in her teens, celebrates learning, redemption, and virtue, three principal themes of her work subsequent.

11. The American writer Alex Haley traveled more than a half million mile to authenticate his novel *Roots*.

12. Sparrows, small birds of the finch family, have stout beak adapted seed eating and are useful to farmers in destroying weed seeds.

13. After children are able to speak or understand a language, they communicate through facial expressions and by making noises.

14. Only in the past 20 years scientists have begun to realize that ozone layers of the atmosphere are being seriously damaged.

15. Historically, no artists have presented clearer or the more complete records of the development of human culture than sculptors have.

II. Cloze Test

Ⓐ Dad Baboons Help Their Daughters Mature 狒狒爸爸帮助女儿成长

Having daddy around when they are growing up is good for little _____ (1) -even if they are little baboon girls. While that's well known _____ (2) people, it's a bit of a surprise for non-human primates.

But a report _____ (3) Monday's online edition of Proceedings of the National Academy of Sciences _____ (4) that female baboons in Kenya raised in groups with their fathers matured _____ (5) and had a longer reproductive life than other baboons.

Males had not _____ (6) thought to be engaged in a level of care that would make _____ (7) difference to their offspring, said Susan Alberts, an associate professor of biology _____ (8) Duke University.

Alberts and colleagues studied groups of yellow baboons _____ (9) near Kenya's Mt. Kilimanjaro. In these groups both males and females have several partners. _____ (10) presence of the father in a group gave the daughters a jump-start _____ (11) sexual maturity, a measure of fitness, the researchers said.

"For young females, _____ (12) their major opponents in life are adult females and fellow juveniles, the _____ (13) of any adult male may be helpful," Alberts said in a statement. _____ (14) do not share food after their mothers cease nursing, but the father's _____ (15) during early maturity may still help daughters get more to eat if _____ (16) father reduces any harassment of their offspring.

"Sons also experienced accelerated maturation _____ (17) their father was present during their immature period, but only if their _____ (18) was high-ranking at the time of their birth," the researchers found.

For _____ (19), the major competition for food is other males, so only the presence _____ (20) a high-ranking father would help, the researchers said.

The research was funded by the National Science Foundation and a Marie Curie Outgoing Fellowship.

β Eyes to the Skies Getting Bigger 观望太空的眼睛越睁越大

A telescope arms race is taking shape around the world. Astronomers are drawing up plans for the biggest, most powerful instruments ever constructed, capable of peering far deeper into the universe — and further back in time — than ever before.

The building boom, which is expected to play out over the _____ (1) decade and cost billions of dollars, is being driven by technological _____ (2) that afford unprecedented clarity and magnification. Some scientists say it will _____ (3) much like switching from regular TV to high-definition.

In _____ (4), the super-sized telescopes will yield even finer pictures than the Hubble Space Telescope, _____ (5) was put in orbit in 1990 and was long considered superior _____ (6) its view was freed from the distorting effects of Earth's atmosphere. _____ (7) now, land-based telescopes can correct for such distortion.

Just the names _____ (8) many of the proposed observatories suggest an arms _____ (9): the Giant Magellan Telescope, the Thirty Meter Telescope and the European Extremely Large Telescope, _____ (10) was downsized from the OverWhelmingly Large Telescope. Add to those three _____ (11) ground observatories a new super eye in the sky, NASA's James Webb _____ (12) Telescope, scheduled for launch in 2013.

With these proposed giant _____ (13), astronomers hope to get the first pictures of planets outside our _____ (14) system, watch stars and planets being born, and catch a glimpse _____ (15) what was happening near the birth of the universe.

"We know _____ (16) nothing about the universe in its early stages," said Carnegie Observatories _____ (17) Wendy Freedman, who chairs the board that is building the Giant Magellan _____ (18). "The GMT is going to see in action the first _____ (19), the first galaxies, the first supernovae, the first black holes to _____ (20)."

When scientists look at a faraway celestial object, they are seeing it as it existed millions and millions of years ago, because it takes so long for light from the object to reach Earth.

III. Reading Comprehension

Passage One

The Brain and the Computer
大脑与计算机

Considering that the brain can be compared to the electronic computer, it may be useful to ask if one computer, the brain, has any advantages over the other, the electronic computer.

First, compare the amount of energy needed to operate the brain and that needed to run a computer. It has been calculated that the entire brain runs on very little energy as compared with a machine. A machine with as great a capacity as the brain — assuming one could be built — would need at least one million times as much electrical power to continue operating.

But the computer is a faster worker than the brain. The advanced calculators are thousands upon thousands of times faster than the brain, and models yet to be built will probably be yet speedier.

Memory is of great importance in "Computer-type" operations. The number of bits of information that can be stored determines the ability of the system to do complex operations. The more bits stored, the more complex the calculations that can be made. In 1962, advanced electronic computers could store about 40,000 bits of information. Here, the brain shows its distinct advantages: although the number of bits stored is certainly not known, it has been estimated at many millions of bits.

One specialist has said that to build a machine to imitate the capacity of the human brain, it would be necessary to make it the size of a very tall building. "The brain is like a computing machine, but there is no computing machine like the brain."

Humans, however, may not continue to have this superiority in the future. Recent developments in electronic equipment, for example, *Sceptron*, have rapidly changed our ideas. Each Sceptron is extremely small, which may mean that is will soon be possible to make a calculator as complex as the human brain — with the same bit storage capacity — and be able to fit it neatly in a desk.

There is one great and very important distinction between humans and machines. While electronic devices may think, "hunger" for electricity, and in other ways imitate animal and human behavior, men have desires, hungers, thirsts, and a complex existence of which the brain is a major, but not the entire, aspect. Human hopes and fears are not like those of the electronic mechanisms, nor will they be so long as we continue to construct thinking machines whose function is only to think as they are programmed.

The use that man makes of automation, decision-making machines, and the other results of cybernetics is dependent on man himself. As Norbert Wiener states in his book *The Human Use of Human Beings* mankind is faced with two possible destructive directions in which cybernetics could develop, influencing all of society. One is that machines that do not learn will obey all instructions and never vary in their approach to problems. The other is that man may find himself in the position of someone who has released an angry force. Machines that can learn and make decisions on the basis of their learning are not obligated to decide in ways that please or improve humanity. Men cannot give machines responsibility for mankind; final choices must always be made by, and in favor of, men.

〰〰〰〰〰〰〰〰〰〰〰〰〰〰〰〰〰

1. The energy needed to operate the human brain is _____ that needed to run a computer.

　　A. much more than　　B. as much as　　　　C. far less than　　D. no more than

2. The computer's ability to make complex calculations depends largely on its _____.

    A. size   B. speed   C. memory   D. operator

3. As far as current computers are concerned, they _____.

    A. approach the capacity of the human brain

    B. have the same hopes and fears as humans

    C. can learn and make decisions just like humans

    D. store much less information than the human brain

4. According to the passage, one important difference between humans and machines is that _____.

    A. humans have more complex feelings

    B. humans can think while machines can't

    C. machines have a longer life than humans

    D. machines can imitate human behavior only

5. Cybernetics could have a negative effect on society when machines _____.

    A. try to please some people

    B. change their approach to problems

    C. don't know how to obey human instructions

    D. make decisions unfavorable to humans

Passage Two

Surgeons of the Future Will be Robots Injected into Your Body
未来的外科医生是注射到人体内的机器人

Tiny crew members inside a microscopic submarine are injected into your bloodstream for an incredible mission that will take them deep inside your body to perform delicate surgery!

It sounds like the science fiction plot for the 1966 movie "Fantastic Voyage", but this amazing scenario is close to becoming science fact — Japanese researchers are designing "microrobots" that will battle illnesses from inside human organs.

"The microrobots are almost like shrunken men, zipping around through the veins to destroy cancer or repair damaged tissue," explained Kenzo Inagaki, a deputy director of Japan's Ministry of International Trade and Industry — which is putting up a staggering $170 million for the project.

The ground-breaking undertaking will begin in April. It will give doctors the ability to fight diseases in areas of the human body that were previously unreachable except by surgery, says Hiroyuki Fujita, a spokesman for the fantastic project that will involve six universities and giant companies like Toyota, Hitachi, Nikon and Toshiba.

Researchers estimate it will take 10 years to carry out the plan, but they say that when it's completed it will dramatically change medicine as we know it! One robot they are planning is a "small pill" — a submarine-shaped capsule you swallow that can be guided to a diseased area inside your body.

"It will be about two-fifths of an inch in diameter, and enclose a tiny robot," said Fujita.

"In fact, the submarine' would be an incredibly tiny lab able to analyze conditions within the body."

Once it enters the stomach, the robot could be steered either by an external remote control or by a built-in guidance system.

When it reached a diseased area, the robot would be able to diagnose a condition close up and treat it with just the right amount of medication.

"Once it has served its purpose, the pill will harmlessly exit the body through the waste system," he said.

A second robotic device is a "micro-intelligent catheter" about one-fifth of an inch in diameter.

The catheter, a tube withy a camera and a laser on the end, could be threaded into the gallbladder and pancreas.

"Its tiny size will eliminate much of the pain and discomfort experienced by today's patients when much larger catheters are used," he said. "The probe will send doctors an accurate picture of what is happening inside without surgery."

And its laser tip will enable physicians to operate internally. "Doctors will be able to use it to cut away cancerous growth, destroy blood clots or to repair breaks in the tissue," said Fujita.

Ironically, these tread-setting medical developments planned by the Japanese come from research started years age in the Massachusetts Institute of Technology in the US — but these efforts faltered because of a lack of funding.

〰〰〰〰〰〰〰〰〰〰〰〰〰〰〰〰〰〰〰〰〰〰〰〰

1. "Tiny crew members" in the first paragraph refers to _____.
    A. sailors   B. workers   C. tiny robots   D. mechanics
2. Researchers predict that birth of microrobots _____.
    A. will make all fatal diseases curable
    B. will make many surgeons unemployed
    C. will bring about a great revolution in medicine
    D. will make internal and external medicines unnecessary
3. We learn from this selection that in Japan, the project _____.
    A. is under way
    B. has gained financial support
    C. has been claimed to be unreachable
    D. has been abandoned by universities and companies
4. Which of the following statements is true?
    A. The robot could enter one's body to cure the diseases from inside.
    B. Capsules of medicines will go into the body together with other devices.

C. Once the robot is inside the body, it can't be directed by an external remote control.

D. When it has fulfilled its mission, the pill will dissolve in blood.

5. In the US this research work was in a shaky state mainly because _____.

A. it lacks public support

B. it suffers one setback after another

C. it fails in its competition with Japan

D. it is short of money

Passage Three

Breakthrough Mine-detection Turns Ocean Floor "Transparent"
突破性的探雷技术使得海床"一览无余"

Since 1776, when naval mines were invented, navies have rightfully feared the stealthy and relatively simple weapons, which can disable or destroy warships and paralyze vital shipping. Navies worldwide employ a host of mine-detection technologies and techniques, most of them complicated, expensive, and far from perfect. So a simpler, more effective method for detecting these mines, developed by a physicist at North Carolina State University, could make big waves in naval headquarters around the globe.

Unlike current mine-detection techniques, the patented methodology finds objects buried in the ocean floor without the use of complex, unreliable modeling and without the usual arrays of sonar transmitters and receivers. Instead, the method records the return echo of a sonar transceiver's "ping", then time-reverses and transmits that signal. The following echo clearly shows buried objects, and suppresses the response from the seafloor itself, making the underwater terrain "transparent."

Dr. David M. Pierson, then a doctoral student in physics at NC State, demonstrated the new approach in research he conducted with Dr. David E. Aspnes, Distinguished University Professor of Physics, in late 2003. The project was supported by a grant from the Office of Naval Research. Pierson has since joined the Applied Physics Laboratory of Johns Hopkins University in Baltimore, where his work is supported in part by the US Navy.

"The method has not been explored as a solution to this problem until now," said Pierson. "Using time reversal on the return echoes back scattered by buried mines gave us results we considered amazing."

According to Aspnes, the young physicist's research is a breakthrough. "Time reversal is a technique that has been used before in various contexts, including optics and acoustics, but before Pierson's work the advantages of time reversal for isolating targets in backscattered signals were never before recognized."

Using time reversal to find buried mines requires only one transceiver, said Pierson, although more can be used, and the method isn't limited by the composition of the ocean floor. "Previous methods had to incorporate a lot of complex modeling of the seafloor and the ocean environment," Pierson said, "and required sophisticated software and hardware systems. My time-reversal technique not only simplifies the needed equipment, but also can be implemented using existing sonar equipment, with minor software changes. More elaborate analyses of echoes are also made possible."

What Pierson has done, said Aspnes, is to demonstrate a new approach that uses sonar but is simpler and works better than any previous method. "In Pierson's approach," he said, "a ping' is first transmitted from a sonar transceiver. The return echo is then recorded, time-reversed, and transmitted. He discovered that in the next echo the response from the seafloor was suppressed, but the echo from buried objects was enhanced. This enhancement is seen even if the signal from the buried object is too small to be detected in the first return."

The NC State discovery should please naval mine-detection experts, who now use everything from dolphins to divers to sophisticated software modeling and elaborate sonar arrays in their grim work. And it should send those who design such mines back to their equally grim drawing boards.

1. Before the NC State discovery of a new method for detecting naval mines, _____.
   A. naval mines did not receive adequate attention from warships
   B. there was no need to worry about naval mines
   C. it was reasonable for navies to be afraid of mines
   D. it was reasonable for navies to make big waves to deal with naval mines

2. The word "patented" in the first sentence of the second paragraph most closely means _____.
   A. powerful　　　B. new and unique　　C. potential　　　D. careful

3. Pierson's project has been financed by _____.
   A. the office of Naval Research　　　B. the US navy
   C. both A and B　　　D. a physicist at NC State University

4. Which of the following is NOT true about the current mine-detecting techniques and the new approach?
   A. The currently used techniques require more equipments, and divers or dolphins are often involved in finding naval mines.
   B. The currently used techniques are unable to find mines if the sonar receives too faint echo.
   C. The new approach requires only one sonar transmitter and one receiver in detecting naval mines.
   D. The new approach uses time-reverse technique so that it can clearly find the situation of the ocean floor.

5. What does the last sentence of the passage imply?
   A. Those mine designers are defeated and they have to face the difficult task of designing new mines.
   B. Those mine designers had better take up painting they are good at.
   C. It is more difficult for those mine designers to work with drawing boards than to design mines.
   D. Those mine designers should have more practice with drawing boards before they can successfully design new mines.

New Findings on Memory Could Enhance Learning
关于记忆的新发现有助于学习

New research in monkeys may provide a clue about how the brain manages vast amounts of information and remembers what it needs. Researchers at Wake Forest University Baptist Medical Center have identified brain cells that streamline and simplify sensory information, markedly reducing the brain's workload.

"When you need to remember people you've just met at a meeting, the brain probably doesn't memorize each person's facial features to help you identify them later," says Sam Deadwyler, Ph. D. , a Wake Forest neuroscientist and study investigator. "Instead, it records vital information, such as their hairstyle, height, or age, all classifications that we are familiar with from meeting people in general. Our research suggests how the brain might do this, which could lead to ways to improve memory in humans."

The researchers found that when monkeys were taught to remember computer clip art pictures, their brains reduced the level of detail by sorting the pictures into categories for recall, such as images that contained "people," "buildings," "flowers," and "animals." The categorizing cells were found in the hippocampus, an area of the brain that processes sensory information into memory. It is essential for remembering all things including facts, places, or people, and is severely affected in Alzheimer's disease.

"One of the intriguing questions is how information is processed by the hippocampus to retain and retrieve memories," said Robert Hampson, Ph. D. , co-investigator. "The identification of these cells in monkeys provides evidence that information can be remembered more effectively by separating it into categories. It is likely that humans use a similar process."

The researchers measured individual cell activity in the hippocampus while the monkeys performed a video-game-like memory task. Each monkey was shown one clip art picture, and after a delay of one to 30 seconds, picked the original out of two to six different images to get a juice reward.

By recording cell activity during hundreds of these trials in which the pictures were all different, the researchers noticed that certain cells were more active when the pictures contained similar features, such as images of people but not other objects. They found that different cells coded images that fit different categories.

"Unlike other cells in the brain that are devoted to recording simply an object's shape, color or brightness, the category cells grouped images based on common features, a strategy to improve memory," said Terry Stanford, a study investigator. "For example, the same cell responded to both tulips and daisies because they are both flowers."

The researchers found, however, that different monkeys classified the same pictures differently. For example, with a picture of a man in a blue coat, some monkeys placed the image in the "people" category, while others appeared to encode the image based on features that were not related to people such as "blue objects" or "types of coats."

While such categorization is a highly efficient memory process, it may also have a downside, said the researchers.

"The over generalization of a category could result in errors," said Deadwyler. "For example, when the trials included more than one picture with people in it, instead of different images, the monkeys often confused the image with a picture of other people." The researchers said that learning more about how the brain remembers could have for reaching benefits.

"If we can understand in advance how the brain works when decisions are made, we can predict when the brain will make a mistake, and correct it," said Tim Pons, Ph. D. , an expert in monkey research and team member. "This finding about how large amounts of information are processed by the brain will help us ultimately achieve that goal."

1. According to Sam Deadwyler, a neuroscientist, when we meet people we need to remember, the brain probably memorizes _____.

   A. their facial expressions

   B. their eyes, noses, mouths, etc.

   C. such things as their hairstyle, height, or age

   D. their stance or manner of speaking

2. In the new research monkeys were used. They were taught to play with _____ so as to find out how the brain memorizes things.

   A. video-games   B. pictures   C. people   D. words

3. According to the passage, which of the following is NOT true about hippocampus?

   A. It is an area of the brain containing category cells.

   B. It processes sensory information into memory.

   C. Its importance for memory is limited to facts, places and people.

   D. It is likely to be injured by a kind of brain disease resulted in old age.

4. Although category cells play an important part in the memorizing process, they cannot solve all the problems of memory, because _____.

   A. over generalization could make mistakes

   B. the new findings are still far-fetched

   C. it is not easy to carry out the trials in humans

   D. the new findings are not accepted by most scientists

5. What is the significance of these trials in monkeys?

   A. They help us know more about how monkeys memorize things.

   B. They help us understand the benefits of learning from animals.

   C. They can help us have a thorough understanding of the brain's memorizing mechanism.

   D. They tell us that knowing more about how the brain remembers could result in better learning.

第十六单元　各种语法点

I. Grammar: Miscellaneous Grammatical Points

A Multiple Choices

1. The man was prejudiced _____ all people of color.

   A. for   B. to   C. against   D. with

2. The medical record shows that it was the drug, not the disease, _____ killed him two years ago.

   A. the effects of which   B. the effects of it

   C. finally   D. that

3. _____ she was living in Paris that she met her husband Terry.

   A. Just when   B. Soon after   C. It was while   D. During the time when

4. While crossing the mountain areas, all the men had guns for protection lest they _____ by the local bandits.

   A. be attacked   B. were attacked   C. must be attacked   D. would be attacked

5. So quickly is technology advancing _____ is a possibility today may be a reality tomorrow.

   A. that   B. that which   C. if what   D. that what

6. The traveler was soaked to the skin, for there was no shelter _____ the rains anywhere.

   A. of   B. from   C. in   D. against

7. Taj Mahal in India is perhaps one of the most beautiful buildings in the world, where I spent _____ moonlit night.

   A. many a   B. plenty of   C. a great many   D. a great deal of

8. It was quite some time _____ the president managed to save his firm from bankruptcy.

   A. while   B. before   C. when   D. ever since

9. We thought she'd come just for a visit, but it seems she is staying _____.

   A. not longer   B. for long time   C. for long   D. for good

10. In my opinion, he is _____ imaginative of all the contemporary poets.

   A. quite the most   B. very the most   C. by far the most   D. rather the most

11. My approach is not to learn everything about something, but _____ something about everything.

   A. rather to learn   B. rather learn   C. to rather learn   D. rather learning

12. Pumas, which are larger, cat-like animals, will not attack human beings if they _____ undisturbed.

    A. leave   B. left   C. are left   D. have left

13. _____ the door than someone started knocking on it.

    A. I had closed no sooner   B. I had no sooner closed

    C. No sooner have I closed   D. No sooner I closed

14. My friend Paul was badly taken in when he paid $1,000 for that second-hand car; it was not worth _____.

    A. that all much   B. that much all   C. all that much   D. much all that

15. Everybody knows that the earth is spherical, _____?

    A. doesn't he   B. doesn't she   C. don't they   D. doesn't it

16. Most doctors recognize that medicine is _____.

    A. as art as much it is a science   B. much an art as it is a science

    C. as an art as much it is a science   D. as much an art as it is a science

17. Scrambled eggs with bacon _____ the standard American breakfast.

    A. is   B. are   C. is to be   D. are to be

18. The police chief announced that he would soon inquire _____ the deaths of two young girls.

    A. about   B. into   C. of   D. after

19. At 4 o'clock this morning, I suddenly woke up and seemed _____ some one scream in the street.

    A. to hearing   B. to have heard   C. hearing   D. having heard

20. The sick _____ been cured and the lost _____ been found.

    A. has has   B. have have   C. has have   D. have has

21. Professor Foster, who teaches English literature at California State University, divides his time _____ teaching, writing and lecturing.

    A. during   B. from   C. among   D. between

22. The meeting was to _____ at ten o'clock, but the chairman had not turned up by eleven o'clock.

    A. start   B. have started   C. is starting   D. be started

23. It was not until he entered the airport _____ he realized that he had forgotten to bring his air ticket with him.

    A. before   B. when   C. after   D. that

24. The signal made by the watchman could mean nothing _____ than a halt to the advance.

    A. much   B. better   C. rather   D. other

25. It is easy to think that a witness who saw a crime _____ will be able to give all the answer.

    A. to be committed   B. to commit

    C. committing   D. being committed

26. _____ , the box will break into pieces.

    A. If handled carelessly   B. Handling carelessly

    C. To handle carelessly   D. If handling carelessly

27. The workers went on strike against the government's plan _____ the prices of daily necessities.

    A. raises   B. raised   C. raising   D. to raise

28. I think she must be a pop music lover, _____ ?

    A. mustn't she   B. don't I   C. isn't she   D. doesn't she

29. The blind can _____ see than the deaf can hear.

    A. no longer   B. no more   C. no better   D. no sooner

30. For him to be reelected, what is essential is not that his new policy works, but that the public believe that it _____ .

    A. is   B. does   C. has done   D. is done

ß Error Correction

1. Be careful to give the caterers an accurate count of the number of people whom you expect to have gone to the wedding reception.

2. The children soon forgot that it was them, their parents, who had encouraged them to continue their education.

3. For centuries large communities of people lived on houseboats in parts of the world where the climate is warm and the waters are calm.

4. Swans, noted for graceful movements in the water, have been the subject of many poetries, fairy tales, legends, and musical compositions.

5. Not until six thousand years ago did man develop the first bows and arrows, and began to make pottery and the first fish hooks.

6. I am excessively grateful for the many kindnesses you have shown my son.

7. Chosen the most outstanding student on his campus made his parents very happy.

8. The news may be true but as I heard it only from second-hand I am not likely to give it credence until I have it confirmed.

9. Thousands of people died even though there was a worldwide effort to send food and medicine to the starved people.

10. The advantages of the photovoltaic cell are its zero pollution, its durability, and its ability for producing energy directly from the sun.

11. All oil lamps being fashioned from a wick floating in a bowl of oil functioned according to the principle of capillary action.

12. The new telephone system can carry many more telephone conversations at the same time as the old one, and can carry them much farther without amplification or regeneration.

13. Bill will present a paper at the conference describe his new approach to eliminate a certain kind of water pollution.

14. The amount of the Antarctic Peninsula are thought to contain copper deposits are similar to those in the Andes Mountains of South America because the two areas were once contiguous.

15. This year, as the past, the oil company will sponsor a television series based on major literary works.

II. Cloze Test

A Heavy Rain Can Trigger Earthquakes 暴雨会引发地震

Huge downpours of rain can trigger earthquakes in landscapes riddled with _____ (1) and channels by increasing pressure within underlying rock, _____ (2) a new study.

It was already known that rainfall could cause tremors, but the _____ (3) of water needed is much more than previously thought, says Steve Miller, a geologist _____ (4) the University of Bonn, Germany.

In recent years, _____ (5) have documented small earthquakes that occurred after heavy rainfall in Germany, Switzerland and France. All _____ (6) low in magnitude-meaning they could _____ (7) detected by seismographs, but not felt by humans.

Some experts have _____ (8) that although the rainfall was heavy, the fact that rain could _____ (9) an earthquake at all suggests that it takes extremely little to _____ (10) a tremor. They concluded that the Earth's crust in a delicate _____ (11), teetering on the edge of a slight shake-up at any moment.

_____ (12), in the new study, Miller disagrees, pointing out that _____ (13) the three documented events happened in a specific type of landscape _____ (14) as karst.

Other geologists studying rain-triggered earthquakes did note that they _____ (15) in karst geology, but they did not delve into the possible _____ (16).

Karst landscape features a distinctive topography of soft carbonate rock riddled _____ (17) deep fissures, underground channels and cave systems.

These characteristic features are carved out _____ (18) carbonate bedrock-typically limestone or dolomite-is _____ (19) slowly by the action of slightly acidic rainwater over thousands of _____ (20). And these structures, says Miller, are key.

B Nature Gives Way to Virtual Reality 自然让位于虚拟现实

As people spend more time communing with their televisions and computers, the impact is not just on their health, researchers say. Less time spent outdoors means less contact with nature and, eventually, less interest in conservation and parks.

Camping, fishing and per capita visits to parks are all declining in a shift _____ (1) from nature-based recreation, researchers report in Monday's online edition of Proceedings of the National Academy of Sciences.

"Declining _____ (2) participation has crucial implications for current conservation _____ (3)," wrote co-authors Oliver R. W. Pergams and Patricia A. Zaradic. "We think it probable than any major _____ (4) in the value placed on natural areas and experiences will greatly reduce the value _____ (5) place on biodiversity conservation."

"The replacement of vigorous outdoor activities by sedentary, indoor videophilia _____ (6) far-reaching consequences for physical and mental health, especially in children," Pergams said in a statement. "Videophilia has been _____ (7) to be a cause of obesity, lack of socialization, attention _____ (8) and poor academic performance."

By studying visits to national and state park and the _____ (9) of hunting and fishing licenses the researchers documented declines of between 18 percent and 25 _____ (10) in various types of outdoor recreation.

The decline, found in both the United _____ (11) and Japan, appears to have begun in the 1980s and 1990s, the period of _____ (12) growth of video games, they said.

For example, fishing peaked in 1981 and had _____ (13) 25 percent by 2005. Visits to national parks peaked in 1987 and dropped 23 _____ (14) by 2006, while hiking on the Appalachian Trial peaked in 2000 _____ (15) was down 18 percent by 2005.

Japan suffered similar declines, as visits to national parks there dropped _____ (16) 18 percent between 1991 and 2005.

There was a small growth in backpacking, but _____ (17) may reflect day trips by some people who _____ (18) were campers, wrote Pergams and Zaradic. Pergams is a visiting research assistant professor of biological _____ (19) at the University of Illinois at Chicago, while Zaradic is a fellow with the Environmental Leadership Program, Delaware Valley, in Bryn Mawr, Pa.

_____ (20) fishing declined, hunting held onto most of its market, they found.

"This may be related to various overfishing and pollution issues decreasing access to fish populations, contrasted with exploding deer populations," they said.

The research was funded by The Nature Conservancy.

.... # III. Reading Comprehension ....

Passage One

Mental Illness and Diagnosis
精神病及其诊断

Like medical doctors, mental health professionals often use diagnosis as a way of categorizing patients and their problems. The use of diagnoses can, at times, help guide treating professionals as to the nature of the problems a patient faces, the origins of those problems, and potential treatment options. Diagnosis can also sometimes be used to straightjacket patients into ill-defined and ill-fitting categories that lend a scientific appearance to socially constructed biases. For example, a diagnosis of major depressive disorder is often used by psychiatrists and managed care companies as an argument that a person has a "biologically-based mental illness" and thus must receive a biological treatment, such as antidepressant drugs or, more rarely, electroconvulsive treatment. The assignment of the diagnosis mandates a treatment prescription despite considerable controversy among researchers and practitioners as to the relative effectiveness of drug treatment versus psychotherapy.

Some conditions bear enough of the characteristics usually associated with illness to be reasonably referred to as mental illnesses. But the jury is still out as to the extent organic factors play in schizophrenia. While there is increasing evidence of organic factors-including genetic factors and illness in the pregnant mother — playing a role in this condition, no organic factors at this point are known to be either necessary or sufficient. Similarly, there exists evidence suggesting that schizophrenia is a condition qualitatively distinct from other modes of living. On the other hand, there exists evidence questioning this view of schizophrenia as a clearly distinct illness. There is evidence that schizophrenia is the extreme end of a larger spectrum of "conditions." And environmental factors clearly play a role in the prospects for the development of the condition and in its course.

If one concludes that schizophrenia is, indeed, largely a biological condition, then it would be reasonable to describe it as an illness. But what if one decides that environmental factors play a large role?

Once we get beyond the clearly organic conditions, the category of mental illness becomes metaphorical. There is nothing wrong with this. People make sense of the world largely through metaphors. The illness metaphor can be illuminating, but it can also be blinding. The question is whether applying it to the emotional problems and issues people face reveals hidden aspects, or covers over important characteristics. Thus, mental illnesses are like other physical illnesses in that they often appear to be involuntary and they can interfere with normal functioning and/or cause distress.

However, many uses of the mental illness construct ignore its metaphorical quality. Thus, it is sometimes presumed without question that anything diagnosed as a mental illness should be treated, despite the fact that the majority of those identified in epidemiological studies as having such a condition do not seek treatment. Others go so far as to form an equation whereby mental illness equals illness, illness means physical condition, and physical condition requires physical treatment. This logic underlies much of the overuse of medications and the downplaying of psychotherapy for problems in living that characterizes the last few decades.

Each of the three links in this equation is fallacious, of course. As I discussed above, mental illness may resemble other illnesses in certain ways, but in most cases definitely is not same thing. Certainly, if one extends the concept of illness to include mental conditions with no obvious organic cause then illness does not mean physical condition and there is no necessary reason that it should be treated, much less treated by physical interventions.

〜〜〜〜〜〜〜〜〜〜〜〜〜〜〜〜〜〜〜〜〜〜〜〜〜〜〜

1. The passage is mainly about _____ .
   A. the way mental illness is diagnosed and treated
   B. the value of psychotherapy in treating mental patients
   C. the improvements made in treating mental illness
   D. the danger in characterizing mental conditions as illness

2. The author uses the example of schizophrenia to make the point that _____ .
   A. mental illness is a kind of physical illness that needs treatment
   B. there is no conclusive evidence that mental conditions have a physical basis
   C. environmental factors rather than organic ones cause mental illness
   D. schizophrenia is most likely to be inherited from the maternal parent

3. In what way is the illness metaphor blinding concerning "mental illness"?
   A. Mental illness is often mistaken as a physical condition to be corrected.
   B. Applying the metaphor to emotional problems yields no ready treatment.
   C. The metaphor gives the impression that mental illness does not need treatment.
   D. The metaphor often confuses medical professionals about the severity of the illness.

4. One of the consequences resulting from "the equation" is the _____ .
   A. overuse of psychotherapy in treating mental illness
   B. ineffective medication for both mental and physical illnesses
   C. frequent use of medical treatment for mental illness
   D. ignorance of the sufferings of the mental patients

5. The word "fallacious" in the last paragraph most probably means _____ .
   A. misleading   B. critical   C. obscure   D. unnecessary

Passage Two

It's the Solution
这就是解决问题的方法
by Nell Boyce

human eggs don't freeze well — or so IVF specialists have always thought. But biologists in New Jersey now say they have overcome the problem, by abandoning the idea that eggs should be frozen in a solution that resembles body fluids.

The researchers have obtained high survival rates after cryopreserving and then thawing mouse eggs. If their technique also works with human eggs, then women whose eggs are frozen — before they undergo chemotherapy that damages their ovaries, for example — will have a better chance of becoming mothers.

Fertility centres routinely freeze sperm and embryos, but only a few births have been reported using frozen eggs. James Stachecki of the Institute for Reproductive Medicine and Science of St. Barnabas Medical Center in West Orange, New Jersey, wondered if the saline solution sued to freeze eggs was to blame.

Cells must be surrounded by a more concentrated solution during freezing. This pulls water out of the cells by osmosis and reduces the chances of ice crystals forming, which can damage cell structures. Cryobiologists usually use a saline designed to mimic body fluids.

But Stachecki suspected that sodium ions from such solutions were getting into the eggs and poisoning them. Instead, he decided to try a solution containing choline ions, which do not readily cross cell membranes. Choline is an organic molecule found in many plant and animal tissues, and is a constituent of B-complex vitamins. Cryopreservation experiments on other types of cells using choline solutions had produced promising results.

Using hundreds of mouse eggs, Stachecki and his colleagues found that the choline solution allowed 90 percent to survive freezing and thawing. And when the surviving eggs were fertilized, 60 percent developed into the ball of cells called a blastocyst.

"The results are very encouraging," says Rogery Gosden, a reproductive biologist at the University of Leeds. With conventional saline, only 50 percent of eggs survived freezing and just 10 percent of those fertilized went on to form a blastocyst.

"The plan now is to do more work in humans to test how well it works," says Stachecki. Several women have already volunteered to donate their eggs for the research. If the new technique works for humans, it may allow easier egg banking at fertility clinics.

1. New Jersey biologists differ from IVF specialists in that _____.
   A. they believe human eggs are like mouse eggs
   B. they believe women's ovaries will be damaged if egg-freezing technique is not used
   C. they don't try to preserve eggs in a solution that resembles body fluids
   D. they will provide women with better chances of becoming mothers

2. The passage indicates that _____.
   A. fertility centres seldom use frozen eggs for birth purposes
   B. survival rates with frozen sperm and eggs have not been satisfactory
   C. human eggs can hardly survive freezing conditions
   D. saline solution is no longer used to freeze human eggs

3. One reason cryobiologists use the saline solution is that _____.
   A. it can to a certain extent prevent ice crystals from forming within the cells
   B. it can function as body fluids
   C. it does not pull water out of the cells by osmosis during freezing
   D. it is a concentrated solution that freezes more easily and quickly

4. It seems that saline solution is characterized by the fact that _____.
   A. its sodium ions might harm the eggs

B. its choline ions do not readily enter cells

C. its choline exists in many plant and animal tissues

D. it will be a promising solution in cryopreservation

5. All of the following, EXCEPT _____ , are factors that encourage Stachecki's further cryopreservation experimentation.

A. higher percentage in mouse egg fertilization with choline solution than that with saline solution

B. choline solution's allowing for repeated egg freezing and thawing

C. the presence of a body of volunteers for the experimentation

D. the possibility of the new technique's effectiveness with human eggs

Passage Three

Synchronized Sex
性的同步

by Menno Schilthuizen

When the biological clocks of males and females are out of sync, their sex lives suffer. Or at least it does if they are melon flies, Japanese entomologists have found. They say that differences in daily rhythms might even promote the evolution of new species.

Takahisa Miyatake and Toru Shimizu of Okinawa Prefectural Agricultural Experimental Station made their discovery while studying the melon fly *Bactrocera cucurbitae*, a notorious pest of melons, couregttes and other members of the gourd family. By selective breeding from flies that were quickest to mature and mate, they built up a population of fast developing individuals. In a similar way, they also bred a line of slow developers. After 25 generations, the slow developers' larvae took more than 12 days to mature, while the fast developers matured in just 6 days.

To their surprise, Miyatake and Shimizu noticed that this was not the only difference between the two lines. In nature, the melon flies mate around dusk. But among the fast developers, sexual activity peaked in late afternoon, one hour before dusk, while the slow developers only started getting interested in sex around three-and-a-half hours after nightfall. "Apparently, both rhythms are regulated by the same clock gene," says Miyatake.

To see how this would influence the ability of the slow and the fast lines to crossbreed, the researchers marked flies from both lines, put them together in cages, and watched to see which mated with expected, which as most matings took place between males and females from the same line. The finding, which will be reported in the journal *Evolution*, suggests that differences in body clocks could cause new species to evolve.

Miyatake says the behaviour of some species suggest they may have arisen this way. "Many closely related species of insect differ in their daily mating time," he says. "For example, the only thing that separates two other flies, *Bactrocera tryoni* and *bactrocera neohumeralis*, is the fact that the former mates at dusk, the latter in the daytime."

"This is interesting work," says Jeffrey Feder, an evolutionary geneticist who studies fruit flies at the University of Notre Dame in Indiana. "It is very exciting that Miyatake and Shimizu have shown how selection on the larvae can affect the mating pattern in adults and prevent crossbreeding."

Feder agrees that the effect could be important in the evolution of new species, especially when insects undergo a shift in lifestyle. For example, if a population of flies starts feeding on a new fruit that rots quickly, this could select for fast-developing larvae with a different mating time and which would not breed with the ancestral stock. "This is getting at the heart of what Darwin was saying in On the Origin of Species," says Feder.

1. It can be inferred from the first paragraph that _____.
   A. the Japanese entomologists have experimented with lots of insects on their sex lives
   B. melon flies are their only object of study
   C. melon flies differ from other insect species in their sex lives
   D. melon flies' sex lives have been confirmed to be affected by their biological clocks

2. Takahisa Miyatake and Toru Shimizu's selective breeding produced _____.
   A. new species of melon flies
   B. surprising differences between fast-developers and slow-developers
   C. the same clock gene that regulates melon flies' mating time
   D. 25 generations of larvae that differ in duration of maturation

3. Most matings occurred within the same line because _____.
   A. different lines are regulated by the same clock genes
   B. each individual line is subject to the same body clock
   C. the lines are not familiar with each other's mating patterns
   D. one line develops faster than the other line

4. Feder thinks that Miyatake and Shimizu's discovery is interesting partly because _____.
   A. it helps distinguish different species
   B. it suggests a way of preventing crossbreeding among fruit flies
   C. mating patterns among fruit flies have been discovered
   D. selection on the larvae has been part of their experiment

5. Which Darwinian theory is Feder referring to by his example in the last paragraph?
   A. Survival of the fittest.
   B. All related organisms are descended from common ancestors.
   C. The earth itself is not static but evolving.
   D. The Variation of Animals and Plants Under Domestication.

Clever Kitty
聪明的猫咪

by Duncan Graham-Rowe

The most ambitious artificial brain yet designed is taking shape in a laboratory in Colorado. The brain's developers aim to link it to a robot kitten called Robokoneko, which they hope will become one of the first superstars of artificial life.

"Observers won't need a PhD to appreciate that there is a brain behind it," says Hugo de Garis of Advanced Telecommunications Research in Kyoto, Japan, the brain's principal architect.

Genobyte, a company in Boulder, Colorado, is building De Garis's Cellular Automata Machine (CAM) brain under contract. It will contain nearly 40 million artificial neurons, compared with the few hundred neurons that most other specialists in artificial intelligence are working with. The CAM brain differs not only in its immense scale, but also in the fact that its neurons are real electronic devices rather than software simulations.

The CAM brain uses a special type of computer chip called a Field Programmable Gate Array (FPGA). Unlike conventional chips, the circuits in FPGAs can be reconfigured by altering the connections between their transistors. When De Garis conceived his project six years ago it was greeted with skepticism. "Many of my colleagues thought I was nuts," he says. But it has now become a practical proposition with the development of a new and exceptionally robust FPGA made by Xilinx, a company in San Jose, California.

The CAM brain will run on 72 linked FPGAs. At any one time these devices will act as a "module" containing 1,152 interconnected neurons. But the devices will be repeatedly reconfigured to represent 32,768 different modules. The brain remembers how the modules connect to each other, and uses the outputs of the modules it has already processed as inputs for others. A cycle through these modules, representing 37.7 million neurons, will be repeated 300 times every second.

To model the brain, De Garis uses some 450 million autonomous "cells" representing components such as the neurons themselves and the axons and dendrites that connect them. Each cell consists of several transistors within an FPGA. The CAM brain is scheduled for completion in March.

Neural networks must be fine-tuned to perform particular tasks. But no human programmer could write the software needed to refine a network as complex as the CAM brain. Instead, this will be generated using an approach that simulates biological evolution. Through random mutations and breeding of the "genetic material" that describes the structure and connections of the network, the program will be evolved over many generations to get the optimum design. Robokoneko will not be built until this work has been completed on a computer simulation of the robot cat. Some experts, however, doubt whether building ever bigger neural networks will bring any fundamental insights into the mysteries of cognition, such as how the brain builds a representation of the world. "The point is that these puzzles are not puzzles because our neural models are not large enough," argues Igor Aleksander, a neural systems engineer at Imperial College London.

The CAM brain's developers admit that they can't predict exactly how it will perform when it is linked to Robokoneko. But they hope it will for the first time allow a robot to interact with stimuli in its environment to develop the sort of intelligence seen in animals. "What is so special about this neural network is a much higher degree of biological relevance," says Michael Korkin of Genobyte.

1. By saying "Observers won't need a PhD to appreciate that there is a brain behind it", Hugo de Garis probably means _____.
   A. the robot kitten will be very much like a real-life kitten
   B. normally observers need PhDs to help appreciate artificial life
   C. anybody will see that there is a brain connected to the robot kitten
   D. only PhDs can understand the artificial brain
2. Which of the following is NOT mentioned as a difference between the CAM brain and other artificial brains?
   A. The CAM brain is made under contract, while other brains are not.
   B. The CAM brain is more complicated than other artificial intelligence in terms of the number of neurons.
   C. Other artificial intelligence uses software simulations as its neurons.
   D. FPGAs are used in CAM brains but not in other artificial intelligence.
3. According to the passage, de Garis's project came to be accepted mainly because of _____.
   A. the existence of 72 FPGAs
   B. the Xilinx's successful production of a FPGA
   C. the promising future of the artificial brain
   D. its possible wide-spread application in real life
4. In which of the following ways does the CAM brain seem to be working?
   A. 72 FPGAs are interconnected to 1,152 neurons.
   B. The brain can remember and use outputs and inputs from the FPGAs.
   C. Reconfigurable FPGAs, by way of the storage capacity, work fast in the form of millions of neurons.
   D. Millions of cells and transistors are used to power the FPGAs.
5. The passage seems to suggest all the following EXCEPT _____.
   A. the CAM brain, complicated as it is, cannot perform all tasks as we wish
   B. current software writers cannot effectively program the CAM brain to do complex tasks
   C. effective software for the CAM brain will take a long time to develop
   D. the building of the CAM brain finally leads to people's understanding of how knowledge is obtained

Model Test One
模拟测试（一）

Section 1: Vocabulary and Grammar

This section consists of 3 parts. Read the directions of each part before answering the questions. The time for this section is 25 minutes.

Part 1　Vocabulary Selection

In this part, there are 20 incomplete statements. Below each statement, there are 4 choices respectively marked by letters A, B, C, and D. Choose the word or phrase which best completes each statement. There is only ONE right answer.

1. The argument about the interpretation of the sentence _____ on the meaning of one word.
   A. hinged　　　B. hindered　　　C. headed　　　D. hunted

2. One of the old soldiers was penitent that they _____ all the prisoners after the battle.
   A. assassinated　B. eliminated　　C. massacred　　D. murdered

3. They will fight against _____ in order to create a fairer society.
   A. privacy　　　B. privilege　　　C. rights　　　D. power

4. Donkeys and camels are still widely used in some parts of the world as beasts of _____.
   A. cargo　　　B. freight　　　C. burden　　　D. lading

5. Professor White, my respected tutor, frequently reminds me to _____ myself of every chance to improve my English.
   A. assure　　　B. inform　　　C. avail　　　D. notify

6. He based his holiday plans on the _____ that his girlfriend was coming with him.
   A. hypothesis　B. synthesis　　C. thesis　　　D. crisis

7. Nowadays advertising costs are no longer in reasonable _____ to the total cost of the product.
   A. proportion　B. correlation　　C. connection　　D. correspondence

8. I promise never to get drunk _____.
   A. hence　　　B. therefore　　　C. henceforth　　D. thereby

9. His speech had at least the _____ of being short.
   A. value　　　B. merit　　　C. excellence　　D. perfection

10. After the _____ to the river the soldiers camped for the night.
    A. excursion　B. pilgrimage　　C. hike　　　　D. expedition

11. The pollution preventing project as well as several other issues is going to be discussed when the Congress is in _____ again next spring.
    A. assembly　　B. session　　　C. conference　　D. convention

12. Do you think that's a _____ Picasso?

    A. congenial   B. genial   C. genius   D. genuine

13. These causes produced the great change in the country that modernized the _____ of higher education from the mid-1860s to the mid-1880s.

    A. branch   B. category   C. domain   D. scope

14. You should _____ the gears of your car.

    A. degenerate   B. dedicate   C. lubricate   D. generate

15. His red hair and short _____ made him easy to recognize.

    A. statue   B. statute   C. stature   D. status

16. Each species has certain _____ features.

    A. distinguish   B. distinguished   C. distinct   D. distinctive

17. High boots were the _____ for women last year.

    A. vulgar   B. vintage   C. vogue   D. vague

18. The condition of the accident victim is deteriorating. I doubt if he will _____ .

    A. pull through   B. pull out   C. pull across   D. pull over

19. To _____ his great ambition of becoming well-known all over Denmark, Andersen, though very young, left home for Copenhagen to make his fortune.

    A. hold up to   B. let up to   C. hang up to   D. live up to

20. We all know that normal human daily cycle of activity is of some 7 − 8 hours' sleep alternating with some 16 − 17 hous' wakefulness and that, broadly speaking, the sleep normally _____ the hours of darkness.

    A. testifies to   B. caters to

    C. coincides with   D. reckons with

Part 2　Vocabulary Replacement

This part consists of 15 sentences; in each sentence one word or phrase is underlined. Below each sentence, there are 4 choices respectively marked by letters A, B, C, and D. Choose the word or phrase that can replace the underlined part without causing any grammatical error or changing the principal meaning of the sentence. There is only ONE right answer.

1. Some critics have praised James Michener's epic novels for their facts but deplored their characterization.

    A. emulated   B. ridiculed   C. lamented   D. complimented

2. The hotel manager became suspicious of those people who were loitering in the lobby.

    A. bustling   B. chatting   C. meddling   D. loafing

3. The situation is bound to deteriorate.

    A. come about   B. continue   C. become worse   D. improve

4. Many types of lilies with ornate blossoms are cultivated for their beauty.

    A. messy   B. dainty   C. numerous   D. elaborate

5. Parents who speak equivocally may cause their children to become confused.

    A. ambiguously   B. angrily

    C. adversely   D. contemptuously

6. Critics of the Wright brothers thought that the idea of a flying machine was totally preposterous.

    A. attractive   B. boring   C. absurd   D. immoral

7. The officer is gallant in his behavior toward the woman.

    A. brave   B. pertinent   C. obedient   D. courtly

8. An increasing proportion of our population, unable to live without advanced medical involvement, will become progressively more reliant on expensive technology.

    A. interference   B. interruption   C. intervention   D. interaction

9. Alice Walker's graphic depiction of the lives of Black people in the south has established her as one of the most promising contemporary writers in the states.

    A. optimistic   B. humorous   C. somber   D. vivid

10. France's renewal of nuclear testing in the South Pacific last month triggered political debates and mass demonstrations.

    A. assumption   B. consumption   C. presumption   D. resumption

11. They pressed ahead with the liquidation of hostile elements among people.

    A. examination   B. extermination   C. investigation   D. execution

12. The guests were in a jubilant mood as the wedding began.

    A. exultant   B. conciliatory   C. reverent   D. receptive

13. I have been a little bit appalled by the levity with which some of our politicians discuss this issue.

    A. contempt   B. insecurity   C. frivolity   D. compunction

14. The turning point for me is that I finally have the confidence to believe that I can make something of my life, without resorting to crime.

    A. turning to   B. turning over   C. turning in   D. turning up

15. I was surprised to find that they all fell in with my suggestion at once.

    A. turned down   B. agreed to   C. cut off   D. carried out

Part 3   Error Correction

This part consists of 15 sentences; in each sentence there is an underlined part that indicates an error. Below each sentence, there are 4 choices respectively marked by letters A, B, C, and D. Choose the word or phrase that can replace the underlined part so that the error is corrected. There is only ONE right answer.

1. Statistics showed that approximately 40 percent of all marriages in the United States end in divorce.

    A. show   B. have shown   C. shows   D. are shown

2. Were it not for the timely investment from the general public, our company would not be so thriving as it is.

    A. Be it not

    B. Should it not be

    C. It had not been

    D. Had it not been

3. As early as in 1647 Ohio made a decision that free, tax-supported schools must be established in every town to have 50 households or more.

    A. has   B. having   C. having had   D. had

4. Turn on the television or open a magazine, and you often see advertisements showing happy and balanced families.

    A. are often seeing

    B. will often see

    C. have often seen

    D. would often be seeing

5. The trumpet player was certainly loud. But I wasn't bothered by his loudness than by his lack of talent.

    A. more than   B. like   C. as   D. so much as

6. An increase in a nation's money supply, without an accompanying increase in economic activity, tending to result in higher prices.

    A. tends   B. tends the   C. tending   D. will tend to

7. enough logical reasons, the fewer seeds, fewer plants grow.

    A. the plants fewer

    B. the fewer plants

    C. plants grow fewer

    D. the plants grow fewer

8. We were pleased to see that, besides our own villagers, the audience was made up of a fair number of people out of around villages.

    A. off around villages

    B. off villages around

    C. from around villages

    D. from villages around

9. If you want to go to the City Hall from there, take the No. 35 bus.

    A. /   B. an   C. a   D. some

10. I think we will arrive enough early this evening.

    A. enough early arrive

    B. early enough arrive

    C. arrive early enough

    D. early arrive enough

11. The accident clearly resulted as your carelessness.

    A. in   B. on   C. for   D. from

12. Saving time and labor, cartoonists generally draw the hands of their characters with only three fingers and a thumb.

    A. Save   B. Saved   C. To save   D. The saving

13. Hadn't my car broken down, I might caught the train.

    A. would have caught

    B. might catch

    C. could catch

    D. had caught

14. A line segment, which is part of a straight line, begins at one point ending at another.

    A. and ends   B. ends   C. by ending   D. the end is

15. We had better wait for your girlfriend Juliet, <u>didn't</u> we?

    A. don't   B. hadn't   C. won't   D. shan't

Section 2: Reading Comprehension

In this section you will find after each of the passages a number of questions or unfinished statements about the passage, each with 4 (A, B, C and D) choices to complete the statement. You must choose the one which you think fits best. The time for this section is 75 minutes.

Questions 1 –5 are based on the following passage.

Non-indigenous (non-native) species of plants and animals arrive by way of two general types of pathways. First, species having origins outside the United States may enter the country and become established either as free-living populations or under human cultivation-for example, in agriculture, horticulture, aquaculture, or as pets. Some cultivated species subsequently escape or are released and also become established as free-living populations. Second, species of either US or foreign origin and already within the United States may spread to new locales. Pathways of both types include intentional as well as unintentional species transfers. Rates of species movement driven by human transformations of natural environments as well as by human mobility-through commerce, tourism, and travel-greatly exceed natural rates by comparison. While geographic distributions of species naturally expand or contract over historical time intervals (tens to hundreds of years), species-ranges rarely expand thousands of miles or across physical barriers such as oceans or mountains.

Habitat modification can create conditions favorable to the establishment of non-indigenous species. Soil disturbed in construction and agriculture is open for colonization by non-indigenous weeds, which in turn may provide habitats for the non-indigenous insects that evolved with them. Human-generated changes in fire frequency, grazing intensity, as well as soil stability and nutrient levels similarly facilitate the spread and establishment of non-indigenous plants. When human changes to natural environments span large geographical areas, they effectively create passages for species movement between previously isolated locales. The rapid spread of the Russian wheat aphid to fifteen states in just two years following its 1986 arrival has been attributed in part to the prevalence of alternative host plants that are available when wheat is not. Many of these are non-indigenous grasses recommended for planting on the forty million or more acres enrolled in the US Department of Agriculture Conservation Reserve Program.

A number of factors perplex quantitative evaluation of the relative importance of various entry pathways. Time lags often occur between establishment of non-indigenous species and their detection, and tracing the pathway for a long-established species is difficult. Experts estimate that non-indigenous weeds are usually detected only after having been in the country for thirty years or having spread to at least ten thousand acres. In addition, federal port inspection, although a major source of information on non-indigenous species pathways, especially for agriculture pests, provides data only when such species enter via closely-examined routes. Finally, some comparisons between pathways defy quantitative analysis-for example, which is more "important": the entry path of one very harmful species or one by which many but less harmful species enter the country?

1. Which of the following statements about species movement is best supported by the passage?

   A. Human factors affect species movement rates more than its long-term amount.

   B. Natural expansions of species account for their slow natural contractions.

   C. Natural environments created by human activities contribute much to species movement.

   D. Long-range movement of species depends on the geographic extent of human mobility.

2. According to the passage, the US Department of Agriculture _____.

   A. is liable for the fast distribution of the Russian wheat pest

   B. fails to isolate the Russian wheat aphid in limited locales

   C. provides data about foreign species entering the country by regulated routes

   D. is responsible for introducing harmful plants onto federal lands

3. It can be inferred that all of the following affect the movement of species EXCEPT _____.

   A. earth fertility   B. import restrictions

   C. natural obstacles   D. fire disasters

4. To determine the entry pathway for a non-native species is LEAST likely to depend on _____.

   A. whether the species is considered to be a pest

   B. whether the species enters by a closely-checked route

   C. the rate at which the species extends geographically

   D. the magnitude of the average number of the species

5. Which of the following may best express the chief purpose of the last paragraph?

   A. To explain the difficulties in tracing the pathways for long-established species.

   B. To describe the events usually leading to the detection of a non-indigenous species.

   C. To identify the problems in assessing the weight of entry tracks for foreign species

   D. To discuss the role of time lags and geographic expansion of species in species detection.

Questions 6 – 10 are based on the following passage.

Dreams have always held a universal fascination. Some primitive societies believe that the soul leaves the body and visits the scene of the dream. Generally, however, dreams are accepted to be illusions, having much in common with day dreams — the fantasies of our waking life. When dreaming, however, one tends to believe fully in the reality of the dream world, however inconsistent, illogical and odd it may be.

Although most dreams apparently happen spontaneously, dream activity maybe provoked by external influences. "Suffocation" dreams are connected with the breathing difficulties of a heavy cold, for instance. Internal disorders such as indigestion can cause vivid dreams, and dreams of racing fire-engines may be caused by the ringing of an alarm bell.

Experiments have been carried out to investigate the connection between deliberately inflicted pain and dreaming. For example, a sleeper pricked with a pin perhaps dreams of fighing a battle and receiving a severe sword wound. Although the dream is stimulated by the physical discomfort, the actual events of the dream depend on the associations of the discomfort in the mind of the sleeper.

A dreamer's eyes often move rapidly from side to side. Since people born blind do not dream visually and do not manifest this eye activity, it is thought that the dreamer may be scanning the scene depicted in his dream. A certain amount of dreaming seems to be a human requirement-if a sleeper is roused every time his eyes begin to move fast, effectively depriving him of his dreams, he will make more eye movements the following night.

People differ greatly in their claims to dreaming. Some say they dream every night, others only very occasionally, individual differences probably exist, but some people immediately forget dreams and others have good recall.

Superstition and magical practices thrive on the supposed power of dreams to foretell the future. Instances of dreams which have later turned out to be prophetic have often been recorded, some by men of the highest intellectual integrity. Although it is better to keep an open mind on the subject, it is true that the alleged power of dreams to predict future events still remains unproved.

Everyone knows that a sleeping dog often behaves as though he were dreaming, but it is impossible to tell what his whines and twitches really mean. By analogy with human experience, however, it is reasonable to suppose that at least the higher animals are capable of dreaming.

Of the many theories of dreams, Freud's is probably the best known. According to Freud, we revert in our dreams to the modes of thought characteristic of early childhood. Our thinking becomes concrete, pictorial and non-logic, and expresses ideas and wishes we are no longer conscious of. Dreams are absurd and unaccountable because out conscious mind, not willing to acknowledge our subconscious ideas, disguises them. Some of Freud's interpretations are extremely fanciful, but there is almost certainly some truth in his view that dreams express the subconscious mind.

6. According to the passage, the dream world has the qualities of being _____.

    A. inconsistent, illogical, and strange   B. unreal, unreasonable, and odd

    C. vivid, strange, and inconsistent   D. illusionary, fantastic, and uncommon

7. According to the passage, indigestion _____.

    A. will definitely cause frightening dreams

    B. will cause dreams of difficult breathing

    C. belongs to internal causes of dream activity

    D. belongs to external causes of dream activity

8. We can conclude from the passage that _____.

    A. dreams occurring in our sleep are quite different from day dream

    B. dreaming is probably unnecessary in our life

    C. sine human beings dream, so may those more intelligent animals

    D. there is plenty of proof available that dreams foretell the future

9. Which of the following may most adequately sum up the ideas of the third paragraph?

    A. Science and dream sequence.

B. How pain may affect dreams.

C. How the mind conditions dreams.

D. The discomfort in the mind of the sleeper in relation with the dream.

10. Which of the following can be a proper title for the passage?

    A. Dreams and their functions   B. Varieties of dreams

    C. Dreams — what do they mean?   D. Dreams and superstitions

Questions 11 –15 are based on the following passage.

    Edgar Snow was a reporter and a journalist. He was a doer, a seeker of facts. His mature years were spent in communicating to people-he was an opener of minds, a bright pair of eyes on what went on about him. Fortunately, he went to many places, knew many people, saw many things; thus he communicated from depth and involvement. Suspicious of dogma, he stated in his autobiography. "What interested me was chiefly people, all kinds of people, and what they thought and said and how they lived-rather than officials, and what they said in their interviews and handouts about whatthey people' thought and said." In writing about people and the event which shaped or misshaped their lives, his point of view was essentially honest and searching-founded on his own inquiry and resting on a body of truth perceived with vision and with compassion. His valued friend and editor, Mary Heathcote, stated that to Edgar Snow, "true professionalism meant telling the truth as one saw it, with as many of the reasons for its existence as one could find out and as much empathy as possible for the people experiencing it…"

    That he is remembered mostly through *Red Star Over China* is understandable. The accounts in that book were of international importance and the experience for the author in getting those accounts was perhaps the most significant one in his life. Though it is typical of him what, after the acclaim the book received, he commented, "I simply wrote down that I was told by the extraordinary young men and women with whom it was my privilege to live at age thirty, and from whom I learned a great deal." That "great deal" spread from the pages of Red Star to alter the thinking of countless people — including many citizens of China who were led by it to action that drastically affected their own lives and the course of their country's future. An awesome realization of personal responsibility also came about at this point for the young journalist, one he was cognizant of the rest of his life — the discovery, as he heard of friends and students killed in a war they had been moved to join largely because of his reports, that his writing had taken on the nature of political action and that he, as a writer, had to be personally answerable for all he wrote.

    There were other texts which broke through ignorance and prejudice in similar ways: Far Eastern Front, Living China, Battle for Asia, People on Our Side, Journey To the Beginning, to name some of the eleven books he produced, as well as many pages of engaged reporting — of floods and famines, of wars declared and undeclared, of human dilemmas and indignities, of unsung heroes and unheralded sacrifices-a life's study of the impact of people and events from many lands known at first hand.

Ed represents what is best in American journalism — as did his compatriot Agnes Smedley and Jack Belden. They dedicated to action, to communication that would help lessen the need, help correct the injustices. A main objective of theirs, because they were there and they saw, because they were internationalists with concern for human welfare, values and dignity, was to contribute to an understanding of China and the crippling burdens she bore — in a world dominated by arrogance, greed, and ignorance.

11. According to the article, the writings of Edgar Snow were based on _____.

    A. facts of life   B. his own peep-hole view

    C. the officials' taste   D. his prejudiced imagination

12. Which of the following was NOT typical of Snow?

    A. Love of truth.

    B. Sympathy for the common people.

    C. Sense of responsibility for what he writes.

    D. Pride in his success.

13. The author's purpose in writing this article is to _____.

    A. describe the whole life of Snow

    B. praise Edgar Snow and his writings

    C. encourage people to learn from Edgar Snow

    D. encourage people to read *Red Star Over China*

14. According to the article, the life of Snow paralleled _____.

    A. the development of China's revolution

    B. the construction of New china

    C. the course of World War II

    D. all of the above

15. From the author using the phrase "a life's study", we may infer that this article _____.

    A. was written for Snow's life

    B. was written for describing Snow's study

    C. was written after Snow died

    D. was written before Snow died

Questions 16 – 20 are based on the following passage.

What is intelligence, anyway? When I was in the army, I received a kind of aptitude test that all soldiers took and, against a normal of 100, scored 160. No one at the base had ever seen a figure like that, and for two hours they made a big fuss over me. (It didn't mean anything. The next day I was still a buck private with KP — kitchen police — as my highest duty.)

All my life I've been registering scores like that, so that I have the complacent feeling that I'm highly intelligent, and I expect other people to think so, too. Actually, though, don't such scores simply mean that I am very good at answering the type of academic questions that are considered worthy of answers by the people who make up the intelligence tests — people with intellectual bents similar to mine?

For instance, I had an auto-repair man once, who, on these intelligence teste, could not possibly have scored more than 80, by my estimate. I always took it for granted that I was far more intelligent than he was. Yet, when anything went wrong with my car I hastened to him with it, watched him anxiously as he explored its vitals, and listened to his pronouncements as though they were divine oracles — and he always fixed my car.

Well, then, suppose my auto-repair man devised questions for an intelligence test. Or suppose a carpenter did, or a farmer, or, indeed, almost anyone but an academician. By every one of those thests, I'd prove myself a moron. And I'd be a moron, too. In the world where I could not use my academic training and my verbal talents but had to do something intricate or hard, working with my hands, I would do poorly. My intelligence, then, is not absolute but is a function of the society I live in and of the fact that a small subsection of that society has managed to foist itself on the rest as an arbiter of such matters.

Consider my auto-repair man, again. He had a habit of telling me jokes whenever he saw me. One time he raised his head from under the automobile hood to say: "Doc, a deaf-and-mute guy went into a hardware store to ask for some nails. He put two fingers together on the counter and made hammering motions with the other hand. The clerk brought him a hammer. He shook his head and pointed to the two fingers he was hammering. The clerk brought him nails. He picked out the sizes he wanted, and left. Well, doc, the next guy who came in was a blind man. He wanted scissors. How do you suppose he asked for them?"

In dulgently, I lifted my fight hand and made scissoring motions with my first two fingers. Whereupon my auto-repair man laughed and said, "Why, you dumb jerk, he used his voice and asked for them." Then he said smugly, "I've been trying that on all my customers today." "Did you catch many?" I asked. "Quite a few," he said, "but I knew for sure I'd catch you." "Why is that?" I asked. "Because you're so goddamned educated, Doc, I knew you couldn't be very smart."

And I have an uneasy feeling he had something there.

16. By calling his assignment to KP as "my highest duty", the author suggests that _____.

   A. KP is an important position in the army every soldier desires

   B. KP is a job of manual labor which does not require a special level of intelligence

   C. KP is his most important job in the army

   D. he is proud of his position as KP

17. From the first paragraph we can know that _____.

   A. the author did very well in an aptitude test and because of this he got a promotion

   B. although the author did very well in an aptitude test his job remained unchanged

   C. a lot of people flattered the author and suggested that his job be changed as he did so well in an aptitude test

   D. the author had grudge against his superior for he did not receive a lift in his position

18. In Paragraph 3 the author says: "By every one of those tests, I'd prove myself a moron. And I'd be a moron, too." The word "moron" here probably means _____ .
    A. a stupid person   B. a very mean person
    C. a person with high integrity   D. a person with high intelligence

19. According to the auto-repair man, why educated people "couldn't be very smart"?
    A. Educated people often give foolish answers to daily questions.
    B. Educated people usually assume that blind people cannot talk.
    C. Educated people are often clumsy when doing manual work.
    D. Educated people are so affected by their trained reasoning that they frequently lose their common sense.

20. What is the message of this article?
    A. A person becomes more intelligent when he receives more education.
    B. A person who scores high on an aptitude test is also smart on other matters.
    C. Intelligence test is relative because it takes different forms in different situations.
    D. A person who scores low on an aptitude test is unlikely to be able to repair a car.

Section 3: Cloze Test

In the following passage, there are 20 blanks representing the words that are missing from the context. You are to put back in each of the blanks the missing word. The time for this section is 20 minutes.

Some Things We Know about Language

Many things about language are a mystery, and many will always remain so. But some things we do know.

First, we know that all human beings have a language of some sort. _____ (1) is no race of men anywhere on earth so backward that it has _____ (2) language, no set of speech sounds by which the people communicate with one _____ (3). Furthermore, in historical times, there has never been a race of men _____ (4) a language.

Second, there is no such thing as a primitive language. There are many people _____ (5) cultures are underdeveloped, who are, as we say, uncivilized, but the _____ (6) they speak are not primitive. In all known languages we can see complexities _____ (7) must have been tens of thousands of years in development.

This has not _____ (8) been well understood; indeed, the direct contrary has often been stated. Popular ideas _____ (9) the language of the American Indians will illustrate. Many people have supposed that the Indians _____ (10) in a very primitive system of noises. Study has proved this _____ (11) be nonsense. There are, or were, hundreds of American Indian languages, and all of them _____ (12) out to be very complicated and very old. They are certainly _____ (13) from the languages that most of us are familiar with, but they are _____

（14）more primitive that English and Greek.

A third thing we know about language _____ （15）that all languages are perfectly adequate. That is, each one is a perfect _____ （16）of expressing the culture of the people who speak the language.

Finally, we _____ （17）that language changes. It is natural and normal for language to change; the _____ （18）languages which do not change are the dead ones. This is easy to _____ （19）if we look backward in time. Change goes in all aspects of language. _____ （20）features change as do speech sounds, and changes in vocabulary are sometimes very extensive and may occur very rapidly. Vocabulary is the least stable part of any language.

Model Test Two
模拟测试（二）

Section 1: Vocabulary and Grammar

This section consists of 3 parts. Read the directions of each part before answering the questions. The time for this section is 25 minutes.

Part 1 Vocabulary Selection

In this part, there are 20 incomplete statements. Below each statement, there are 4 choices respectively marked by letters A, B, C, and D. Choose the word or phrase which best completes each statement. There is only ONE right answer.

1. There has been a _____ increase in the form's sales.
   A. minor   B. marginal   C. nugatory   D. peripheral

2. People had been conscious of the problem before, but the new book made them aware of its
   _____.
   A. multitude   B. magnitude   C. altitude   D. latitude

3. A mirage is an optical _____.
   A. allusion   B. delusion   C. elusion   D. illusion

4. He felt insulted at the comment that his writing was all _____.
   A. junk   B. pollutant   C. garbage   D. waste

5. The Empire State Building was _____ on a grander scale than previous skyscrapers.
   A. executed   B. conceived   C. restrained   D. applauded

6. I bought a new sweater in a newly-open clothes-market. But what a pity it was that the sweater
   _____ when I washed it.
   A. shrank   B. contracted   C. shortened   D. condensed

7. Because of the strong sun the new sitting-room curtains have _____ from dark blue to grey.
   A. fainted   B. bleached   C. paled   D. faded

8. Corporations and labor unions have _____ great benefits upon their employees and members
   as well as upon the general public.
   A. conferred   B. granted   C. flung   D. submitted

9. A man has to make _____ for his old age by putting aside enough money to live when old.
   A. supply   B. assurance   C. provision   D. adjustment

10. The returns in the short _____ may be small, but over a number of years the investment
    will be well repaid.
    A. interval   B. range   C. span   D. term

11. I am not _____ with my roommate, but I have to share the room with her, because I have nowhere to live.

    A. concerned   B. compatible   C. considerate   D. complied

12. The judge ruled that the evidence was inadmissible on the grounds that it was _____ to the issue at hand.

    A. irrational   B. unreasonable   C. invalid   D. irrelevant

13. _____ to some parts of South America is still difficult, because parts of the continent are still covered with thick forests.

    A. Orientation   B. Access   C. Procession   D. Voyage

14. The movement of the moon conveniently provided the unit of month, which was _____ from one new moon to the next.

    A. measured   B. reckoned   C. judged   D. assessed

15. Foreign disinvestment and the _____ of South Africa from world capital markets after 1985 further weakened its economy.

    A. displacement   B. elimination   C. exclusion   D. exception

16. The restaurant is frequently _____ by tourists because of its famous cooking.

    A. patronized   B. serviced   C. utilized   D. congregated

17. Although the rates are high in comparison with other modes of transport, the savings in insurance and packing costs help to _____ this.

    A. compensate for   B. ward off   C. interfere with   D. ensue from

18. _____ , I picked up the phone and rang my sister in Australia.

    A. Off impulse   B. On guard   C. Off guard   D. On impulse

19. Medical scientists are _____ a breakthrough in cancer research.

    A. striving for   B. struggling against

    C. fighting against   D. contending for

20. I don't _____ building the park near a jet-port, which might make people suffer from defective hearing.

    A. subscribe to   B. ascribe to   C. describe to   D. contribute to

Part 2   Vocabulary Replacement

This part consists of 15 sentences; in each sentence one word or phrase is underlined. Below each sentence, there are 4 choices respectively marked by letters A, B, C, and D. Choose the word or phrase that can replace the underlined part without causing any grammatical error or changing the principal meaning of the sentence. There is only ONE right answer.

1. The destitute family is given an allowance.

    A. impoverished   B. anomalous   C. scandalous   D. perpetual

2. Frostbitten fingers and toes should be treated with lukewarm water.

    A. frigid   B. tepid   C. boiling   D. steamy

3. In 1937 Eleanor Roosevelt, who was a <u>discerning</u> stateswoman in her own right, became the first wife of a United States President to hold a press conference.

   A. perceptive   B. controversial   C. generous   D. respected

4. Some physicists have proposed that sunspots and solar wind have <u>negligible</u> effects on the earth's weather.

   A. undetermined   B. insignificant   C. unusual   D. indisputable

5. Giant horned dinosaurs like triceratops were probably among the favorite prey of the <u>ferocious</u> Tyrannosaurus rex.

   A. fierce   B. gigantic   C. prehistoric   D. piyeous

6. One out of five bridges in the United States is <u>outmoded</u>.

   A. incessant   B. intimate   C. obsolete   D. concrete

7. At first, the <u>delivery</u> of color pictures over a long distance seemed impossible, but, with painstaking efforts and at great expenses, it became a reality.

   A. transaction   B. transmission   C. transition   D. transformation

8. I was unaware of the critical points involved, so my choice was quite <u>assumptive</u>.

   A. rational   B. arbitrary   C. plausible   D. excessive

9. He stood aside, registering the <u>vivacity</u> of the school life.

   A. magnificence   B. confrontation   C. animation   D. panorama

10. There remains, of course, the risk of capital <u>depreciation</u>.

   A. depression   B. devaluation   C. deprivation   D. devastation

11. The Polynesians, who colonized Hawaii sometime between A. D. 500 and A. D. 1000, found uses for many <u>indigenous</u> plants.

   A. tropical   B. simple   C. native   D. strange

12. Alaska boasts of several climates due to its <u>lofty</u> mountains, warm ocean currents and frozen sea.

   A. towering   B. countless   C. rugged   D. ageless

13. You must be tired, but try to <u>hang on</u> till all the work's finished.

   A. stop working   B. keep working   C. wait   D. rest

14. She <u>all but</u> fainted when she heard the news.

   A. all over   B. seemingly   C. almost   D. obviously

15. Though she isn't British by birth, she's British citizen <u>by virtue of</u> her marriage to an Englishman.

   A. on account of   B. depending on   C. by means of   D. judging from

Part 3   Error Correction

This part consists of 15 sentences; in each sentence there is an underlined part that indicates an error. Below each sentence, there are 4 choices respectively marked by letters A, B, C, and D. Choose the word or phrase that can replace the underlined part so that the error is corrected. There is only ONE right answer.

1. To be equal to other things, a man who expresses himself effectively is sure to succeed more rapidly than a man whose command of language is poor.

    A. Were other things equal   B. Other things to be equal

    C. Other things being equal   D. Being equal to other things

2. We have been told that under no circumstances we may use the telephone in the office for personal affairs.

    A. may we use   B. we should use   C. did we use   D. we could use

3. Even though they had been living side by side for twenty years, the two neighbors are not very friendly to each other.

    A. had lived   B. have been living   C. having been lived   D. having been living

4. There is a man at the reception desk who seems very angry and I think he means making trouble.

    A. to make   B. to have made   C. to having made   D. having made

5. In spite of relatively costly, the diesel engine is highly efficient and needs servicing infrequently.

    A. Despite   B. It is   C. There is   D. Even though

6. Uniform acceleration occurs according to the rate of change remains the same over successive and equal intervals of time.

    A. if   B. under   C. because of   D. no matter

7. One who desires and impulses are not his own has no character.

    A. his   B. whose   C. whom   D. of whom

8. These surveys indicate that many crimes go having been unrecorded by the police, mainly because not all victims have reported them.

    A. unrecorded   B. to be unrecorded

    C. have been unrecorded   D. to have been unrecorded

9. He doesn't often agree with me. He thinks different from me.

    A. different to   B. different with   C. differently from   D. differently to

10. Japan is in the east of China.

    A. at   B. to   C. on   D. by

11. Professor Lee's book will show you how you have observed that can be used in other contexts.

    A. that you have observed   B. that how you have observed

    C. how that you have observed   D. how what you have observed

12. Supposing you can't write, what would you do?

    A. may not   B. couldn't   C. are unable   D. wouldn't

13. But for his help, I wouldn't succeeded.

    A. wouldn't have   B. hadn't   C. didn't   D. haven't

14. I have kept that portrait when I can see it every day, as it always reminds me of my university days in Cambridge.

    A. which   B. where   C. that   D. whether

15. Pass me the butter, <u>don't</u> you?

    A. will   B. won't   C. do   D. wouldn't

Section 2: Reading Comprehension

In this section you will find after each of the passages a number of questions or unfinished statements about the passage, each with 4 (A, B, C and D) choices to complete the statement. You must choose the one which you think fits best. The time for this section is 75 minutes.

Questions 1 – 5 are based on the following passage.

Sen. John F. Kerry's 11 – day mini-campaign on the theme of national security appears unlikely to produce sensational headlines or seize the country's attention — which is, on balance, to his credit. At a moment when the crisis in Iraq dominates the national discussion, Mr. Kerry is resisting the temptation to distinguish himself from President Bush with bold but irresponsible proposals to abandon the mission, even though that course is favored by many in his party. Nor has he adopted the near-hysterical rhetoric of former vice president Al Gore, who has taken to describing Iraq as the greatest strategic catastrophe in American history and calling US handling of foreign detainees an "American gulag."

Instead, Mr. Kerry is in the process of setting out what looks like a sober and substantial alternative to Mr. Bush's foreign policy, one that correctly identifies the incumbent's greatest failings while accepting the basic imperatives of the war that was forced on the country on Sept. 11, 2001. In his opening speech on the subject Thursday, Mr. Kerry reiterated one of the central tenets of Mr. Bush's policy: Lawless states and terrorists armed with weapons of mass destruction present "the single greatest threat to our security." He said that if an attack on the United States with unconventional weapons "appears imminent I will do whatever is necessary to stop it" and "never cede our security to anyone" — formulations that take him close to Mr. Bush's preemption doctrine.

Yet Mr. Kerry focused much attention on the president's foremost weakness, his mismanagement of US alliances. The Bush administration, he charged, "bullied when they should have persuaded. They have gone it alone when they should have assembled a team." Not only is the truth of that critique glaringly evident in Iraq and elsewhere, but Mr. Kerry is also right to suggest that repairing and reversing the damage probed will require a new president. Though Mr. Bush has belatedly changed course in response to his serial failures in Iraq, there is no evidence that he would pursue a more multilateral foreign policy if reelected.

Mr. Kerry's promise to "launch and lead a new era of alliances for the post 9/11 world" nevertheless does not add up to a strategy by itself. Tensions between the United States and countries such as France, Germany and South Korea predate George W. Bush and will not disappear if he leaves office; leaders in those nations have their own ambitions to challenge or contain American power. Strong alliances require a common strategic vision — and the vision offered so far by Mr. Kerry is relatively narrow. His Thursday speech focused on combating threats and on reducing dependence on Middle East oil; this week he will set out policies to block the spread of nuclear weapons. But he has had little to say about the good that the United States should seek to accomplish in the world. In an interview Friday, the candidate stressed that he has set out the "architecture" of his foreign policy and will talk more about goals and values in coming weeks. Thus far he has spoken more about protecting American companies and workers from foreign competition — something that hardly promotes alliances — than about fostering democracy in the Middle East or helping poor nations develop.

The emerging Kerry platform suggests that ultimately he would adopt many of the same goals as Mr. Bush. In his latest speech he rightly warned of the terrible consequences of failure in Iraq and, like Mr. Bush, embraced elections and the training of Iraqi security forces as the best way forward. His proposal for a U. N. high commissioner represents a slight upgrade on the deference already given by the White House to U. N. representative Lakhdar Brahimi; his call for a NATO-led military mission already has been aggressively pursued by the Bush administration, with poor results. There are, in fact, few responsible alternatives to the administration's course. Mr. Kerry's argument is that he has a better chance of making it work. It's not a bold offer to voters — but it's probably the right one.

1. The fact that Mr. Kerry did not propose to abandon the Iraq mission might _____.

   A. leave him in a disadvantaged position in the campaign

   B. result in a draw against President Bush in the campaign

   C. do him good instead of harm in the campaign

   D. bring about a general disappointment among the public

2. The second paragraph suggests that _____.

   A. Mr. Kerry and Mr. Bush both support the war on terrorism

   B. Mr. Kerry and Mr. Bush have very different views on national security issues

   C. Mr. Kerry prefers a more sober and substantial foreign policy than Mr. Bush

   D. Mr. Kerry has nothing new to offer in his opening speech

3. Mr. Kerry's attack against the president focused on _____.

   A. the latter's use of force against Iraq

   B. the difficulty in reassembling US alliances

   C. the need of a new president in directing the Iraq mission

   D. the latter's practice of unilateralism

4. In the author's view, the "good that the US should seek to accomplish in the world" might be

   _____.

   A. creating a strong alliance with France, Germany and South Korea

   B. combating threats and reducing dependence on Middle East oil

   C. fostering democracy in the Middle East or helping poor nations develop

   D. protecting American companies and workers from foreign competition

5. The author seems to suggest that _____.

   A. only when Mr. Kerry is in power can we judge whether he is right in his policies

   B. Mr. Kerry has not made powerful proposals in favor of his election campaign against Mr. Bush

   C. Mr. Kerry always follows Mr. Bush in his foreign policy guidelines

   D. Mr. Bush is still leading in the campaign

Questions 6 – 10 are based on the following passage.

The term *control* is highly — and unjustifiably — unpopular. Some of its unpopularity can be traced to educational and philosophical writings that have addressed issues of freedom, self-determination, self-worth, individuality, and other humanistic concerns — concerns often equated with liberal and permissive child-rearing and educational methods. They are the concerns that define the spirit of these times. No teacher wants to be nonliberal and restrictive. And there is little doubt that the deliberate exercise of control *is* restrictive. Is control therefore unethical?

There is, of course, no simple answer. If there were, there would be little controversy, and behaviorists and humanists would have much less to disagree about.

Consider, first, that control is not only inevitable but also necessary. There is no doubt that teachers, by virtue of their position and by virtue of their duties, have control. Indeed, it is not at all unreasonable to insist that the exercise of control is one of the teacher's most important duties. We are not speaking here of a fear-enforced control that might have been characteristic of some of yesterday's schools. Control can be achieved, or at least facilitated, in a variety of gentle ways, some of which can be learned.

Parents too control their children (or at least try), often by setting limits for their behavior. Part of the successful socialization process requires that children be prevented from engaging in behaviors that might be injurious to themselves or to others. Thus, parents do not permit their children to play with the dinner as it is cooking on the stove, to insert knives into electrical outlets, to jump off ladders, or to swim in dangerous waters. Less extreme instances of control involve the teaching of socially appropriate behavior, of values and morals — of "shoulds" and "should nots". It is less by accident than by virtue of parental control that children learn not to deface wall, steal other people's property, or kill the neighbor's god. In short, certain standards of behavior are learned at least partly as a function of parental control. Whether that control involves reinforcement, punishment, models, reasoning, or a combination of these and other strategies, we cannot avoid the fact that control is being exercised.

The classroom situation is not really very different. Teachers have often been described as acting *in loco parentis* — in the place of parents. More precisely, teachers have been urged to act in all ways as might a wise, judicious, and loving parent. And there is, in fact, no great incompatibility between values held in highest esteem by those who describe themselves as humanistically oriented and the techniques of behavior control that have been described by science. Love, empathy, warmth, genuineness, and honesty can go a long way toward ensuring a classroom climate corducive to and learning and development. In spite of these highly desirable qualities, however, discipline problems are not uncommon in classrooms. That teachers should judiciously administer rewards and punishment in an effort to maintain an effective educational environment does not mean that they care less for their students; indeed, in might well indicate that they care more.

6. The passage indicates that the current educational spirit is characterized by _____.

    A. unjustified control

    B. unpopularity

    C. liberal and permissive educational methods

    D. deliberate exercise of restrictions

7. Which of the following might behaviorists agree with?

    A. Students should not be granted too much freedom.

    B. Educational environments should ensure that students' individuality is fully promoted.

    C. Teachers are not to control, but to practice their duties.

    D. Parents are not humanistic enough towards their children's education.

8. Instances of parental control provided in the passage are aimed at _____.

    A. justifying the educational use of control

    B. informing educationalists of what is the right thing to do in the education of children

    C. persuading the public of the importance of ethics education

    D. assessing whether parents or teachers are more important in the education of children

9. It is indicated in the passage that _____.

    A. teachers have not been acting in the same ways as loving parents

    B. scientific use of control is of no big contradiction to humanistically oriented approaches in children's education

    C. discipline problems cannot be solved in humanistic ways

    D. punishment administered by the teacher is indicative of care for the children

10. Which of the following can be an appropriate title for the passage?

    A. Control or Liberty?

    B. Teacher's Control or Parent's Restriction?

    C. The Ethics of Control

    D. How to Use Control Scientifically?

Questions 11 – 15 are based on the following passage.

    Davis, California, like many other American cities, has been threatened by unchecked growth, swarming automobiles, and steeply rising energy costs. But unlike towns and cities which leave energy policy to the federal government or energy corporations, the citizens of Davis have acted on their own.

    After lengthy debate, Davis' City Council moved to curb growth. It turned against the automobile and embraced the bicycle as a means of transport. It sponsored an inquiry into energy uses and endorsed a series of measures aimed at reducing energy consumption by as much as one half. It cut back the use of petroleum-derived pesticides on the thousands of trees and shrubs that shade the city's streets, adopting instead a policy of biological control for insects. The city's own cars and trucks have been transformed into a fleet of compact vehicles. When a Davis employee has to get around town, he borrows a bike from the city rack. Davis even passed a law formally and solemnly sanctioning the clothesline.

The citizens of Davis have been involved in progressive city planning and energy conservation since 1968, when they persuaded the City Council to facilitate bicycle transportation by developing a system of bikeways. The City's general plan for development, drawn up in 1972, was based on questionnaires distributed to residents. When a survey of residents showed that automobiles represented 50 percent of energy consumption and space heating and cooling accounted for 25 percent, transportation and building construction became important focal points in the Davis plan.

Armed with survey information revealing that a building's east-west orientation on the lot, as well as its insulation, window area, roof and wall colors, overhang shading, and other factors greatly influenced space heating and cooling needs, the City Council drew up a building construction code which greatly reduced the cost of winter heating and eliminates the need for air conditioning even on Davis' hottest (114°) day. To demonstrate to local builders and developers methods for complying with the new code, Davis built two model solar homes, a single-family dwelling which takes advantage of natural southern exposure sunlight and a duplex adaptable to difficult siting situationswhere direct sunlight is blocked. Many of Davis' measures simply facilitate natural solar heating or sun-shading. Where most communities require that fences be built close to houses, Davis realized that practice meant blocking winter sunlight. New fences in Davis must be placed closer to the street, giving residents the benefit of natural solar heat in winter. Reducing required street widths provides more shade and saves asphalt to boot.

Davis' other energy conserving moves run the gamut — from a city ordinance encouraging cottage industry (to cut down on commuting and the need for new office building construction) to planting evergreens on city streets to reduce leaf pickup in the fall, from a ban on non-solar swimming pool heaters to a recycling center that supports itself by selling $3,000 worth of recyclables a month.

11. It can be inferred from the passage that Davis' City Council felt that _____.

    A. bicycles are healthful because they promote physical fitness

    B. control of automobile traffic is an essential part of energy management

    C. Davis citizens are always ready to do the most modern, up-to-date thing

    D. survey results should always determine legislative actions

12. Why did Davis build model solar homes instead of just one?

    A. To show what they could do when they put their minds to it.

    B. To show that even the hottest days could be mastered without air conditioning.

C. To demonstrate that even multiple dwelling in difficult locations could be solar powered.

D. To indicate that other cities were inadequate to the job.

13. The purpose of this article is probably to _____.

    A. congratulate Davis on their fine work

    B. help Davis spread their message

    C. chide the federal government for not doing enough to help cities like Davis

    D. hold up Davis as an example to other cities

14. It appears that Davis is _____.

    A. a "good old American town"

    B. committed to social justice

    C. a medium-to-small-size city

    D. blessed by a strong radical element in the population

15. The passage supports the conclusion that _____.

    A. Davis does not have much industry

    B. Davis cannot go any further than it already has toward being energy efficient

    C. the days of the automobile are numbered

    D. planning can solve all our problems

Questions 16 – 20 are based on the following passage.

The income-tax deadline approaches and some taxpayers' thoughts turn to it. Test time approaches and some students' thoughts turn to it. Temptation appears and some spouses consider it. Nowadays, cheating is on the rise. "You want something you can't get by behaving within the rules, and you want it badly enough, you'll do it regardless of any guilt or regret, and you're willing to run the risk of being caught." That's how Ladd Wheeler, psychology professor at the University of Rochester in New York, defines cheating.

Cheating represents the triumph of the "Brazen Rule" over the "Golden Rule", says Terry Pinkard, philosophy professor at Georgetown University in Washington D. C. "The Golden Rule says, Do unto others as you would have them do unto you. 'The Brazen Rule says, Do unto others as they would do unto you if they were in your place. '" Many experts believe cheating is on the rise. "We're seeing more of the kind of person who regards the world as a series of things to be manipulated. Whether to cheat depends on whether it's in the person's interest." He does, however, see less cheating among the youngest students.

Richard Dienslbier, psychology professor at the University of Nebraska in Lincoln, believes that society's attitudes account for much of the rise in cheating. "Twenty years ago, if a person cheated in college, society said: 'That is extremely serious; you will be dropped for a semester if not kicked out permanently, '" he says. "Nowadays, at the University of Nebraska, for example, it is the stated policy of the College of Arts and Sciences that if a student cheats on an exam, the student must receive an 'F' on what he cheated on. That's nothing. If you're going to fail anyway, why not cheat?"

Cheating is unethical, Pinkard says, whether it's massive fraud or failure to tell a store cashier you were undercharged. "You're treating other people merely as a means for your own ends. You're using people in ways they would not consent to. The cheater says, 'Let everybody else bear the burden, and I'll reap the benefits.'"

Cheaters usually try to justify their actions, says Rohert Hogan, chairman of the psychology department at the University of Tulsa in Oklahoma. "They never think it's their fault." Cheaters make justifications because they want to feel good about themselves, adds Wheeler. "They don't want to label themselves as a cheater. Also, they may be anticipating the possibility of getting caught, so they work on their excuse ahead of time." The most common justifications, psychologists say, include:

"I had to do it."

"The test was unfair."

"Everybody does it, and I have to cheat to get what's rightfully mine."

"The government wastes the money anyway."

"My wife (or husband) doesn't understand me, and we've grown apart."

Cheating is most likely in situation where the stakes are high and the chances of getting caught are low, says social psychologist Lynn Kahle of the University of Oregon in Eugene. In his study, a group of freshmen were allowed to grade their own tests, while secret, pressure sensitive paper indicated who changed answers. To raise the pressure, students were given an extremely high scores as the "average" for the test and told that those who failed would go before an inquiring board of psychologists. About 16 percent of the male students changed answers; among the females, about 30 percent cheated.

Everybody cheats, a little, some psychologists say, while others insist that most people are basically honest and some wouldn't cheat under any circumstances.

Despite the general rise in cheating, Pinkard sees some cause for hope: "I do find among younger students a much less tolerant attitude toward cheating." Perhaps, he says, the upcoming generation is less spoiled than the "baby boom" students who preceded them — and therefore less self-centered. "There seems to be a swing back in the culture."

16. The purpose of this passage is to _____.

A. convince the reader that cheating is immoral

B. discuss the varieties of and reasons for cheating

C. describe how cheaters cheat

D. suggest how to curtail cheating

17. According to the passage, which of the following is true?

A. It is ethical to cheat unless money is involved.

B. Failure to tell a store cashier you were undercharged is not considered cheating.

C. There has been a general rise in cheating.

D. Most cheaters are college students.

18. According to the passage, with which of the following would the author probably NOT agree?

    A. Cheating is often the result of intense pressure.

    B. Cheating is cheating, whether on a test or on income tax forms.

    C. Cheating is widespread and society is too tolerant.

    D. The Brazen Rule is a better rule than the Golden Rule.

19. When a person is caught cheating, it is most likely that he _____.

    A. pretends to apologize for what he has done

    B. pretends that he has no knowledge of what is going on

    C. ascribes his misconduct to some external motivation

    D. denies the fact in fearful anticipation of escaping punishment

20. Regarding the future of cheating, the author seems to be _____.

    A. depressed   B. optimistic   C. amused   D. bewildered

Section 3: Cloze Test

In the following passage, there are 20 blanks representing the words that are missing from the context. You are to put back in each of the blanks the missing word. The time for this section is 20 minutes.

Where do you really come from? And how did you get _____ (1) where you live today? DNA studies suggest that all humans today _____ (2) from a group of African ancestors who — about 60,000 years ago — _____ (3) a remarkable journey.

The Genographic Project is seeking to chart new _____ (4) about the migratory history of the human species by _____ (5) sophisticated laboratory and computer analysis of DNA contributed by hundreds of _____ (6) of people from around the world. In this unprecedented and real-time _____ (7) effort, the Genographic Project is closing the gaps of what science _____ (8) today about mankind's ancient migration stories.

The Genographic Project is a five-year _____ (9) partnership led by National Geographic Explorer-in-Residence Dr. Spencer Wells. Dr. _____ (10) and a team of renowned international scientists and IBM researchers, are _____ (11) cutting-edge genetic and computational technologies to analyze historical patterns in DNA _____ (12) participants around the world to better understand our human genetic roots. _____ (13) three components of the project are: to gather field research data _____ (14) collaboration with indigenous and traditional peoples around the world; to invite _____ (15) general public to join the project by purchasing a Genographic Project Public Participation Kit; _____ (16) to use proceeds from Genographic Public Participation Kit sales to further _____ (17) research and the Genographic Legacy Fund which in _____ (18) supports indigenous conservation and revitalization projects. The Project is anonymous, non-medical, _____ (19), non-profit and non-commercial and all results will be placed in the _____ (20) domain following scientific peer publication.

练习参考答案
第一单元

I. Grammar
A. Multiple Choices

1. B   2. A   3. C   4. C   5. D   6. C   7. D   8. A   9. C   10. B
11. D   12. C   13. A   14. B   15. B   16. C   17. D   18. D   19. B   20. D
21. C   22. A   23. A   24. B   25. A   26. C   27. A   28. C   29. D   30. A

（2. 此句中的 room 为不可数名词，解释为"余地，空间"。

11. 此句中 as well as physics 为插入语；主语 mathematics 为单数名词。

14. 此句中 bacteria 为复数，其单数形式为 bacterium。）

B. Error Correction

1. media → medium
2. pain → pains
3. supply → supplies
4. human being → human being's
5. defect → defects
6. attract → attracts
7. much → many
8. were → was
9. authorities → authority
10. remain → remains
11. confirm → confirms
12. leafs → leaves
13. were → was
14. jewelry → jewel
15. informations → information

（1. 此句中 media 为复数，其单数形式为 medium。

2. 此句中 pain 作不可数名词时解释为"痛苦"；作可数名词时解释为"努力"。

9. 此句中 authority 为不可数名词时解释为"权威，权力"；为可数名词时解释为"权威人士，当局，官方"。）

II. Cloze Test
Passage A

1. to   2. rather   3. Whether   4. phenomenon   5. women
6. not   7. have   8. compete   9. strictly   10. some
11. in   12. Insistence 13. means   14. sports   15. to
16. Strict   17. from   18. minds   19. a   20. has

Passage B

1. ancient   2. were   3. ancient   4. until   5. be
6. Olympic   7. myths   8. struggle   9. demigod   10. of
11. he   12. the   13. the   14. their   15. the
16. of   17. in   18. sport   19. initially   20. to

III. Reading Comprehension

Passage 1: 1. C   2. D   3. B   4. D   5. A

Passage 2: 1. C 2. D 3. C 4. B 5. A

Passage 3: 1. C 2. B 3. A 4. D 5. C

Passage 4: 1. B 2. D 3. A 4. C 5. B

第二单元

I. Grammar

A. Multiple Choices

1. A 2. C 3. B 4. A 5. B 6. C 7. D 8. C 9. B 10. B

11. D 12. A 13. B 14. D 15. D 16. A 17. A 18. B 19. C 20. B

21. A 22. B 23. C 24. C 25. B 26. D 27. D 28. D 29. B 30. B

B. Error Correction

1. quicklier → more quickly   2. considerable → considerate

3. fresher → fresh   4. historic → historical

5. coldly → cold   6. invaluable → valueless

7. the most east end → the east end 8. ill → sick

9. best → better   10. continual → continuous

11. possibly → possible   12. strangely → strange

13. great → greater   14. president → presidential

15. tenser → tense

(2. 此句中 considerable 意为"相当多的"；considerate 意为"考虑周到的，为他人着想的"，更符合句意。

 3. 此句中 when bought and eaten fresh 是时间状语从句 when they are bought and eaten fresh 的省略形式，形容词 fresh 做主语 they 的补足语。

 7. 此句中，有了 end，就没有必要再用 most 了。而且，表示方向的最高级有特别的拼写方式，如，"最东面"应该是 easternmost。

 11. 此句中，形容词 possible 作宾语 the rapid growth of the publish business 的补足语，因宾语太长而前置。）

II. Cloze Test

Passage A

1. different 2. sweeping 3. for 4. will 5. a

6. come 7. instead 8. canvas 9. while 10. knives

11. the 12. paint 13. cheap 14. Hold 15. Using

16. blade 17. would 18. different 19. Pressing 20. into

Passage B

1. had 2. few 3. raised 4. they 5. The

6. influenced 7. form 8. marked 9. tour 10. in

11. by 12. material 13. new 14. variety 15. Group

16. pursued   17. was   18. patient   19. autograph   20. mourned

III. Reading Comprehension

Passage 1: 1. C   2. A   3. C   4. B   5. C

Passage 2: 1. C   2. B   3. D   4. C   5. D

Passage 3: 1. C   2. C   3. D   4. A   5. B

Passage 4: 1. A   2. C   3. B   4. B   5. D

第三单元

I. Grammar

A. Multiple Choices

1. A   2. C   3. B   4. D   5. C   6. A   7. D   8. C   9. D   10. C

11. A   12. B   13. C   14. B   15. B   16. A   17. B   18. A   19. A   20. B

21. B   22. D   23. B   24. C   25. A   26. A   27. B   28. C   29. D   30. B

(11. 此句中，alone 在此为副词；lonely 只能作形容词用。)

B. Error Correction

1. universal → universally   2. pretty → prettily

3. lately → late   4. specially → especially

5. widely → wide   6. formerly → formally

7. fastly → fast   8. incredible → incredibly

9. unusual → unusually   10. nearly → near

11. enough careful → careful enough   12. indoor → indoors

13. most → almost   14. too far → far too

15. complete → completely

II. Cloze Test

Passage A

1. stay   2. wide   3. class   4. can   5. hotel

6. theme   7. in   8. keen   9. most   10. especially

11. modern   12. discovered   13. close   14. rated   15. and

16. The   17. as   18. out   19. lovers   20. as

Passage B

1. thick   2. to   3. quarters   4. and   5. wards

6. he   7. for   8. journey   9. the   10. with

11. village   12. homes   13. fertilize   14. electricity   15. heads

16. precious   17. this   18. style   19. the   20. coastal

III. Reading Comprehension

Passage 1: 1. A   2. C   3. D   4. C   5. B

Passage 2: 1. C   2. D   3. B   4. C   5. D

Passage 3: 1. C   2. B   3. D   4. D   5. B

Passage 4: 1. C   2. D   3. D   4. C   5. D

第四单元

I. Grammar

A. Multiple Choices

1. B   2. A   3. B   4. C   5. B   6. C   7. D   8. D   9. B   10. B

11. C   12. D   13. A   14. D   15. B   16. A   17. C   18. A   19. B   20. C

21. D   22. C   23. A   24. A   25. C   26. B   27. B   28. D   29. B   30. C

(11. 此句中，look sb. / sth. in the face 为固定词组，解释为"正视"。)

B. Error Correction

1. very next day → the very next day   2. the cash → cash

3. a fine weather → fine weather   4. same → the same

5. leading part → a leading part   6. a bottom → the bottom

7. a room → room   8. on trail → on the trail

9. with the laughter → with laughter   10. at a length → at length

11. an → a   12. the air → air

13. the women → women   14. greater population → a greater population

15. a → an

II. Cloze Test

Passage A

1. has   2. unlike   3. reason   4. was   5. late

6. an   7. of   8. poor   9. road   10. holiday

11. of   12. the   13. be   14. range   15. it

16. surrounded   17. private   18. very   19. range   20. and

Passage B

1. when   2. to   3. site   4. site   5. which

6. peninsula   7. lead   8. place   9. burden   10. backed

11. need   12. around   13. more   14. checking   15. explore

16. and   17. to   18. destination   19. drop   20. that

III. Reading Comprehension

Passage 1: 1. D   2. C   3. B   4. A   5. C

Passage 2: 1. C   2. A   3. B   4. A   5. C

Passage 3: 1. B   2. D   3. B   4. D   5. C

Passage 4: 1. A   2. B   3. C   4. C   5. D

第五单元

I. Grammar

A. Multiple Choices

1. A   2. A   3. C   4. C   5. D   6. B   7. C   8. B   9. C   10. A
11. D   12. C   13. B   14. A   15. B   16. A   17. A   18. C   19. C   20B
21. C   22. A   23. A   24. A   25. B   26. B   27. B   28. A   29. B   30A

（1. 此句中，be reported to do sth. 是固定用法；此处用完成被动式 be reported to have been done 更符合句意。

此句中两处 's 皆为 has 的缩略形式，所以用现在完成时的被动形式。

27. 此句中，被动语态的动名词短语 being jailed 作介词 besides 的宾语。）

B. Error Correction

1. translated → been translated
2. amplify → be amplified
3. being given → been given
4. completed → was completed
5. exposed → been exposed
6. didn't find → was not found
7. follow → be followed
8. have been → have
9. seeing → being seen
10. had broken → had been broken
11. has calculated → has been calculated
12. swept → were swept
13. calls → is called
14. be lasted → last
15. crippled → was crippled

II. Cloze Test

Passage A

1. nation   2. the   3. such   4. or   5. than
6. usefulness   7. much   8. psychological   9. enormous   10. The
11. in   12. in   13. was   14. but   15. were
16. word   17. necessary   18. Any   19. today   20. societies

Passage B

1. human   2. preserve   3. examining   4. such   5. or
6. or   7. well   8. crime   9. the   10. the
11. therefore   12. inform   13. role   14. is   15. the
16. how   17. decay   18. most   19. and   20. institutions

III. Reading Comprehension

Passage 1: 1. C   2. D   3. A   4. C   5. A
Passage 2: 1. D   2. C   3. B   4. A   5. A
Passage 3: 1. B   2. C   3. B   4. C   5. D
Passage 4: 1. A   2. D   3. B   4. C   5. D

第六单元

I. Grammar

A. Multiple Choices

1. C 2. A 3. A 4. D 5. A 6. C 7. C 8. D 9. C 10. B
11. C 12. C 13. A 14. A 15. B 16. A 17. A 18. A 19. C 20. D
21. B 22. D 23. C 24. D 25. B 26. B 27. A 28. A 29. A 30. C

（5. 此句中，recommend 后面的宾语从句用虚拟语气，即 passengers（should）not smoke during the flight。

6. 此句为与过去事实相反的虚拟句，条件句用的是 if I had realized you were busy 的倒装形式。

7. 此句为虚拟句，前部分为隐蔽式条件句，可还原为 If there had not been electronic computers, much of today（s advanced technology would not have been achieved.

13. 此句中，insist 后跟的宾语从句用虚拟语气，即 he（should）do everything he could to make sure of Mary's happiness。

16. 此句为假设条件被隐蔽的虚拟句，可还原为 If Mary had received my letter, she would have replied before now。

21. 此句为与现在事实相反的虚拟句，且后部分用倒装形式，还原后即为 if there should be a sudden loud noise。

26. 此句为假设条件被隐蔽的虚拟句，可还原为 If they had been done by hand, the millions of calculations would have lost all practical value by the time they were finished.

28. 此句中的 or 意为"否则"，此句为假设条件被隐蔽的虚拟句。

30. 此句为倒装形式的虚拟条件句，相当于 If there should be any trouble with the boiler，与将来可能情况相反。）

B. Error Correction

1. devoted → be devoted
2. could be → (should) be
3. was → were
4. go → went
5. might get → (should) get
6. arrived → had arrived
7. was called → (should) be called
8. am → were
9. is → be
10. was → were
11. make → have made
12. must take → (should) take
13. is → were
14. went → (should) go
15. I had known → Had I known / If I had known

（1. appropriate 后面的从句用虚拟语气。
7. suggest 后面的从句用虚拟语气。
11. 此句为假设条件被隐蔽的虚拟句。
15. 此句为与过去事实相反的虚拟句。）

II. Cloze Test

Passage A

1. deep 2. a 3. its 4. action 5. a

6. His	7. widely	8. as	9. of	10. days
11. his	12. been	13. running	14. support	15. candidates
16. in	17. poisonous	18. when	19. more	20. the

Passage B

1. from	2. president	3. against	4. had	5. said
6. Clinton	7. was	8. and	9. war	10. more
11. signature	12. however	13. kept	14. new	15. president's
16. develop	17. second	18. could	19. after	20. Bush

III. Reading Comprehension

Passage 1:	1. D	2. C	3. A	4. B	5. A
Passage 2:	1. B	2. C	3. A	4. B	5. D
Passage 3:	1. D	2. A	3. C	4. D	5. D
Passage 4:	1. C	2. C	3. A	4. B	5. D

第七单元

I. Grammar

A. Multiple Choices

1. C 2. A 3. A 4. A 5. D 6. C 7. C 8. A 9. A 10. D
11. C 12. A 13. C 14. D 15A 16. C 17. C 18. B 19. C 20. A
21. D 22. C 23. B 24. C 25. B 26. A 27. A 28. A 29. C 30. D

(6. 此句中, be considerate of sth. 为固定词组, 意为 "某事考虑周到"。

11. 此句中, abide by 为固定词组, 意为 "遵守 (法律、决定等)"。

17. 此句中, be reconciled to 为固定词组, 意为 "顺从、听从"。)

B. Error Correction

1. upon → in
2. count on → count for
3. equal with → equal to
4. out → from
5. of which → in which
6. over → through
7. for → at
8. along → for
9. for → of
10. with → by
11. on → in
12. from → by
13. out → beyond
14. among → between
15. from behalf of → on behalf of

(2. 此句中, count much for 为固定词组, 意为 "关系重大, 很有价值"。

15. 此句中, on behalf of 为固定词组, 意为 "为……的利益"、"代表某人"。)

II. Cloze Test

Passage A

1. that 2. or 3. its 4. written 5. development

6. with	7. fast	8. you'll	9. of	10. difference
11. word	12. what	13. above	14. behavior	15. rights
16. served	17. for	18. crops	19. raised	20. meaning

Passage B

1. as	2. there	3. ourselves	4. responses	5. what
6. United	7. to	8. today	9. the	10. other
11. of	12. argue	13. schools	14. of	15. such
16. take	17. about	18. you	19. aware	20. listen

III. Reading Comprehension

Passage 1:	1. D	2. C	3. B	4. A	5. B
Passage 2:	1. A	2. C	3. B	4. B	5. D
Passage 3:	1. D	2. A	3. C	4. C	5. B
Passage 4:	1. C	2. A	3. A	4. D	5. B

第八单元

I. Grammar

A. Multiple Choices

1. D	2. B	3. A	4. D	5. A	6. B	7. A	8. A	9. C	10. B
11. B	12. A	13. B	14. B	15. D	16. C	17. D	18. C	19. D	20. C
21. B	22. B	23. C	24. C	25. A	26. C	27. C	28. B	29. C	30. A

（2. 此句中，which 引导的非限制性定语从句代表前面整个句子的内容。

4. 此句为介词提前的定语从句，即 up to half of them are from overseas。

9. 此句中，as 是代词，指代逗号后面的主语从句。

13. 两个逗号之间的部分为插在主句当中的定语从句。

19. 此句中，which 引导的非限制性定语从句代表前面整个句子的内容。

23. 此句为介词提前的定语从句。

24. 两个逗号之间的部分为插在主句当中的定语从句。）

B. Error Correction

1. who → in which	2. whom → whose
3. that → which	4. which → with which
5. which → whose	6. what → as
7. when → that	8. them → which
9. where → which/that	10. which → that
11. when → which	12. that → where
13. where → of which	14. which → whom
15. which → whom	

（3. 此句中，which 引导的非限制性定语从句代表前面整个句子的内容。

7. 此句中，关系代词 that 在定语从句中作宾语，不能用关系副词 when 替代。）

II. Cloze Test

Passage A

1. Story	2. Visitors	3. focuses	4. learning	5. uses
6. is	7. with	8. route	9. a	10. the
11. be	12. onto	13. adding	14. fascinating	15. stages
16. get	17. stations	18. then	19. will	20. incentive

Passage B

1. marry	2. follows	3. folk	4. pinning	5. serenading
6. ends	7. the	8. of	9. often	10. parents
11. until	12. in	13. families	14. are	15. for
16. urban	17. rural	18. child	19. home	20. duties

III. Reading Comprehension

Passage 1:	1. B	2. C	3. B	4. A	5. C
Passage 2:	1. D	2. B	3. B	4. D	5. C
Passage 3:	1. D	2. A	3. C	4. D	5. C
Passage 4:	1. A	2. D	3. B	4. D	5. C

第九单元

I. Grammar

A. Multiple Choices

1. B 2. C 3. A 4. B 5. A 6. D 7. C 8. A 9. A 10. A

11. A 12. A 13. B 14. C 15. D 16.1B B 18. C 19. B 20. A

21. B 22. C 23. C 24. C 25. B 26. A 27. A 28. A 29. C 30. A

（6. 被动语态的现在分词短语 being played 用作 those（roles）的定语，表示"正在被扮演的角色"。

20. 过去分词 seen 表被动；when seen alone 相当于时间状语从句 when it is seen alone。

23. 现在分词 appearing 表主动；when appearing at the door 相当于时间状语从句 when she was appearing at the door。

24. 现在分词 thinking 表主动；when thinking about substances 相当于时间状语从句 when they are thinking about substances。

27. 现在分词短语 taking place 相当于定语从句 that are taking place。)

II. Error Correction

1. believed → believing   2. Seeing → Seen

3. were → being   4. involving → involved

5. Have → Having   6. adding → added

7. earning → earned   8. keeping → kept

9. picking → being picked   10. gathering → gathered

11. is called → called   12. is required → required

13. unpreparing → unprepared   14. Having eaten → Eating

15. depended → depending

（3. 此句中，so many representatives being absent 为带主语的独立分词结构，表示原因。

  7. 此句中，earned 意为 that are earned 或 that have been earned，作定语用，修饰 interest。

  11. 此句中，过去分词短语 called polygons 作定语，修饰 a class。

  13. 此句中，过去分词 unprepared 当形容词用，意为"未做好准备的"，在本句中作主语 they 的补足语。）

II. Cloze Test

Passage A

1. family   2. connected   3. go   4. dialect   5. goes

6. membership   7. between   8. significant   9. Arrernte   10. stations

11. within   12. from   13. the   14. areas   15. belongs

16. traditions   17. are   18. their   19. There   20. to

Passage B

1. differed   2. to   3. the   4. than   5. The

6. In   7. percent   8. Expanding   9. founders   10. of

11. high   12. system   13. universal   14. century   15. local

16. on   17. seeking   18. as   19. institutions   20. the

III. Reading Comprehension

Passage 1: 1. A   2. C   3. D   4. D   5. C

Passage 2: 1. B   2. C   3. A   4. B   5. A

Passage 3: 1. A   2. C   3. B   4. C   5. B

Passage 4: 1. B   2. D   3. B   4. A   5. D

第十单元

I. Grammar

A. Multiple Choices

1. C   2. D   3. B   4. A   5. B   6. C   7. D   8. B   9. B   10. D

11. A   12. C   13. A   14. D   15. D   16. B   17. D   18. B   19. C   20. A

21. C   22. B   23. A   24. D   25. D   26. C   27. D   28. C   29. B   30. C

（10. 此句中，when it comes to sth. 是一种特殊句型结构，意为"说到……"。

  11. 此句中，while 引导状语从句，表示主句和从句内容的对比。

  13. 句中用了 such... that... 结构。

  26. 此句中，for all that 为关联词结构，引导让步状语从句。）

B. Error Correction

1. Although → Now that   2. Since → As

3. since → before

4. until → if

5. after → when

6. if → unless

7. for → as

8. Unless → If

9. as → than

10. so that → in that

11. otherwise → so that

12. even if → in case

13. whether → when

14. Once → Although

15. because → until

II. Cloze Test

Passage A

1. at	2. were	3. resounding	4. fat	5. over
6. that	7. heart	8. of	9. found	10. sizes
11. to	12. heart	13. age	14. levels	15. and
16. differences	17. risk	18. risk	19. Those	20. fat

Passage B

1. was	2. people	3. the	4. government's	5. for
6. at	7. United	8. people	9. of	10. high
11. protein	12. The	13. with	14. overall	15. very
16. you	17. says	18. the	19. allows	20. calories

III. Reading Comprehension

Passage 1: 1. A	2. A	3. B	4. D	5. C
Passage 2: 1. D	2. B	3. A	4. B	5. C
Passage 3: 1. C	2. B	3. D	4. B	5. C
Passage 4: 1. B	2. D	3. A	4. B	5. D

第十一单元

I. Grammar

A. Multiple Choices

1. C 2. C 3. B 4. B 5. B 6. C 7. C 8. C 9. A 10. B

11. D 12. B 13. D 14. A 15. B 16. B 17. D 18. B 19. C 20. B

21. D 22. A 23. D 24. C 25. D 26. D 27. A 28. D 29. D 30. `C

(16. 此句中，must have done 表示对过去动作或已完成动作的肯定判断。

　21. 此句中，can't have done 表示对过去动作或已完成动作的否定判断，意为"不可能做过……"；此处的否定词 not 前置，放在了谓语动词 think 之前。

　23. 此句中，should have done 表示过去本应该做而实际并未做的动作。

　25. 此句中，needn't have done 表示过去的或已完成的、但没有必要做的动作。

　27. 此句中的 should 意为"竟然"。)

B. Error Correction

1. don't need → needn't
2. Dares → Dare
3. must take → must have taken
4. Will you → Would you
5. will be → must be
6. may eat → may have eaten
7. can → must
8. would better → had better
9. should give → should have given
10. should → can
11. ought to report → ought to have reported
12. to come → to have come
13. will → should
14. had far better bought → had far better have bought
15. may → should

(1. 此句中，need 既可用作情态动词，也可用作一般动词。作情态动词时，常用于否定句和疑问句中，其否定式是 needn't do sth.；作一般动词时，要用助动词 do 构成否定式和疑问式。)

II. Cloze Test

Passage A

1. corporations	2. the	3. skills	4. they	5. multinational
6. States	7. warehouses	8. countries	9. becoming	10. Time
11. Internet	12. products	13. form	14. the	15. than
16. more	17. are	18. Some	19. communities	20. operations

Passage B

1. Or	2. come	3. and	4. sellers	5. sites
6. make	7. a	8. it	9. They	10. catalogs
11. call	12. have	13. location	14. customers	15. with
16. Consumers	17. most	18. before	19. going	20. duplicate

III. Reading Comprehension

Passage 1:	1. A	2. B	3. C	4. C	5. A
Passage 2:	1. C	2. A	3. D	4. B	5. C
Passage 3:	1. B	2. A	3. B	4. C	5. C
Passage 4:	1. A	2. D	3. D	4. A	5. C

第十二单元

I. Grammar

A. Multiple Choices

1. D	2. B	3. D	4. B	5. D	6. B	7. C	8. A	9. C	10. D
11. C	12. B	13. A	14. A	15. A	16. D	17. B	18. A	19. C	20. C
21. C	22. C	23. A	24. C	25. A	26. D	27. A	28. B	29. C	30. B

(12. 词组 turn out 解释为"生产"。

14. 词组 come off 解释为"成功，达到预期的效果"。

21. 词组 count on 解释为"依赖，指望"。

24. 词组 drag down 解释为"使下降，使衰退，使滑坡"。

27. 词组 round off 解释为"加工、润色，使之圆满、完善"。

28. 词组 bear on 解释为"对……有影响"，这里指"摩擦"。)

B. Error Correction

1. break out → break away
2. broke apart → broke down
3. come with → come up with
4. pointed about → pointed out
5. calls in → calls for
6. boils off → boils down
7. took on → took down
8. gives up → gives in
9. meet their ends → make ends meet
10. make a stand → take a stand
11. put out → put on
12. sets to → sets in
13. hang around → hang on
14. push around → push aside
15. turned out → turned against

II. Cloze Test

Passage A

1. accounts
2. rise
3. began
4. became
5. one
6. highly
7. peak
8. directly
9. particularly
10. Mercantilists
11. never
12. priority
13. simple
14. in
15. did
16. The
17. expense
18. ideas
19. more
20. wider

Passage B

1. marketing
2. exchanging
3. occur
4. whom
5. the
6. they
7. be
8. defined
9. such
10. confined
11. exchanged
12. in
13. is
14. and
15. scope
16. sale
17. is
18. can
19. of
20. managerial

III. Reading Comprehension

Passage 1: 1. D   2. C   3. C   4. A   5. B

Passage 2: 1. A   2. B   3. D   4. C   5. C

Passage 3: 1. D   2. D   3. B   4. A   5. C

Passage 4: 1. D   2. D   3. C   4. A   5. B

第十三单元

I. Grammar

A. Multiple Choices

1. C   2. A   3. B   4. B   5. C   6. A   7. C   8. B   9. D   10. A

11. C   12. B   13. C   14. D   15. D   16. A   17. A   18. C   19. D   20. D

21. D   22. A   23. A   24. C   25. D   26. C   27. C   28. A   29. D   30. D

（4. 此句用进行时表示对对方经常性行为的抱怨。

15. 一般现在时用于对真理性事实的表述。)

B. Error Correction

1. reflected→reflect
2. did→was doing
3. have to → will have to
4. will use up → will have used up
5. have been able → will be able
6. varied → varies
7. develop → developed
8. couldn't → can't
9. awards → awarded
10. threw → thrown
11. will finish → finish
12. had been → are
13. stole → stolen
14. have presented → had presented
15. watched → watching

II. Cloze Test

Passage A

1. that	2. into	3. manufacturing	4. Service	5. professional
6. services	7. proportion	8. notably	9. A	10. tend
11. example	12. only	13. industries	14. rapid	15. the
16. the	17. service	18. allow	19. functions	20. in

Passage B

1. aspect	2. that	3. and	4. In	5. hazards
6. use	7. greatest	8. affect	9. nature	10. to
11. generated	12. always	13. may	14. in	15. safety
16. geology	17. results	18. pressures	19. rock	20. occurs

III. Reading Comprehension

Passage 1: 1. B 2. D 3. B 4. B 5. C
Passage 2: 1. D 2. C 3. B 4. C 5. C
Passage 3: 1. C 2. C 3. A 4. B 5. A
Passage 4: 1. D 2. C 3. B 4. A 5. B

第十四单元

I. Grammar

A. Multiple Choices

1. B 2. D 3. A 4. B 5. A 6. D 7. B 8. C 9. B 10. D
11. C 12. B 13. D 14. A 15. D 16. D 17. C 18. A 19. B 20. C
21. B 22. A 23. A 24. A 25. C 26. A 27. C 28. A 29. A 30. C

(2. 此句中, 代词 that 指代前句中的 system。

8. 根据句意可判断, 代词 those 指代 the students。

13. 此句中, him and me 为 the finalists 的同位语, 在句中作介词 to 的宾语。)

B. Error Correction

1. some → any
2. their → his/her

3. someone → anyone
4. the other → other
5. another → the other
6. their → theirs
7. This → It
8. which → whose
9. before → until
10. those → that
11. the other → each other
12. him → his
13. something → anything
14. every → each
15. either → any

（7. 此句中的 it 为形式主语，真正的主语为 that 所引导的主语从句。）

II. Cloze Test

Passage A

1. and	2. because	3. In	4. be	5. is
6. In	7. or	8. to	9. has	10. much
11. from	12. for	13. At	14. However	15. in
16. For	17. has	18. in	19. are	20. over

Passage B

1. such	2. at	3. up	4. of	5. Since
6. themselves	7. though	8. to	9. a	10. cause
11. if	12. apply	13. far	14. than	15. no
16. at	17. to	18. in	19. least	20. one

III. Reading Comprehension

Passage 1: 1. C   2. B   3. A   4. D   5. B
Passage 2: 1. D   2. A   3. D   4. D   5. B
Passage 3: 1. D   2. C   3. D   4. A   5. B
Passage 4: 1. D   2. A   3. B   4. D   5. C

第十五单元

I. Grammar

A. Multiple Choices

1. B   2. D   3. D   4. B   5. A   6. B   7. D   8. B   9. A   10. B
11. B   12. A   13. A   14. B   15. D   16. B   17. C   18. B   19. A   20. A
21. A   22. C   23. C   24. B   25. A   26. C   27. C   28. B   29. C   30. A

（5. 此句中的 it 为形式宾语，作主句谓语动词 think 的宾语；that 引导的从句为真正的宾语；a pity 作宾语的补足语。

8. 此句中的 it 为形式主语，that 引导的从句为真正的主语。

13. 此句中 what 引导的部分为主语从句；that 引导的部分为表语从句。

16. 此句中，the large number of bookstores 是本句的主语，所以系动词用第三人称单数。

23. 此句中，the girl's being educated 是带逻辑主语的动名词短语，用作句子的主语。

27. 此句中，object to（doing）sth. 是固定搭配。

28. 此句中，with which to regulate them 是介词提前的定语从句，修饰 sundials。）

B. Error Correction

1. work → working

2. relativity → relative

3. container → contains

4. consisting of → consists of

5. build out → build up

6. giving → given

7. different → different to

8. to live → living

9. single → a single

10. subsequent → subsequently

11. mile → miles

12. adapted→ to adapt

13. After → Before

14. scientists have begun → have scientists begun

15. the more → more

（1. 此句中，dedicate sb. / sth. to（doing）sth. 是固定搭配。

8. 此句中，be worth（doing）sth. 是固定搭配。

14. 此句为 only 置于句首的倒装句。）

II. Cloze Test

Passage A

1. girls
2. for
3. in
4. found
5. earlier

6. been
7. any
8. at
9. living
10. The

11. on
12. because
13. presence
14. Baboons
15. presence

16. the
17. if
18. father
19. sons
20. of

Passage B

1. next
2. advances
3. be
4. fact
5. which

6. because
7. But
8. of
9. race
10. which

11. big
12. Space
13. telescopes
14. solar
15. of

16. almost
17. director
18. Telescope
19. stars
20. form

III. Reading Comprehension

Passage 1: 1. C   2. C   3. D   4. A   5. D

Passage 2: 1. C   2. C   3. B   4. A   5. D

Passage 3: 1. C   2. B   3. C   4. D   5. A

Passage 4: 1. C   2. B   3. C   4. A   5. D

第十六单元

I. Grammar

A. Multiple Choices

1. C   2. D   3. C   4. A   5. D   6. B   7. A   8. B   9. D   10. C

11. A   12. C   13. B   14. C   15. C   16. D   17. A   18. B   19. B   20. B

21. D 22. B 23. D 24. D 25. D 26. A 27. D 28. C 29. B 30. B

（5. 此句用的是 so... that... 结构，连词 that 引导结果状语从句，what is a possibility today 为结果状语从句中的主语部分。

20. 此句中，the sick 和 the lost 表示一类人，谓语动词用复数形式。

30. 此句中的 does 替代前面的 works。）

B. Error Correction

1. have gone → go

2. them → they

3. lived → have lived

4. poetries → poems

5. began → begin

6. excessively → exceedingly

7. Chosen → Being chosen

8. from → from（删去）

9. starved → starving

10. for producing → to produce

11. being fashioned → fashioned

12. as → than

13. describe → describing

14. it → the needle

15. as the past → as in the past

（4. 此句中，poetry 为诗歌的总称，为不可数名词。

11. 过去分词短语 fashioned from a wick floating in a bowl of oil 作定语，修饰 lamps。

13. 现在分词短语 describing his new approach to eliminate a certain kind of water pollution 作定语，修饰 a paper。）

II. Cloze Test

Passage A

1. caves   2. suggests   3. amount   4. at   5. geologists

6. were   7. be   8. suggested   9. trigger   10. produce

11. balance   12. Now   13. all   14. known   15. occurred

16. implications   17. with   18. when   19. dissolved   20. years

Passage B

1. away   2. nature   3. efforts   4. decline   5. people

6. has   7. shown   8. disorders   9. issuance   10. percent

11. States   12. rapid   13. declined   14. percent   15. and

16. by   17. that   18. previously   19. sciences   20. While

III. Reading Comprehension

Passage 1: 1. D   2. B   3. A   4. C   5. A

Passage 2: 1. C   2. B   3. A   4. A   5. B

Passage 3: 1. D   2. A   3. B   4. B   5. A

Passage 4: 1. C   2. B   3. C   4. A   5. D

Model Test One

Section 1: Vocabulary and Grammar

Part 1   Vocabulary Selection

1. A   2. C   3. B   4. C   5. C   6. A   7. A   8. C   9. B   10. C
11. B   12. D   13. C   14. C   15. C   16. D   17. C   18. A   19. D   20. C

Part 2   Vocabulary Replacement

1. C   2. D   3. C   4. B   5. A   6. C   7. D   8. A   9. D   10. D
11. B   12. A   13. C   14. A   15. B

Part 3   Error Correction

1. C   2. D   3. B   4. B   5. D   6. D   7. B   8. D   9. C   10. C
11. D   12. C   13. A   14. A   15. B

Section 2: Reading Comprehension

1. D   2. A   3. B   4. D   5. C   6. A   7. D   8. C   9. B   10. C
11. A   12. D   13. B   14. D   15. C   16. B   17. B   18. A   19. D   20. C

Section 3 : Cloze Test

1. There	2. no	3. another	4. without	5. whose
6. languages	7. that	8. always	9. of	10. communicated
11. to	12. turn	13. different	14. no	15. is
16. means	17. know	18. only	19. understand	20. Grammatical

Model Test Two

Section 1: Vocabulary and Grammar

Part 1   Vocabulary Section

1. B   2. B   3. D   4. A   5. B   6. A   7. D   8. A   9. C   10. D
11. B   12. D   13. B   14. D   15. C   16. A   17. A   18. D   19. A   20. A

Part 2   Vocabulary Replacement

1. A   2. B   3. A   4. B   5. A   6. C   7. B   8. B   9. C   10. B
11. C   12. A   13. B   14. C   15. C

Part 3   Error Correction

1. C   2. A   3. B   4. A   5. D   6. A   7. B   8. A   9. C   10. B
11. D   12. B   13. A   14. B   15. A

Section 2: Reading Comprehension

1. C   2. A   3. D   4. C   5. B   6. C   7. A   8. A   9. B   10. C

11. B   12. C   13. D   14. C   15. A   16. B   17. C   18. D   19. C   20. B

Section 3: Cloze Test

1. to   2. descend   3. began   4. knowledge   5. using

6. thousands 7. research   8. knows   9. research   10. Wells

11. using   12. from   13. The   14. in   15. the

16. and   17. field   18. turn   19. non-political 20. public

全国翻译专业资格（水平）考试问答

问：什么是"翻译专业资格（水平）考试"？

答："翻译专业资格（水平）考试"（英文：China Accreditation Test for Translators and Interpreters — CATTI）是为适应社会主义市场经济和我国加入世界贸易组织的需要，加强我国外语翻译专业人才队伍建设，科学、客观、公正地评价翻译专业人才水平和能力，更好地为我国对外开放服务，根据建立国家职业资格证书制度的精神，在全国实行统一的、面向社会的、国内最具权威的翻译专业资格（水平）认证；是对参试人员口译或笔译方面的双语互译能力和水平的认定。

问：证书由谁颁发？其有效范围如何？

答：翻译专业资格（水平）考试合格，颁发由国家人力资源与社会保障部统一印制并用印的《中华人民共和国翻译专业资格（水平）证书》。该证书在全国范围有效，是聘任翻译专业技术职务的必备条件之一。根据国家人力资源与社会保障部有关规定，翻译专业资格（水平）考试已经正式纳入国家职业资格证书制度，该考试在全国推开后，相应语种和级别的翻译专业技术职务评审工作不再进行。

问：谁负责组织实施全国翻译专业资格（水平）考试？

答：根据国家人事部《翻译专业资格（水平）考试暂行规定》的精神，翻译专业资格（水平）考试在国家人力资源与社会保障部指导下，由中国外文出版发行事业局（以下简称"中国外文局"）组织实施与管理。中国外文局组织成立全国翻译专业资格（水平）考试专家委员会。

全国翻译专业资格（水平）考试考务工作，分别由国家人力资源与社会保障部人事考试中心和国家外国专家局培训中心具体承担。即：国家人力资源与社会保障部人事考试中心负责考务工作，国家外国专家局培训中心承担口译考试考务工作。

问：通过翻译专业资格（水平）考试可以实现什么目标？

答：首先，通过该考试，可以对社会上从事和有志于从事翻译工作的人员的翻译能力和水平作出比较科学、客观、公正的评价。

其次，翻译专业资格（水平）考试，是对全国翻译系列专业技术职务单一评审模式进行的一项积极的、富有改革意义的重大举措。通过翻译专业资格（水平）考试，取得翻译专业资格（水平）证书的人员，用人单位可根据需要，按照《翻译专业职务试行条例》任职条件要求聘任相应的专业技术职务。从2005年开始，英语二、三级翻译专业资格考试在全国推开；从2006年开始，法、日语二、三级翻译专业资格考试在全国推开；从2007年开始，英、法、日、阿、俄、德、西七个语种的考试在全国范围进行。2008年，七个语种的翻译（中级）、助理翻译（初级）职称只能通过考试取得，各地区、各部门不再进行翻译、助理翻译职称的评审工作。

此外，在翻译专业实行资格考试制度，可以规范国家翻译人才资格标准，提高翻译人才队伍整体素质，为翻译市场提供高质量的服务。

问：翻译专业资格（水平）考试与职业资格证书制度是什么关系？

答：翻译专业资格（水平）考试已纳入国家职业资格证书制度的统一规划和管理。

问：翻译专业资格（水平）考试等级与专业能力是如何划分和要求的？

答：翻译专业资格（水平）考试等级划分与专业能力：

（一）资深翻译：长期从事翻译工作，具有广博科学文化知识和国内领先水平的双语互译能力，能够解决翻译工作中的重大疑难问题，在理论和实践上对翻译事业的发展和人才培养作出重大贡献。

（二）一级口译、笔译翻译：具有较为丰富的科学文化知识和较高的双语互译能力，能胜任范围较广、难度较大的翻译工作，能够解决翻译工作中的疑难问题，能够担任重要国际会议的口译或译文定稿工作。

（三）二级口译、笔译翻译：具有一定的科学文化知识和良好的双语互译能力，能胜任一定范围、一定难度的翻译工作。

（四）三级口译、笔译翻译：具有基本的科学文化知识和一般的双语互译能力，能完成一般的翻译工作。

问：资深翻译、一级翻译取得的方式是怎样的？

答：资深翻译实行考核评审方式取得，申报资深翻译的人员须具有一级口译或笔译翻译资格（水平）证书；一级口译、笔译翻译实行考试与评审相结合的方式取得。资深翻译和一级口译、笔译翻译评价的具体办法另行规定。

问：二级口译、笔译翻译和三级口译、笔译翻译取得的方式是怎样的？

答：二级口译、笔译翻译和三级口译、笔译翻译实行统一大纲、统一命题、统一标准的考试办法。申请人可根据本人所从事的专业工作，报名参加相应级别口译或笔译翻译的考试。

问：翻译专业资格（水平）考试报名条件是什么？

答：凡遵守中华人民共和国宪法和法律，恪守职业道德，具有一定外语水平的人员，不分年龄、学历和资历，均可报名参加相应语种、级别的考试。

问：考试由谁命题？

答：根据《翻译专业资格（水平）考试暂行规定》，中国外文局组建翻译专业资格（水平）考试专家委员会。该委员会负责拟定考试语种、考试科目、考试大纲和考试命题，研究建立考试题库等有关工作。

问：翻译专业资格（水平）考试如何与专业技术职务聘任制接轨？

答：二级口译、笔译翻译和三级口译、笔译翻译的相应语种实施全国统一考试后，各地、各部门不再进行相应语种的翻译及助理翻译专业技术职务任职资格的评审工作。

取得二级口译、笔译翻译或三级口译、笔译翻译资格（水平）证书，并符合《翻译专业职务试行条例》翻译或助理翻译专业技术职务任职条件的人员，用人单位可根据需要聘任相应职务。

问：外籍及港、澳、台地区的翻译人员是否可以参加考试？

答：经国家有关部门同意，获准在中华人民共和国境内就业的外籍人员及港、澳、台地区的专业人员，符合本规定要求的，也可报名参加翻译专业资格（水平）考试并申请登记。

问：此考试设置哪些语种？

答：翻译专业资格（水平）考试现设英、日、法、阿拉伯、俄、德、西班牙七个语种。

问：各语种、各级别考试如何分类？

答：各语种、各级别均设口译和笔译考试。口译考试分为《口译综合能力》和《口译实务》两个科目，其中二级口译考试《口译实务》科目分设"交替传译"和"同声传译"两个专业类别；笔译考试分为《笔译综合能力》和《笔译实务》两个科目。

问：该考试各语种、各级别的难度如何？

答：本考试各语种、各级别的难度大致为：三级，外语专业本科毕业，并具备一年左右的口笔译实践经验；二级，外语专业本科毕业，并具备3－5年的翻译实践经验；一级，具备8－10年的翻译实践经验，是某语种双语互译方面的专家。

问：全国翻译专业资格（水平）考试每年举行几次？

答：英语二级、三级翻译专业资格（水平）考试每年分两次进行，英语同声传译类考试和其它语种的考试每年只进行一次。每年的5月份（具体日期以考前通知为准）举行二级、三级英语、日语、法语、阿拉伯语笔译和口译交替传译类考试；11月份（具体日期以考前通知为准）举行二级、三级英语、俄语、德语和西班牙语的笔译、口译交替传译类及二级英语口译同声传译类考试。相应级别的职称评审在我国不再进行，即：今后相应语种的翻译专业人员获取助理翻译（初级）、翻译（中级）专业技术职务不再通过职称评审的办法，而必须通过参加相应级别的翻译专业资格（水平）考试获取职业资格，从而获得聘任相应专业技术职务的任职资格。

问：一个人是否可以同时报考口笔译两种证书的考试？

答：考生根据本人的实际水平和能力，可以同时报考同一语种、同一级别的口笔译两种证书的考试；也可以报名参加不同语种、不同级别口笔译证书的考试。

问：各科目考试时间是如何规定的？

答：二、三级口译、笔译考试均分两个半天进行。

二、三级《口译综合能力》科目、二级《口译实务》"交替传译"科目以及英语同声传译考试时间均为60分钟；

三级《口译实务》科目考试时间为30分钟；

二、三级《笔译综合能力》科目考试时间均为120分钟，《笔译实务》科目考试时间均为180分钟。

问：各科目考试的方式如何？

答：各级别笔译考试采用纸笔作答方式进行，口译考试采用听译笔答和现场录音方式进行。相应级别笔译或口译两个科目考试均合格者，方可取得相应级别、类别《中华人民共和国翻译专业资格（水平）证书》。

问：口笔译考试侧重什么？

答：考试侧重评价考生的实际翻译能力和水平。

问：考生如何报名？

答：各语种、各级别考试口译试点城市的BFT考点具体负责口译考试报名工作；笔译试点城市的人事考试中心具体负责笔译考试报名工作。详情可登录 http://www.catti.net.cn 以及 http://www.catti.cn 网站查询。

问：报名时须注意哪些事项？

答：参加考试的人员，应符合《翻译专业资格（水平）考试暂行规定》中的条件。由本人携带有效身份证明到当地考试管理机构报名，领取准考证。凭准考证、有效身份证明按规定的时间、地点参加考试。

问：何时能够查询成绩？

答：考试结束后两个月左右。

问：是否有翻译考试培训机构？

答：有。由中国外文局认定的培训机构统一使用"全国翻译专业资格（水平）考试指定培训机构"名义。详情可登录 http://www.catti.net.cn 网站查询。

问：各语种考试有相关用书吗？

答：各语种考试有考试大纲、指定教材和辅导用书等。中国外文局授权外文出版社独家出版发行相关考试图书，任何单位和个人不得盗用中国外文局指定机构名义编写、出版与翻译专业资格（水平）考试有关的书籍。未经中国外文局授权，不得全部或部分使用翻译专业资格（水平）考试试题作为编写、出版、翻印、复制、发行、培训的内容。

问：考试大纲、指定教材及辅导用书的编写发行情况如何？

答：各语种考试大纲由中国外文局全国翻译专业资格（水平）考试办公室组织专家编写，授权外文出版社独家出版发行；在考试办公室的指导下，外文出版社负责组织专家编写各语种考试指定教材及辅导用书，并独家出版发行。

问：如何能购买到相关的考试用书？

答：参考人员可在全国各大书店购买翻译考试相关图书，或直接与外文出版社联系，网址：http://www.flp.com.cn，读者服务部电话：010-68995852，68996188。也可登陆中国网（http://www.china.com.cn）首页"专题库"栏目里的"科教文卫"分类找到相关图书的信息。

问：继续教育与证书登记的目的是什么？

答：实行翻译专业资格（水平）证书定期登记和继续教育制度，是为了适应时代的发展以及社会对翻译专业人员实行规范的行业管理的需要，也是与国际惯例接轨的一种形式。通过继续教育，可以促使持证的翻译专业人员继续努力钻研翻译业务，不断更新知识，不断提高业务能力，保持应有的翻译专业水平，为用人单位使用翻译人才提供客观公正、科学有效的依据。

问：已经通过翻译专业资格（水平）考试并获得翻译职业资格证书的人员，是否必须参加继续教育并办理证书登记手续？

答：是的。2004 年 1 月 1 日后取得翻译专业资格（水平）证书的证书持有者必须接受相关的继续教育并进行证书定期登记。翻译专业资格（水平）证书有效期为三年，在有效期满前 3 个月，持证者应到中国翻译协会办理证书登记手续。

问：翻译专业资格（水平）证书持有者继续教育和证书登记由哪个部门负责？

答：中国外文局全国翻译专业资格（水平）证书登记管理办公室为翻译专业资格（水平）证书

持有者继续教育和证书登记的管理机构，设在中国外文局全国翻译专业资格（水平）考试办公室。中国外文局委托中国翻译协会负责持证者继续教育和证书登记的具体实施工作。中国翻译协会行业管理办公室是继续教育与证书登记工作的常设机构，联系方式：北京市西城区百万庄大街24号；邮编100037；电话010-68997177。中国翻译协会网站 www. tac-online. org. cn。

问：证书登记和继续教育工作的监督管理单位是哪里？

答：中国外文局全国翻译专业资格（水平）考试办公室负责对继续教育（或业务培训）和证书登记工作进行检查、监督和指导。

问：继续教育的主要内容是什么？

答：继续教育（或业务培训）的主要内容是对证书持有者进行职业道德教育、翻译业务培训。

问：二级口译英语同声传译类考试在何时、何地开始实施？

答：2005年11月12日，二级口译英语同声传译试点考试首次在北京进行。

问：二级口译英语同声传译类考试科目是如何设置的？

答：二级口译英语同声传译类考试设置《口译综合能力》和《口译实务（同声传译类）》两个科目。

问：二级口译英语同声传译类考试对报名资格有何要求？

答：（一）根据《翻译专业资格（水平）考试暂行规定》（人发〔2003〕21号）和《二级、三级翻译专业资格（水平）考试实施办法》（国人厅发〔2003〕17号）考试报名有关要求，凡遵守中华人民共和国宪法和法律，恪守职业道德，具有一定外语水平的人员，均可报名参加同声传译类《口译综合能力》和《口译实务（同声传译类）》两个科目考试，考试合格可取得相应证书。

    （二）通过二级口译英语交替传译类考试并取得证书的人员，可免试《口译综合能力》科目，只参加《口译实务（同声传译类）》科目的考试，考试合格可取得相应证书。参加《口译实务（同声传译类）》科目考试的人员，在报名时应提交《中华人民共和国翻译资格（水平）证书》（二级口译英语交替传译类）。